9

CRADLE OF SECRETS

CRADLE OF SECRETS

Emma Lorant

HEADLINE

First published in 1993
by HEADLINE BOOK PUBLISHING PLC

10 9 8 7 6 5 4 3 2 1

British Library Cataloguing in Publication Data

Lorant, Emma
Cradle of Secrets
I. Title
823 [F]

ISBN 0-7472-0845-X

Typeset by
CBS, Felixstowe, Suffolk

Printed and bound in Great Britain by
Mackays of Chatham PLC, Chatham, Kent

HEADLINE BOOK PUBLISHING PLC
Headline House
79 Great Titchfield Street
London W1P 7FN

To Colin and Richard, the wish come true

ACKNOWLEDGEMENTS

Thanks are due to the many friends who read, and commented on, the manuscript. In particular Nickie Bertolotti, Joy Cotter, Gillian Geering, Michael Ridley and Richard and Ruthi Warburg who all took the trouble to read several drafts and to make constructive criticism.

1

It was when she found the four-leaf clover that Lisa Wildmore knew, without a shadow of a doubt, that she'd give birth to twins. What Lisa did not, could not, know was that that would just be the beginning.

She was walking Seb to Crinsley Farm for his first birthday party. Meg Graftley had absolutely insisted on it. 'Born and bred in Lodsham,' she'd laughed at them both, brown eyes twinkling, sleeves rolled up above her elbows. 'That calls for a proper Somerset cream tea.'

Seb's legs dangled over Lisa's bare shoulders. She clasped his hands and jogged him to their gate. Alec would be driving them back. No need to trundle the pushchair the long way round by road.

'Look at that, Seb!' Lisa called to her little boy, amused, as a lone duck plodded heavily along the road in front of their drive. 'Look at that big, fat duck!'

The drab bird turned to squawk annoyance, two V-shapes of open beak exploding curses at them, the flailing wings threatening attack.

'Quack, quack; quack, quack!' Lisa parroted her, bouncing Seb up and down but keeping well out of the bird's way. Beady eyes gleamed as the duck ruffled her feathers towards them. Lisa retreated hastily behind their wrought-iron gate.

'Not being very nice, is she?' Lisa asked Seb. 'I always thought ducks were supposed to be friendly.'

A squeal of brakes made Lisa wince. The passing motorist slowed down for just a moment, swerved a wide curve towards the gate and away again, then revved up and roared off. To Lisa's astonishment there was no flurry of scattered feathers, no limp body to be seen. The large and angry bird had disappeared. In its place she saw two normal-sized farm ducks waddling contentedly along the road.

All the same, Lisa thought heatedly, the locals drive too fast. Some of the feedstuff lorries clattered along these meandering lanes at outrageous speeds.

'Best jump on the verges,' Meg had suggested, right from the start, when they'd first met the Graftleys. 'The drivers don't go too near the rhynes if they can help it.'

'You mean they're afraid of drowning in those ditches?' Lisa had wanted to know. 'I've never seen much water in them.'

'Well,' Meg had shifted her eyes away, 'that depends. We've had mostly fair weather since you settled here. There can be some nasty mishaps at times.' Her face had brightened slightly, though Lisa had noted the lines around her mouth were deep with tension. 'That's mostly if a driver's had a jar too many,' Meg had said, her shoulders more relaxed. 'What really worries them is the banks giving way when wet. The milk tankers'll slip right in. Devil of a job to get them out again.'

Today, Lisa told herself briskly, pushing unwelcome thoughts away, was a red-letter day. She wanted to savour it, to walk with her little boy who had just learned to do so. Seb was a toddler now. She was the mother of a child, she'd brought him safely through babyhood. That first year had been hard work, but the rewards were all she'd hoped for. She radiated happiness.

Scanning right, left, right Lisa darted across the road and stepped the few yards more towards the iron gate. Splinters of cracking paint spiked her fingers as she undid the latch. She could already see the chimneys of Frank Graftley's farm, embraced by willows sifting the wind, four hundred yards across the moor.

Lisa squeaked the old five-bar open and walked through. She turned to click the bolt and caught sight of her home. The large, late-Victorian house she and Alec had bought nearly two years ago perched serene and confident on its little knoll. Mellow red brick, a slate roof, tall chimney stacks, set high above the wetlands to avoid winter floods.

'A square house,' Rex Smollett, the local builder, had pronounced it approvingly. Somerset dialect for solid, she and Alec had gathered. 'Plenty of space for a good-sized family,' the builder had added, eyeing Lisa's slim body.

Much later Lisa was to realise that it had all started then, almost from the moment when they first arrived. The omens were there, if she'd only known how to interpret them. A jungle of elders had overshadowed their long drive, twisting, menacing. Some said elder was the tree Judas hanged himself on. The juice of elderberries stripped by birds had stained the drive a bloody red, a darker liquid oozing out as the Audi's tyres crushed them. Alec had arranged for the landscape gardeners to uproot the unsightly hedge as soon as possible.

'You don't want to cut them down,' Rex had warned them, reverting to the vernacular, a curiously urgent tone edging his voice. 'They be a good safeguard.'

'Safeguard?'

Rex, remembering himself, had looked uncomfortable. 'It's only an old saying,' he'd muttered. 'Now these here drains—'

'A safeguard against what?'

He'd shrugged broad shoulders. 'Witches,' he'd said, unwillingly, with finality. 'Spells and suchlike. As I was saying—'

'But the Witch Laws were repealed in 1954,' Alec had smiled; that rather condescending smirk Lisa could do without.

'Witch Laws?' Rex had repeated scornfully. 'Which laws, more like. Laws don't matter; you can't never be sure what they get up to on the moor,' he'd continued gloomily. There had been, Rex had told them, a tarring and feathering in the village as late as 1963. He wasn't a village man, himself; he lived in Glastonbury.

There *was* a feeling of a bygone age. Lisa could sense it, hovering, like the white mist that often ghosted the Levels.

She giggled nervously, thinking back. Seb joined in with her, kicking his little legs. Lisa began to tire and eased him onto the low stone wall built onto a little hump-backed bridge. A sea of green to cross before they reached the next field. Grass pollen rose in clouds as they waded through. Nothing but sedgemoor stretching as far as the eye could see, and only Glastonbury Tor, crowned by St Michael's tower, to break the flat landscape. All permanent pasture, the ancient wetlands drained by willow-fringed rhynes first dug almost two hundred years ago. They edged the roads and skirted the fields, trickling their waters into wide, straight drains, then on into the rivers. But the tougher sedge grasses had long gone, eradicated by modern weedkillers.

Lisa coaxed her little boy on, walking him slowly, patiently, through the tall, sweet-smelling grasses. Her hands idled through meadow foxtails, Yorkshire fog and the abundant velvet bent, all in full bloom. She flicked thumb and forefinger across the seedheads beginning to form, enjoying the sensation of juicy kernels digging into delicate fingertips. Sow thistles speared yellow everywhere, and blue cornflowers glinted through the hazy brown-crimson of flowering knapweed heads. Frank Graftley was cherishing an old-fashioned sward, profuse with local wild flowers.

'No fertilisers here,' he'd told Alec earnestly when they'd first really got to know the Graftley family, early last year. 'Not even organic ones.

We're keeping this meadow just the way they did in the Middle Ages.'

'Only one cut of hay,' Meg had explained to Lisa. 'Later, when the season's getting on.' The farmer's wife had screwed perceptive eyes into her slow, widening smile as she walked Lisa round her henhouse. 'Here, have a dozen; we've got that many.'

Meg kept the eggs from her special flock of Rhode Island Reds for her own family. 'We give a few to neighbours,' she'd told Lisa. 'But we don't sell them.'

Lisa had basked in the warm glow of friendship.

'The wild flowers are really coming on,' Meg had said. 'And I counted ten kinds of butterflies already.'

And now Lisa was established here, walking her own son through the Graftley meadow on a glorious late-summer day. She thought there could be no greater happiness in all the world: Sebastian's first birthday, another baby on the way. The peaceful drone of bees gathering nectar mingled with Seb's little shouts of delight.

''Ut'er'y,' Seb clapped his hands while a painted lady butterfly sailed serenely past his nose. ''Etty.'

The meadow seemed to be alive with the beautiful insects. Small tortoiseshells, settled on cornflowers, teetered drunk with nectar.

'Butterfly, Seb.' Lisa moved to the side of the meadow and sank thankfully onto a hummock at the edge, a sudden heaviness in her legs confirming her new pregnancy. She watched her firstborn crawl, grasping ineffectually at two slow, drifting scarlet admirals. Meg was quite right; the luxuriant growth was attracting masses of fluttering insects. A great flock of high brown fritillaries soared up as Seb stood and blundered further into the meadow. The butterflies seemed to be everywhere, flaps of warm umber speckled brown waving against the light, flying a halo around him. Enveloped in beauty, Lisa thought tenderly, eyes soft with love for her son. They hardened into surprise as she saw Seb standing up, his chubby fingers crumpling cinnamon wings.

''Utter'ly,' Seb said.

The child balanced uncertainly on buckling legs, both hands now grasping the flailing wings. The furry, wormlike body between them looked bloated, almost twice its normal width. Seb's fingers trickled a yellow liquid as the body throbbed, broadened. Lisa gasped to see the butterfly appear to split in two. Brown-flecked wings twirled out and whirred.

''Utter'*lee*,' Seb insisted, pulling his hands apart. He had a fritillary in each hand, wings beating, flapping against small fingers.

'Let them go!' Lisa cried out. 'You'll kill them, Seb,' she said, lowering her voice, wondering why she was so distraught. The child must have chanced across a mating pair and separated them. She brushed aside the fleeting impression that both insects had been males as she irritably waved clouds of butterflies away. They seemed dense enough to choke them, casting a shadow, almost obscuring the intense sunlight with their outstretched wings.

'Let's clean your fingers on this tuft.' Breathing deep to calm herself, Lisa took Seb's hands and cleaned off the worst of the yellow mess with grass, then used her handkerchief on the rest. She pulled the little boy back to the meadow edge with her and sank down again, kissing his curls, cuddling him close to her.

A soft breeze stirred the grasses into graceful dance. Lisa looked up and around. A billow of woolpack cumulus crossed the blazing sun, darkening patches of meadow, saturating greens into viridian and jade. Yellowing willow leaves, first signs of autumn, feathered onto rhyne water, floated, then sank away to mud.

Seb twisted away from Lisa and teetered back into the meadow. She noticed a large rabbit near the child, standing on its hind legs, long ears erect, unblinking eyes. A buck, she supposed, it was so enormous. The eyes glittered bright, fixed steadily ahead, completely unafraid. And, as Lisa watched, astonished at how close the animal stayed, she tensed to see several more, surrounding Seb. All the same size, all simply standing there, staring with gleaming eyes. She felt a tremor of unease, a momentary fear.

''Unnies,' Seb prattled, stretching a hand towards the furry shape nearest to him.

Lisa was nervous of his touching them. Those eyes glowed mean and somehow menacing. She clapped her hands to chase the animals off. At first they did not move, just glared at her. Then, relieved, she saw the whole warren scatter away.

Relaxed once more, Lisa sank back and looked around. Lush clover, beloved by the clouded yellow butterflies, was growing near her feet. Red clover heads swayed drunkenly above the fine sheep's fescue and a thicket of trefoil leaves. Lisa tossed her sandals off and absently began to examine the leaves in turn. Each leaf, three lobes of vivid green, seemed to wink at her. So fresh-looking, so healthy, she thought, a feeling of deep contentment spreading through her body and coiling into her limbs.

She looked past the barbed-wire fence which separated the meadow from the field beyond and her eyes, bored with green, searched colour. Flecks of creamy white seemed to beckon to her as she became aware of slightly different vegetation – white-veined clover leaves, larger, almost gross, growing in clumps a little further off, right where the meadow edged on to Frank's trial pasture. Lovely, unusual, she thought vaguely as she caught sight of an especially large clump of leaves growing by the barbed wire.

'Look at the pretty clover, Seb,' she called to her little boy, holding out her hand for his and pulling him towards it. 'I think we're going to find a four-leaf one. That's specially for luck!'

And then she blinked, amazed, as the leaf she was now concentrating on turned out to have four lobes, not three. She could have sworn there were just three a moment ago, even though she'd been quite sure of finding one with four. Startled, delighted, sensing good fortune, she picked it eagerly to show Meg and Alec.

'Look, Seb,' she almost shouted, turning to him. 'I've found one. A lucky four-leaf clover!'

'Cloner,' he lisped.

She laughed. 'Clover,' she said. 'V. Clov-ver. Can you say that?'

'Clowler,' he smiled at her.

'Very nearly right,' she said. 'Try again. Clo-ver!'

'Cwo-ver,' he mimicked her as best he could.

'Watch,' she turned to him, her dress swirling a circle in the grass. The red clover goblets above the streaked foliage seemed larger than the rest. She picked a flower and pulled the petals off in chunks. They were massed solid, tight as she had never seen them before. Plucking some seemed to make no difference. 'It tastes really good.'

Seb pushed petals into his mouth.

'Don't eat them,' she grinned at him. 'Just suck the nectar out.'

'Well, fancy a townee like you knowing that. And how's the birthday boy?'

Lisa looked over towards the old-fashioned wooden gate Frank Graftley had put up only a couple of weeks ago.

'Meg! I didn't notice you were there. We were just coming.'

'You think my teas aren't filling enough so you're stuffing yourself up.' The brown eyes steadied. 'Not too much, mind. That's not good for you.'

As russet as a cider apple, and as round, Meg Graftley unlatched the new gate and waited for Lisa and Seb to amble through.

'Not good for you? You mean the clover?'

'The cattle and the horses are really sweet on it, but it's dangerous for sheep. Makes them swell up. Get off, Mikey, do,' she urged a towhead clambering up beside her. Bare feet swung across the top bar as he grinned his gapped teeth at her and pivoted himself on the swinging gate. Another boy, a slightly younger version of Michael, suddenly emerged from behind Meg and twirled himself up onto the top bar and at his big brother. Both boys tumbled off, breathless, in front of Lisa.

'You've got your hands full in the holidays, I see.'

'Not really. Alan and Mikey just came along with me to meet you. Frank has them with him most times, thank goodness. Or they're round Don, helping with the chores.' She turned to smile. 'Well, it does start the boys on farming ways, and they can do their bit.'

'Isn't Don about today? He isn't sick or anything, is he?'

'Sick? Don? Never missed a working day for Frank, nor for his Dad before him.' Meg laughed. 'Steady as a rock, old Don. He's about, right enough. Just Alec asked to talk to Frank and Don together. Said the boys would get in the way of it.'

The thought crossed Lisa's mind that Alec might find his own children 'got in the way' of his life. So far his interest in Seb had been somewhat peripheral. And her husband had been decidedly grudging about her getting pregnant again.

'Alec mentioned there's been another fertiliser breakthrough.'

'Flaxton's special,' Meg said. 'That Multiplier stuff we've been testing out. Some of the clover leaves have doubled up – two for the price of one.'

Lisa smiled vaguely, then slipped her sandals on. 'So now I've got a one-year-old.' Delightedly she swung her son up in her arms and held him away from her, her hands under his armpits, cloverleaf in her mouth. 'I can't believe I've actually got him there.'

'You're a good mother, Lisa,' Meg told her, sober now. 'I own I didn't think you had it in you when you first came here. But you've really blossomed out.' There was a slight pause as she eyed her friend's son. 'And Seb's very advanced for his age,' she added thoughtfully, looking him over. She tousled her own two sons' hair and pushed them playfully together. 'Not like my two pumpkin heads!'

'I don't know about Mikey and Alan,' Lisa said gaily, 'but I know Paul and Phyllis are just as forward as Seb; and much sturdier, I'd say.' It irritated Lisa that her son was so slight compared with the Graftley twins, born a mere nine weeks before him.

Meg was clearly pleased. 'A bit stockier, maybe, but they don't talk as much as your Seb.' Her eyes shone joy. 'But even if they weren't blooming, there's nothing like motherhood, when all's said and done.' She straightened up. 'Get that gate shut, Alan. Purdle along now. The twins'll be finishing their nap and wondering where I've got to.'

'I'm pregnant again,' Lisa confided to Meg, speaking softly. 'Found out this morning, Seb's birthday! Isn't it wonderful?'

'Very true, my duck. After all the trouble you had before you settled here. Right in the air, I swear it.'

'And I found a four-leaf clover,' Lisa told her, holding it out.

Meg took the clover leaf and looked at it carefully. 'There's that many with leaves doubled into two sets of three,' she said. 'But this one's different.'

'I know!' Lisa could hardly contain her delight. 'It's a good luck charm; means my wishes will come true.' Her eyes shone happiness. 'Guess what? I have a hunch it'll be twins this time.'

'Twins?' Lisa was surprised to hear her friend sound startled, almost shocked. 'Whatever makes you say that?'

'Just intuition, really. And wishing on that four-leaf clover.'

The pause before Meg spoke again made Lisa search her friend's face.

'Would you want that?' Meg sounded oddly unenthusiastic about the idea.

'I'd love it,' Lisa said, exulting in the thought. 'I'd really love it. Why? Did you prefer having one at a time?'

'Not me.' Meg laughed, a curiously brittle laugh. 'The more the merrier, as far as I goes. Just that – well, women are made to have one at a time, I reckon. Country folk don't much go for twins and such.' She paused and turned back to look at Lisa. 'The saying is that clover is bad for women in the family way.'

'Really? D'you think that's true?'

'Well . . .'

Lisa could see Meg hesitating. Afraid to worry her, perhaps. Meg always insisted Phyllis had a clubfoot because, being a twin, she'd been crowded in the womb.

'Phyllie does seem to have a bit of pain. Not much, really, just the odd twinge.' She paused, then blurted out, 'Frank's the one who got flummoxed, went on about her foot needed straightening, right from the start. Made her have the operation when she was only just born.'

'The doting father.' Lisa laughed Meg's unease away; Meg did not favour medical intervention except as a last resort. Lisa felt Frank's concern did him credit, though she was surprised he thought an early operation necessary. It didn't quite fit the image she had formed of him – a man who did not tolerate interference. 'Phyllie always looks quite fit to me,' she continued.

The child had often outpaced her twin Paul in spite of the brace on her foot; Seb wasn't even in the running.

'And I thought you said Alec doesn't want more than two young'uns altogether.' Meg's glow of contented motherhood, so evident only a few moments before, had been replaced with troubled eyes, the soft lips drawn grim.

Lisa saw Sally and Jean, both darker than their brothers but with the Graftley smile, skipping towards them bearing trugs brimming with peas.

'We've picked along all the rows, Mum.'

'Thank you, my dears. We can all have a go at shelling.' She lifted Seb up high, then brought him down again. 'You'd like to help us with that, eh, Sebbie? You're such a big boy now.'

2

Crinsley farmhouse, its stone walls keeping the inside cool, sprawled long and narrow. A cobbled courtyard separated it from a scramble of outhouses Lisa always found somewhat daunting. It seemed that everything the Graftleys touched multiplied. They had six children, and the Graftley Friesians, speckling black and white against the glossy green of their thriving pastures, bore ever-sturdier calves.

'Frank reckons fertilising with Doubler hasn't just increased the grass and milk yields; he reckons the old orchard trees have taken on a new lease of life,' Meg explained.

'I do that,' her husband agreed quietly. Lisa's eyes, as yet unaccustomed to the dark after the brilliant sunshine, had not spotted the farmer sitting by his empty fireplace, draining a mug of something she suspected was the scrumpy he made every autumn. 'Just for us and a few friends,' Frank had expounded to her several times. 'Can't abide that stuff they peddle in the shops. Cider's meant to be still, not that frothy rubbish they sell.'

Frank's cider came straight out of his hogshead barrels, at least twenty of them stacked neatly in one of his barns. Lisa turned dutifully to smile at him. He seemed obsessed with having more of everything.

'Dangdest thing,' he said, looking right at her. 'Reckoned we'd have to grub the old trees out and buy apples in. But no, we had a decent crop last year.' He turned to Alec whom Lisa could now make out sitting across the fireplace from Frank, politely taking tiny sips at his cider.

'And Flaxton's little baby doesn't stop at increased crop yields,' Alec put in sagely. 'It boosts profits very nicely, thank you. There's reason to suppose that sales of Doubler will increase exponentially.' He placed the pewter mug on the floor beside his chair and opened his briefcase. Alec did not much care for cider, Lisa knew, though he'd been careful to drink his whack whenever he was with Frank. 'In fact, their latest figures suggest that their market share has tripled in a single season. It's really quite astonishing.'

The newly qualified accountant Lisa had married eight years before, when she'd given up teaching at Hornsby Art College, had almost immediately joined the prestigious City firm of Grew, Donsett and Tyler. Two years ago he'd been invited to become a partner of the renamed Grew, Donsett, Tyler and Wildmore. Alec had been elected their man out West, chosen to open an office in Bristol.

'Bristol,' he'd told Lisa at the time, 'is going to be the second city in the UK. All the banks are moving out of London. Lloyds has already built Bank House in Wine Street.'

The first organic fertiliser from Flaxton, enthusiastically called Doubler and more than living up to its name, had been as good for the firm of accountants instructed by Flaxton as it had for West Country farmers shrewd enough to switch to organic. Small farmers, hardly able to make ends meet before, found themselves able to sell their produce at a good price; they flocked to buy Flaxton's products.

On the back of Flaxton's success, Grew, Donsett, Tyler and Wildmore had quickly become *the* leading agricultural accountants. Flaxton's headquarters was sited in an old mansion set in the Mendips. Their chief executive, Nigel Carruthers, owned a country estate there, near Priddy. Alec, astute as ever, had rapidly worked out that this dynamic West Country firm would expand, in fact be quoted on the stock exchange, before much longer. That was why he'd looked for his country house near Wells, the smallest city in England.

'Good schools there,' he'd explained to Lisa when she'd objected to moving to such a remote rural area. 'Millfield's in Street, and Wells Cathedral School has a very good reputation.' It was the assuredness with which he'd talked of schools that had persuaded her to move from London.

Doubler, based on algae and patented worldwide, was obviously a winner. Now Flaxton were testing their latest product, Multiplier, first manufactured eighteen months before. The new fertiliser incorporated plankton, and promised to be an even greater success than Doubler. Somerset was the trial ground again, and the Graftley farm had been chosen as the first experimental site.

'Somehow or other,' Alec said as he peered through steel-rimmed glasses at his balance sheets, 'though the chemists haven't worked out the reasons yet, they think the strain of plankton they're using for Multiplier encourages the shedding of extra ova in mammals, and increased egg-laying in fowl.' Alec beamed round the room as though he, personally, had invented Multiplier. 'Give your chickens corn fertilised with it, and you'll have more free-range eggs than you can handle!'

'We can always sell them,' Frank put in coolly, setting down his mug. 'Get a good price for them.' He got up and sauntered over to Alec.

'What d'you mean, "plankton"?' Lisa asked. 'Is Multiplier completely organic?'

'Absolutely. No artificial ingredients at all.' Alec was drawing his finger along the lines of figures. 'Just look at these projections we've been working on.'

'Manufactured like Doubler, or is it a new process?' Lisa wanted to know.

'What? Yes, of course.' He looked over his shoulder at the farmer peering suspiciously at the figures. 'It is completely organic, Lisa, I told you. Algae are purely vegetable matter; plankton contains some animal organisms. Primitive animal organisms,' he added hurriedly. 'But that's still organic.'

'Easy to tell by seeing the bigness – healthy enough,' Frank assured Lisa. 'No need for you to worry none.'

'Isn't plankton something whales live on?' Lisa persisted, holding Seb on her lap and helping him drink the Graftleys' goat's milk from a cup. Most children, Meg had assured her, tolerated it better than cow's milk.

'Exactly,' Alec agreed. 'The stuff can be produced rapidly and in vast quantities. And I'll wager the eggs will be larger as well as more of them.'

'The hens are mine to see to,' Meg put in. 'I just run a few for ourselves. No need for more than that.' She looked across at Alec's papers, then at her husband. 'I just like them to scratch around for their grub,' she said firmly. 'I reckon feed fertilised with Multiplier makes them double-yolk.'

'Folk like the double-yolkers,' Frank gruffed, frowning at his wife. 'If we get a surplus, we can always sell some,' he repeated. He cut the end off his Havana, placed it in his mouth, and lit it. It smouldered like a gun which had just fired.

Meg's eyes slid away from him and she said nothing further.

'I know you need the money, Frank,' Alec said wickedly, the left side of his mouth rising more than the right. 'You want to buy more privatisation issues to add to your little portfolio.'

Frank grinned. A brawny man, his neck and arms a deep, darkened reddish-brown, his curly black hair showing wisps of grey, he still moved gracefully and quickly. 'Only doing my bit for my country.' He reached easily towards the floor, lifted his pewter mug to his lips again and took a long, deep swallow.

'We saw an enormous duck on our way over,' Lisa told them. 'Didn't we, Seb?'

''Ack, 'ack.'

'Mark's dillies?' Frank smiled down at Seb. 'Runs a team of Khaki Campbells alongside the moor. Stops the lorries going too fast.'

'Not a team,' Lisa said. 'At first there was just one. A bit aggressive, actually, and round enough to look like a pregnant duck!'

'Dillies lay eggs,' Frank said, staring at Lisa.

She smiled away her irritation; she wasn't that much of a townee! 'Of course. It's just that this one was so bloated, somehow. And she rather took against our being there, didn't she, Seb?' She turned to face Frank, keen to understand what he had meant. 'How can they slow the lorries down?'

He chuckled. 'The drivers either cut their speed to allow for them, or mow 'em down.' He grinned. 'Works, either way.'

Lisa shuddered at the calculated callousness of it. 'I did notice a driver brake,' she agreed. 'I thought he'd run the fat duck over, but he swerved, and when he'd gone there were two ordinary ducks waddling along, without a feather out of place. They seemed quite amiable, as well.'

The farmer stared at her, his eyes blank, then turned to Alec. 'The problem now is not how to increase yields, but how to stop them getting out of hand. Twin lambs are fine, but more'n that and it can be bad all round.' He drained his mug and looked up slowly. 'Don came across a set of triplets only the other day.'

Frank looked across the room at the silent Don sitting by the window and putting back the cider. Lisa had often marvelled at the man. Quite old, seventy at least, she judged, but he was as sinewy and firm as many a younger man.

'Arr,' he said, drinking deep. 'Not allus t'best thing. 'T'were the one wi' the twin lambs; us forgot to tag 'un. Next time us looked 't'were three on they! Her couldn't handle they wi' jest two teats, and littl'uns were missin' out. Missus had to hand-rear 'en. 'T'won't do.'

'All money in the bank,' Alec put in hurriedly.

'Not if them dies of starvation, it bain't.'

'I think it might encourage rabbits, too,' Lisa put in. 'Seb and I came across a whole warren of them.'

'Coneys?' Don asked, suddenly animated, looking up. His eyes, Lisa noticed, were almost colourless. A light, blue-grey. 'You saw they in the homeground?'

'Really big ones,' Lisa told him eagerly. 'All standing on their hind legs. They weren't even afraid of us.'

'We'll put paid to them tomorrow.' Frank crashed his mug down. Bronze drops spurted down the pewter into a pool, the quarry tiles glistening red. 'We'll shoot the whole lot of those damn critters.'

Lisa, shocked at the threat of such wholesale slaughter, felt a lurch in her belly. A churning feeling stirred the contents of her stomach. Seb's weight on her lap felt heavy. She tried to shift him further down her knees as heartburn made her flinch.

'Go and see Daddy, Seb.'

He trotted off obediently. Lisa could feel colour flood her shoulders and reach into her face and hair as blood surged round her body.

'You all right, my duck?' Meg's voice seemed distant.

Lisa grasped the table in front of her, lowering her head between her arms to drain the blood.

'I'll fetch some water.'

Alec was by her side, putting his arms round her shoulders, then squatting next to her, keeping Seb from trying to climb back onto her lap. Her hair felt sticky, plastered to her forehead.

'Up we go!' Alec heaved the little boy against his shoulder. 'I expect it's the new baby,' he said, softly, whispering into Lisa's ear. 'Would you like me to run you home?'

'Dare say it's because of the clover she had a go at.' Meg put a filled glass of water on the table. 'They say it's not good for pregnant women.'

'Clover? Lisa *ate* clover?'

'Just sucked a bit of nectar out.' Meg laughed at him, but her brown eyes were veiled. 'Only a drop. She'll be as right as rain again tomorrow.'

Lisa sipped slowly from the water Meg had brought over for her. The cool liquid helped calm her. She dipped her fingers in and spread a few drops over fiery cheeks.

'Morning sickness in the afternoon,' she managed to gasp. She pushed back her chair and headed for the bathroom. The dark, unfamiliar house made her nervous. She drew in great gulps of air, then felt as though her body were distended, bloated up. Just like the sheep Meg had talked about, it occurred to her.

The firm direction of Meg's hands steered her through a door. 'I'll light the lamp.'

Kneeling by the lavatory bowl Lisa allowed the contents of her stomach to erupt. An odd, intense yellow stained the bowl. It reminded her of something – she couldn't quite place it. In any case, quite different from the trickle of innocuous white she'd sicked up when carrying Seb. She looked at the lurid colour and felt prickles of panic stabbing through her body. The vivid, buttercup hue of egg yolks came to mind – Meg's double-yolked eggs – and precipitated further retching. Perhaps deeper-coloured vomit was a sign of twins, she tried to soothe herself.

Another turn in her belly brought on a further spasm which seemed to relieve Lisa of whatever her body had taken such exception to. The liquid was now clear, she was glad to see. Quite suddenly she felt all right again.

Flushing the bowl and splashing her face and hands with water, she rubbed a towel briskly over her face. No further problems; just pregnancy nausea of a slightly different kind. She'd check it out with her GP.

'Each period of gestation is different,' Roger Gilmore had intoned over the telephone that very morning, ringing through confirmation of conception. 'Just take it easy. You've got a toddler on your hands as well, this time.'

'It's nothing at all,' she reassured Alec as she hurried back into the room where the others were. 'I think it's just that Somerset clover is so rich – like everything else around here! When I pulled off a chunk of petals you couldn't even see that they had gone.'

Sally and Jean had set the big table by the window: freshly baked bread, Meg's own clotted cream, the new season's strawberry jam, farm butter, lardy cake, scones. And a birthday cake – Victoria sponge covered in chocolate icing – for Seb. A large, solitary candle was at its centre.

'I'll just light that,' Frank said, walking over. 'Now then, Seb. Blow it out, like a big boy!'

'A nice cup of tea,' Meg offered Lisa. 'Put you right.'

'I'd love some of that delicious wholewheat bread,' Lisa said eagerly. 'I really feel quite hungry now.'

'Eating for two,' Meg laughed. 'Spread some of my butter on that, and add a bit of jam.'

Lisa tucked into Meg's food with relish. All wholesome, homemade produce; she was making a good start on feeding the new life within her.

'You are wonderful, Meg,' Lisa said, looking in awed admiration as Meg brought in another cream-filled bowl.

'I do make a good dollop of clotted cream,' Meg agreed, putting it down. 'But the girls laid the tea.' She laughed. 'Praise where praise be due. They're turning into proper little maids.'

3

'Lisa! Wake up!'

She saw Alec looming by the huge bay window, staring across the Levels. Following his gaze she looked through the old glass, watched it distort the scene like a fairground mirror. Moorland expanded outwards below them, interspersed with willows and ringed by the Mendips painted a deep slate blue. As she watched, the glass twisted double-bent willows into witch shapes, black and menacing. She could distinguish them quite clearly: pointed hats, broomsticks, billowing skirts. A whole coven of them down by the Sheppey flowing its way sinuously towards Bridgwater Bay.

'Lisa!'

Why was he shouting her name? Alec was, apparently, intent on peering at the grassland, his face away from hers. Lisa was aware of dark grey clouds gathering forces, obscuring the hills, marching across the vast expanse of sky brooding over the pastures. The wind scrolled shapes into wet grass, snaking the different greens into a glittering damask spread out in front of her. It winked at her, sudden eddies of white-flecked highlights eyeing her. First one, then two, suddenly hundreds of eyes gleamed at her, held her tight. Not eyes; circles on wings, she saw. Hundreds of butterfly wings hovering over the Levels, hugging the turf. She tried to shut them out and found she could not do so.

The patter of rain turning to hail began to beat hard against the window panes; Lisa could almost feel the hailstones knocking into her. The wind, only a sigh to start with, began to shriek. It's blowing so hard it's rocking a house as solid as Sedgemoor Court, she thought uneasily. Twenty-two inches of solid brick walls; a square house! How could a mere hailstorm cause such movement?

'That's our lot, then,' she heard Alec say, his voice distinct and clear above the hail splattering against the glass. 'After this one our family's complete.'

'Supposing I want three?' Alec's assumption infuriated her. If he refused to father more—

'Then you'll have to make sure you're carrying two,' he grinned at her. That lopsided grin, the left side of his mouth higher than the right. His look unbalanced her, made her feel she was about to fall. She clutched at the shutters to steady herself and felt them opening. The vast spread of wood squeaked wide. She stepped away, shouting a warning to Alec, then watched him turn his whole body towards her. Amazed, she saw he was holding Seb in his arms. But there was something odd about Alec's face now. It seemed to be split in two, one side grinning at her, the other scowling.

Lisa braced back against the woodwork and tried to catch her breath. Something was wrong; something to do with her family. She rubbed her eyes and looked again, startled. Someone else was standing there. Who was that with Alec? The figure turned and she could see it was another man. A thickset, bulky man, shorter than Alec, booted feet planted firm, astride.

Frank, Lisa recognised, astounded. A different Frank; the Frank of eighteen months ago, before they had got to know the Graftleys well. Unfriendly, almost hostile. Keeping his distance, his eyes slits against outsiders, his shoulders hunched away. The dark, curly head, without the grey, was lowered over something lying in a box. Small fingers waved unsteadily above the sides. A baby lying in a carrycot.

Frank had a pillow in his hands. He lowered it over the cot, pushed it down, pressed hard . . .

'Stop!' Lisa screamed. 'You'll smother it!'

He turned to her, his small eyes spots of venom. 'Bain't human,' he told her. A cold, firm voice. 'Bain't nothing there but vermin. Old Don'll be shooting the whole lot of them damn critters.'

She saw them, then; dozens of rabbits, shot dead, their corpses lying in the meadow.

'Darling, wake up! It's me!'

And she saw Seb, apparently in Alec's arms; he was also on the floor and on the chairs. He seemed to have split into little Sebs all over the place.

Lisa clutched her belly in sudden terror that she'd lose the new baby only just conceived. It seemed to quicken within her, grow from embryo to foetus within seconds, split into two . . .

As she felt the split, an image of one embryo appeared. A large oval, pulsating, then slowly, inexorably expanding, its nucleus broadening.

And then it divided into two, tearing apart like an amoeba, separating into two nuclei, apparently identical; two distinct beings, pulsing with energy, beating their rhythm of life in unison. Two oval forms, she saw, swimming in fluid, throbbing with vigour.

As she watched, one form began to take shape, to grow, to swell, to bloat, then to dwarf the smaller one. The large embryo opened up what looked like a giant maw. Lisa saw it slither towards the smaller one and engulf it in its jaws. She felt a pinching, tearing pain within her, then saw the huge mouth close tight over the second embryo and swallow it. The larger embryo had absorbed the smaller one, had obliterated it from life.

'Lisa!'

A grey mist swam across the image. The pinching turned to shaking; her shoulders were shaking in horror at what she'd seen. She held her hands over her abdomen, protecting it.

'No!' she called out. 'No! Don't do that!'

'Darling,' she heard. She recognised Alec's voice, urgent and low. 'Wake up! You're having a nightmare! Lisa!'

The grey mist completely shrouded her, then turned to a cold, measured, festering sensation inside her. Cold, she felt so cold. And that sinking feeling; as though she were being sucked into a chasm, a cataclysmic series of events she could not control.

Her hands were interlocked, hard below the still-flat belly she clasped to herself. She could hear Alec talking to her, his voice caressing, could feel his hands against hers, stroking, trying to relax them. Her eyelids began to tremble. The gloomy grey turned into the soft, orange glow of the bedroom lamps.

'Are you all right, pet?'

'I suppose so.' Lisa struggled to open her eyes properly. Alec was sitting on her side of the bed, his hands now on her shoulders, sliding across her back, holding her to him, embracing her.

'I couldn't seem to wake you up. What was it?'

'I dreamed you'd turned into someone else.' She looked at him carefully, then round the room and down at herself. Only a crumpled nightdress to remind her of the scene in her dream. 'It was so real . . .'

'All that rich clotted cream at Meg's, I expect,' he soothed her, stroking her blonde, damp hair with his right hand, his left arm holding her to him. 'And that idiotic business of sucking clover.' He kissed her hair. 'I'm just the way I always was.'

'And Seb – Seb turned into several little Sebs.'

'You're dreaming of a baby brother for him.'

'And the new baby split in two.' She shuddered as she remembered the vividness of it. 'Split right down the middle; divided in half like an amoeba.'

'It was a nightmare, sweet; all over now. Nothing to worry about.'

'Like a fertilised ovum dividing into identical twins,' she continued stubbornly.

She felt his arms tighten round her, hard. 'Determined to copy Meg, aren't you?'

'Completely, exactly the same as each other,' she felt impelled to carry on. 'Split into two equal foetuses; well, embryos maybe.' She shuddered again, seeing the giant maw opening up, then devouring the second embryo. 'And then one of them swallowed the other one.'

She could not shake the image off, it was so real, so tangible.

'That's what you get for wishing for two for the price of one!' Alec rumbled good-naturedly. She felt his chest against her own, the pyjama buttons pressing into her. 'It's all right now; it was just a dream. There's no need to worry. You know what the obstetrician said.'

'I know; he went on and on about the fertility drugs not affecting this pregnancy. But my dream was about identical twins; nothing to do with that.'

'Twins are twins.'

Lisa bolted upright, pushing her husband away from her, eyes blazing. The placid disposition nurtured by their serene, country life style seemed suddenly transformed into her previous, rather more stormy, temperament.

'No, they're not. Fertility drug twins are formed by two ova released and fertilised at the same time: fraternal, two-egg twins. Identical twins are formed in a quite different way. They're produced by the splitting of a single fertilised ovum into two, usually within the first two weeks of pregnancy.'

'Whatever, Lisa,' Alec cut her off impatiently. 'We really don't have to worry about more than one baby this time; this pregnancy is quite different from the first.'

'I'm not an idiot, Alec. I know fertility drugs often lead to multiple births. And you know I haven't taken them this time.' She paused, and looked at Alec. 'But twins can just happen, too, you know!'

He released her, stood up, and walked towards the bottom of the bed. He heaved the duvet on to it, pulling it over her.

'I see you've done your homework.'

She had. When the Hammersmith had kept her waiting. That's when she'd decided to do a little research of her own. She couldn't stop herself from feeling annoyed, even now.

'I *can* still read, Alec. Motherhood doesn't deprive one of one's wits.'

It rankled, the memory of the way the doctors had brushed off her first efforts at enlisting their help in becoming pregnant.

'Come back in a year,' they'd told her brusquely and dismissively. 'That's the time we allow for infertility. If you're still worried then, we'll run some tests.'

'I'm worried now,' she'd told them, keeping her voice steady and flat. 'We've been trying to have a baby for two years.'

Obviously they hadn't heard her. 'You've taken the contraceptive pill for a long time,' the specialist had told her judgmentally. 'Twelve years altogether, I think you said.'

Practised birth control – of course, she only had herself to blame!

'It would have been different if you'd had a baby right away, when you first married.' A shrug. 'You need to give your body time to adjust before assuming you're infertile,' the Hammersmith consultant had insisted.

Lisa was then thirty-six and worried that time for having babies was running out for her. Time for adoption had already passed; parents over thirty-five were not considered suitable.

All the same, she'd had no option but to play along with the doctors. No other fertility clinic would look at her if her notes told them she'd already been to the Hammersmith.

Lisa settled back onto her pillows. They had given her the fertility drugs eventually, but she still hadn't conceived – until they'd moved to Somerset. In the end that was all it took. Not their stupid pills, but good, country air and wholesome food. That's what had done the trick. The doctors could keep their dangerous chemicals; Lisa intended to live a purely natural life.

'Let's not worry about all that history now. Just leads to nightmares,' Alec insisted. He put his arms back round her shoulders, drawing her to him, nuzzling her neck. 'You're pregnant again, and everything is fine. I'll soon relax you!'

An almost irresistible feeling of aversion came over Lisa. She held her breath, at first allowing her husband to fondle her without withdrawing, just holding herself back, unresponsive, but forcing her body out of rigidity. In some way she could not quite understand she felt

Alec would be threatening her unborn child – children – if she allowed him to go inside her. She'd discussed this point at length with the medical profession at the time she'd finally conceived Seb. According to them, intercourse caused no danger to a foetus.

According to them. For this second pregnancy Lisa preferred not to take any chances. She'd decided to sound Meg out as well, as delicately as she could. 'Are there any special problems about carrying more than the one?' she'd asked her, diffident, insisting on carting the tea things out to the scullery after Seb's party.

'Problems? Before the birth, you mean? Not then; didn't even know I was carrying twins until the seventh month!' Meg had said, her voice unusually high.

'You mean there were problems later?'

Meg's eyes had slid away. 'Susan noticed I was bigger than before; she's the midwife in charge, so she organised a scan. That showed them, right enough.'

'That's when it became harder? In the last few weeks?'

'Not so you'd notice.' Meg's dishes had been clattered into her cupboards, the doors shut tight.

'And what about – well, you know, Frank?'

Meg had looked at her shrewdly, face to face. 'Frank's just like any other man,' she'd said, shrugging. 'But he never caused me any trouble.'

So that hadn't been what had worried Meg.

Alec's lips were on Lisa's, eager and pressing. 'You're choking me,' she spluttered, gasps of coughing successfully wrenching her out of his arms. 'I think I must be getting a cold.'

Startled, annoyed, he lifted his head away from her explosive hacking without, however, releasing her.

'It's all that ridiculous composting you've decided to go in for,' his voice hissed in her ear. 'You overdo it, and then you complain you're tired, or not feeling well.'

The coughing eased and he reached towards his groin, his lips flirting now, caressing her ears, her hair, her eyelids. She struggled, heaved against him, began to cough in earnest.

He let her go, climbed over her to his side of the bed, reached his hand out to turn off the light, and pulled the duvet away from her to spread over himself. Lisa lay back, recovering her breath.

'You really are becoming tricky, Lisa. I never know where I am with you.'

'It's just a cold,' she murmured, putting out her hand. 'It's brought on by a virus; nothing to do with making compost.'

Her husband turned away from her. His silence made her uncomfortable. It stirred her imagination yet again. Alec, she knew, could have lived quite happily without any children. Now that he had a son, she sensed he felt that was all he needed. He was prepared to tolerate a sibling for Seb; more than that, Lisa was clear, he would not put up with.

''Night,' she purred. 'I expect it was just the nightmare. I'll be fine tomorrow.'

'I'll get Saunders in to stack the compost for you, if you insist on making it,' Alec announced. 'You'd think Doubler would be good enough for you. You can even have a go at Multiplier, if you want.' He heaved the duvet up and down. 'You're not Meg Graftley, you know. She's got the muscles for all that; you haven't. I wish you'd bear that in mind.'

Listening to her husband's deep breaths of sleep Lisa felt isolated, unsure. What was wrong with her? Why was she causing trouble? She now had everything she'd always dreamed of. A healthy son, a comfortable country house set in idyllic surroundings, another baby on the way, a perfectly good husband doing well in his profession. What else could she possibly want?

A large family. Lisa wanted a family like Meg's – half a dozen children, company for each other, tumbling over the house. An earth mother; she wanted nothing more than to be an earth mother.

The four-leaf clover appeared in her mind again. Four leaves erupting from a single stem. One for hope, one for faith, one for love, and one for luck, as the saying went.

'It'll bring me luck,' she whispered to herself. 'I know it will bring me luck.'

4

Ian Parslow, the obstetrician at the Bristol Infirmary, was no less condescending than the one Lisa had consulted at the Hammersmith. She wondered vaguely why he had such a good reputation.

'We're actually looking at the ultrasound, Mrs Wildmore,' he was telling her, an edge of irritability creeping through the bedside manner. 'You can see for yourself – one baby!'

He showed them how they could tell it was a boy. Lisa, used to graphic representation, immediately caught on. Parslow smiled knowingly at Alec who was doing his best to decipher the vague, blurred impressions of a twenty-week foetus. 'You can't always see, but he is lying exactly right.'

Was she imagining it, or was Parslow looking rather intently at the monitor? It was impossible to say, but Lisa sensed he was holding back. Her instincts told her that her new pregnancy was different from her first; she tried to imprint the pictures on her brain, intending to read up on scans later. Had this bland specialist detected an intriguing irregularity? An unusual slant, perhaps, which might be worth discussing with a colleague but best kept a secret from the parents? It made her uneasy to see the doctor's eyes flit busily from blob to blob, then write a note on his pad.

'Is there a problem, Mr Parslow?'

The obstetrician's head jerked up to look at her. The jowls firmed into determined optimism as he shifted his eyes rapidly away from hers and looked at Alec. Something was not quite normal, Lisa was sure; but this man was not about to admit it.

'A well-formed foetus, Mrs Wildmore. Nothing at all to worry about.'

If anyone was worrying, it wasn't Lisa. It was simply that she had no means of knowing what the scan actually told them. Her dream came back to her: was there a small blob within a bigger one? Is that what Parslow had noted down? She'd read about such cases; perhaps that was why she'd dreamed of one. She watched as the doctor traced out the shapes to Alec, outlining a human in the making. Ultrasounds were not really of interest to Lisa, though Alec was insisting on the whole battery of medical tests.

'You're almost forty, pet,' he constantly reminded her, as though somehow she were trying to deny it. At least this test was not intrusive; as far as she knew, at any rate.

Lisa was beginning to find the repetitious references to her chronological age threatening. Was Alec tiring of her, looking for someone younger? She *had* begun to age. Careful observation of young men's reactions told her that. She wasn't quite as girlish, maybe; more womanly. But not completely past it, either. Glances still followed her when she deliberately passed close by to men using pneumatic drills, or cleaning shop windows. They still whistled – most of the time. And last month, when Trevor had come to stay, he'd congratulated her on her appearance.

'I don't know how you do it, sweet, I really don't,' he'd said. 'All the other mums I know are so *frumpy*.' Her agent had thrown his expressive hands into the air and gazed, apparently delighted, at her clothes. 'And ethnic is so clever for the country. You look wonderful, darling. Brimming with health.'

Dear Trevor; he'd kept her spirits up all the long months when she was carrying Seb. He'd told her how trim she was, encouraged her to continue with her painting. He'd even praised her Somerset landscapes. Though prettier – just kitsch, if she was honest with herself – than her London work, he'd managed to find the right outlet. Not at the usual gallery.

'There's this new chap on my list now,' he'd told her. 'Tiny place off New Bond Street. Marvellous for country scenes. Leo's expanding by leaps and bounds; moving to Albemarle Street in a couple of months.'

Alec, by contrast, was continually harping on possible misfortunes. 'Things can go wrong, you know. We wouldn't want a Down's syndrome child or one handicapped by any other congenital disease, now would we?'

Lisa was not at all sure about terminating the life within her even if the doctors pronounced it inadequate. The summary execution of an unborn baby just because the medics had decided it might not be perfect did not immediately appeal to her.

But she was feeling calmer, happier, than she'd ever felt before, and she had no intention of upsetting this blissful state for the sake of arguing a point which might never come up. Perhaps the cows around her exuded something catching to make her feel so tranquil. She had become, she felt, positively bovine.

Composed, she smiled at Ian Parslow. A slow, unhurried, knowing smile; mirroring Meg. If the baby could lie in such a way that one might not see its gender, perhaps he was lying in such a way as to obscure a second one, she reasoned to herself, serene.

Lisa watched her husband as he examined the scan with more than his usual superficial interest in matters concerning gestation.

'That's really extraordinary,' he said. 'I'd no idea one could see the foetus so clearly.'

'A perfectly normal pregnancy.' Parslow turned affably towards Alec, then rapidly back to the machine. Had Alec noticed how the man hid behind platitudes? Lisa again had the odd feeling that he was not being candid, that the image contained something the consultant was not entirely happy with. 'An unusually clear picture,' he insisted. 'Your wife is doing very well.'

Lisa felt the blood begin to spurt at the deprecating tone, the oblique method of communicating with her. What was 'an unusually clear picture' supposed to convey? Something exceptional, clear to him, but which he had no intention of discussing with them? And she was doing well to cope with it in her body?

'In that case there won't be any difficulty about my having the baby at home,' she said sweetly, automatically smiling though the doctor's back was turned to her. Only the throbbing pulse in her neck showed that calm had deserted her.

Mr Parslow seemed to freeze; then he turned from the scan to look at Alec again. 'We do like to have our older mothers in.'

'I don't think, pet—'

'You just said all is well, Mr Parslow,' Lisa interrupted, but smiled again disarmingly. '"A perfectly normal pregnancy" I think you said.'

The doctor turned to glance at her, his hooded eyes sweeping almost immediately back to the flickering images on the monitor.

'There's no suggestion of a possible abnormality, is there?' she asked softly, forcing her voice low and self-effacing.

He was, apparently, still examining the scan. 'I do assure you, Mrs Wildmore, none at all. There's no reason for anxiety. If you're at all worried, I can prescribe something to calm you down.' He pulled a prescription pad towards himself as he smiled reassuringly at Alec. 'It's just a matter, as I said, of preferring—'

'I prefer not to take any medication, thank you,' Lisa said, as amiably as she could. She had promised herself to be particularly careful during her pregnancies. She'd even thrown out some of her favourite pigments – chrome yellow and cobalt violet – aware that her habit of licking her paintbrush could leach poison to her foetus. All she was suggesting to Parslow was to have her baby in as natural a way as possible. She smiled determinedly again. 'And if everything is fine, I'll go for a home birth.'

'But, pet—'

'Dr Gilmore is perfectly willing to take it on, and I've already seen the midwife. Of course, if the scan had shown anything unusual, however trivial, I know you'd feel happier if I came in.'

'There would be no question about it then.' Parslow actually turned to look at Lisa fully before returning to the machine. 'As you can see, there's clearly just one baby. He's not even particularly large.'

The barely concealed exasperation, the put-down, made Lisa even more determined. She flicked her eyes over the screen. The vague, shadowy forms it displayed were not what she was concerned about. Her body was reacting in a different way this time; she was as certain of that as she'd ever been of anything. Apart from that first attack of nausea – mercifully not repeated – she had felt movement in the very first six weeks; definite movement. Gilmore had, naturally, dismissed that as gas. But she'd still felt it. The images in her dream came back in force. She was convinced that, somehow, this baby would turn into more than one, even if he hadn't done so at this stage.

'My wife goes in for small babies,' Alec said. For some reason he found this fact threatening to his virility. 'Our firstborn weighed in at only six pounds.'

Lisa and Seb, visiting Crinsley Farm, found Meg and her twins in the converted barn she used as a dairy. Meg was making butter.

'Was it exhausting, Meg? And did you get much bigger right from the start?' Lisa pestered.

Meg didn't answer immediately. 'I told you before,' she finally brought out. 'Didn't notice anything special. Susan was the one who said about me being bigger – quite late on, mind.'

Lisa heard the evasiveness and waited.

'Well, I was bulkier, somehow. Thought I'd put on a bit of weight.'

'But before you actually knew? Did you notice anything special early on?'

'Felt like a football ground towards the end,' Meg sidestepped, rather peremptorily. 'They seemed to be having a game between them.'

It was not that Meg wasn't being sympathetic, or supportive. But Lisa realised that her friend not only did not share her enthusiasm for the possibility of a multiple birth, she was positively against it. Lisa could see no reason for this attitude. Phyllis and Paul were enchanting little toddlers; pretty, bright and always on the go. Phyllis was the ringleader, the stronger one.

'Let go that pushchair,' Meg had scolded Phyllis last time they were out walking. 'You're pushing Paul in the rhyne.'

Lisa had wondered how a child as young as Phyllis could possibly have such strength. The clubfoot was a very minor defect; Phyllis wouldn't even know she'd had it by the time she became an adult. On top of that, the twins were the darlings of their older sisters, and of Don. Dour by nature, normally too shy to speak to anyone, Don Chivers seemed to take a special interest in Paul and Phyllis. Lisa had noticed him looking into the double pram, heard him say a word or two to them. Meg had told her that Don had never shown any special regard for her other children. 'Those two young'uns get to him, somehow,' she'd boasted to Lisa. 'Phyllie specially; always round her.'

'But what about the birth?' Lisa persisted. 'Anything difficult about that?'

'Don't know that I remember all that much about it.' Meg's eyes looked sad, almost dejected. She'd talked volubly about the birth of her other children often enough. Made jokes, put Lisa at ease during the last few days before she'd given birth to Seb.

'You mean the gas and air?'

'Gas and . . .? No. No, I didn't bother none with that.' Meg turned away, giving Lisa the distinct feeling that she was hiding something. But what? 'The births were easy enough. All done in fifteen minutes.'

'You are lucky!' Lisa breathed, enjoying the three toddlers tumbling about on the dairy flagstones. 'Isn't it wonderful? They clamber over each other but never seem to come to any harm!'

'Like kittens, I reckon; keep their claws sheathed.' Meg still sounded grudging.

'It would be lovely to have two.'

'One way to get round Alec,' Meg agreed, but she seemed broody, oddly reserved. She noticed Lisa look at her and brightened. 'Quite a bit of hard work, of course. Especially when you get a lively one, like Phyllie. Had that new pram in tatters almost from the start.' Meg smiled. 'And she's not one for sleeping. Happen Paul goes through the night, you can be sure she won't!' Meg seemed more cheerful as, confident in her mothering, she bundled a toddler under each arm and carried them, squirming, to the pushchair she kept handy. 'But you get used to it.'

Lisa watched her dexterously place one child in a seat while still holding the other under her arm. Then she wagged her finger at Phyllis to stay in place while she went over to the other side and settled Paul. She strapped them both into their seats.

'Can't afford to turn your back for a minute; what one don't think on, the other will.'

Meg started to scrub down. Always meticulous, this time she seemed to be exerting unnecessary energy. She polished the gleaming churn, her face and body red.

'Don don't like the look of it,' she finally blurted out, returning to her butter, patting it into box shapes all over again. 'Makes me feel agitated. What Don don't know about farming just isn't worth the knowing.'

'Don doesn't like the look of what, Meg?'

'All those multiple births. Keeps saying it "bain't natural".'

'I expect he just remembers the way things were done in his young days,' Lisa said absently, not sure what Meg was getting at, or why she took so much notice of Don. 'Lambs are bred for twinning now; means double the profit. Farming must have changed out of all recognition since he was young.'

'Too much of a good thing. The hens are laying more than ever they did, and mostly double-yolkers. Seems creepy, somehow.'

'Would you rather they didn't lay at all?' Lisa laughed.

Meg had a way of looking along her nose which Lisa did not much care for.

'What I mean,' she added hurriedly, 'is that it might all just as easily go the other way. You said yourself, it all evens out in the end. You can't fool nature.'

Meg shrugged her ample shoulders and heaved a milk container to one side.

'Take some of my goat's milk cheese,' she urged Lisa. 'I've started making ewe cheese as well. Better for you than factory cheddar, any day.' She wrapped small cylinders of cheese in greaseproof paper. 'And mind now, goat's milk is better for babies than cow's milk. We have plenty enough; there are two nannies, now.'

'That's really sweet of you. I'm going to try breast feeding again. Perhaps I'll have more luck this time!'

'Always the best,' Meg agreed. 'You could try taking basil tea. Just the job for stimulating milk.'

'Really?'

'Easy to make.' Meg smiled. 'And just get Alec to bring Seb over if you're pushed,' she went on. 'You know, if you feel tired.'

'It's wonderful to know you'll stand by,' Lisa said gratefully. She was already sure she'd need Meg's help.

'Susan is very good,' Meg reassured her again. 'She saw me right.'

'Didn't Gilmore insist on hospital once the scan showed two?'

'Gilmore? We didn't bother none with him. No, it was all agreed between Susan and me. We managed very nicely, thank you!'

'I hope I'm not early,' Lisa said absently. 'Susan's going on holiday just before I'm due. Even Dr Gilmore might be away then.'

'The relief midwife seems sound enough,' Meg put in quickly. Speed wasn't Meg's way, Lisa knew. It meant the relief midwife's reputation was not yet established.

'What about Gareth Witherton? He's the new doctor in the practice, isn't he? I thought he was supposed to be specially keen on home confinements.'

'I know nothing about him, so far.' Meg rushed for Seb who was about to place his plastic duck in her butter churn. 'We don't often feel poorly. Frank puts it down to sticking to organic grub. Pays to pay that bit more attention to proper food.'

'And now Flaxton's fertilisers are producing results beyond inorganic farming anyway.'

There was just a moment too long before Meg answered. A premonition of danger flitted through Lisa's mind, then disappeared.

Meg looked her usual self as she hefted the double pushchair over a drainage gully. 'That's you lot out of harm's way.' She gently kissed her twins. The love in her voice was entirely reassuring. She turned back to Lisa, her eyes faintly clouded. 'I know,' she said. 'I know Multiplier is organically based. Should be just the job.'

'But you don't entirely trust it?'

'Don't rightly know. Nothing you can put your finger on for sure. Too good to be true, somehow. Something for nothing.'

Meg collected her butter, gleaming gold, a faintly acrid smell in the air. She looked at Lisa leaning back against the wall. 'Just got to sluice the floor. Be through in a minute,' she said, concern in her voice. 'Then you can have a sit down. Anyway, all due to that special plankton they use, Frank says. Fancy Multiplier being developed here, in Somerset!'

'The grass looks marvellous.'

'Almost a bit too lush.'

The field beyond the home meadow was drowsing in unusually warm winter sunshine. The latest herd of bullocks was huddled under the whitethorn hedge to the left of the field, the animals swishing their tails and keeping away from the sun. A few, thirstier than the rest, were exposing themselves to danger by stepping into the rhynes lining the pastures and now only trickling water. It had been a dry winter.

'Frank'll need to get the water pumps going,' Meg was saying anxiously. 'What with the size of the herd, there's not enough for them to drink. We had one die only the other day.'

'Did you?' One out of so many did not seem terrible to Lisa.

'Costs a mint to get the knackers out. Can't get nothing for a dead animal,' she explained to Lisa. 'Even for pet food. Against the new regulations.'

Lisa looked uncertainly at the animals now crowding down towards picturesque withies edging a rhyne. 'But you've had lots more than usual this year, haven't you?'

'The odd thing is that when Frank goes out to tag them, he often finds they know. They try to get away from him. None of them likes the tagging, of course, but they do seem to know he's going to do it. Maybe Multiplier makes them brighter as well as fatter!' Meg laughed.

'Can't be bad,' Lisa said, vaguely remembering that Don had also mentioned tagging lambs, and that one of them had managed to dodge him.

Phyllis bent down to her foot, pulling at the brace, fretfully kicking her leg.

'Come on, Phyllie. We'll be taking that off soon.'

The child kicked petulantly, with strength enough to displace the double pushchair.

It seemed to be taking the strain well. Lisa examined it critically. 'Is this a good type of pushchair?'

'Can cope with Phyllie's temper,' Meg snorted. 'Got to be strong for that.'

5

'Guess what?' Alec was on the phone, excitement mounting in his voice. 'It's been confirmed. Multiplier not only increases herb yields by a factor of three, it seems to affect the meat yield as well!'

'Meat yield?' Lisa, feeding Sebastian his lunch, had no idea what Alec was so fired up about.

'Has the effect of making cows produce calves with quicker growth rates, and they go on to become bigger beef cattle.'

'Really?'

'And the ewes produce lambs with bigger yields on both wool and meat; but that's almost too much of a good thing.'

Sebastian made an ineffectual stab at the food on his plate. Lisa steered his spoon into the mashed potato while balancing the receiver on her shoulder. 'It is?'

'People think it's mutton, not lamb.'

'Of course.'

Lisa heaped a few pieces of carrot into Seb's mouth but tried to encourage him to feed himself. The new baby was due in a couple of weeks, and could be early; Seb would need to do as much for himself as possible. 'You're going to have a baby brother soon,' she cooed at him. 'Won't that be lovely? Then you can play with him.'

'Bother,' Seb said dutifully.

Lisa laughed; bother was right even if he didn't know it.

'Lisa? You there? Okay if I bring Frank round?' Alec was asking her. 'We need to go over some figures and our place is quieter than theirs – at least for the time being,' he added, not altogether jocularly.

'He'll have to take pot luck.'

'I'll pick up some scrumpy,' Alec chortled down the phone. 'By the time we get round to the meal he won't know the difference.'

Lisa marvelled again at Alec's confidence. He was the newcomer; Frank's family had lived in Somerset for generations, all experts at cider-making – and sampling.

'You mean you won't,' she teased him, telling herself she'd take a couple of gallon jars to Meg's and have them filled. 'I'll get supplies in for you,' she told him. 'See you later.'

She hung the phone back on the wall hook and turned to Seb. 'Janus,' she said. 'Your little brother's going to be called Janus.'

The twenty-month-old looked at her and suddenly spat potato all over the table, at the same time knocking off his mug of apple juice.

'Seb!' Lisa caught herself shouting. 'That's a horrid thing to do.'

'*Another* helping? Sure you're feeling all right?' Alec asked his wife. 'You don't normally eat that much.'

'I'm simply ravenous,' Lisa explained. 'The business of eating for two, I suppose.'

'You look rather uncomfortable.' Alec's forehead furrowed into deep slits as he peered at Lisa, then poured more cider for Frank. 'Quite a bit bigger than last time. I swear you've billowed out since we started the meal.' He walked towards his wife and stared at her. 'You can hardly reach the table. I thought this was supposed to be another tiddler.'

Though larger than with her first child, Lisa had, until recently, remained remarkably trim. The angular look had softened to a gentle roundness, a hint, even, of plumpness. But she was still small and dainty. Fragile wrists gave away a delicate bone structure and the bump of baby, though evidently there, had been by no means massive. Until two weeks ago. That's when she'd noticed an extraordinary increase in her appetite, a sort of greed she could not control. She'd eaten constantly, watching herself expand to quite unprecedented proportions.

'The muscles aren't as tight as the first time,' Lisa explained. A languorous calm, a feeling of composure, made her sound plausible. 'I expect it just shows more.'

Alec looked at her pensively but made no further comment. She smiled, covering the curious sensations she felt in her body by pointing to her husband's favourite pudding – crème caramel. 'More for you?'

He laughed and passed his plate. 'I suppose you must be okay if you're up to thinking about feeding me!'

'What about you, Frank?'

'Good grub, that.' He smiled as he handed her his plate.

Though the baby wasn't due for a fortnight, Lisa was prepared for an earlier delivery. None of the antenatal checks had shown signs of anything other than a single baby, but Lisa stuck to her original conviction. Twins, she knew, were often premature.

'My carrycot's a mess,' she'd insisted to Meg a month ago, watching her stack her baby equipment to give to Cancer Relief. 'Could I possibly use one of yours?'

'You can have both if you want,' Meg had said, looking at her sharply. 'We won't be having more. Six are enough young'uns for anyone. You still thinking about twins?'

'Mr Parslow ruled out any possibility,' she'd said, annoyed at Meg's quick interpretation.

'But you aren't taking any chances,' Meg had concluded for her. 'Parslow may be a specialist, but he's only a man. And you certainly seem bigger this time. I can hardly credit it.'

Everything was going well so far. Seb was safely tucked away in his cot, Alec was crunching figures with Frank, and what she was experiencing might well turn out to be a false alarm. But even if it were not, she was determined to hold out until the last minute before calling in the medical profession. If she were to be two weeks early, they might be disposed to rush her off to hospital. Lisa's instincts called for a home delivery; her whole being screamed out for it. Something unusual was going on, she knew there was. And the only way she could remain in charge was to give birth in her own home.

She felt some further movements in her womb; not really contractions, more like a lively infant turning inside her.

'I'll leave you two men to it,' she excused herself as soon as they'd finished supper. 'I'm feeling a bit tired.'

Alec looked up. 'Positive you're all right? Shall I give the midwife a ring?'

'I'm fine, Alec, don't fuss. I'll just have an early night.'

'We'll be doing the straightening up for you,' Frank smiled at her. 'Don't you worry none about that.'

She saw Alec's lips tighten but he started clearing the table amiably enough. She smiled her thanks and walked upstairs to her bedroom. That faint slither of worry she thought she'd subdued was beginning to insert itself into her mind again. Was she being pig-headed, risking the new life within her? If it were twins, and they were about to be born, they must be tiny to have escaped detection.

The turmoil in her belly seemed to have subsided, but not its size. Lisa, lying on her bed, patted her bump, feeling round its edges for the two sets of limbs she was convinced she'd find. Nothing, really. But Alec had a point; she was enormous, a Humpty Dumpty puffed out so much she could hardly keep her balance. That odd, enveloping feeling of fullness that she did not remember from her first pregnancy was quite disturbing. She heaped cushions behind her back and to the sides to keep herself upright and wrapped the duvet round herself.

A sudden lurch in her abdomen made her gasp. Her eyes grew round as she saw the bump move under the duvet. The thick down seemed to hoist itself up. A trick of the light, perhaps. She pushed the covering off, impatiently flinging it over to Alec's side, and looked down at her belly. Visibly expanding now, like a gigantic balloon being blown up, it was still veiled by her large, encompassing nightdress. Mouth open, she watched the fabric straining at the seams.

The feeling of something biting into her suggested to Lisa that she was merely sitting on a fold of nightdress caught underneath her. Smiling at this simple explanation, she raised herself on her left elbow, lifted her buttocks up and pulled the nightie up under her armpits with her right hand. The effort required appeared to be tremendous, and Lisa lay back to catch her breath. She felt much more comfortable with nothing to restrain her body. She lay back thankfully, wondering whether she needed to get yet another, larger maternity nightdress.

The trickle between her legs did not register right away. When she finally understood what was happening she found she could not move. The trickle had become a steady stream. Horrified, Lisa watched a bright yellow fluid exuding out of her. It oozed out of her body, visibly diminishing the size of her belly.

Her waters must have broken. She tried to reach an arm to the phone on Alec's side. It was as though she were held fast. A vice-like grip kept her on the bed, her body unable to move, while the contents of her womb began to stir in earnest.

Lisa stared at her belly and gulped. It was expanding sideways, elongating into a huge rugby ball. She could feel the being within her struggling, his limbs pummelling her womb, stretching it. Appalled, she tried to call out. Her throat muscles seemed to have petrified. She saw the central bump under her abdominal wall elongate, then flatten. She felt a tearing, rending sensation. Not painful, but it worried her. She was convinced there'd been some sort of change within her. Not the feeling of bearing down she remembered when in labour with Seb; more a sudden widening, an odd sense of the bump changing shape.

With some surprise she now saw that her navel was slightly sunk in again, for all the world as though she had *two* bumps rather than one. But her abdomen was quite still now. And her muscles were under her control again.

Gently she slid her hands around herself. She fingered two solid protuberances, top and bottom. It felt as though there were two heads – she could swear there were two heads! A slight tingling within herself made her bold enough to explore further. Two sets of limbs! Twins after all, she thrilled. Those doctors . . .

The urge to urinate was suddenly overpowering. Gingerly raising herself up to a sitting position, she levered her legs carefully off the bed, planted her feet on the carpet, and stood up. She was appalled to feel liquid still trickling down her legs. Incontinent? Surely not.

Hurriedly stuffing some tissues between her legs she waddled to the lavatory. A flow of liquid, rather more than she would have expected and still that curiously deep yellow colour, dribbled steadily out of her. Buttercup yellow; that did seem odd. Something strange, something remarkable, was happening within her. Yet she did not feel threatened, attacked. She was convinced she was about to give birth to twins, and she awaited their arrival with eager anticipation.

Her sense of certainty was short-lived. The banal truth, that all that size was simply because she'd retained extra fluid, suddenly flashed across her mind. Her body had produced the hormones necessary for the birth; that's all it was. That's really what she'd been feeling; not twins, but the baby changing position, being pushed down the birth canal. Naturally all that extra fluid would be draining out.

'Remember the second time can be very fast,' the midwife had warned her more than once, and stressed it again at the last check-up. 'I'd rather you called me for a false alarm than left it too late.'

'Alec!' Lisa cried out, standing in the corridor and walking over to the balustrade guarding the staircase. She could hear ripples of laughter interspersed with low, rumbling tones. The men, no doubt, were finishing the cider, good-humoured, ripe with money and plans for investments.

She tried a few more calls. There was no response from downstairs. She lowered herself carefully down the stairs, clinging to the banisters, edging down step by step. She tried hard not to dislodge the contents of her womb in any way. Suppose she gave birth while she was walking down?

'It's started, Alec.' She was standing by the open living room door, hiding her dishabille behind it. Neither man heard her.

She opened and shut the door with a bang and tried again. 'Alec! I think it's started.'

'I'll be there in a minute,' she heard him say. He thought she was calling him to come to bed.

'The *baby*, Alec. I think he's decided to be early!'

It was Frank who took the matter in hand; Alec had clearly had too much cider to hear, let alone take charge.

'Best ring the midwife,' he said at once, picking up the receiver and tapping the number on the keypad. 'Meg said Susan Andrews be seeing to you. Better than the doctor, any time.'

Lisa forgot her nervousness about wearing only a nightdress in front of Frank and came into the room to slip down on an easy chair. The strain of standing was beginning to be too much for her.

'No answer.' Frank looked uncomfortably at Lisa. 'Perhaps she's out on another case.'

The holidays, Lisa remembered now. Susan might already have left. 'Oh, dear.' Lisa felt panic rising. Had she made a terrible mistake, jeopardised the unborn by not ringing for help before? She forced herself into composure. 'Susan did leave me another number,' she told them, catching her breath as an unmistakable contraction began. 'It's on the fridge door, Alec. Under the big magnet.'

'Right.' Alec stood up and lurched towards the kitchen. He returned with the small card in his hand and tapped the number in.

'Alec Wildmore here,' she heard him say as she eased herself back into the chair. 'I think my wife's in labour. Can you come over right away? That's right, Dr Gilmore's patient. Susan Andrews left us your number. Directions? D'you know your way across the moors?'

'Tell her to look out for the Land Rover at the Tin Bridge,' Frank put in quickly. 'I'll lead her back. Don't want her lost; not now.'

'She'll be there in twenty minutes,' Alec told them, taking three attempts to replace the receiver in its cradle.

'I'd best let Meg know what's happening.' Frank smiled at Lisa, tapping his number in. 'No need to worry yourself none; she'll be round for young Seb first thing tomorrow.'

'I'll help you up the stairs.' Alec placed his arm behind Lisa and inched her up the wide staircase, along the corridor and to the guestroom bed she'd already prepared.

'Let me lift you up,' Alec said anxiously as he eased her swollen body on to the mattress. Lisa lay back, feeling a deep contraction. The birth process was in full swing; there was no longer any doubt about it. She felt around her belly again. One large, round ball shape at the top; she couldn't mistake that. Was it really two babies, or was it that the one Parslow had seen on the scan had not been lying right? A breach position, perhaps? That's what he'd seen, and avoided telling her because it usually righted itself. Her heart began to flutter as she pulled the covering over herself.

'Bit premature, aren't you?' Alec asked, concerned.

'A little,' Lisa found herself saying, breathing deep to sound serene and unflustered. 'Two weeks is nothing either way. No need at all to fuss. Everything's ready.'

The sound of the front door opening and crashing shut again alerted Lisa to the outside world. She could hear voices, then a heavy, unknown tread climbing the stairs. Rita Connolly, presumably; the relief midwife.

'Decided to make a start, have we?' a raucous voice greeted her.

A large, raw woman, Lisa noted with alarm. Not a bit like the bird-like Susan whose quick, sure movements had always given her confidence. Rita stood stolid, panting with the exertion of climbing the stairs, looking for somewhere to put her bag. She settled for the bedside table, opened the bag wide and extracted a white overall and some surgical gloves. Lisa flinched as cold, plastic-coated hands pressed roughly at her.

'No mistaking the waters have broken; you're in quite a state.' Rita pushed herself upright again and regarded Lisa unsmilingly. 'I'd better ring Doctor,' she said, lugubrious and prim. 'He'll want to order the flying squad.'

The woman's assumption that Lisa would simply do as she was told sent blood back into her brain. Something deep inside her insisted she had to stay at home to deliver. She had to be where she, or at least Alec, was in control. Every nerve in her body told her that.

'From Bristol?' she asked, panting between contractions coming at two-minute intervals. 'It's rather far to go up there at this stage, isn't it? What if the baby's born?'

'They're very well set up to deal with that.' Rita consulted a massive notebook which, it seemed to Lisa, must take up most of the space in her bag. 'Little nipper's on the early side; best to play safe.' She rummaged in the bag and unearthed a Biro. 'Not to worry,' she said, looking at Lisa with pursed lips. 'Lots of older mothers have prems. You'll be all right, I'm sure.'

'As he's a prem I'd rather he wasn't born in an ambulance.' Lisa stopped suddenly; the contractions were getting very close together.

'This phone connected?' Without waiting for an answer Rita sat on the side of the bed. The mattress dipped and Lisa slid towards the midwife, who got up rapidly. 'Dr Witherton? Rita Connolly. I'm at Sedgemoor Court. Mrs Wildmore; the elderly multigravida, yes. Preterm, I'm afraid.'

Witherton! That meant Gilmore, too, had left for his holiday. These substitutes would be unlikely to take responsibility for a home confinement. Terror clutched at Lisa. The only way she could stay at home was to be quick about it; get it over with before their precious ambulance arrived. She gathered her strength together and began to push, bear down, try to force the foetus in her birth canal to earlier delivery.

It seemed to work. No sooner had she started than her uterine muscles began to expel in earnest. Encouraged, she pushed harder.

'How d'you do.'

Lisa, immersed in what she was doing, looked up to see a man standing beside the midwife in the room.

'One of Susan's,' the midwife trumpeted. 'She went gallivanting off on holiday last night, so we'll have to do the best we can without her.' The voice suddenly dropped. '... Waters ... deep yellow ... could be ...'

The doctor's head, Lisa saw, was bent towards Rita. His eyes were still on Lisa, and he parted his lips in a smile. 'I'm Dr Witherton. Roger Gilmore's away till the week after next,' he said gently to her. 'I'm sorry, Mrs Wildmore, you're just going to have to put up with a pair of strangers, I'm afraid. I ought to just examine you.'

Examine, Lisa thought acidly, was rather a grand word; he moved her nightdress up and looked at her.

'I won't do an internal,' he told her, stepping back almost instantly, 'in case I precipitate things. But I'm not entirely satisfied; you're rather early.' He paced gravely up and down the room.

'Only two weeks,' Lisa gritted through clenched teeth.

'I really think you'll be better off in hospital. They've got all mod cons in case we run up against a problem.'

A problem? What reason had *he* to think things might go wrong? Could he tell just by looking at her, or was there something in the notes? Why couldn't he say exactly what he thought?

'I'd much rather go ahead with a home birth,' Lisa breathed through contractions. 'That's what I agreed with Dr Gilmore. I've got everything ready—'

'Prems often need expert attention,' Witherton said.

'It's only two weeks—'

'There are some indications of foetal distress.'

Foetal distress. Is that what she'd been experiencing? A foetus desperately trying to fight his way out of her body? All her instincts told her Witherton had got it wrong. The baby would be safer here than in some aseptic hospital. They'd pounce on any little defect there, insist on interfering. *She* wanted to be in charge, to be the judge of what to do for her own offspring.

'I can't take responsibility for his being born at home. I really do advise you to go to hospital. The flying squad is excellent, you know.'

'I'll take the risk,' Lisa said curtly. 'The contractions are coming very close together now.'

'Foetal distress? I thought you wanted this baby?' Alec had come into the room and right up to her, his flushed face near to hers.

'The baby could be starved of oxygen. And if he dies, it's tantamount to murder,' the doctor intoned in sepulchral tones, addressing Alec. 'Do you want that on your conscience?'

'We'd better do as he suggests, pet,' Alec encouraged her. 'I honestly think that that would be the best solution.'

'It's *my* body; I don't want to go to hospital!' Lisa cried out, clasping the sheets to herself. She couldn't think; she could only feel terror at the thought of medical intervention.

'He's my son, too, Lisa. You heard what Dr Witherton said. He's in distress. His brain might be deprived of oxygen . . .'

The contractions were powerful now; strong and painful. Even if she'd wanted to argue further, she hadn't the energy.

Dr Witherton walked over to the phone. 'You'll be in excellent hands. They're very well rigged out, you know. They'll be able to cope if the baby needs special care.'

Wearily she realised there was nothing further she could do. Apart from pray, of course. Her hands round her swollen belly, Lisa caressed her bump, and folded her palms in an attitude of prayer.

6

'Quite the little shrimp, isn't he?' Rita's loud voice dismissed the newborn she was weighing. 'He's only just on five and a half pounds.'

'He's two weeks early,' Alec said coldly. 'I'm much more worried about his being all right until the special unit arrives. They're taking their time, aren't they?'

'Your little lady pipped them to the post, old man. But we won't need them now,' Dr Witherton said. 'This chappie's very fit. Look at that hold!'

The new infant gripped the doctor's hand in such a vice that he could support his own weight. As the doctor demonstrated this feat to Lisa, the baby's big blue eyes seemed to gleam, then wink conspiratorially at her.

'Doesn't he need special care?' Alec was clearly mystified at the sudden change in attitude. 'I thought anything under five and a half pounds was considered delicate.'

'It isn't only a question of weight; and anyway, he's virtually there.' The doctor smiled, as though he personally had been responsible for producing a lusty child. 'He may be small, but there's no mistaking those lungs. He could become an opera singer with a pair like that!'

'He's certainly going to be a six-footer,' Rita said, reading the tape measure she was placing from the top of the baby's head to between his heels. 'He measures fifty-eight centimetres; that's nearly twenty-three inches.'

'Really?' Witherton went over to look. 'That's quite unusual,' he told Alec. 'The average is more like twenty.'

'And just look at those eyes!' Lisa thought she could hear admiration in Rita's tone. 'If I didn't know better, I'd swear he was focusing from about four feet. Looking me over.'

Lisa lay back, watching, listening. They weren't paying any further attention to her. They'd delivered her safely, they were now busy with the new baby, absorbed in their own world. Whatever problems they had anticipated had not appeared. But she knew there was more to it than that – another human being more. She could feel further life stirring within her: a sudden turn as, she imagined, the second baby engaged his head in the birth canal.

Was it another baby? Or was she simply so determined to have twins it was a sort of pseudo pre-birth experience?

'The bump doesn't seem to have gone down that much,' she tried softly.

'What, dear? I'll bring your baby over in a minute.'

'There still seems to be quite a bump,' Lisa repeated, raising her voice a decibel.

'Just extra fluid, I expect. There did seem to be a lot of that.' The midwife glanced at the new mother over her shoulder, her tone bored and long-suffering. 'You'll get rid of it in no time,' Rita added, bringing the baby over and patting her shoulder. 'What are you going to call him?'

'Janus,' Alec announced. He walked after Rita, peering at his new son. 'He's even smaller than Seb was.' He smiled indulgently at Lisa. 'My wife goes in for small babies,' he explained to Witherton, 'but then she's quite a dainty little thing herself.'

'A cup of tea would be most—'

'The second one is coming,' Lisa gasped, bearing down. She had been right, and this time even the medical profession could not dismiss what was happening.

Rita, caught in the act of sitting down, stood up again. 'Second one?' She laughed. 'Doesn't like to give us time to get our breath back, eh, doctor? It's just the afterbirth, my dear.'

Witherton had approached Lisa rapidly. One last, strong push and the baby's head crowned.

'It *is* another one! My goodness!' Witherton was clearly astonished. 'And you had no idea, of course.'

The actual birth, quicker even than the first, seemed ridiculously easy to Lisa. The child's first cry was almost as powerful as his brother's. This child also appeared healthy. Thinking back, Lisa found it even harder to understand the shifting of Meg's eyes, her reserve.

'Twin boys! Isn't that lovely. And another respectable five and a half pounder!' the midwife announced, awe creeping through her voice. 'Fancy that. Normally one twin's quite a bit smaller than the other.'

'Looks like another long one, too.'

'Not quite such piercing eyes,' Rita said slowly, thoughtfully. 'That's the only difference I can see.'

Alec was standing by Janus in his carrycot, staring from one new arrival to the other. Lisa could not see his expression, could only guess at his reactions.

'We could call this one Jeffrey,' she heard him say, gruff and low. 'My father's name was Jeffrey.'

Lisa, almost delirious with the fact that she had, indeed, given birth to twins, decided not to make an issue of the name. She didn't care, she had two more healthy sons, the four-leaf clover had come through with flying colours.

'Where on earth shall we put him?' Alec now wanted to know. 'We haven't made any sort of provision for two babies.'

'Don't worry about that.' Rita was cleaning the second infant's nostrils. 'Just pull out a drawer from a chest; that'll do nicely.'

'There's all the rest of Meg's old gear in the airing cupboard,' Lisa told them, feeling smug. 'Including another carrycot.'

She saw Alec's mouth drop open, then close without comment.

'All nice and warm. I asked her to let me have her old things, just in case we ran short of anything.'

'I suppose,' Witherton mentioned to Alec, dropping his voice, 'your wife resisted the idea of twins. Many women simply cannot cope with that. It's only natural; it is a great deal of extra work.' He smiled encouragingly at Lisa. 'I'll be very glad to counsel you. Mother and child care is my speciality, you know.' He turned to look as Rita brought in the second carrycot. 'And we'll make sure you have sufficient help.'

'The scan showed only one—'

'Not possible.' The doctor brushed Alec aside. 'Fraternal twins are conceived within days of each other. Identical twins do often develop later, but not as late as after a scan. The embryo can only split within two weeks of fertilisation. Some sort of mix-up in the notes, I expect.' He smiled again. 'I'm afraid getting the paperwork right is one of our greatest difficulties.'

He evidently misinterpreted the slight dismay on Lisa's face. 'Don't distress yourself, my dear.' Witherton patted her arm. 'They're definitely yours, whether the paperwork was right or wrong!' He laughed uproariously.

'There's still something moving,' Lisa said nervously, turning to the midwife for support.

Even Rita's impatience was held in check this time. 'Don't worry, love. That really is the afterbirth. And you'll lose that little bit of flab before you know it, when you get your muscle tone back.'

This time, Lisa thought grimly to herself, she was quite keen that the medical profession should have produced an accurate diagnosis. She was perfectly content with twins.

'They are both all right, are they?' she heard Alec ask. He sounded anxious, even a trifle suspicious.

'Beautiful little boys. Perfectly formed in every way.'

'No defects?'

'Ten fingers and ten toes; all present and correct,' Rita put Alec down, back to her old form.

'I'm being serious.'

Witherton took over. 'As far as I can tell, they're completely normal. They're both unusually long, and the first one has a remarkable grip. Their eyes are extraordinarily well developed. The first little lad almost seems to be focusing at a range of distances, even at this stage. No need to worry, Mr Wildmore. You have a pair of strong, healthy sons. You're very lucky.'

They were identical: big ears, wide mouths, the silken fuzz of premature hair so fair as to be almost invisible, deep frown lines across their foreheads. And there was a tiny mark, right on their lower left earlobe, identically present on them both.

'No need to check whether there's one afterbirth or two,' Dr Witherton laughed, 'we know these two are monozygotes – identicals. Have you seen those little indentations on their ears? Exactly the same, in exactly the same spot!'

How would she and Alec be able to tell them apart, Lisa wondered rather vaguely to herself. Perhaps it was just tiredness which gave her the uncomfortable, almost unnerving, feeling that there was no difference between them whatsoever. It was positively uncanny.

Alec had, by now, put the second baby in one of Meg's cots and marked it 'Jeffrey the Second'.

'Could you bring them a little nearer?' Lisa's eyes, sharpened by motherhood, had noted a difference after all. The firstborn, Janus, had a somewhat pointed skull. 'Janus has a differently shaped head,' she announced triumphantly.

'That's temporary,' Witherton pointed out. 'The head is very soft, you see. The bones aren't closed; the top – the fontanelle – is open, to avoid damage when pushing through the birth canal. The second twin has obviously profited from his brother's work and was able to slide through with his head much squarer.'

'It'll sort itself out quite quickly,' the midwife told them. 'You can't rely on that staying different for more than a few weeks at most.'

Lisa, content, had exactly what she'd wished for – two more sons, Janus and Jeffrey. Both strong, thin bodies; limpid blue eyes, squat noses. She would sort out how to tell them apart another time. An overwhelming sense of motherhood, of flesh of her flesh, flowed through her, warmed pink into her cheeks.

'Could you bring the cots right up to the bed?' she asked Rita. 'I'd like one on either side.'

The midwife moved the cots without a murmur. 'They'll be with you for life,' she said. 'You'll never be free of them.'

Lisa stretched out sensitive fingertips, felt the silky fuzz on her newborns' heads, pulled Janus to her and brushed her lips over his eyes. They opened wide, brilliant, aware. A surge of happiness brought tears to Lisa's eyes. She put him back and picked Jeffrey up, snuggled him to her breast, oblivious of the rest of the world.

'Right then, mother, you're on your own,' Rita announced, packed up and ready to leave.

Lisa smiled, nodded at her absently.

'They look just like Seb when he was born,' Lisa mentioned to her husband as soon as they were alone.

'I know,' he laughed. 'We seem to have reproduced ourselves in a set of three.'

'By the time they're ten or eleven people might think they're triplets.' It just slipped out, as though preprogrammed. Lisa had no idea why she felt impelled to talk of triplets. 'The doctors could be wrong again,' she worried. 'That bulge has not gone down at all. I *might* be carrying another one.'

He laughed at her. 'Honestly, Lisa. You really are taking this obsession of yours too far. First you imagine you're . . .' He stopped and looked at her again, and frowned. 'I suppose they did mix up the scan, or misread it, or something,' he finally conceded. 'Though I can't see how. After all, we both saw the one baby.'

'They can't have it both ways, Alec. Either they didn't interpret the scan properly – and we simply allowed them to do it for us – or the foetus split later.'

'Or they were lying in such a way that one completely obscured the other,' Alec said gently. 'That could account for it.'

'I thought of that as well.' She smiled and sat up straighter in the bed;

she felt exhilarated, unwilling to go to sleep. 'I did think that tiresome Parslow was holding something back. Perhaps he saw some sort of shadowing.'

She hoped that's what it was. Instinct told her there was more to it than that, that Parslow had identified something but had not recognised its significance. But still, so what? She had her twins, healthy, strong. Nothing else mattered.

'D'you really think you might be carrying another baby? Is it possible for one to be born later?'

'I looked it up when I was doing my researches,' Lisa explained. 'It's happened in the past. Quite rarely, of course, but twins have been born one or two weeks apart. If that can happen with twins, presumably it can also happen with triplets.'

Alec was not smiling now. 'I certainly hope you've got that wrong,' he said. 'We planned a family of two.'

You may have, Lisa thought coldly to herself. I planned on rather more.

7

Lisa was lying on the couch in her conservatory, revelling in the luxury of having some time entirely to herself. The twins were sleeping in their prams beside her, and Seb was still at Meg's. She had, she thought, about half an hour before he was due back.

'Don't you at least need a home help?' Alec had nagged at Lisa several times in the last few days.

'I'm managing extremely well,' she'd snapped at him, pursing her lips and narrowing her eyes. 'Rita gives the babies their bath, and I don't want anyone else around them, spreading germs. Lucky it's such torpid weather; I don't even need to dress them most of the time. And God bless Pampers!'

Help, Lisa felt, meant someone constantly about, someone she'd feel obliged to talk to, someone who'd want to chat over coffee and biscuits, require regular cups of tea. Lisa preferred her own way of coping; after all, Meg managed a much larger family *and* her chickens and goats. For the moment Lisa wanted as little interference as she could get away with. There was a sense, she realised vaguely, of not wanting to be spied on.

Alec's returning interest in her body was a different issue. Something impelled her to try to keep him away for the time being, though why she felt this she could not understand. There was, after all, no longer any reason for it. She shelved the problem neatly by insisting he help her with the two o'clock morning feed. As she expected, that knocked him out.

In any case, he wasn't at home all that often. The launch of Multiplier, due around the time of the twins' birth, had unexpectedly been postponed. The delay had infuriated Alec; all his hard work, all the time he'd spent, were wasted. Flaxton, overwhelmed with pre-launch orders of what promised to be an even more commercially important fertiliser than Doubler, needed Alec's presence both in Bristol and in London.

'And do you really have to go on wearing that awful gear?' Alec had demanded several times, exasperated.

For some reason she could not explain even to herself Lisa continued to wear her maternity clothes. The bump, she had to admit when she examined her body in the bath, though marginally there, was flattening rapidly. Was she disturbed, suffering from post-partum depression? Did her conviction that another child would soon appear mean some sort of mental illness? She'd heard of women becoming psychotic after childbirth. Was that why she was so irritable with Alec, so on edge? Perhaps she'd ask Meg for some of the valerian tea she'd always sworn by.

'Drugs can be addictive.' Meg had shaken her head when Lisa had brought the subject up. 'I grow the roots right in my own garden; got to be better for you.'

The sound of crunching gravel on the drive shook Lisa out of her thoughts; probably Meg already, she realised. She walked to the conservatory door and saw Meg and Sebastian, hand in hand, coming towards her. Seb was sobbing, wiping his eyes. He pulled away from Meg as soon as he saw his mother, and ran towards her as fast as he could.

'Kitty dead, Mummy!' he cried out, tears smudging down his face.

Lisa lifted him into her arms. 'There, now, Seb; you know sometimes kitties get ill—'

'All kitties dead!'

'Frank drowned all five of them,' Meg greeted her, subdued. 'Forgot he did promise one to Sebbie. He's that upset.'

'There now, darling. We'll find another kitty for you, promise.'

'I'll pick out another one for him,' Meg said uncomfortably. 'Don't know what Frank was thinking of, drowning all five of them.' She smiled vaguely at Lisa. 'Sebbie does like the calicoes specially. Thought I spotted one at Mark's the other day.'

'Come along now, Sebbie, it's going to be all right. There'll be another kitty for you soon.' She cuddled the little boy to her as she turned to Meg. 'It is good of you to take such trouble, Meg. You mean Mark Ditcheat's got a new litter? That would be lovely.'

Meg walked over to the prams and peered in, then swept her eyes over Lisa. 'Still in your smocks? I'd have thought you'd be fed up with them by now,' she said, looking at Lisa critically. 'You're so little anyway, and you got your figure back right away. Different for me; nothing else for me to wear.'

'They're much more comfortable in this heat,' Lisa insisted evenly, annoyed at Meg's indiscretion. 'I'm sorry, Meg. I'd offer you a cup of tea, but I'm so pressed for time . . .'

'No call to worry, just bringing Seb back,' Meg said quietly, searching Lisa's face. 'And Frank asked me to let you know he didn't forget the milk. Don'll drop it off later. He won't be long. It's market day; he's taking some of the Jerseys in.'

'We can survive for at least another hour,' Lisa joked. 'After that the racket will be intolerable.' She glanced at the prams affectionately.

'Seems the goat's milk is doing them a power of good. Natural's best, whatever those doctors do say.'

'I know.' Lisa could not help sounding proud. 'They didn't lose a single ounce. Rita says she's never come across prems putting weight on right away. Janus looks almost plump! I told her your two did just as well. She was very impressed.'

'She comes from London,' Meg dismissed Rita as irrelevant. 'But I never did see a baby put on weight as quick as your Janus. Not even Phyllie.'

Lisa laughed, delighted. She was assured now in her motherhood; she was no longer infertile, pitied and patronised. On the contrary, she was admired, looked up to. Even sophisticated London friends, normally uninterested in babies, were clamouring to see the twins, though Lisa was keeping them at bay. 'Janus certainly loves his food. And they do seem to be thriving on the bottle.'

'You're settled on not giving the basil tea another go?'

'I can't manage to feed two of them, Meg. And there's so much to do, I'm always rushing round. It's very kind of you, but I simply haven't got the energy.'

Lisa felt guilty about rejecting Meg's kind attempts to help her breast feed the infants. Meg was doing all she could to support her, and yet . . . Lisa realised she was acting almost churlishly towards Meg and smiled brightly to cover up.

'There is something I'd like to try, though, Meg.'

Meg's eyes lightened into friendliness. 'And what be that, then?'

'You mentioned about valerian tea. A sedative, you said, better than any tranquilliser.'

'Having problems sleeping?' The eyes questioned her, sought out intimacy.

'Rather het up, I suppose,' Lisa admitted unwillingly. 'I'm always worrying.'

'I'll send some roots round with Don,' Meg immediately reassured her. 'Steep an ounce in a cup of cold water for a day or so. Doesn't taste too good, mind. And see you don't take too much.'

'I won't.' In spite of Meg's obvious concern, Lisa could not rid herself of the feeling that Meg was holding out on her somehow; that she knew something, some other facet, about having twins which she refused to share with Lisa.

What made Lisa even more uncomfortable was her own changed attitude to Meg's children. She felt them to be a threat to her babies in some mysterious way she simply couldn't account for. Surely she wasn't prejudiced by Phyllis's defect? It wasn't contagious, after all. The clubfoot had, according to Meg, simply been caused by the position in the womb. Two foetuses, naturally, had less room to play with. And Meg's twins had been considerably larger than her own. But what really upset Lisa was the look of the brace on Phyllis's leg. It seemed so obtrusive, so ugly. Perhaps the valerian tea would calm her down about that as well.

Meg kissed the top of Seb's head. 'I know you're pressed. I won't keep you.' She made no immediate move to leave, however, but stood, staring at the infants lying asleep near the shaded windows. 'They're getting on all right, are they?'

'Getting on?'

'No little problems?' She looked at Lisa, then back at the infants. 'You know, like my Phyllie. Always best to make sure you catch small troubles directly.'

Lisa remembered that Meg had not wanted medical interference when Phyllis was first born. It was Frank who'd insisted on the operation. Even the doctors had maintained it was a borderline case. Why was Meg advocating doctors now? It seemed entirely out of character for the woman who believed in using herbs rather than modern drugs to cure the occasional minor ailments her family suffered from.

'They're perfectly all right, Meg.'

'Just remember, I can drive you over to the doctor's any time,' Meg said, waving goodbye to Seb and finally moving off.

Lisa hugged Seb to herself, stroked his hair, enjoyed the feel of his strong, energetic limbs. She always made a point of spending time with him when he came back for lunch, before the twins' two o'clock feed.

'More kitty,' he insisted. 'Miaow, miaow.'

'*More* kitty, Seb?' Lisa felt for her little boy and his distress. 'You mean you'd like a new kitty now. We'll find one for you very soon.'

'More, more,' he persisted.

His insistence on more of everything was beginning to fray her nerves. Lisa kissed him, then brought his paintbox out. He splashed seven similar shapes all over the paper.

'More kitty,' he repeated.

Lisa took the brush and added ears and tails to five of the vague blobs he had sloshed down. Meg had said there'd been a litter of five.

'More, Mummy!'

She added ears and tails to two more blobs. That seemed to satisfy him.

The rumbling of a farm vehicle in the drive alerted Lisa to Don's arrival with the milk. She hurried through to the kitchen and was surprised to see him, milk churn in his left hand, moving round the outside of the house, towards the conservatory. She went out by the back door and followed him.

He turned as he heard her feet crunch gravel behind him. 'A'rternoon, missus. Brought t'milk.' He stood awkwardly, looking beyond her, making no move to hand her the small churn whose contents she always emptied straight into the bottles in the steriliser.

'That is kind of you.' Something about Don's intense stare, his stolid stance, made her feel uneasy, made her wonder why he continued to stand there. 'Thank you so much.'

He made no move to leave. There was evidently something he was nerving himself up to say. Lisa noticed his leathered cheeks, lined in a dozen runnels. She was startled to find herself thinking what an unusually attractive face it was. The open, light grey eyes, honest and clear in sun-creased skin, had the direct, sympathetic look of a man who cared. Then she remembered Don had no children of his own. His wife hand-reared any orphan lambs on the farm instead. And he had, Meg had told her, taken a special interest in Meg's twins. So why was she so nervous of him?

Don was staring through the windows of the conservatory. 'Them in they prams?' The low, diffident voice had finally emerged. It took Lisa by surprise. Was he really concerned about her babies? Though smiling occasionally at Seb, he hadn't ever spoken to him, or paid any attention to him. Perhaps Don was captivated, like so many others, by the special charm of identical twins.

'You'd like to see them?'

He nodded, expressive eyes sweeping towards the door and waiting for her to go in ahead of him. He followed almost on her heels, put the milk churn on the floor, and peered first at one infant, then at the other. Lisa expected a perfunctory glance into each pram followed by a quick retreat. Instead, Don took his time, moving his eyes slowly backwards and forwards from one baby to the other. At last the small, spare man turned to her.

'Be them stout littl'uns?'

'The doctor said they were exceptionally healthy,' she said, mystified.

'Got t'same mark on they ears,' Don said. 'Doctor seen she?'

'It's just a little mark, nothing to worry about,' Lisa explained. Don's powers of observation were impressive.

'Hard to tell they apart.'

'I know,' Lisa agreed, laughing now. 'I dress them in different colours just to make sure we know which is which. Yellow for Janus and red for Jeffrey,' she said, pointing to the tiny T-shirts over their nappies.

'I's green,' Seb put in, looking up at Don and jiggling Janus's pram handle vigorously up and down.

'Seb's favourite colour is green; he's the eldest, so he was allowed to choose,' Lisa put in quickly, taking the little hands off the handle. She always tried to remember to include Seb. He'd been upstaged by two infants, not just one.

Janus, woken by the violent movement, opened his eyes.

'You'll probably need earplugs now,' Lisa said. 'He expects the instant appearance of the bottle when he wakes, and he's got a very healthy pair of lungs.' Lisa lifted Janus out and held him up for Don to see. The infant's eyes opened wide. Lisa was struck again by the piercing gleam that seemed to glow from them, then noticed Don's eyes broaden as Janus focused on him. The stockman stepped back, crashing into the goat's milk, spilling white liquid all over the quarry floor. He twisted back down rapidly to right the churn, but at least half a pint of milk had oozed along, creeping towards the sisal rug. A large stag beetle, lurking at the sides, began to crawl towards the milk.

'Sorry, missus. Bain't that cackhanded, usual.'

Lisa hated the sight of the big black carapace moving slowly towards the white liquid. She was about to scoop it up and throw it out when she saw Don's heavy leather boot move towards it, then crush it. The beetle's shell crunched open.

'Don't worry,' Lisa breathed, stunned by the speed with which he'd acted. 'Could you just hold Janus a minute? I'll fetch a cloth.'

It seemed to Lisa that there was more than reluctance in Don's eyes as he looked uncertainly at the child, then took him from her awkwardly. She dashed out to fetch a cloth and pail, wondering why Don had stayed so long and become so clumsy. Coming back through the door she saw Don fingering Janus's left ear. The child, leaning at an odd angle, looked as though he might slip out of Don's arms.

Lisa sprinted forward in alarm, dropping the pail with a clatter. Don, startled, grasped the yellow T-shirt, successfully stopping the child from crashing to the floor.

'Clothes don't stay on they tight enough,' he said as she rushed towards them, holding out her arms. 'Best use some'utt else.'

Lisa covered her irritation with a grin. This man had nearly dropped Janus onto the hard quarry-tiled floor. Was he presuming to tell her how to look after her own children?

'Metal be best,' he said, head down. 'Bain't on for they to rid theyselves o' metal.'

He handed Janus back to her and took the cleaning gear to mop up the mess, slowly and carefully. Unhurriedly he crunched on several beetles and dropped their dead bodies into the pail. Then he backed out of the conservatory door. The eyes which had seemed so clear before were veiled.

'Us'll bring more milk,' he said, not looking back.

'When am I going to be allowed to see my new grandsons?'

'I told you, Sarah. They're very delicate. The midwife says they shouldn't be exposed to too many people's germs.'

'Poppycock. You just don't want me around.'

'If that's the way you want to interpret it.'

Lisa was already in bed, though it was only half past seven. Feeding the babies every four hours round the clock and looking after Seb made her snatch at any extra time she could get for sleep. But it was more than that. She simply could not rid herself of a feeling that something disconcerting was about to happen; a nervousness which showed itself in constant checking that the new infants were still all right.

Don had upset her. His odd reference to metal kept coming back to her, reminding her of tabbing on the farm. What on earth had he meant?

'I'm sorry, Sarah. One of the babies is crying; I'll have to go.'

Lisa was more than usually reluctant about a visit from her mother-in-law. It was not that she harboured any special dislike of her, but something motivated her to keep her children, and herself, away from absolutely everyone, not only locals.

'It's the heatwave,' she lied smoothly to Sarah. 'And Rita thinks it would be best if no one visits for at least a month,' she added. 'There's measles about. That could be fatal for such tiny babies.'

'Wouldn't it be useful if I came down?' her mother-in-law asked, subdued. 'At least I could take Seb off your hands.'

'He really isn't any problem,' Lisa almost shouted. 'Actually he's very good at helping me.'

Seb, though sadly neglected compared to the days before the twins' birth, showed no apparent jealousy of his younger brothers. He merely followed Lisa about, handing her nappies, staring at one or other of his brothers lolling in his carrycot or pram, and watched silently as his mother fed them.

'You're telling me a child not yet two is more help than I would be,' Sarah said dryly. 'I quite see that.'

Lisa was once more overwhelmed by a presentiment of disaster, a feeling of an unknown, inexplicable dread hanging over her. She swung out of bed and ran along the corridor, holding the portable phone, intent on checking the infants yet again.

'What's that odd noise?'

'I'm on my way to the nursery; the portable tends to pick up static.'

'They're crying *again*? You need some time off, Lisa. You'll wear yourself out completely.'

If only her mother-in-law would stop ringing her, Lisa thought dully. If only people would leave her to get on with it, stop telling her how to run her life. As far as she was concerned, she'd worked out a splendid routine. She didn't need their help.

8

It was two weeks to the day of the twins' birth – Friday – that Lisa woke before the clamouring for the six o'clock feed. A hot flush suffused her body; she was uneasy, about to get up and look at the twins although there was no sound, no crying to alert her. Alec was by her side, sleeping heavily. And, as she turned away, she made out a little figure standing just inside the bedroom.

'Hello, Mummy,' Seb husked hopefully, shadowy by the creaking door.

Was that what had woken her? Seb had managed to climb out of his cot and she had heard him coming?

'Ssh,' she sibilated at him. 'You should be asleep.' She got out of bed as softly as she could, lifted Seb up and tiptoed him back to his room. He squirmed out of her arms and stood, pulling at her hand. A tearing at her guts; her little boy was hoping for some time alone with her. She had neglected him, sending him off to Meg's first thing every morning, too busy to do much with him even at lunchtime. Just like yesterday; no sooner started on helping him with painting his kittens than Janus and Jeffrey had demanded their feed.

'More,' Seb announced, confident. He took her hand and tried to pull her with him towards his door. 'Seb got more bother.'

Something was wrong; she knew immediately something was wrong. A fast pulse drummed reverberations into her ears as she realised the twins' nursery door was wide open. Had Alec left it like that? But there was no sound of crying; their rhythmic breathing told her they were still asleep.

'It's not time to get up yet, Seb,' she told him gently, calmed by the sound of mingled breathing. She disengaged her toddler's hand. 'Go back to sleep.'

'More,' he told her again, eagerly. 'More, more.'

'More what, Seb?' He was keen on his food, additionally so now that his baby brothers were potential rivals for it. 'It isn't time for breakfast yet.'

'More bother.'

More bother? Did he mean more mother? He wanted to see more of his mother? She hated the look of resignation on his earnest little face. Was that what he was desperately trying to tell her? He wanted to see more of her?

Her heart contracted as she forced herself to remain with him for a few moments. She bounced him in her arms, stroked his hair out of his eyes, tucked him up in his cot again and softly sang 'Pop Goes the Weasel' to him.

'More *bother*, Mummy,' he insisted again, his voice becoming louder. He loved nursery rhymes, but this time there was something distracting him from them. And her. All the time she spent in Seb's bedroom she had to stifle an odd nervousness which urged her towards the nursery. The babies were all right, she kept repeating to herself. There were no noises off, no need at all to get worked up.

Even so, she left Seb after only one verse to go through to the twins' room and was, at first, relieved to see Jeffrey sleeping soundly in his cot, the relaxed sleep of the recently born. A weight off her shoulders, she turned to the other cot.

Her heart thudded into her throat, then palpitated crazily.

Was she seeing double? It was still not quite day, cotton curtains blocking out the strengthening light, but surely she could make out *two* infants' heads in the second cot?

She pulled herself together. Alec must have put the twins in one cot, by mistake. So tired out after the two o'clock feed that he had lumped Jeffrey together with Janus instead of putting him in his own carrycot.

No, it couldn't be that. She'd just checked on Jeffrey. Gulping, keeping her eyes away from the second cot, she swished the curtains to the sides; she could not face the harshness of electric light. Turning round from the window she held her breath, eyes turned to Jeffrey's cot. One small head and, lower down, his body bare except for a Pampers nappy, his limbs sprawling, the coverlet thrown back. He was sleeping peacefully, his breathing even, normal. She looked at him, forcing her mind to accept what her eyes saw. Tortuously, reluctantly, she twisted her body round to look at the second carrycot. Two heads, close together, crowded in the small cot; two babies, both completely naked, boys, identical, the nappy that had been on Janus popped open and lying loose. The cover had been kicked beneath two pairs of legs.

A cold finger of terror held her shoulders tight as she stopped concentrating on irrelevancies and the real situation forced itself upon her: three infants where there had been two, two in the cot where there had been one. She stood, rooted to the spot, and gaped at the four legs in front of her. She looked towards the top – two heads. Two separate infants lying side by side; even at her most idiotic she could not mistake two for one.

Lisa pinched herself. Was she asleep? Another nightmare? If so, it was terribly vivid, more lucid than her ordinary dreams. Had Seb crawled into a cot, retreating, somehow, back to infancy? She made herself return to his room; he was safely surrounded by the bars of his own cot.

'More bother,' he assured her again, smiling at her.

More bother – he meant more *brother*. He knew! He'd simply accepted what seemed to him a fact in his short experience of life, something she could not begin to understand. She stood at the foot of his cot, wanting to stay, wanting to ask him questions, knowing she had to leave.

She forced herself back into the twins' room. She had to switch on the electric light, flood the room with illumination, disperse the deceptive flickers of strengthening daylight. A trick of shadows, perhaps; that's what it had been. Clouds scudding over the sky, creating double images. She looked again.

Three babies; two naked, crowded together in one carrycot. Another in the second cot, with his nappy on. All three identical. She tried to still her heart now beating at twice its normal rate, tried to subdue her horror, gasped, drank down great draughts of air.

The single infant in the carrycot, no doubt woken by the sudden brightness, began to stir and open his eyes, to mewl, then cry demand for his feed. The response to mother him took over. Lisa lifted him out of his cot and swayed with him, cooing to him, her back turned to the other cot. This was Jeffrey, her second twin, born just two weeks ago. She took the prepared bottles of goat's milk from the small fridge they'd set up in the nursery and placed them in the bottle warmers. The routine she'd worked out – changing the first infant to wake him while she warmed the bottles – occupied her sufficiently to stop her from thinking. Force of habit made her sit in the rocker as she fed Jeffrey, her eyes firmly fixed on his little face, prattling at him, making baby noises, enjoying the sensation of his weight against her breast. He sucked the teat lustily, quickly, as though sensing that now he had two rivals.

Distracted, unable to come to terms with what she'd seen, Lisa fed Jeffrey until a growing din from two more babies forced her to place him in his cot and prop the bottle on a towel so he could feed himself.

She turned round. Two red, squalling infants. As far as she could tell, identical. Where had the second baby come from?

And there it was again. That odd, deep yellow stain. The open nappy, Lisa saw, was wet and faintly yellow. But the bedding, and the babies' legs, were covered in a deeper wet, a curious, permeating substance.

She took the gauze nappy she always kept slung over her shoulder and rubbed it gently against one leg. The yellow soaked into the gauze, leaving the leg quite clean. Just urine; she was making a fuss about a little urine. Then she understood. The heat had concentrated the urine, and it was highly coloured. No wonder Janus had asked for so much food, gobbled it up. She should have given him water. Foolish of her. What she had done was to offer him large quantities of goat's milk. Whatever Meg said, it occurred to Lisa, the stuff was too rich. Janus had looked quite puffy yesterday.

As she watched, the two babies turned puce, their mouths wide open, screaming for food. Which child should she pick up? They decided for her, the cries of one drowning out the other. She put a dummy in the less insistent mouth, then carefully put her hands under the raucous one's arms and lifted him up.

He was a baby; a baby like the one she had just fed. Quickly, expertly, she cleaned him up, powdered him and placed a nappy on him. Was he Janus? Who could tell? She held him to her, nestling her face against his, feeling her motherhood. This was her child, her son.

Settling him in an easy chair, Lisa propped the bottle for him to feed himself. It was time to pick up the third baby. Would this one disappear as soon as she touched him? Had she brought a phantom baby on herself with her superstitious wishing for twins on a four-leaf clover? The First Commandment said: 'Thou shalt not have false gods before me.' Was this her punishment for breaking it?

Gingerly, Lisa forced her hands to support the third baby under his armpits. She held him up to look at him. The dummy dropped out of his mouth and he began to whimper. He looked so helpless, so lost, she could not resist him. She pressed the little body secure against herself, felt his responsive heartbeat, wrapped her arm tenderly behind his neck, took in his baby smell. He was as solid, as tangible as the other two. Her warmth had calmed him for a moment; he gazed at her with trusting, baby eyes. She sighed; she could not see the slightest difference, the faintest mark, to distinguish him from the two infants she had just seen to. A baby; adorable, enchanting.

She hoisted the child onto her left arm and hip, balancing him as she walked over to the other two. Tiny baby fingers gripped tight as she settled the bottles at better angles. Third bottle in the fridge, she told herself briskly. The twins were such eager feeders that she always made an extra bottle for topping up.

The child on her arm puckered his mouth for a teat. Lisa settled back in the rocking chair and offered him some goat's milk. He sucked as ardently as either of his brothers, his left-hand fingers wisping over hers. His brothers! This was *her* baby. She and Alec had yet another son.

Should she tell Alec how she found him? She toyed with what that would imply. And there was no doubt in her mind: he would immediately call in the medical profession.

Doctors – she shuddered at the thought. The doctors, if they got the faintest whiff, the slightest suggestion, that something out of the ordinary had happened, would take over. There would be searching questions, a clinical atmosphere, disinfectants, aggressive nurses. Tests, she could already see; revolting, disgusting, possibly painful tests on her three infants and herself.

Hospitals – they'd insist she go to hospital, be prodded by unsmiling consultants, obsequious interns. The children taken care of in a different part, nursed by strangers, Seb left alone . . . She could say goodbye to her dream of motherhood. She must not allow even the slightest suspicion of this event to get to the doctors. They'd all conspire to take away her children; they would tear them right out of her loving arms.

The baby on her lap had emptied the bottle. He seemed gentler than either of the other two, quieter. He lay, limpid and tranquil, in her arms, his blue eyes open. Her heart went out to him as love flowed over her. The soft, intelligent eyes seemed to invite her to hug him, burp him. She would not – could not – be deprived of this happiness. She was his mother; she was the mother of them all.

The baby gurgled at her, stroked at her hands. Delicate, fluttering hands, so unlike Janus and his hard, strong grip. She was convinced that he was the new arrival; he might look the same, but his personality was quite unlike either of his brothers'. Lisa was sure she was holding her latest son.

Tenderly she laid him on one of the coverlets on the floor, burped Jeffrey and put him back into his cot, and removed the third infant from the easy chair, then burped him, too. This one was Janus; there was no doubt in her mind. She could not mistake that clear, bright, penetrating look, those gleaming eyes. His lips began to move as though he were trying to communicate. He put strong, grasping arms round her neck; she had to extricate herself and was surprised at the strength it took.

She prattled at Janus, returned him to his carrycot, picked up the new baby and wrapped him in her nursing apron. She sat back in the rocker, held the infant to herself, tried to calm the turmoil in her mind, to think. The baby bubbled at her; the blue eyes blinked, composed. Small fingers twined themselves endearingly round one of hers. He looked content, his eyelids lowering down, trusting her. She was his mother; he belonged to *her*.

She looked down at herself. Her normal slim figure was back again. The extra bump she'd mentioned to the midwife had definitely gone.

The new child was obviously her latest offspring. He had to be, he looked exactly like her other babies. He was so sweet, so trusting. Her love, her passion, her very existence were all involved with these babies. She had identical triplets now, and she had no intention of giving any of them up.

Intent on her thoughts, she had not heard a noise and was horrified to see the door opening, slowly and quietly. Was Alec up already? What should she do? She squeezed the infant in her arms, held him protectively against her breast. He'd have to pry him loose . . .

'Hello, Mummy.' Seb edged in, smiling winsomely up at her. 'More bother.'

'Seb,' she whispered hoarsely, putting her arm round him, covering the top of his head with kisses. 'Sweetheart, I told you. It isn't time to get up yet. Come on, darling. Back to bed.'

'More bother,' he said again, looking at the baby in her arms, at the baby in the cot. 'Mummy got more bother.'

'Another little brother,' she agreed, lowering the infant she was clutching. 'We'll have to think of names for him.'

'Yames,' he said eagerly.

'Mummy's very busy, Seb. Go back to your room and I'll bring your special book.'

He looked at her, she thought, almost conspiratorially.

'Yames,' he said, clearly trying to pronounce the J. 'Mummy got Yames.'

'James?' she said, almost to herself. Seb clearly understood she was holding the new infant, and wanted to call him James. Well, why not let him name his new brother?

Could he have . . .?

She was letting her imagination run away with her again. He might be bright and very forward for his age, but he couldn't spin a new baby out of thin air any more than she could.

She was shaking now, trying to control her trembling. The infant on one arm, she led Seb back to his room. She did not dare to put the baby down to lift the little boy back into his cot.

'Sit on the sheepskin rug, Sebbie. Play with your helicopter book, there's a good boy.'

Lisa walked towards the guestroom, hugging the new baby to herself. She had mentioned to Alec that she might go and lie down in there after the early morning feed so as not to deprive him of that last precious half-hour or more of sleep.

Seb had seen the third infant, Seb had understood that there were three. And he knew the one in her arms was not Janus; he knew he was 'another one'. She wasn't clear how he could spot the difference, but he seemed quite sure; and he'd confirmed what she instinctively felt. Whatever the actual case, the one on her arm was the one she'd call James.

'More bother,' he'd said. Of course that's what he'd been trying to tell her before. He'd already seen the new child, had come to fetch her. How had it happened? It was simply crazy. How *could* it have happened? Babies did not appear out of nowhere.

Had she given birth to a third infant? Sleepwalking, unaware? Was she so tired she'd done it all in a sort of trance? Cleaned up after herself? That was the only possible sane explanation; the only thing that *could* have happened. She'd tell Alec the simple truth: this was her child – their child.

Quaking, shivering in spite of the hot, humid weather, Lisa took the new baby and lay back, exhausted, on the guestroom bed. She pulled the covers over them both and waited for Alec to get up.

9

'Lisa?'

She could hear Alec's slippers sliding into the twins' room and out again; up early and looking for her. The thudding in her chest threatened to choke her. Her mind, gone numb, refused to function. She waited, tense, unprepared, hoping love for her children would inspire the right words to say to Alec. Would he accept that James was his latest son, *his* flesh and blood? Because, in fact, that's what he was, whatever the circumstances of his birth.

It all depended on her; her grit, her character, what sort of mother she really was. Fail in her motherhood, and she'd fail her whole family, stand to lose all three babies, perhaps all four children. Who'd believe *her* that Jeffrey was not the same as Janus, was not involved?

'I'm in here,' she called unsteadily, but raising her voice enough to carry into the hall from the guestroom.

She heard his footsteps, already halfway down the stairs, stop and return, his tread now firm and decisive.

'You don't have to go to quite such lengths on my account,' he began as he swung the door open and stood, his eyes adjusting to the curtained room, looking towards her.

'Hello, darling,' she greeted him, a determined smile wreathing her face.

He went to pull back the curtains. Turned against the light, his expression was hidden from Lisa. But the thrown back head and shoulders showed Alec's instant doubt that all was well.

'Is something wrong?' he asked, eyes fastening on the bed, seeing she was in rather than on it. Lisa watched, the roots of her hair rising, as he focused. She saw him take in the baby's head beside her on the pillow, tasted salt on her parched lips.

Alec's jaw fell open as he came nearer, peering at the infant cradled in her arms. He stopped, looking from her to the child and back again. 'Which one of them is that? I just checked their room; I could have sworn I just saw both of them!'

He turned on his heel, crashed out of the room and back into the nursery, reappeared at once.

'My God!' Alec stared, disconcerted, at the baby, then back at Lisa. 'Is that really what I think it is?'

'We have another son,' Lisa said, partly uncovering the baby wrapped in the apron.

'So you *did* have another one.' Alec gulped, his eyes round goggles, then closing to slits, almost, she felt, accusing her of causing another child by mentioning the possibility.

'Darling—'

'How could you possibly have produced another baby? Didn't Witherton examine you?'

He was assuming she had given birth again. If she had not panicked in the first place, she would have known that that would be his reaction. What else *could* he think?

'There was one unexpected birth already, Alec.' Her voice sounded husky; she cleared her throat, forcing her voice into a calm, low throb. 'Witherton didn't even examine the afterbirth; you remember, he said there was no need.'

'Why didn't you call me? Have you rung the midwife?'

'I only just had time to get on the bed,' Lisa explained.

'What I can see of him looks *exactly* like the other two,' Alec announced, switching on the overhead light and bending over the new baby, examining him. 'Well, exactly like *Janus*, actually.' He looked again, intently. 'Same head shape. Bit thinner, of course.' He fingered the gaudy apron round the baby and pulled it back. 'You simply had him, just like that?'

'Giving birth is a perfectly natural activity.'

Alec frowned at her. 'Not all that natural stuff again, Lisa. In our society women have medical attendants.'

'He arrived before I even knew it.'

'The birth canal's still wide, I suppose.' He nodded, mystified but trying to come to grips with the situation. A deep crease of concentration as he looked again. 'His face looks the same as the other two *now*; not crumpled up, or highly coloured, or anything.'

Lisa shivered involuntarily; Alec was pretty sharp, after all. Perhaps he'd work it out.

'I'm sorry, darling.' He put his arms round her, kissing her. 'I shouldn't tire you with all these questions. You must be cold and exhausted. I'd better make a hot drink before we do anything else.' He took off his dressing gown and wrapped it round her shoulders. 'It does just seem so incredible – *another* baby.'

'Grown on, I suppose,' Lisa reasoned as much for herself as for Alec. 'He's had more time.'

'Identical triplets; that's quite remarkable.' Alec stared again at the new arrival. 'How are we going to tell them apart?'

'Bracelets,' Lisa said instantly. 'I'd like to put silver identification bracelets on their left wrists or ankles.'

The words slipped out as though rehearsed. She had absolutely no idea why she was saying this, but the moment she had uttered it she felt a sense of calm, as though the bracelets would solve any problems that might arise. The vision of something strong, securely strapped to each child's wrist, was oddly comforting. In her enthusiasm she was raising herself up in bed, hoisting the infant on to her lap.

'You really shouldn't move like that, I'm sure,' Alec said, leaning towards her. 'I'll do that for you. I'd better get a nappy on him.' He bent to scoop up the infant wrapped in his unusual swaddling clothes.

'Better not wake him,' Lisa said hurriedly. Her arms curled protectively round her child. 'Perhaps if you could fetch one for me?'

As he went out Lisa lay back, a feeling of serenity overpowering her, an almost heady feeling of bliss replacing her previous tense anxiety. Alec had simply assumed that she had given birth again; he had not really questioned it. And James was Alec's flesh and blood as much as he was hers.

By the time Alec came back into the room, holding a packet of Pampers and a towel, Lisa had closed her eyes and drifted into a sort of dream.

'Are you all right, darling?' He sounded anxious. 'You look all in. I'll ring the doctor right away.'

Lisa opened her eyes and smiled; a full, beatific smile. 'Just taking a catnap,' she reassured him easily. 'Plenty of time for all that later.'

'We ought to get someone,' he said, reaching for the phone.

Lisa put her hand on his. 'I'm fine, darling; honestly. Nothing to worry about. I know the drill by now. There's no rush about the baby, either. He's sleeping soundly, as you can see.'

'But . . .'

Her obviously placid acceptance of the new baby seemed to get through to him at last. He grinned assent and sat down by her. 'You must have known,' he said slowly, a wondering admiration in his eyes.

'You must have known right from the start.'

'Only about the twins,' Lisa said softly.

'Hold on, I'll get the kitchen scales.'

When he returned, Lisa did not stop him from taking the baby and weighing him; five pounds eleven ounces. 'That really beats everything.' Alec laughed, delighted now. 'Exactly one ounce less than Jeffrey weighed in yesterday. He must have gained at almost the same rate, even if he couldn't quite keep up with Janus.'

The new child looked identical to Janus, not Jeffrey. After only two weeks, Jeffrey and Janus were already easier to tell apart. Lisa realised that James would soon develop along his own lines as well, though he looked exactly like Janus now; except that he was lighter than the Janus of yesterday. Extra fluid – Janus must have been retaining fluid. That's why he'd looked so bloated yesterday. Rita had mentioned something about his looking really puffy.

Lisa smiled uncertainly. 'And he may lose a bit of weight at first,' she reminded Alec, although she guessed he was unlikely to. Neither Janus nor Jeffrey had lost a single ounce.

'Not if he's like his brothers,' Alec boasted, looking quite proud, even sounding enthusiastic. 'Rita said she'd never seen anything like it.' He paused. 'When, exactly, was this one born?'

'I fed the babies,' Lisa said. 'And changed them and everything. Then I felt a bit overdone, so I came in here to lie down.'

'That's when it happened? Just like that?'

'He'd arrived before I even knew what had happened.'

Alec stared around the room, then at his wife. 'He'll need a name,' he said at last.

'Seb wants to call him James.'

'Seb?' There was shock in Alec's voice. '*Seb*'s seen him?'

Adrenaline surged through Lisa; how would she explain that Seb already knew? 'He heard me feeding the twins,' she smiled, freezing cheek muscles tight. 'He likes to come and help.'

Alec looked at her searchingly. 'So he already knows?'

'Yes.'

'And you didn't send him to fetch me?'

'He wanted to stay with me, Alec. Yet another baby brother – it must be as much of a shock for him as it is for us. I wanted to play it down, not make too big thing of it.'

'An extra baby brother, another son, that's nothing to make a fuss about!' He looked at her quizzically. 'I quite see that.'

'Really, Alec. I'd only just had time to wrap the baby up and pull the sheets over us—'

'I thought you said Seb watched you feeding the twins?'

'I sent him back to bed, but of course he was still awake. I expect he heard me come in here. You know I encourage him to have some time on his own with me, between feeds. It's the best I can do for him at the moment.'

'And where is he now?'

'I asked him to go back to his room and play.'

'And he wanted him called James?'

'"Morc bother", he said.'

'He's got that right.'

'And when I said he needed a name he said "Yames".'

'All right, darling. If that's what you want, we'll call him James.' He clearly intended to soothe her, keep her calm. 'I can't help thinking, you know. Perhaps those pills that chap in Bristol insisted on you taking right at the start – fertility drugs have side effects.'

'Vitamin pills, organic vitamin pills. I took the same ones when I was carrying Seb.'

'It still doesn't make any sense. He said there was just the one.'

'It doesn't really matter now, does it, darling?'

'As long as there aren't any more surprises.'

'I rather think that's it,' she said, patting her flat abdomen. 'What's really bothering me is how we're going to be sure we can tell the three of them apart before we get the bracelets in place.'

A stirring in her unconscious; a conviction that she needed the children labelled.

'Perhaps we'd better put a piece of sticky plaster on his wrist right away,' she said brightly. 'Just to make sure. Even if we can tell which is which ourselves, supposing something happened to us? No one else would know.'

'If you insist.' He brought a plaster over and Lisa placed it on the baby's wrist. 'He's much more like Janus than Jeffrey,' Alec repeated, awed. 'I wouldn't have believed it possible. I can't see *any* difference.'

Lisa wrapped the shawl Alec had brought tightly round the child. She didn't want Alec to look too closely, or to realise that if he looked the image of Janus, it was because Janus had lost significant weight.

'I suppose it's because he also had to do all the work for himself,' Alec said, frowning. 'So his head would be affected in the same way.'

Lisa kissed the top of her new son's head tenderly. The same, intense baby smell as the other two infants.

'I suppose that's what it must be.' Alec sounded glum. The smile, now lukewarm, reminded Lisa that he had originally wanted a family of two. Now there were four.

Lisa looked down at her latest son and silently agreed with Alec that that was enough. 'Perhaps you should ring the midwife now,' she suggested. The strain of the last little while had exhausted her, the thought of possible battles ahead made her feel drained. 'Just so that she can check out that everything's okay.'

He looked at her sharply. 'You feeling off?'

'Just tired.' Lisa had no intention of letting the woman examine *her*, but she did want a professional to visit, to acknowledge the new child, to give him, so to speak, the necessary credentials. Fortunately Rita Connolly would still be on duty. Her brusque manner, her constant assumption that her time was more precious than her patients', would now be welcome traits.

What about the physical evidence of a birth? Insist that Alec had thrown the afterbirth away. Identical multiples sometimes had several afterbirths, sometimes a single one. In this case, clearly, Janus and Jeffrey had shared an afterbirth, James had had one to himself.

Was that, medically speaking, feasible? No need to talk about it; just say Alec had helped her clear up, and it had gone. The navel was a trickier proposition. She'd find a rubber band to twist round it.

'I'll give the surgery a ring,' Alec agreed, making for the door.

'And could you bring me a couple of gauze nappies and some clothes,' Lisa called after him. 'And the cot from the airing cupboard.'

'You've got *another* cot in the airing cupboard?'

'Meg gave me both of hers.'

'I'm going to put them side by side to see,' Alec said, coming back into the room with Janus. 'They really are indistinguishable.'

Janus, on Alec's arm, opened his eyes. It seemed to Lisa that the child understood exactly what was going on. He looked at her and – grinned. She could swear it wasn't wind.

'Don't wake them up,' Lisa whispered at Alec. 'It's the last thing we need. And we don't want to mix them up, either.'

Janus, as though he understood her, closed his eyes. Freed from their penetrating look, a sudden inspiration came to Lisa. 'Let's put a bit of sticky plaster on Janus, too, now that you've brought him. A transparent one, so we can be sure to tell one from the other.'

She wanted something fastened to Janus which he could not take off, something tight on his body, clamped to it. A tag – she wanted Janus tagged. Just like Don's lambs, she realised. That's what she had in mind.

10

The heavy, lumbered tread on the stairs alerted Lisa to Rita's arrival. She burst into the guestroom without knocking, her face flushed bright red, her eyes squinting in disbelief.

'Your husband said you'd had another one,' she accused Lisa.

'Isn't he lovely? The spitting image of his brothers.'

Meg's second carrycot was on its stand a few feet from the bed Lisa was lying on. The midwife went over to the cot and pulled back the covering to look at the child. 'Out for the count, I see.' She turned suspicious eyes on Lisa. 'I really find it almost impossible to believe.'

Lisa smiled sweetly through the panic flooding her brain. 'It is extraordinary, and so little trouble.' What *could* the woman make of it? She couldn't deny the child, and how else could she explain his presence?

'Medical history, I'd say.'

Panic turned to consternation as Lisa chose her words with the utmost care. 'Well, hardly that,' she said as casually as she could. 'It's quite well recorded, about further births at a later stage.' She couldn't resist a certain snideness. 'I did mention there was still a bump and that it was moving.'

Rita Connolly, if she heard, ignored this. 'I suppose I ought to examine you.' She opened her bag and pulled on plastic gloves.

'Dr Witherton has been in.' Lisa drew the bedding round herself protectively.

'Just to make sure you're all right.' In her peremptory way the midwife was already tugging at the sheets covering Lisa.

Lisa held them tight. 'It's not obligatory, is it? I'm a bit tired now. And I expect you want to get on, in any case.'

'Of course, Mrs Wildmore.' Seeing the clenched hands holding back the sheet, Rita stopped, her lips pursed. 'It's just—'

'As I said, Dr Witherton has been in to see me. He was very happy with everything.'

This was quite true. The GP had called in briefly to see that all was going along well. But that was yesterday, on his way home. He had not stayed long, and he certainly had not suggested to Lisa that he should examine her.

'I'll leave all that to Roger; he's your doctor, after all. He'll be back tomorrow,' he'd encouraged Lisa. 'And I'm afraid I'm leaving for Majorca myself first thing. You'll begin to think none of us can stay the course.'

Deprived of Lisa, Rita busied herself checking the new infant. 'The oddest thing of all is the way the umbilical appears to be at the same stage as that of the other two. I suppose Dr Witherton put on the elastic. Except for that, I can't tell the difference between him and the others.' The midwife looked doubtfully at Lisa. 'Can you?'

Lisa took a deep breath. 'He's very gentle,' she said, love for the baby suffusing her body. 'Extraordinary how differences in temperament show at such early stages.'

Rita snorted.

'I know how busy you are,' Lisa said placatingly. 'And that you're due for your break. And Friday's your specially busy day as well – I remember you mentioned that. Sorry to hold you up at all.' Lisa looked at the midwife and pulled her lips back in a travesty of a smile. To her relief it seemed to work.

'I'm always glad to come when I'm really needed,' the midwife said quickly, still checking over the infant, clicking surprise. 'I'll just see to him.' She looked faintly embarrassed. 'I don't think I've got time to bath the other two as well.'

'Of course,' Lisa agreed smoothly.

She settled back against the pillows. She was astonished at how easily the holidays, and the general confusion, had allowed her to fudge the issues. Rita was off on holiday later today; next time a midwife was due to call – this evening or tomorrow morning, Lisa judged – it would be Susan Andrews. And before that visit, Lisa would insist Alec get Gilmore over.

Alec put his head round the door, acknowledging Rita with a bare nod. 'Everything okay for a couple of minutes? D'you think Meg will lend a hand until reserves arrive?' he asked Lisa anxiously. 'I simply have to get these figures straight.'

Alec's vital meeting in Bristol this morning, with potential Flaxton clients from the States, could be delayed but hardly cancelled. Doubler had finally passed the stringent Food and Drug Adminstration laws.

Nigel Carruthers, Flaxton's chief executive, was keen to sign up American distributors and to alert them to the outstanding test-site performance of Multiplier.

'Don't worry,' she soothed him. 'Meg's always over for Seb as soon as she can get away. She'll take over.'

Lisa had the feeling of *déjà vu*, a scene rehearsed and now played out. Meg had offered to take Seb every morning for a couple of weeks after the twins were born. Lisa had accepted gratefully; it made her feel less guilty about not having time for him. Now she'd simply ask Meg to keep him until teatime for several days. Lisa was sure she would be willing to do that.

But there was one thing which nagged at her, one thing she could not shake from her mind however hard she tried. She wanted the triplets – manacled, flashed through her mind – permanently identified. The sticky plaster could come off at any stage.

'You don't, by any chance, have any identification bracelets with you, do you?' she asked Rita.

The midwife chuckled. 'No, I don't, but I can ask Susan to bring some round.'

'That would be wonderful. Enjoy your holiday.'

'The best of luck,' Rita said, bumping the door open with her ample rear. 'You'll need it.'

Lisa forced her facial muscles into one last smile, then fell back against the pillows, exhausted. The doctor; she still had to convince the doctor. Her strength seemed to have deserted her. Tears came; floods of relief welled over her lower lids and onto her cheeks.

'Gone, has she?' Alec was bringing her a tray with cereal, toast and marmalade, Seb in tow. 'Poor darling. You look completely bleary-eyed. That battleaxe is the limit. Did she upset you?'

'Not really. I'm just tired. I suppose I will need an extra pair of hands for a day or two. Perhaps Social Services could send round a home help.'

'Already organised.' Alec grinned, pleased with himself. 'I'd better ring the agency for a nanny.'

A nanny? Through her exhaustion Lisa could see the dangers looming up. A nanny would know immediately if there were another . . . splitting. How could she stop it happening again? A sudden horror that Jeffrey might also have reproduced himself left her blood drained from her face. How could she check?

'You're really white, darling. Didn't she even make sure that you're okay?'

'Are the twins – the other two triplets – all right?'

'I'll go and check.'

'If you could bring their cots in here,' Lisa suggested.

'You want them all in here with you?'

'That's right.'

'You won't get any peace.'

'If you wouldn't mind,' Lisa directed firmly. It was extraordinary how everybody seemed to think they knew better than she did.

'You'll get completely overdone.'

'It's all right, Alec. I'm fine. Native women just carry on after childbirth.'

But Jeffrey was not Janus, she calmed herself. In some strange way, she knew that only Janus could split. Neither Jeffrey nor James would cause that sort of problem.

'You're not a native woman, Lisa,' Alec said impatiently.

He did, however, bring the other children through. Two cots, two babies, still sleeping. Lisa breathed a sigh of relief.

'When's Meg due, did you say?' he asked, aligning the last cot at the far end of the room.

Lisa's blood began to ebb again. Meg. Now there was a real stumbling block. Meg was likely to ask for details, prod for specific answers. She was far more of a threat than anyone else.

'Round half past ten,' she said, faint, subdued.

'You need a sleep,' Alec said gruffly.

Somehow she had to avoid seeing Meg, at least until she could get her act together. 'I tell you what, darling. When the home help arrives, why don't you take Seb round to the Graftleys? It's on your way, and you can tell them the news.'

He smiled. 'Good idea.'

'Stay with more bother,' Seb told them, settling down beside Lisa. 'Like bother.'

'When you've been to see Auntie Meg.' Lisa smiled at him, her heart aching at sending him off. 'Why don't you fetch your clothes, then I'll put them on for you.'

As the little boy trotted off she turned to Alec. 'Ask Meg to come back with him when her twins are napping,' she suggested. 'I'll tell her all about it then.'

Something was trying to surface in her mind. She put Seb's T-shirt on back to front in her confusion. What? Why was she so sure there'd be no further infants? Had she, after all, really given birth to James?

A loud, tempestuous knocking at the side door brought Lisa out of her reverie. 'That must be the home help, Alec.'

'Say goodbye to Mummy, Seb. I'll get back as quickly as I can make it, darling.' He bent down and kissed her; a full kiss, on the lips. Had she misjudged him? Was he actually pleased to have four sons?

Seb in his arms, Alec dashed out. Almost immediately there was a demure rap on the open door of the guestroom.

'Mrs Wildmore?'

'Do come in.'

'I'm Maureen Donahue.'

'Hi. It's really sweet of you to come at such short notice.'

'I didn't mind. It's ever so exciting, isn't it?'

As though on cue, the triplets demanding their ten o'clock feed brought conversation to an abrupt end. Lisa carefully directed Maureen to bring the babies to her, one by one, and then to change and burp them.

By the time the babies were in their cots again, it was already noon. The front door bell rang out.

'That'll be Dr Gilmore.'

He arrived, bronzed from his holiday but out of breath. 'I hear you've sprung a surprise on us,' he greeted Lisa.

'An extra one was a bit over the top,' Lisa agreed, smiling at him. Rita must have finished her rounds very quickly and sent her notes in; that was unusually efficient.

'You're still feeling weak?'

'Weak?'

'The twins are a fortnight old, aren't they? Most modern mothers get up a day or two after the birth, you know.' He laughed indulgently. 'I know, you're trying to put off the evil day when you'll have to do all the work yourself.'

Twins? So he hadn't heard about the triplets yet.

'The most recent one was only born this morning,' Lisa rushed out at him. 'Actually I'm feeling fine; nothing to it at all. Rita Connolly's been in already and dealt with everything.'

'You mean you only had the second twin this morning?' He looked completely baffled, rummaging through his bag. 'I know we're not brilliant at notes in the practice, but that's a bit too much. I'll have to talk to the office staff.'

'Another baby after the twins, Dr Gilmore.'

He looked completely blank.

'I've got three babies – triplets. The latest one arrived this morning.

Look.' She pointed to the three carrycots lined up at the far end of the room. 'There they are.'

He simply stood and gaped at her, then turned his head in their direction.

'Do sit down.'

'Yes, thank you; yes.'

Hearing Maureen moving about nearby, Lisa called to her to make more tea. By the time she turned back to the doctor he had composed himself.

'I'd no idea, Mrs Wildmore. No idea at all. I do apologise. I thought the notes said twins.' He stood, his back to the window, irresolute, frowning, confused, then wandered towards the cots.

'Proverbial peas in a pod,' he grunted. 'Rita looked them over and everything?'

'Indeed she did,' Lisa assured him. 'She's off herself tonight, as you know. Susan will probably be in later.'

'Susan's back, is she?' The relief was audible. 'No problems, then.' A new thought seemed to cross his mind. 'But Rita was here to assist you, I take it?'

'She was an enormous help. I really don't know how I'd have managed without her. She came at once, as soon as my husband called her,' Lisa burbled on, determined to complete the spiel she had rehearsed until it felt like second nature. 'And my husband simply had to get to Bristol for a meeting, you see; and my friend Meg has taken on looking after my little boy.'

He did not seem to hear a word of all this. 'No complications with the birth?'

'It was very easy,' Lisa trilled on. 'They're all three quite small, of course,' she breathed, then stopped the flow when she saw Maureen Donahue bringing a tray with tea which she placed beside Lisa's bed. 'Milk and sugar?'

The doctor turned from the cots, beads of moisture on his forehead, wiping his face with a handkerchief. 'You certainly sound chirpy.'

'It *is* a big thrill; a family of four in no time, after all that trouble with infertility.'

Another deep frown as the GP tried to come to terms with the odd situation. 'These drugs,' he said, nodding gravely. 'Wonderful what they can do, of course. Sometimes there are unexpected side effects.'

'Chocolate biscuit?'

'I really must get on; so much to do after my holidays, you know.

Some of my patients simply won't have anyone else.'

'Of course.' Released from the problem of convincing a doctor about what had happened, Lisa wondered whether she dared ask him about identification bracelets.

'Perhaps your lady help can let me in later,' Gilmore suddenly suggested.

He'd worked out something was wrong, after all! That dopey look had hidden his real understanding. Lisa braced herself for battle. 'You'd like to come again?'

'I hope you won't think it an imposition; you must be overwhelmed.' He smiled ruefully. 'But I would so like my daughter to see the babies. *Triplets* in the practice, *and* identical. I don't think we've had a set in my time before.'

'Any time,' Lisa said. 'And if you could ask Susan to bring identification bracelets. They're so alike, you see. We don't want to mix them up.'

'Of course,' he beamed. 'No difficulty about that. I can let you have those right away.' To Lisa's amazement he took three plastic bracelets out of his bag. 'Not very fashionable, I'm afraid, but they'll do the job.'

[illegible]

[illegible]

[illegible]

[illegible]

[illegible]

[illegible]

[illegible]

11

'You're a dark one,' Meg said, leading Seb by the hand and bringing him in to Lisa. 'Fancy springing another one on us!'

'It did rather take me by surprise.' Lisa smiled guardedly. 'I don't suppose you've got time for a gossip?'

'Not really,' Meg grinned at her, 'but if you think I'm not going to make it, you can think again.'

Lisa watched her friend's face carefully. Did she have any inkling about the way the new child had appeared?

'I know I mustn't tire you, so I won't. But I'm just dying to know what happened. Beats anything I've ever come across before; never heard of anything like it.'

'Apparently such cases have been written up – at any rate about twins. And I kept telling Rita there was still a bump.'

'Not so's you'd notice,' Meg said. 'Some people are that lucky.'

'I felt it move, I told you, didn't I?' Lisa insisted. 'Of course no one took any notice of what *I* had to say.'

'But the scan only showed the *one*.' Meg looked at Lisa searchingly. 'I know you think those doctors don't know what they're on about, but the scan's just a machine.'

'It must have happened after that.'

'That's not right, Lisa. You know what they do say – it's right early on the embryo can split in two.' Meg looked at her. 'They're identicals, aren't they?'

The smile froze on Lisa's face. She had no idea Meg had followed her pregnancy as carefully as that, nor that she knew so much about how identical twins come into being. 'Really?' Lisa managed to ask, gulping down the orange juice she was drinking to cover her confusion. She looked cautiously towards Meg. 'Did Susan tell you that?'

But Meg had already shifted her eyes from Lisa to the cots. 'Or three, it do appear.'

'Doctors are always changing their minds about the latest theories.

First the fertility medics told me taking the pill stops you conceiving when you come off it. Now they all maintain it's the other way round. They say that's when you are most likely to conceive. I expect they misread the scan or something.'

'Mine showed as two on the scan,' Meg said. 'Ever so clear.' She was staring into the cots, looking first at one baby and then at another. 'With you they kept telling you it wasn't twins, let alone triplets.' Meg walked over from the cots and looked Lisa right in the eye. 'And you saw the monitor yourselves, isn't that so?'

'You had a scan at seven months, Meg. Mine was at twenty weeks. One could have read almost anything into it. We simply interpreted it the way the specialist told us to.' Lisa adjusted the pillows behind her and sat up. 'And that slithery Parslow knew something was up, I could tell at the time. He wasn't going to tell *us* of course. We're only the parents.'

'He did, did he?' Meg sounded almost excited at the prospect. 'You think he really saw something amiss? And didn't let on?'

'I don't know about amiss. He saw something he wasn't sure about. Could have been one foetus right on top of another, making the image more distinct, I suppose. That's Alec's theory.'

'Then one would have had to be blocking two more of them.'

'Whatever.' Lisa was genuinely beginning to tire. The strain of the day had begun to exhaust her. And Meg's shrewdness was not as easily countered as the paternalism of the medical profession. 'What's it matter, anyway? The triplets are here, see for yourself.'

Meg walked slowly over to the cots again, Seb clutching her hand, pointing to the cot James was in and saying 'More bother,' as though he couldn't stop.

'Brother, Seb. You've got another little brother.'

'Bwuther.'

The child's preoccupation was making Lisa feel concerned. Had he seen something she had not? Had he confided what he'd seen to Meg? Lisa resolved to find someone else to help look after him; and find her fast. Meg knew something was up, that was clear.

'They really look alike. Specially these two,' Meg continued, standing between the cots holding Janus and James. 'Which one's the latest, did you say?'

'Yanus, Yeffwey, Yames,' Seb said, pointing them out in turn.

'Seb knows which is which better than any of us,' Lisa tried out, watching for a reaction from Meg. There wasn't any. 'Uncanny, isn't it?

Dr Gilmore's brought identification bracelets to strap round their ankles. Otherwise even we might mix them up.' She laughed, forcing gaiety into her voice. 'We can't rely on Seb entirely.'

'So it's the one with the bit of sticky on his wrist, that it? James, you calling him?'

'The plaster, yes; we put it on before the doctor got here. I didn't want to rip it off.'

'Funny thing about their eyes.'

'Their eyes?'

'They say babies only focus at around eight inches early on. The one in the middle cot is looking straight at me; a real knowing look. Janus. He the first one you had? Just like my Phyllis.' Meg's expression was looking for an echo.

Lisa was not going to acknowledge that astute, far too perspicacious look. Why was Meg comparing Janus to Phyllis? Phyllis was Paul's fraternal twin, quite different from Janus's relationship to Jeffrey. What could Meg possibly think Phyllis and Janus had in common?

'The doctors say they can't smile for ages, too,' Lisa sidetracked as casually as she could, 'but Seb smiled at me within the first week.'

'You know what comes to mind?' Meg stood stolidly beside the cots, comparing the three babies.

It was all Lisa could do to stop herself from shuddering. Meg was going to come right out with it, tell her she knew. She'd just deny it. Whatever Meg said, she'd simply call her bluff. There was no way that Meg could *prove* anything.

Lisa put her arms round Seb and busied herself looking at the drawing he'd brought back for her, her eyes scanning the paper with its criss-crossed crayon marks.

'What Don's been on about,' Meg persisted.

'Is this our house?' Lisa looked at Seb and pointed to an accidental triangle on the piece of paper he had given her.

'House,' Seb agreed happily.

'You know Don; Don Chivers.'

Lisa's hands, shaking a little, began to fold Seb's paper into two, then four.

'No, Mummy! S'my dwawing.'

'Sorry, darling.' She kept her features rigid, her voice breathy, neither denying nor admitting to knowing Don.

'Our stockman, Lisa.'

Lisa's face remained blank as she straightened out the piece of paper and solemnly handed it back to Seb.

'The one who does all the donkey work; keeps tabs on which cow calved and that.' Meg turned her head to look at Lisa again. 'Susan Andrews is married to his nephew. 'Course you know Don!'

'Really?' Lisa looked at Meg, genuinely surprised. It was amazing, the intricate network of relationships in the area. 'I'd no idea he and Susan are part of the same family.'

Lisa remembered Don Chivers' visit only too well, the way he'd talked about securing metal to her babies, because clothes didn't 'stay on they tight enough'. Most of all she remembered Don had maintained that when he forgot to tag one of a pair of newly born twin lambs, it had turned into two the next time he'd looked. The parallel with Janus could not be denied. Don knew it could happen. That was why he'd wanted to see the twins, why he'd scrutinised them so carefully. He'd guessed it might happen with one of them.

She could picture him now, reluctant to hold Janus; he'd looked for something, recognised it, been unnerved by it. So he'd tried to tell her what was needed, tried to tell her how to protect her children.

Lisa was not going to challenge his suggestion this time. She'd get permanent metal identification bracelets fastened to the triplets as quickly as she could.

She forced her lips into an upward curve and crinkled her eyes. 'Of course I know Don, Meg. He's brought the goat's milk over a couple of times. Sorry, I'm still feeling groggy.'

'He said it right at the start, and he keeps saying it, time and again: "that many lambs bain't natural".'

Lisa's pulse began to race. Play dumb, deny it, say how ridiculous.

'We had seven lambs from the one ewe just the other day.' Meg looked at Lisa again. 'Don said he couldn't believe what his eyes told him.'

'Seven? From one ewe?' It sounded crazy, but not necessarily what Lisa was terrified Meg would say. Lisa took a deep breath. 'That does sound over the top. Has anything like it ever happened before?' Her voice sounded tremulous, even to herself. She coughed slightly.

Meg was not to be deterred. 'Been known. British record was set in early 1991.'

'How can you possibly be sure they were all from the one ewe?'

The sixty-four thousand dollar question.

''Cos Don delivered them.'

Delivered them. She was safe; Don hadn't confided his real suspicions to Meg. These multiple lambs had not split *outside* the womb. Maybe they had split late; very late on, perhaps. But no one could know that. That was, of course, how Jeffrey had been produced – by the foetus splitting just before birth. Janus – Lisa was sure that it had to be Janus – had split inside the womb; that's what she'd felt, that's what she'd seen happening when she watched her abdomen change shape, elongate sideways. Now she understood why the doctors had not been able to find any trace of twins. Lisa's muscles relaxed and she smiled broadly.

'He could see the ewe having trouble with the first one. Couldn't credit it when more kept popping out, and all identically marked. He'd never heard of such a thing before.' Meg looked directly at Lisa, challenging her. 'This is your lot then, that right?'

The relief was so enormous Lisa felt light-headed. 'Honestly, Meg. You really are letting your imagination run away with you. Not very likely, is it?' She patted her flat stomach.

'I reckon it has to be down to that Multiplier stuff. May be organically based, but it's not right, somehow.'

Even if that were true, Lisa wondered how it could possibly have affected her. She laughed; a high, shrill laugh. 'In case you haven't noticed, Meg, I'm not a farm animal, and I don't eat grass.'

'But you did suck clover petals,' Meg reminded her. 'I told you then, three leaves and that could bring on triplets.'

Actually what Lisa remembered was that Meg had said it made sheep swell up. And something about country lore maintaining that clover was bad for pregnant women. And the clover she'd found had had four leaves, not three. A four-leaf clover, in Lisa's mythology, was meant to bring good luck. The luck that she had asked for was twins; it had overdone that bit. 'Honestly, Meg. Just one suck at the nectar, to show Seb.'

'It made you sick. And you did have the butter and cheese I made from milking the Jerseys pastured on the home meadow. And the cream. You remember, when you found out you were carrying again.'

'Of course I remember. You said you didn't fertilise that pasture; you said you ran it like a medieval field.'

'Meadow; we do. But there's always drift, you know. All the fields around are fertilised, like the rest of the farm. The one Frank set aside for special testing of Multiplier is upalong the home meadow. I saw those cows crane their necks to get at the grass on the other side of the fence. Especially the clover. Always at it; it draws them, somehow.'

'They've been twin calving, then?'

'No, matter of fact. They calved earlier on. We've been keeping them as milch cows. So those don't really count; they're only just in calf again now.'

Meg, Lisa could see, was clearly toying with the idea of foetuses splitting in the womb at a late stage. Encouraged, she would believe in it. Challenged, she might be thrown off the scent, or at least driven into defensive silence. Either way, it didn't really matter too much. How long before the real, shattering truth of splitting *outside* the womb dawned on her?

'So let me get this straight. You think that because I sucked nectar out of a few clover petals and ate your homemade butter and cheese –' she looked at Meg defiantly, 'and don't forget the yoghurt, that's what I really went to town on, I ate that every day – my baby split into three inside the womb at a much later stage than normal.'

Perhaps Meg *had* put her finger on the cause. She'd steer right away from the Graftleys' dairy produce, even though Meg had assured her that the goats and chickens were completely isolated from any sort of fertiliser. Meg was determined on that, in spite of what Frank said; she always stood up to him on that point. But the fertiliser could leach from one part of the farm to another; and, anyway, maybe Frank used Multiplier on Meg's part of the farm behind her back. He was always greedy for extra produce.

Meg laughed uncomfortably. 'It does sound completely daft, put like that. Reckon what Don keeps saying about the stock is getting to me.' She took a deep breath, her eyes solemn. 'But there is something you should know. Something I never told—'

'Lisa? Is everything okay?' Alec came bounding up the stairs, back home as fast as he could make it. Lisa was delighted to hear his voice.

'Oh, hello, Meg. Helping us out again?'

'Just brought Seb back, Alec. Well, I'd better run. Sally and Jean'll be getting the twins their tea. I like to be there to see to them myself.'

'We really can't go on making use of Meg,' Alec said as soon as she had gone. 'I've been on to the agency. They can't find us a nanny. They say we're just too far out in the sticks.'

'I see.' Lisa wasn't sure whether to be depressed or relieved.

He grinned, obviously pleased with himself. 'I did have a bit of luck about a mother's help, though.' He hugged her.

'I thought you just said they didn't want to work in the country.' Lisa broke away from him, familiar churnings in her stomach making her tense and unyielding.

'Not the agency girls; useless, really. No, at the office of all places.' He beamed. 'I suppose I was bragging a bit. Anyway, old man Carruthers was there, chairing the meeting with the Yanks. He sounded really taken with the whole business of the new arrival, asked me all kinds of questions.' He grinned again. 'He's only got one baby daughter; I suppose he felt inferior for once.'

So that was it. Alec was proud of his sudden brood – macho father of triplet sons.

'Carruthers? You mean the man you work with at Flaxton? Rather a bimbo for a second wife?'

'That's the one.'

'What kind of questions? What did he want to know?'

'How we know for sure that they're identical. That really got to him.'

'So what did you say?'

'Told him about that little mark on their ear. He really saw the force of that. Went over the ground time and again.' Alec grinned delightedly. 'Then he told me his niece is absolutely potty about young children. Marvellous with them, by all accounts.'

'His niece? Wouldn't she be too young?'

'Not really – remember, Diana's his second wife. He was talking about his sister's daughter – they live in Wedmore. It's absolutely ideal. She could cycle over, or one of her parents can drop her off. At a pinch I could always pick her up myself.'

'So how old is she?'

'Just on sixteen, he said.' Alec hugged her shoulders. 'You smell of new-mown hay, without the ghastly pollen that goes with it.' He stood up and walked over to the triplets' cots. 'Excellent family background and all that; nothing to worry about there. And simply adores babies.'

'Why isn't she studying for something?'

'Bit of a dunce at school, apparently. They think a good reference from people like us would help her get into a training school for nannies. Her GCSEs are hopeless.'

It might just suit, Lisa thought to herself. A professional nanny would expect to take over the children's care, decide for herself whether the triplets wore identifying bracelets or not. No, an unqualified young girl, not too bright, willing to learn from Lisa, someone who adored children, that could be just the thing.

'I suppose we'd better give her a try,' Lisa agreed, settling back. 'As you say, we can't take advantage of Meg's good nature for ever.' Far too shrewd. She'd worm things out of Seb, put two and one together.

A mother's help would keep Meg at a distance, make sure she didn't see too much of the triplets, let alone air those impossible theories of hers.

And what about Don? The man obviously knew what was happening on the farm, suspected it had to be connected with the new fertiliser. And if Don suspected, Frank must, too. Was that why the launch of Multiplier had been delayed so long?

She shrugged that away; whatever was happening on the farm was not connected with her. After all, Dr Gilmore had accepted James's late arrival. No, she was safe. Don wasn't likely to go against what had been accepted by the medical establishment. He could only speculate about her children, he couldn't possibly *prove* anything.

Alec suddenly cupped her face in his hands and kissed her. A long, drawn-out kiss of love, of pride. 'What a clever girl you are; four sons in under two years.'

So he was going to forgive her? Perhaps even be glad to have such an unusual family? 'Anytime,' she murmured.

'That's going too far,' he rumbled into her ear, kissing her forehead, her hair. 'I think we ought to leave it at that. Unless you can promise me twin daughters.'

'No guarantees,' she said. Though she knew very well that if there were to be more infants, they would be boys.

12

A tall, slim, fragile-looking girl with long, side-swept black hair cascading over her left shoulder, Geraldine Fitch-Templeton stood on the Wildmores' doorstep several days later. A large, black Mercedes was sleeking discreetly down the drive as Lisa opened the door.

Geraldine teetered into the hall on high, spiky heels and looked around at the corniced ceilings and the massive staircase. Apparently they were considered satisfactory. She shook off an outer layer of supple suede. Then, somewhat theatrically and rather incongruously, Lisa felt, she drew a neatly folded overall out of a crumpled paper bag.

Lisa eyed her suspiciously; the petulant look, the high heels she hadn't bothered to wipe on the doormat, the crumpled bag. But the sight of the neatly folded overall lulled Lisa into a sense of seemliness. It was only when Geraldine had donned the overall that Lisa returned to her original impression. Two large, fresh daubs of red – tomato ketchup, or perhaps tomato soup – leered at her like saucer eyes. Looking below the red patches, Lisa noticed the stitching on one of the patch pockets had been torn away, and that two front buttons were missing.

'Perhaps you'd better bring another overall tomorrow,' she managed to say. 'I'll put this one into the machine with all the other washing.'

Geraldine agreed happily, an impish grin spread wide. Seb, unaware of his mother's reservations, tried to make friends.

'I got bwuthers,' he told Geraldine proudly. 'More bwuthers.'

He tried to pull her up the first tread of the staircase and so on to the triplets' room. Geraldine, retreat cut off by Lisa, tottered beside him up the stairs. Lisa made a list in her head: flat heels, hair kept neatly tied back, no dangling jewellery. It was going to be an uphill task.

'He's telling you about the triplets,' Lisa interpreted for her as they walked into the babies' nursery.

A look of boredom crossed Geraldine's face as she looked at the eager little boy. She unclasped the hand he'd confided to her and walked towards the cots. But the sight of the three identical infants appeared to rouse latent maternal feelings.

'Ooh, look at that!' she giggled. 'Don't they look *sweet*! May I hold one of them?'

'Sit down,' Lisa said hurriedly. 'I'll bring one over to you.'

Janus, Lisa saw, was still awake, but not crying. He was lying in his carrycot, his eyes a little dulled. He'd brought up some of the mid-morning feed. Lisa suspected that he was still losing weight. Was something wrong with him?

Susan Andrews, right from the first visit after her holiday, had been sure the goat's milk was causing problems.

'I thought goat's milk was supposed to be better than cow's,' Lisa had queried, surprised, on that first visit after Susan had taken over from the relief midwife. 'Seb really thrived on it.'

'I'd switch to formula,' Susan had said, quiet, assured, checking the babies' weight against Rita's notes. 'Janus has lost almost six ounces.'

'I know,' Lisa had agreed, thankful that Susan couldn't know the real reason. 'It is odd. He used to be a lusty feeder, positively greedy compared to Jeffrey!'

'I'm sure he's allergic to the goat's milk,' Susan had insisted. 'Did you notice any bloating, early on? Face on the puffy side? Always a sign.'

Bloating? What did she mean by bloating? Had Rita put something about that in the notes? Lisa thought that unlikely. 'Just a bit chubby,' she'd told Susan, guardedly.

'Well, never mind. We'll get him round. Each child develops at a different pace,' Susan had soothed her. 'I'll bring some formula tomorrow.'

'Cow's milk, you mean?'

Susan had looked thoughtful at first, then smiled at her. 'I thought we might try soya bean modified to resemble human milk,' she'd said. 'Let's put both Janus and James on it.' She'd hesitated, looked uncomfortable. 'And Jeffrey. Well, all three. To make things easier,' she'd added. 'Give it a try; you can always change to something else if that's not right.'

Susan's attitude had made her wonder whether Don had, after all, mentioned his suspicions to his family.

Lisa picked Janus up. She smiled at him and lowered him onto Geraldine's lap.

A wistful Seb laid a hand on the rocker arm supports and stood silent, looking on, as Geraldine sat rocking Janus on her knee. Long earrings dangled in sympathy. Lisa's heart leapt as she saw Janus's eyes begin to gleam, a little hand apparently about to reach out to grasp the glittering gold. She intercepted the child's intention with her fingers. Was that a flash of irritation at her interference? She could have sworn he tried to shake her off as though impatient. He was much too young for all that; she was beginning to imagine things.

'And you'll have to take those shoes off, Geraldine, before I can let you carry a baby around. You could easily trip.'

The girl tossed off her shoes; they scrambled sideways on the floor, gaping and hazardous.

Lisa looked at them, lying askew, black patent leather reflecting up at her. 'Someone could trip over those,' she explained wearily.

At once the firm body coiled forward, Janus held in mid-air, as the shoes were kicked under the rocker. Would this girl really do? Lisa saw her edging Janus on one side and taking hold of his wrist.

'What a darling bracelet,' she said, twisting the baby's arm to read the inscription. 'Is it silver or platinum?'

'Be careful of his arm! Turn the *bracelet* if you want to see what's written on it.'

'Oops, sorry. That *is* a clever idea,' Geraldine went on, unperturbed. 'D'you leave them on all the time, even at night?'

'They stay on round the clock,' Lisa said, standing full height. 'I was going to alert you about that. No one but their father or myself is to take them off – *no one*, you understand.'

'What about me? I shall be—'

'No!' Lisa broke in, shrill, then forced her voice calm and reasonable. 'I have to make that a really strict rule. I can't even allow the midwife, or the health visitor, to take them off.'

Mascara-fringed eyes opened wide; Lisa had the girl's full attention now. 'You mean you could really mix them up?'

'Other people could, and I'm not taking any chances. I can't always be around.'

'Would it matter that much?'

'Of course it could matter!' Lisa insisted as emphatically as she dared. 'Supposing one of them was on medication? Giving it to the wrong baby could cause a tragedy!' Lisa, triumphant now, felt confident about underlining her wishes. 'Janus, for instance, has been feeling a bit queasy. He might need something to settle him. So you're *never* to take the bracelets off, under any circumstances whatsoever.'

'Of course, Mrs Wildmore. I won't forget.'

'It's rule number one.' Lisa walked over to examine Janus's bracelet. The silver encircled his wrist snugly, intact, five ornate capitals spelling out

JANUS

Geraldine got up, the baby's head lolling slightly back, and walked with him, looking around the nursery. Lisa watched nervously.

'And there's another thing, Geraldine.'

'Do call me Gerry.'

'Gerry. Be very careful of their heads. Make sure your arm is under the curve of the neck; they need the support at this age.'

'Like this, d'you mean?'

'Exactly, just like that. You won't forget now, will you?'

A whispering at the back of Lisa's mind, a feeling of uncertainty; it would not be safe to leave this girl alone with her children. She felt unguarded, vulnerable to this stranger who had invaded her home. Her family was now exposed to prying eyes.

'Did you know you were going to have triplets?'

Why was this girl so curious, asking so many questions? 'I suspected there was more than one,' Lisa said shortly. She took Janus from Geraldine; his nappy needed changing. 'Disposable nappies are very simple to put on; the gathered bit goes at the back.'

'This milk looks different, somehow. Sort of grey.' Geraldine slithered long fingers round the spare bottle still in its warmer. 'Is it a special formula?'

'We're trying out soya at the moment.'

'You're vegan?'

'No.' Lisa explained. 'We started off with goat's milk. But Susan Andrews – that's the midwife – thinks Janus may be allergic to animal milk. Soya does seem to suit him better.' She turned back to Geraldine. 'But whatever concoction we use, always spray a bit of it on the inside of your wrist. It should feel neither hot nor cold.'

She forced a smile as the explanation of each humdrum task mollified her into accepting that these children were quite ordinary infants. 'Always hold them up against the support of your shoulder and your arm when you're giving them a bottle; it gives the air bubbles a chance to rise.'

'Very good, aren't they?'

'They've only just been fed.' Lisa grinned at her new helper. 'You haven't heard them in full cry.' She laughed. 'You might consider changing those earrings for earplugs when you have.'

Geraldine laughed back at that.

'Seriously, they'll pull at those long earrings. Perhaps you could wear some which don't dangle.' She studied the girl – exceptionally pretty, expertly made up, expensively dressed. 'And your hair; it's really lovely, but perhaps you'd keep it pinned out of the way while you're with us.'

Geraldine looked up at Lisa, eyes showing dark. 'If you really think that's important.'

'I do. And now perhaps you'd look after Seb in the playroom,' Lisa directed her. She replaced the sleepy Janus in his cot. 'He loves being read to. I'll help Mrs Donahue get some lunch together.'

The new mother's help arrived with alacrity as soon as Lisa called that the meal was ready. 'Where's Seb?' Lisa asked, looking round for him.

'I suppose he's still playing. Seb!' Geraldine bellowed without moving. 'Lunch!'

'Ssh! You'll wake the triplets. Perhaps you'd go and fetch him, Gerry.'

The girl appeared thin to Lisa, almost anorexic. That didn't turn out to be the case. It seemed incredible that anyone so thin could eat so much. And she also ate voraciously, as though she feared the food that she'd been given would be taken away if she were slow to get it down. She wolfed her first helping, accepted more, disposed of that, looked round for thirds and maybe fourths.

'I'm afraid it's raining.' Lisa looked disconsolately out of the playroom window. 'I'd hoped you and Seb could go for a nice walk. You'll just have to stay in and amuse him indoors.'

'We could play hide and seek,' Geraldine suggested. 'It's a lovely big house for that.'

'Up to a point.' Lisa wasn't altogether happy at this idea. 'The triplets' room, my studio and the bedroom, and Alec's study, are strictly out of bounds.'

'I's hide!' Seb said happily, and ran off into the living room.

The girl seemed oddly snoopy to Lisa, but at least she could entertain

Seb. Maybe she could even learn to bottle feed a triplet while Lisa watched her, instructed her in the art.

Lisa found herself going into the nursery to check again that the silver bracelets were secure. She knew she was becoming obsessive about checking them but she simply could not stop herself.

'How's Geraldine working out?' Alec asked her that evening. 'She didn't say much about the children when I drove her back.'

'Bit on the clumsy side,' Lisa said dully, tired but content. Geraldine was an awkward girl; two broken cups, a baby bottle cracked on the kitchen tiles and coffee spilt on the living room carpet was the score to date. Worse, she'd only just been prevented from wedging Seb's fingers in the nursery door. In spite of these misadventures, Lisa felt she could not do without her. Whatever her shortcomings, she would serve to keep others away.

'She'll get into the swing of it after a while,' Alec bantered easily. 'Her people seem awfully nice; offered me a drink.' He smiled at his wife encouragingly. 'I thought she sounded quite promising. Bubbly, full of fun.'

'She wants to bring her dog.'

'A dog? She's got a dog?'

'A terrier,' Lisa said indifferently. 'A bull terrier, she said. Apparently her mother's people breed them.'

'Good little dogs.'

'I don't know that I can cope with a dog as well.'

'Just make her keep it outside, Lisa. You've got to have some help. I checked again. The agency can't find anyone who'd consider working in such a rural area.'

Misgivings pushed aside Lisa allowed Geraldine to bring her dog, Duffers. Seb seemed to enjoy playing with him and this, in turn, persuaded Geraldine to pay at least some attention to the little boy.

'He needs his boots on when it's wet,' Lisa sighed, seeing Seb's ruined shoes and wet socks.

'Sorry, old thing.' The girl laughed cheerfully at the child. 'Let's see what we can do to get them on.'

'For goodness sake, Gerry! Change his socks first!'

'What a muggins,' the girl said, amiably enough, crashing upstairs in muddy shoes which left a brown-stained trail to Seb's bedroom.

There could be no complaints on the grounds of cheerfulness, Lisa was aware. She decided to concentrate on training the girl in the easy task of looking after Seb.

13

'See who it is, will you, Gerry?'

Lisa, immersed in giving the triplets their two o'clock bottles, resented any disturbance. She still considered it unsafe to leave Geraldine alone to cope with the feeds. But the girl's weekday presence did give Lisa a chance to do some painting in the afternoons, while the triplets were napping.

'Someone who says his name is Trevor Sayles,' Geraldine shouted up the stairs. 'Says he's a friend of yours.'

Trevor? Trevor was on her doorstep? Though Lisa was fond of her agent, she felt edgy about a visit now, at this very moment. If he caught sight of her in her present state, he could only be embarrassed.

Lisa removed the bottle from the suckling Jeffrey and heaved herself and infant up from the rocker to walk out into the corridor.

'Ask him in, Gerry,' she raised her voice from outside the open nursery door.

'What?' Geraldine shouted from the bottom of the stairs.

The girl really had the most atrocious manners. Lisa hoisted Jeffrey onto her shoulder, appalled at the grubby condition of her clothes and her untidy hair, but decided to advance towards the head of the staircase. Geraldine was standing next to Trevor, smirking at him.

'Run back to check on Jansy, there's a dear,' Lisa called to her, an urgent tone in her voice. 'He's still finishing his bottle.'

Geraldine swung herself reluctantly up the stairs and pushed past Lisa.

'Trevor!' Lisa tried to sound enthusiastic, welcoming. 'What a surprise.' She concealed her body by allowing Jeffrey to slide down into obscuring arms. 'Do go on through to the living room and fix yourself a drink. I'll be with you as soon as I can.'

Trevor, his foot on the first step, stopped short as he noticed her backing off. 'Sorry, Lisa.' He smiled discomfiture as he retreated. 'I really should have given you a bell before dropping in. Just happened to find myself in Bath, you know. Thought I'd take my chances of saying hello to the new arrivals.'

His voice tailed off. He'd evidently taken one look at her dishevelled appearance, heard the sounds of wailing in the background, and regretted coming near her. Had he come to say he could no longer sell her paintings? That she was simply wasting her time? And his, of course.

''Lo, Uncle Tweff.' Seb, grasping his helicopter book, had no inhibitions about going down to Trevor.

'Hello, young man. Doing a good job keeping your brothers in order?'

'Lots bwuthers,' Seb agreed solemnly.

'Thought you could use some help.' Trevor bent down to the little boy. 'Another member of the family.' He flourished an enormous teddy from behind his back.

Seb's eyes grew round. 'More bwuther?' He turned to Lisa hovering near the balusters. 'More yame.'

'You'll have to think of another name beginning with J,' Lisa directed Trevor. 'I'll expect you to have sorted that out by the time I come down.'

She laughed as she turned rapidly back to the nursery. Trevor had called for a social visit; she was beginning to see bogeys where there were none.

'Want me to take over?' Geraldine suggested as soon as Lisa walked in, holding her arms out for Jeffrey. 'Jiminy's asleep already; I can manage perfectly well.'

The girl seemed keen to help, to take responsibility. Had she misjudged her, not given her a proper chance? In her eagerness not to keep Trevor waiting, she decided to delegate more than she usually did to Geraldine.

'Remember to burp him,' Lisa instructed her. 'Don't put him down until he's brought up at least one good burp.'

'He's done his bit, I think,' Geraldine said, grinning, as Jeffrey broke wind explosively. 'Haven't you, Jeffers?'

'Then I'll leave you to finish Janus,' Lisa announced, lifting the liveliest of the triplets out of his cot; he had emptied a whole bottle. Susan Andrews had been absolutely right about changing to the soya formula. The child was back on form, thriving and lusty. 'He's had one bottle, but he's demanding more.'

'Old gobble guts.' Geraldine deposited Jeffrey in his cot and expertly took Janus over. As Lisa left she saw the girl settle herself back in the rocker. 'He wolfs the stuff down as though he needed to eat for two. If he isn't careful he's going to be quite tubby.'

Janus had been changed and was fully dressed; Lisa had checked again that his bracelet was secure. What could possibly go wrong? 'I'll leave you to it, then,' she told Geraldine. 'Make sure he goes straight down when he's finished, otherwise he'll get bad-tempered.'

Lisa eagerly started to strip her clothes off on the way to her bedroom. The nursing apron, the old skirt with its residue of milk, the pushdown socks, the moccasins. She opened her wardrobe door and contemplated her pre-triplet clothes for the first time since she had given birth. A rush of excitement, of possible escape from infants for just a short time, took her by surprise. The gay, red floral print in a cool cotton, with a wide skirt and billowing sleeves, appealed to her. Even if her figure wasn't quite back to normal, this dress would fit.

Now in her underwear, Lisa pulled off her bra and pants. She felt like looking good. Her pink lace bustier and thong briefs, she thought, topped by her smooth, silk slip. No tights; just her white sandals with the medium heels.

Naked now, Lisa tossed her hair over her face and brushed it briskly, then tossed it back again. She was beginning to feel more like a normal woman. She rolled deodorant under her arms, stepped into her underwear, slipped on the dress and sandals, and put on a glowing red lipstick. Was she keeping Trevor too long? Her reflection smiled back at her; not bad. She could use some green eye shadow. She examined herself again and saw with satisfaction that the triplets had not deprived her of her looks.

'Lisa, darling.' Trevor jumped up, removing Seb and the new teddy from his lap. He stretched both arms out to embrace her. 'You look marvellous. Motherhood must be a beauty treatment.'

'Finally made it, Trev. Sorry to keep you.' Lisa displayed white, even teeth at him, remembering too late that she had forgotten to spray on toilet water. 'I hope Seb's been looking after you. What brought you to Bath?'

'There's quite a good little gallery in Queen Square,' he told her, watching her carefully. 'I thought they might well be interested in a West Country artist.' He grinned at that. 'If you can stand the label.'

'I suppose that's what I am. In a sort of way.'

'The moorland landscapes go down well, even in London. I don't doubt they'll be a runaway success in Bath. There's always a steady market for local scenes,' he said, nodding at her latest rendering of Glastonbury Tor displayed in pride of place over the mantelpiece.

'You think I've gone soft, don't you?' Confronted with her agent, Lisa looked at her work in a more demanding way. The representational rendering of wind-bent willows fringing pastures replete with Friesians, with the ubiquitous Tor raising its breast-like shape behind them – these were the scenes tourists delighted in.

'Darling. Of course I don't.' He put his arm round her shoulders and guided her to one of her sofas. 'It's only natural that your work should take on a slightly more traditional look.' He settled himself next to her and took her hand. 'What the punters really go for is the exquisite detail. It is quite breathtaking, you know.'

'Too photographic,' Lisa said, annoyed with herself.

'Your style will change again, my dear. Please don't push at this stage. Anyway, you're selling well, so why knock it?' he pattered on, obviously aware of her feelings and intent on bolstering her. 'D'you keep anything liquid other than milk?'

'Didn't you help yourself? I think Alec's got a decent selection.'

'Not that awful sour cider you're so ridiculously proud of,' Trevor went on, a slight furrow deepening his forehead. 'The place seems to be overflowing with the local brew.'

'I know you aren't a scrumpy fan,' Lisa laughed at him. 'Even Frank's. I was going to offer you an Islay malt. Weren't you treated to a snifter last time?' She pushed several bottles aside and pulled out the whisky. 'It's Alec's latest find. Acquired taste, of course; and turns expensive. At least I've warned you.'

'Another yokel product?'

'I believe they pride themselves on it – huge exports to Japan.'

'Hardly a recommendation,' Trevor said. 'But I'll give it a go. Can't be as bad as Farmer Frank's.'

'Keep your voice down, Trev.' Lisa sounded conspiratorial, even to herself. She saw him register surprise. 'Flaxton is Alec's most important client at the moment, and Frank Graftley is Flaxton's blue-eyed boy and a good friend.'

'Is the place bugged?' Trevor whispered, grinning at her. 'I thought the triplets were only four weeks old.'

Lisa giggled delightedly. 'You are good for me, Trev. Thanks for coming down.' She lowered her voice, glancing at the living room door. 'Just Geraldine's on the prowl, and she's related to the Flaxton bigwigs. She'll have finished the triplets off by now.'

'One has to hope not literally, I suppose,' he grinned. 'I thought you said she wallowed in magazines whenever there's a pause in the milk-tippling.'

'Murder most foul. But only when nothing else is going on. Bit of a nosy parker, actually. Loves to snoop around; fancies herself as a feisty female sleuth.' She poured some whisky into a tumbler. 'Ice? Or will Malvern do?'

'Malvern is fine.'

'Something for her to do when the children are napping. Anyway,' Lisa mouthed at him, 'there's a new man about. She's hardly to know she doesn't stand a chance against Leo.'

The loud banging of the side door knocker made them both jump.

'Anyone at home?' The noise of the old door opening and the soft Somerset tones alerted Lisa to Meg's arrival.

Seb had already rushed to greet her with excited shouts of 'I got more bwuther, Auntie Meg. Yasper.'

'The trusty Meg?' Trevor asked softly.

Lisa frowned; her afternoons were sacrosanct. Was there something wrong, or was Meg deliberately ignoring her signals not to interrupt the painting sessions?

'*Another* brother?'

From the sound of the yelp, Lisa realised, dismayed, that Meg had not put such a possibility entirely out of court.

'Oh, he *is* a big one.' The drop to a normal tone was clear. 'That's your new teddy, then.' Meg walked cautiously through. 'Lisa? You down here? Hello. Didn't mean to – oh, you've got company. I'm ever so sorry. I was just passing and I thought you'd be pleased to know—'

'This is Trevor Sayles, Meg, the clever lad who sells my paintings. Apparently he's discovered a new outlet in Bath, so he's come down to see whether I've done any new work.'

'Oh dear, you're talking business. I didn't mean to butt in none. Give you a ring later,' Meg said, retreating rapidly.

Lisa hesitated. Meg would consider it a social slight if she allowed her to go. There had been a distinct cooling off since Lisa had felt obliged to change from the goat's milk. If she didn't invite her now, Meg would take it as proof that Lisa preferred her one-time London friends to her new ones in Somerset.

'Do stay,' she invited Meg, using a detached tone to convey that she should not stay long. 'We were just going to have some tea. Why don't you join us?'

Meg looked uncertainly at Lisa, then turned to Seb. 'That teddy's almost as big as you are. Special present, that it?'

'Uncle Tweff's pwesent.'

'What a lucky boy.' Meg turned, awkward and bemused, to look at Trevor; he was standing, politely waiting for her to sit down.

'I'd love a cup of tea,' she said at last. She sat back heavily, pulling Seb next to herself on the sofa opposite Trevor.

Trevor, seated again, turned attentively to Meg. 'I've heard so much about your farm, Mrs Graftley.'

'Oh yes?'

'I gather you have a wonderful herd of pure Jersey cows; quite unusual for this area, I'm told.'

'We do run a few, though we stick to Friesians mostly.'

'And Rhode Island Red chickens – I understand those have nearly died out.'

Meg was beginning to thaw out. 'I go in for a few laying hens, just enough eggs for us and a few friends.'

Lisa leaned through the kitchen hatch and placed the tea tray on it. 'Everything all right, Meg?'

There had not been any further references to multiple calvings or oblique intimations about odd happenings in the farm animal world for a couple of weeks now.

'The chickens are double-yolking quite a bit,' Meg admitted, Lisa thought, somewhat reluctantly.

'Is that bad?' Lisa could see Trevor struggling to find the right words. 'I rather like double-yolked eggs myself.'

'Bad for the hens,' Meg said, sombre now. 'Bit of a strain on them.'

'Of course; I hadn't really thought of that.' Trevor, urbane, was still bent on relaxing her. 'Lisa tells me you make the most fabulous clotted cream.'

There was a hint of a smile.

'And you even make your own cheeses. I do admire that.'

'Just the way we live,' Meg said, matter-of-fact, but Lisa could see her beginning to feel at ease with Trevor. His charm was working. 'Always wondered how chaps like you go about selling pictures,' Meg went on, rushing her words. 'It's not the same as selling cattle. How d'you get folk interested?'

'It's a question of choosing the gallery that has the right clientele.'

'Well, now. How can you tell?'

'Nothing fancy, I'm afraid. I just look at what they're selling at the moment, and work it out from that.'

'I thought paintings come in all sorts.'

'You're quite right, of course,' Trevor smiled expansively. 'Some galleries go in for abstract work, others like the more representational. Whatever they prefer, one has to have the right appeal. It's exactly what I've been telling Lisa. Her recent landscapes are so brilliantly evocative of this area, they're bound to be in demand locally. A splendid new market for her work.'

'You'll want to hear my news, then.' Meg turned to Lisa and saw her placing the teapot on the open hatch. She got up to take it through for her. 'It'll give you more of a chance later on, when the triplets get underfoot.' She was evidently very pleased with herself. She paused dramatically, placed the teapot on the table in front of the sofa and began to set out the cups and pour the tea. 'Anne Marsden is thinking of starting a playschool in the village. Only five hundred yards down the road. She's taken on Lodsham House.'

'Really? A playschool?'

'Thought you might like to put your name down in a hurry. She can take on twenty. Your young'uns would amount to a fair slice of that.'

'That is thoughtful of you, Meg. What ages is she going to start them at?'

'Whatever's wanted, she said. She'll hire the staff according.'

'So Seb could go right away, and she might take the triplets when they're up to it?'

'Dare say she'd find that a feather in her cap,' Meg said slowly. 'Folk like to mix with triplets and such. That and my twins'd get her off to a flying start.'

Perhaps, after all, it wasn't just the goat's milk which had caused the slight rift between her and Meg, Lisa thought. Perhaps her friend's nose was out of joint now that she had produced triplets to rival the Graftley twins.

Meg drained her cup and stood. 'I'd best be going, Lisa. You'll be wanting to finish your business before the triplets wake.' She patted Seb on the head. 'And I've got to see to Frank's tea.'

'I'll pack up the painting I promised you,' Lisa said quickly, springing up.

'Next time I come round,' Meg dismissed that immediately. 'Don't worry now. I'll see myself out.' She hugged Seb and waved goodbye.

'She always as dour as that?' Trevor wanted to know. 'I expected the jolly farmer's wife.'

'You noticed, did you? I thought I might have been imagining it. No, it's only since the triplets appeared.'

'The triplets? What would they have to do with Meg? You mean she felt obliged to help?'

'I don't think it's that, though we did have to impose on her before Alec found Geraldine. I think she might feel threatened.'

'Threatened? By what?'

'She's been the big earth mother up to now. She's lost the title, I suppose.'

'I thought she had dozens of children herself, even more than you,' he teased her.

'Single children, fraternal twins. Not identical triplets.'

Trevor laughed out loud. 'I'd no idea there was a hierarchy of motherhood.'

'Seb, go and take your teddy to show Gerry, will you? Mummy's got to talk business to Uncle Trevor.' She led the little boy out to the hall and saw him up the stairs.

'You're worried about more than that,' Trevor said, his face now grave.

'It's not just the triplets being born,' Lisa blurted out. 'It's how it happened. Meg's got this crazy theory that it's all due to that new fertiliser stuff. You know, Flaxton's Multiplier. She thinks the scan only showed one infant because the embryo split much later than normal, and that that happened because I ate the dairy produce from their farm.'

'I thought you said that the stuff hasn't been released yet?'

'The Graftleys have used it for over two years now, Trev. Their farm's the testing site.'

'So? What's it got to do with you?'

'I drank their milk and ate their cheese and yoghurt, all through my pregnancy.'

Trevor stared at her, trying to understand. 'But I thought it was all organic?'

'It is, and the Jerseys are pastured on the home meadow, which isn't fertilised. But Meg says there's seepage, and that the farm animals have more twins and triplets than usual as well. It's getting me down, rather.'

'Yes,' he said, looking at her. 'I noticed you looked strained as soon as she turned up. Hasn't been implying more than one man or anything, has she?'

Even Lisa laughed at the absurdity of that. 'She's talking about identicals – splits from the same fertilised egg.'

'That's rather technical for me.'

'A fertilised egg can split into two or more to produce several individuals. That happens very soon after conception but Meg thinks that in my pregnancy it took place at a much later stage than usual. She thinks I brought it on myself by sucking at clover petals – there's some sort of local old wives' tale about that.'

'Witchlorc, I suppose. The area has that reputation.' He looked at her thoughtfully. 'Tales of black masses invoking the devil on the Tor. You don't, I take it, think there's anything to that sort of claptrap?'

'Of course not.' Lisa laughed; a hollow, strained sound she hardly recognised. 'But anything's possible,' she added hurriedly, trying to cover herself. Should she – could she – really confide in Trevor what she had suppressed so long? Would he stand by her? She couldn't bring herself to do it. It was too much to ask. 'I – I don't care one way or the other, Trev. I just want to enjoy my children.'

'You've mentioned Meg's blatherings to Alec?'

'Not really. I wouldn't want him to think that that business is getting to me, Trev. He'd think I'd gone completely off my rocker.'

'If all the local hocus pocus is worrying you, you really should tell Alec. They've got no right to hassle you.' Trevor was walking round the room examining pictures, pedantically straightening the frames.

'It's just that . . .' She trailed off, not sure how far she dared go. Trevor must know she was worrying about more than Meg and her innuendoes. He wasn't a fool.

'What's really bugging you, Lis?'

She took a deep breath. 'Their stockman, Don Chivers, maintains some of the farm animals split once they're born unless he tags them.' There. She'd actually said it.

'Split? You mean split open?'

'Split into two separate animals – clone,' Lisa rushed at him. She'd used the actual word, come out with it.

'Clone?' He stared at Lisa. 'What exactly do you mean by "clone"?'

'One animal divides into two identical ones, like an amoeba.'

He laughed out loud at that; a deep, long, belly laugh. 'That really is preposterous. You'll be telling me about the witches' curse next.'

It startled her. 'What makes you say that? Did I tell you about the elders?'

'Village elders, d'you mean? They've been saying having triplets isn't natural?' He giggled. He stood, planting his feet apart. 'Bain't natural,' he intoned in what he took to be a Somerset accent. 'That right?' He grinned. 'Told you to expose them on the Mendips, I dare say.'

Lisa was not amused. 'Elder bushes – we grubbed out a dreadful old elder hedge. They're said to be a safeguard against witches' spells.'

'Honestly, Lis. You're not going to let that sort of bunkum get to you, surely?'

'Not really.' She managed a watery smile. 'It does sound crazy when you talk about it to someone who doesn't live here.'

Trevor was sipping at the malt, walking around the room again. 'Anything in the studio you want to show me?'

'A couple of landscapes completed, a few sketches for new ideas.' She shrugged. 'Not very much, I'm afraid.'

He put his arm round her shoulders. 'Entirely understandable. Amazing what you've managed to do.'

'I'd like to switch back to acrylics as soon as possible.'

'Give it a little more time, Lis. You'll exhaust yourself.' He steered her towards the stairs. 'Let's go and visit the little darlings first. I'm longing to see if I can spot the difference.'

She walked ahead of him and tried to sound carefree, gay. 'Bet you can't. I've put silver identification bracelets on them, just in case, so no cheating. I'll be watching you.'

He'd completely pooh-poohed her reference to cloning. She must have imagined that James was Janus's clone. Trevor had just proved it. Even when she'd spelt it out for him he had rejected the idea; even in theory, even for farm animals.

'I'll have a go.'

He might, of course, change his mind when he saw just how alike they were.

Trevor looked intently at the triplets, lying like little angels in their cots. 'That's pretty awesome,' he said at last. 'I can see why you need the bracelets.' He pointed to Jeffrey. 'That one has a slightly wider forehead. I can't come up with anything else at all.' He straightened up. 'Perhaps it's easier to see differences when they're awake. They must have different personalities.'

'Full marks. The only one who never hesitates between them is Seb.'

'Bright lad, your little Seb. Inherited his mother's eye for detail.'

She looked at Trevor. He did not, apparently, find it strange that she had found it necessary to label her own children, and certainly made no connection between that and what she had told him about Don and his newborn farm animals.

She took a deep breath; she might as well try to draw him out. 'I think Don is beginning to wonder whether I've "tagged" them to stop them splitting into more.'

'The stockman, you mean?' He paused. 'Why would that make any difference?'

He'd heard, then; taken it in, but not understood.

'He hasn't actually said.'

'Just implied it,' Trevor chuckled, 'Somerset fashion. And what, precisely, is supposed to cause this unbelievable phenomenon?'

'I told you, Trev. Meg blames it on the new fertiliser, says it affects a foetus exposed to it.'

'That's absurd.' He sounded almost cross. 'I've never heard of anything so ridiculous, have you?'

14

It was as though Trevor had released her from invisible bonds. After his visit, Lisa felt she was a person in her own right again. A vibrant, good-looking woman who was not only a mother but also a sought-after artist.

'Nigel and Diana are having a celebratory do this Thursday,' Alec purred down the phone. 'They're relying on us to be there.' He seemed quite animated; just why, Lisa was not clear. Simply another office party, she assumed.

'What sort of do?' she asked, sounding cautious and not too eager. She wanted to enjoy something personal, just the two of them, then realised with a start that she hadn't actually been out socially since the appearance of the triplets. Why not go to a party? The babies were gaining weight steadily and slept well between the feeds. The silver bracelets were in place; there shouldn't be any problems.

'Flaxton are launching the new fertiliser at last,' Alec said excitedly, 'At the Carruthers' house. The whole crowd will be there.'

'Meaning?'

'Everyone involved with developing Multiplier, Lis!' Alec sounded impatient. 'Pulling out all the stops,' he said, the sort of drive in his voice which Lisa had not heard for months. 'You'll have a wonderful time, darling. Everyone's really keen to see you again. I said we'd be able to rustle up a babysitter by then.'

Alec's voice throbbed low enough to make the words hard to distinguish. Lisa wondered, vaguely, why Nigel Carruthers was so important to her husband. Of course she knew that Carruthers was in charge of the Flaxton group based in Wells, and Alec's firm's most important client; Grew, Donsett would expect him to represent them. Carruthers was also a keen follower of the Lodsham hunt, but Alec didn't ride, and nor did Lisa. Frank did, but he was hardly Carruthers' type.

'But Thursday's the day after tomorrow.'

'What about Gerry staying on?'

'Geraldine?' The note of anger came through before Lisa could control it. The girl had clearly been making a play for Alec from the very first day. And he had reciprocated; she'd seen his eyes devour Geraldine's legs, travel up to her bosom, on to her hair. And he was always trying to spend more time in her company.

Now wasn't the right occasion to deal with that. Lisa altered her tone to one of calm detachment. 'Geraldine can only just look after herself. You really can't be serious, Alec. Leave a young girl of sixteen in charge of four children under two?'

'They'll be asleep, pet. We needn't get there till eight. No need to fuss.'

'Fuss? For God's sake, Alec, even you must have noticed that occasionally one of them wakes.'

'Gerry seems quite competent to me.'

He was always taking the girl's side. And Lisa had noticed he was only too ready to take her home, even when he'd just driven back from work and was tired out.

'*Competent?* At what, precisely? Snaring men?' The anger slipped out before she could stop herself. Geraldine, for her part, always made sure she needed a lift. She had a magnificent racer bicycle she could use, but didn't bother to.

'What's that supposed to mean?' The voice lowered again, as though asking her to imitate the tone.

'It seems to take you a long time to see her home.'

'A long time? Is that what's bugging you?' He was finally getting her drift. 'I've told you, Lisa, her people usually ask me in for a drink.'

'I've seen the way she looks at you.'

She knew she was being absurd to react like this. There was probably nothing between them at all; at any rate, nothing significant. She was feeling guilty about her reluctance to allow her husband to sleep with her, and had transferred that guilt to jealousy. Even more than Alec, she was determined to avoid a further pregnancy. The threat of such a possibility had made her frigid. She was afraid; afraid she'd have another multiple birth, as she called it to herself. Afraid she'd conceive another cloner was the truth of it. Abstinence, as far as Lisa's present state of mind was concerned, was the only foolproof contraceptive.

'Lisa, I'm in the office. This nonsense will have to wait. Now, yes or no for Thursday?'

'Is it important?'

'Yes.'

'Then take Geraldine! I'm sure she'll do you proud.'

'Stop being idiotic.' There was a pause, and Alec's voice changed to a more caressing tone. 'You know I want to show you off.'

'I'll see if I can think of someone.' Not Meg, she told herself; anyone but Meg.

'I thought of Meg, of course,' Alec was saying, as though reading her mind. 'But naturally she and Frank are guests of honour.'

'Are they?' Of course they were; Lisa had quite forgotten that their farm had been the testing site. They'd worked with Multiplier for over two years now. Lisa suddenly felt enormously relieved. The brittle in her voice turned soft and friendly. That's what had been holding her back. She hadn't wanted to risk Meg alone with the triplets.

'Nellie Kirby will be sitting for them, I expect,' Alec reminded her.

'Right,' she agreed, a gay tone replacing her previous anxiety. 'I'll see if Meg knows someone else we could trust.'

Lisa replaced the receiver without waiting for Alec's reply and tapped in the Graftleys' number. She wondered whether she'd get a cool reception. It had been about three weeks since she had been in touch. 'Meg?'

'Hello, stranger.'

'I hear you're going to the Carruthers' party on Thursday.'

'Right enough.'

'I suppose you're having Nellie round for the children?'

'Quite right, my duck. Is something wrong?'

'No, no; it's just that Alec wants us to go as well. Met any good babysitters lately?'

'Well, now. Let me put my thinking cap on.' A fruity laugh. 'I reckon Betsy would be right for you. Betsy Beste. She lives in the village, next to the Post Office.'

'Like Nellie, you mean?' Nellie Kirby had sat with Sebastian a number of times. Lisa felt safe with her. 'D'you think she could cope with the triplets if they woke up?'

'I reckon she could,' Meg said slowly. 'She comes from a big family. Twelve of them, and she's the eldest.' Meg chuckled down the phone. 'Great pal of Nellie Kirby's.'

Lisa flustered around the triplets, tucking them up in such a way that they'd be quite unsmotherable, checking the windows, seeing to the lights – examining the bracelets over and over. She even woke Janus by checking on the fastener of his. He stared at her solemnly. He looked as sweet, and as innocent, as her two other babies. He turned his head away, as though dismissing her. All too soon she heard the hum of the Audi returning, parking in the drive.

'This is Betsy Beste,' Alec introduced her, towering just behind a short, neat, dark-haired woman in her forties.

Shiny, crinkled black curls revealed one or two white hairs. Mrs Beste bent her head towards her left shoulder. Small, eager eyes lowered immediately after contact with Lisa's.

'She and Miss Kirby are neighbours – well, almost more than neighbours,' Alec said, brandishing open the door and guiding the small figure through into the living room by gently putting his hand against her elbow. 'Miss Kirby has the flat above Mrs Beste.' He held out an expansive arm.

'Hello.' Lisa prised her lips into a forced greeting, tense and uncertain. Suddenly she felt exposed. Was she expected to leave her triplets – all four precious children – not to the familiar and reliable Miss Kirby, but to someone she'd never even met before? She felt Alec had pushed her into this. She drifted vaguely after them, feeling resentful.

'Wasn't it lucky she could come at such short notice?' Alec was looking over his shoulder at Lisa, nodding encouragement, beckoning her to follow through.

Lisa stared at him stonily, then softened her eyes and turned to Betsy Beste. 'You live alone?'

'Oh no, Mrs Wildmore. I live with my husband and my daughter Mandy. She's sixteen now; she hardly needs me any more.'

'I'm sure she does.'

'They grow up ever so quickly,' Mrs Beste sighed. 'So now I'm free to help out. I do so love the little ones, you see. And I only had the one myself.'

Mrs Beste's small, round form was perched, uneasy, on an easy chair, her legs tucked under her. She seemed about to leap to her feet again.

'I'll show you where the children sleep,' Lisa suggested. 'Seb may still be awake. It would be a good idea if he met you just in case he wakes up later.'

Betsy was already standing before Lisa had finished speaking. 'That would be wonderful,' she said. 'Mr Wildmore's been telling me all about your little family. I can hardly wait to see them.'

Lisa began to relax; the stiff pretence of a smile eased off to a genuine one as she led the way upstairs and into Sebastian's room.

''Nigh', Mummy,' he turned towards them, lids lowered, Jasper clutched firmly to his chest.

'He sleeps like a log all night. I don't think he'll give you any trouble.'

'You need that, what with the triplets,' Betsy cooed. 'And *isn't* he a lovely little boy?' Her eyes sparkled at Lisa, wide with enchantment.

Unwinding even more, Lisa pushed open the door to the triplets' room. Light from the corridor slanted across the cots, showing three golden-headed babies sleeping contentedly.

'Oh, that is beautiful,' Betsy whispered as she crossed the room and walked up to the cots. She stood peering at each baby in turn, then tiptoed softly back and beamed at Lisa.

'I'll just show you how the TV works, shall I?' Alec chirruped at them as they came out of the nursery. He clearly wanted to do his bit to make the new babysitter feel at home.

'No, thank you, Mr Wildmore,' she said softly, looking over her shoulder at the cots. 'I think I'll just sit quietly with my knitting. I'll leave the living room door wide open, if that's all right. It's such a big house. That way I can be sure of hearing anything that's going on upstairs.'

'We have a baby-listening device.'

'I like to make sure.' Betsy turned to take one more look inside the nursery before Lisa leaned the door to. 'You have the most wonderful family, Mrs Wildmore. I do envy you.'

A feeling of calm reassurance came over Lisa as she led the way down the broad staircase and into the hall. 'I'll just show you where everything's kept in the kitchen,' she said. 'In case the babies wake up, or there's something you would like.'

Betsy stood, reminding Lisa of a mother blackbird standing poised, head cocked to the side. She listened, nodding dark curls, to Lisa's instructions.

Quite suddenly Lisa knew her children would be completely safe with this woman. Alec, raising his brows at her, caught Lisa's smile of assent.

'Well, we'll be off then,' he said. 'I've put the name and number of the family we'll be with by the phone in case you need to be in touch.

We won't be far away, and we shan't be late.'

'All right?' Alec said smugly in the car. 'She'll do?'

'A miracle,' Lisa breathed easily. 'Especially compared to Geraldine.'

'Let's not go into that now,' Alec said quietly. 'Let's just enjoy ourselves. It's our first outing together since the triplets were born.'

The Audi hummed its way across the moor and the main road to Wells. Despite herself, misgivings began to tug at Lisa. Was she mad to risk her family like this? A complete stranger? What if . . . what if another child appeared? That was the crux of it.

'All babes and no outings make Lisa a dull wife,' she vaguely heard as Alec backed the Audi into the last space in the Carruthers' massive driveway. It was going to be a big party.

The triplets were quite safe; it was inconceivable that Betsy Beste would take the bracelets off.

'Let's make a real night of it. Everybody's here, and there's even a live band.'

The party was in full swing. Lisa edged into a corner, trying to decipher words through the steady beat of music straining her ears. She sipped the frothy snowball Alec had spied for her, allowing the bubbles to release the tension in her veins.

'Hello, my dear.' Meg was a few feet away, a full moon face shining beneath pan make-up inexpertly applied.

'Hello, Meg. What a lovely colour,' Lisa said, unnerved by brilliant taffeta. 'Is it new?'

'Belonged to my old mum,' Meg told her, laughing easily. 'Fits like a glove. Made them big enough in those days. You left Betsy in charge?'

'Yes, thanks.' Reminded, Lisa felt nags of worry through the alcohol. 'D'you think they're going to be all right?'

'Evening, Lisa.' Frank's eyes traced her shape through the black silk hugging slim perfection. 'They'll be all right along of Betsy.'

'Still worrying?' Alec swallowed the smoked salmon he was savouring, took another sip of Pouilly-Fuissé, and looked towards his wife. 'She's got this number.'

'Betsy'd ring the minute there were any problems, Lisa,' Meg soothed.

'You're sure?' Lisa's smooth brow was knotted into deep, vertical stripes.

'Of course she'd ring if anything was up.' Lisa could feel Alec's irritation, his holding back. He took another bite of smoked salmon and emptied his wine glass. 'But if you're going to fuss, why don't you give her a buzz? There's a phone in the hall.'

Lisa almost knocked into Frank in her hurry to get to it. Hands trembling, beads of sweat on her upper lip, she tapped the number in.

A tentative, small voice answered before the second ring.

'Hello?'

'Mrs Beste?' Well, who else could it be?

'Yes, this is Mrs Beste.'

'Hello, Mrs Beste. This is—'

'I'm sorry, you'll have to excuse me for a moment. I think I can hear one of the children crying.'

'—Lisa Wildmore speaking.'

The sound of the phone laid aside at the other end left Lisa rooted to the spot, clenching the receiver in her right hand, drumming the little table with her left. Seconds ticked by as her mind formed dark shadows moving in the triplets' nursery. She blinked and looked away, towards the rich oak of the banisters. Travelling up, her eye registered a series of exquisite prints: Munch's 'Frieze of Life' stepped along the wall by the Jacobean staircase. The eloquence of monochrome stirred her imagination. She wondered idly whether she should make an effort now to escape from her rut of chocolate box watercolours and try something new. Too soon, she realised; it would take too much creative energy.

The poignant round of the mouth opened wide drew Lisa into startled imitation of 'The Cry'. Her eyes, huge saucers, saw again the innocent meadow, then the splitting of the butterfly in Seb's hands, the rabbits proliferating in the field, the clover leaves dividing, over and over. A fungoid mass, black, menacing, began to move, overwhelm the other shapes, blot them out. Fleshy lobes of oozing matter elongated, split, detached themselves, reformed into original shapes. Small specks of white infiltrated them, turned into eyes which opened up and pierced her mind, gleaming at her. Hundreds of eyes, alive along the wall, moving now. Lisa let out a cry of pain at what she saw happening: the unleashing of a force beyond control. It ate up everything; hundreds of identical beings, overwhelming the planet, running amok. She saw them move, growing long, spiky legs. Spiders, spinning their silky prisons . . .

'You all right, Lisa?' Diana Carruthers asked her, tripping by on her way to greet new arrivals.

Lisa shuddered in the warmth of the hall. 'Just checking on the children,' she explained, her throat tight, her hand white round the receiver now pressed hard against her ear.

The voice came back on the line. 'I'm so sorry to keep you waiting. I'm afraid Mr and Mrs Wildmore have gone out.'

Lisa paused for a moment. 'I know, Mrs Beste.'

There was a further silence, then the voice came through again. 'They went out about an hour ago. They left their number, if you want to get in touch with them.'

'No, Mrs Beste. It's me, Mrs Wildmore. I'm just ringing to make sure that there aren't any problems.'

Another long, deep pause. 'That's Mrs Wildmore, is it?' the voice asked cautiously.

'Yes.' Was something terribly wrong? Had a bracelet come loose and . . . Butterflies somersaulted in Lisa's stomach. She saw the quivering flight of a myriad peacocks, gleaming circles of shimmering colour, a chimera of accusing eyes. They milled around her, squeezed her tight. She fought for air, heaved oxygen into her lungs. 'Is everything all right?' she managed to breathe.

'Everything is perfectly all right, Mrs Wildmore. The children are all fast asleep. I look in on them every ten minutes, just to make sure. Sorry to keep you waiting earlier on. I thought I heard a noise.'

'That's absolutely fine,' Lisa, shaking off suffocating worries, almost sang her relief. 'I'm sorry to have bothered you.'

When Lisa returned to the buffet table, Alec was deep in conversation with Nigel Carruthers.

'So this is our dainty lady with the gigantic family,' he boomed at her. 'Know when to stop, I hope?' His eyes were crinkled into a smile, but Lisa felt the cold, calculating pierce of pale, hard eyes sunk well below shaggy brows. 'Identical triplet boys – an extraordinary achievement for such a delicate lady. The mind boggles to think how it was done.' The eyes bored openly into her midriff, then held her own in what seemed a stranglehold to Lisa. What did he mean, 'was done'?

Diana Carruthers swept up to them, flowing through a magnificent Zandra Rhodes, jagged edges of rose and magenta transparent over gold. Her throat was choking with enormous pearls. Lisa watched, fascinated, as they jiggled up and down whenever Diana spoke.

'Darling,' she trilled, shrill above the band. 'I think you're *such* a clever girl.' Lisa cringed nervously into the Caroline Charles which had made her feel so attractive earlier in the evening. 'Have you met

Wilford Gudgeon?' Diana introduced Lisa. 'Sir Wilford farms the thousand acres next to us; and he's Master of the Pakenham Moor pack.' She paused. 'One of the great foxhound packs in the country. And he's just joined the Flaxton board.'

Lisa smiled doubtfully. Diana was an avid rider. Lisa watched her metamorphose from social butterfly into competent sportswoman as she talked to Sir Wilford.

'You live near here?' Gudgeon demanded, his eyes devouring the table laden with food.

'In Lodsham,' Lisa said. 'Sedgemoor Court. Your hounds often run over Mark Ditcheat's fields. He's our neighbour.'

'Of course they do; I remember now,' Diana yelped over the thump of baying music, like a hound herself, grabbing a tray of beautifully presented poultry slices and holding it out for Lisa. 'I'd forgotten that. You must be quite isolated there. May I tempt you to some of this?'

Lisa took a single slice of dark duck meat.

'Any family?' Sir Wilford demanded.

'Four boys under two, Willie,' Lady Carruthers told him. A spike of chiffon twirled itself round Sir Wilford's arm. 'Isn't that just too divine?'

'Four? Under two?' He snorted, thick, florid sinews in his neck swivelling as he examined every inch of Lisa. 'How on earth d'you manage that?'

'Triplets the second time round,' Diana shrieked over the babble, her head pointed forward. 'Quite a brain teaser, isn't it?'

Lisa saw solid red nostrils flare into disdain. 'Triplets? You mean three at one go? That's overdoing it a bit, what?' Gudgeon's loose flesh shook admonishingly at Lisa. 'House must be like a rabbit warren.'

'And so alike they've had to put identification bracelets on them,' Diana giggled, beckoning a maid to offer further food.

Sir Wilford commandeered a whole plate and began to eat from it.

'Isn't that simply gorgeous? Who's your obstetrician?' Diana suddenly asked Lisa, lowering her voice slightly. 'I had Ian Parslow.'

'Actually, that's the man I went to,' Lisa told her. 'The specialist at the Hammersmith recommended him.'

'Brilliant mind,' Nigel put in. 'Absolutely brilliant. He's one of the country's leading embryologists – in DNA research.'

Lisa spluttered on the mouthful of champagne she was about to swallow. Brilliant Parslow might be; as far as she was concerned he was too damned patronising, too smooth; too know-all.

'Did you say bracelets?' The poultry slices were disappearing at an extraordinary rate as Gudgeon's jaws worked steadily. 'Metal, d'you mean?'

'Quite narrow little silver chains, with their names on a tab,' Alec explained.

'Keep 'em on all the time, what?' Gudgeon was still staring at Lisa. What was he asking her?

'It's just so other people don't mix them up,' she told him carefully. 'Just in case of accidents or something. Even identical triplets have quite distinct needs, you know. Janus, for instance, is allergic to goat's milk. It's important to think ahead about that sort of thing.'

'Goat's milk? I thought it was cow's milk which caused so many problems,' Diana put in.

'I suppose it all depends,' Alec intervened. He savoured the wine in his glass. 'This is outstanding, Nigel. Where d'you buy? Harvey's of Bristol?'

'Import it directly from the chateau,' Carruthers told him. 'Only way I can be sure they don't use additives. It's quite disgusting what even the most reputable firms get up to.'

'Additives? You mean they add chemicals to chateau-bottled wine?' Alec sounded quite shocked.

'Many of them do. Prevents even outstanding wine from reaching its full potential.' Carruthers looked grave. 'Basically, wine making depends on yeast fermenting the sugar in grape juice. Add something foreign to unadulterated grape, and you stop the whole process dead.'

Yeast feeding greedily on sugar, swelling up, flowing over . . . Lisa felt hemmed in again, waves of warm, moist yeast ballooning, oozing around her, blurring familiar contours, overwhelming, out of control.

Carruthers waved the bottle over Alec's proffered glass. 'I get them to keep a dozen crates for us; can't persuade them to let me have more. Our quota,' he laughed, and turned to Lisa. 'We're going to have to set *you* quotas, too,' he told her, not altogether jocularly.

'Don't worry about that,' Alec put in quickly. 'We already have.'

Wilford Gudgeon, red jowls flapping as he crammed even more food into his mouth, nodded approvingly as he moved heavily towards the wine. 'Might end up with quads next time,' he said, unsmiling eyes and mouth opening wide as he twisted the bottle to read the label.

'You really must bring the little sweeties over for tea,' Diana chirruped at Lisa. 'Fenella and I'd *love* to see them.'

'So? Any problems?' Alec asked Lisa quickly as soon as he found the opportunity.

'Everything's fine as far as I can gather,' she admitted. 'The woman's a disaster on the phone, but she seems to be a marvellous babysitter.'

15

'Bestie's here, Mummy!'

Seb, up from his nap, nose glued to the playroom window, was watching for the first sign of Betsy Beste. Lisa joined him to see Betsy wave her right arm as she cycled through the gateway, endangering her equilibrium. Her sou'wester glistened with tiny droplets which ran runnels along her sleeves. Drizzling, not raining, Lisa saw. It was going to clear up.

Betsy wobbled the handlebars in an effort to balance the bulging plastic bag sitting in the basket at the front.

Seb was already by the open door. 'Got my puddlers on,' he jumped his greeting in the porch. 'See? I's green.'

Another lurch of the handlebars almost ended in a fall as Betsy narrowly missed Seb's spotted cat. A large black patch over the left side of her face, dwarfing the profusion of smaller spots in ginger and brown on a pristine white body, made her look one-eyed.

'Hold Kitty out of my way, Seb, please.'

Lisa felt a tightening in her chest as she realised Seb's kitten did not just have poor vision; she was going blind, and rather more quickly than the vet she had consulted had anticipated. The child was going to be heartbroken if his pet could not be saved. Seb bent down to keep Kitty from bumping into Betsy.

'Want to see the swans today.'

'Good boy. Let Bestie put her bike away.'

'Jansy's got yellow, and Jeffers red; and Jiminy's blue.'

'What lovely new boots you've all been given. Are they a birthday present to the triplets?'

'They's not any present, they's shoes!'

'My mistake!' Betsy laughed. 'Let's just help Mummy strap the triplets in the pushchair, shall we?'

'I want to see the swans.'

'Then the swans it shall be,' Betsy agreed.

'Meg's bringing the twins over later,' Lisa explained as she helped Betsy to secure the three toddlers in the pushchair harness. 'If you could manage to keep them out for a couple of hours that'll give Geraldine and me a chance to get the birthday tea together.'

Lisa and Alec had decided to celebrate the triplets' birthday on the day the twins were born. Today was J-day.

'Of course, Lisa. I'll take them down the drove. Frank's special foals are in the big field. There's so many of them! And Seb does love to count – he's getting really good at it.'

'We's going to see the swans! You promised.'

'And we'll see the swans on the way.' Betsy was swinging Seb up and down as he chortled happily. 'You're getting such a big boy now, I can hardly lift you any more.'

'He's growing at a rate of knots.' Lisa's carefree laugh echoed round the porch. 'Come on, Gerry. Where have you got to now?'

'Just settling Duffers, Lisa.'

The girl's wretched terrier, Lisa thought irritably. His snuffling, searching snout, his slitted eyes and the way he burrowed after her toddlers worried her. They brought to mind TV pictures showing animals trained to sniff out drugs.

'You said he wasn't to go with them unless I was along,' Geraldine reminded Lisa.

Still cuddling James to herself, kissing soft, golden ringlets haloing his head, Lisa pulled his blue plastic anorak hood up. 'There you are, Jiminy. That'll keep you dry.' He was the most delicate of the three babies.

She turned to Betsy. 'Alec won't be able to make the birthday tea, I'm afraid. He's up in Bristol for meetings all day. But he said he'd be back as soon as he can get away; he'll see them all in bed if nothing else.'

'We'll have a lovely party,' Betsy was cooing at the triplets. 'Six little ones, balloons and jelly.'

'And the rocking horse,' Seb told her proudly.

'Ssh, Seb.' Lisa put her right index finger to her lips. 'That's the triplets' big present. It's still a secret.'

Apparently he hadn't heard. 'Daddy said I'm allowed the rocker, too.'

A fresh-faced Meg had walked her twins over the home meadow. They were clutching spring wild flowers in their hands: yellow tulips, snake's head lilies, cuckoo-pint, even some early purple orchids. Paul made a little bow as he handed his bunch over to Lisa.

'Aren't they lovely? Shall we put them in a jam jar?'

Phyllis loped up to Lisa and solemnly handed her a package wrapped in cellophane. Lisa just prevented herself from stepping away from the child; she was shocked to find herself nervous of her, and forced herself to lean forward to kiss the little girl, taking the package from her. 'And lardy cake as well; you are a dear, Meg.'

'And this should keep us going.' Meg had carted over a large pot of bramble jelly and two pints of clotted cream. 'Fresh from the dairy,' she told Lisa, pride in her voice. 'Sally makes all the cream now; she specially sent this over.'

Had Meg forgotten that Janus was allergic to dairy products? She'd have to try and make sure he didn't get any. 'From the Jerseys?' Lisa felt impelled to ask. 'Where d'you graze them?'

'Worried about producing quads?' Meg teased her gently. 'You expecting again?'

Lisa, taken aback, covered her nervousness with laughter. She had not allowed unwelcome, submerged thoughts into her consciousness during this past busy year. 'Nothing like that,' she said. 'I think I'm very content with what I've got.'

The three babies had filled out, just in the way Rita had prophesied. To look at them now one would never guess they'd been so small at birth. Janus, in particular, was strong and on the podgy side; almost getting fat.

'Betsy still out with them?'

'Taken them to see Frank's special foals.'

A momentary shadow seemed to cross Meg's face. 'Doing very well, mostly,' she said, jovial enough. 'Though we did find a dead one the other day. Did Betsy tell you? We've had far more than we expected. And so alike. You'd swear they were identical, leastways until you see them all together. Frank's had top prices for them.'

'Really?' Lisa had no intention of allowing stories about extraordinary numbers of twins or other multiples to come up. 'I've got a special surprise for—'

'Some of them seem to go lame all of a sudden. Frank don't rightly know why; their legs seem to bloat up, then stiffen. Perhaps we've bred them too fast. The mares bear strong, healthy foals, but—'

'I gather they're outstanding hunting stock.'

'My foot hurts, Mum. Want to take the brace off. You promised.'

'Your sandal's on too tight, Phyllie, that's all it is.' Meg bent to loosen the strap but stopped to glance up. 'Right enough. Frank's really keen on point-to-points, qualifying the hunters for the season.' She straightened up again, helping the child to stand. 'All right, my duck? You can walk straight now.'

'It still hurts, Mum,' Phyllis insisted plaintively. 'Bites into me.'

'You be all right, Phyllis. Enough of that whining,' Meg said sharply.

'Hunters, not hunter, eh?' Lisa interjected. She'd never heard Meg speak as peremptorily as that to any of her children before. 'You *are* getting grand. He's actually going to race them, is he?'

'So he says.'

'Here come the troops.'

Betsy looked out of breath. Lisa rushed down the drive to help her unfasten the children; pushing three one-year-olds up the steep slope was more than either of them could handle alone.

Janus, sitting in the centre, rocked backwards and forwards, raising fat arms and demanding to be first.

'Wait a minute, Jansy. We're going as fast as we can.'

A glint of fury twisted the child's mouth into a long, piercing scream. He turned sideways to pummel little James with flailing fists. The slighter child sat still, leaning away without fighting back.

'Jansy!' In spite of her instinct to unfasten James first and carry him in, Lisa undid Janus's reins and helped him stand. He grasped the pushchair handle and began to force it up the drive with his two brothers still strapped to it. Lisa and Betsy stared in disbelief as the pushchair moved against the incline, then twisted to its side and starting going backwards.

'Take Jansy, will you, Gerry?' Lisa instantly put her foot by the wheels and pulled the brake on. 'I'll take Jiminy; Betsy, you get hold of Jeffers.'

The yapping of an excited Duffers drowned Janus's shrieks as he and the dog pulled Geraldine in different directions.

'Duffers! Heel, boy!' The terrier's barks subsided into snappish grunts. Geraldine hoisted Janus under her arm and strode into the house with him.

Lisa hugged James to herself, covering him with kisses. Janus was so aggressive; the child in her arms had tears on his cheeks, but he responded to her endearments with a smile. 'Everybody in now? Good.'

A momentary hush as they all settled into the playroom allowed the loud knocking at the front door to penetrate.

'That's my surprise.' Lisa, laughing and full of mystery, insisted on answering the door herself. 'Just wait a moment.' She giggled at them all. 'See what I've got for you.'

The strong, low tones of a man's voice edged their way across the squeaks behind the playroom door.

'It's my Daddy,' Seb shouted, bursting through.

'Daddy is coming later, Seb.' Lisa took the child's hand and held the playroom door wide open. 'This is Matthew,' Lisa flourished the young man through. 'Look, Paul. He's got a special rabbit for you.'

Paul and Phyllis, now nearly three, advanced on the rabbit in unison and were about to grasp its ears. They were not quick enough. The terrier, retired to the corner of the room, sprang forward and seized the animal by the neck and began to shake it.

'Duffers!' Geraldine rushed forward. 'Let go, boy. Down.' The terrier stood, his tail wagging furiously, unsure. The girl knelt down beside him and carefully, delicately, and with remarkable aplomb disengaged the dog's teeth from the rabbit. 'Sorry about that, Matthew,' she smiled at the young man standing by.

He stood irresolute, waiting uncertainly, unclear what he was expected to do. Geraldine's smile produced an answering one.

'He can't help going after rabbits; hunting's in his blood. I didn't know you were coming, or I'd have kept him locked out.' Geraldine grinned apologetically at Matthew, clicked the leash into the dog's collar and led him from the room.

The rabbit, stunned but not hurt, sat still, allowing Phyllis and Paul to twist its ears. Janus's eyes began to gleam as he heaved himself to his feet and staggered over. He managed three steps before he propelled himself by crawling instead. A retinue of Jeffrey and James followed him.

'Woa, there, young'uns.' Matthew smiled doubtfully, clearly unnerved by so many human look-alikes.

'I'll take them over here for you.' Geraldine, now minus Duffers, grasped two of the triplets, one under each arm, and began to lend an unusual hand.

'Let's all sit down, shall we?' Lisa suggested.

Cushions were strewn on the floor. The young conjurer, relieved, returned to his rabbit. Within no time at all he had produced two more.

'More, more,' an excited Seb shouted as a fourth rabbit took its place beside the other three already assembled from the basket Matthew was pulling them out of. 'More wabbits.'

Lisa shuddered slightly as she realised Seb might think his triplet brothers had appeared in the same way. 'Rabbits, Seb.'

'More bwabbits.'

A galaxy of pigeons now streamed out of Matthew's pockets. Phyllis and Paul began to rush all round the room to catch them and, with Geraldine's help, Matthew enmeshed the children in masses of brightly coloured silk scarves.

The ecstatic Seb was counting pigeons: '. . . six, seven, eight, *nine*,' he shouted his delight.

James and Jeffrey first watched, round-eyed, then followed Janus's lead by crawling under the gaudy streamers and the paper hats, grasping at them.

Lisa watched Janus, strong and raucous. His eyes gleamed bright as he hoisted himself upright and lunged a hand into Matthew's left arm sleeve. He was so quick the conjurer only just had the presence of mind to draw the bird out of the sleeve with him. A shrill, dominating laugh filled the room as Janus grasped the pigeon's claws and brandished the bird round his head.

Matthew produced more pigeons. They whirled throughout the room. Janus stood up and stretched out his arms. To Lisa's amazement six identical white birds alighted on them. He grinned triumphantly; he showed no fear whatsoever.

'It's time for us to go, Lisa,' Meg finally announced, panting and laughing, rounding up Phyllis and Paul, stuffing paper hats and the remains of crackers into a plastic bag. 'Such a lovely, lovely party. Stroke of genius, bringing in Matthew.'

'I'm glad you enjoyed that. Thought it would give us all a bit of time to catch our breath.'

'I don't know about that,' Meg puffed, now finding it harder than last year to control her twosome. 'Wish I'd brought Sally and Jean along to see to these two.'

'My foot hurts, Mum,' Phyllis wailed. She'd sat down on the floor again and was twisting the brace in an effort to ease her foot. 'Want it off!'

To Lisa's amazement Meg did not immediately take any notice of Phyllis, did not smile. The gaiety had left her face as she turned impatiently to the child. 'It isn't right yet, Phyllie. Doctor'll see to you Monday.' She turned to Lisa. 'We're taking her to Bristol Infirmary.'

'She really does seem to be in pain, Meg. Can't you just take it off?

A day or two can't make any difference, surely.' Lisa looked more closely and saw that the brace was biting into part of Phyllis's foot, the flesh swelling over the ankle.

Meg turned away. 'Frank's so particular,' she said. 'Won't hear of it coming off.' She looked at Lisa, her face drawn. 'But you're right, Phyllie does seem to be in pain. Could I borrow the Volvo to drive us all home? Frank'll bring it back directly.'

'Of course, Meg. What a good idea; and don't worry, I'm not going anywhere tonight. Frank can bring the car back any time before tomorrow morning. Hope Phyllie feels better soon.' She pressed a final balloon into the child's hand as Meg lifted her up and took her two children to the car.

'It really has got late,' Betsy was worrying. 'I'm sorry I can't stay to help you bath them, Lisa. Mandy's got her new boy friend coming round. I promised to give them supper.'

'Don't give it a thought, Betsy. Geraldine and I can manage perfectly well, can't we, Gerry? The triplets are one year old! And I've only got to give them a quick wash,' Lisa said, shunting her infants upstairs with Betsy's help. 'They won't need anything more to eat.'

'I'll help Matthew put his gear away,' Geraldine announced, her back turned to Lisa.

'And I'll make sure the kitchen's clear for you,' Betsy reassured her. 'Shall I just help you undress them and pop them in the bath?'

Within minutes the little boys sat, all four of them, in the bath together. A flotilla of plastic ducks swam between them. Lisa caught her breath as she looked at her family. Four enchanting little boys; perfectly formed, lively, bright.

'Aren't they a picture!' Betsy kissed them goodnight, wiping away a circle of blackberry jelly smeared round Janus's mouth. 'And Sebbie will help you, Lisa,' Betsy went on. 'He's always so good with the babies.'

'Seb help Mummy,' he told Betsy solemnly. 'Help Mummy with more bwuthers.'

'Brothers, Seb.'

'Bye bye, Sebbie; bye bye, Jansy; bye bye Jeffers; bye bye Jiminy,' Betsy called gaily, retreating backwards through the bathroom door. They all waved back at her, splashing their hands, then raising them again.

Lisa knelt on the bathmat and started to bathe her children. She sponged squirming, healthy bodies, enjoyed their beauty, their energy.

Only Janus seemed rather plump and puffy; she made a note that she would cut down on the amount of cereal she gave him.

There was no sign of Geraldine, she noted irritably. Taking her time seeing Matthew off, presumably.

'Sebbie, you come out first.'

He splashed the water harder, hitting his flat palm against it.

'Come on, darling. You've got to be a big boy today and help Mummy get the triplets to bed. Okay?'

He splashed his hand one more time but dutifully got up and let Lisa lift him out. Standing beside the bathtub, Lisa's heart turned over again as she thought of the many times her little Seb had had to take second place in the last year.

'You sing "Baa Baa Black Sheep" to Jeffers while I get Jiminy dried,' she went on, rubbing the towel round Seb and brushing his hair.

'Babababababa,' Jeffrey joined in.

Lisa laughed at her little singing baby. 'Geraldine will be with you in a minute, Seb.' She brushed his teeth, then took the trouble to pull up the stool and sit him on her lap and sing a little song to him while watching the triplets splashing in the bath.

Pyjamas on, Seb ran into the guestroom now turned into the night nursery. Lisa could hear him tumbling on the double bed as he waited for her to bring Jeffrey in for him to sing to.

'Gerry,' she called.

There was no answer.

'Gerree!'

She should have known Geraldine would be chatting Matthew up, a good-looking young man like that. Man-crazy; the girl was man-crazy. However much Alec had denied it, hadn't she seen her fluttering her eyelids at him, wiggling her hips?

Lisa brushed the thought aside. It was time to get the triplets out of the water; she couldn't wait for ever, and they'd be getting cold. It really shouldn't be impossible. Jeffrey first, towel him down and get him ready for bed. Then take him quickly through to the triplets' room to be with Seb.

'Come on now, Jeffers.'

The little boy laughed at her and clapped his hands. She couldn't resist clapping with him, encouraging him. He was just as delightful as her Seb, she thought sunnily. Jeffrey was the one who liked to sing; Janus the one who used his strength. And little Jiminy – he always had a smile, he waited patiently while his stronger brothers clamoured for attention. So alike, and yet so different. Lisa rumpled Jeffrey dry on her lap, then slipped his nappy and red pyjamas on. Bouncing him up and down in time to his singing, she carted him off to his cot.

'Can we play on the bed?'

'No, Seb, it's already late. Jeffers will need to calm down now. Bring him a rattle if he starts to cry.'

Her ear, attuned to noises in a room she wasn't in, had heard odd sounds. There was an ominous sort of gurgling as she left the bedroom and started back along the hall. She began to sprint, suddenly aware that even a moment's inattention could result in a drowning. Fear gripped her; she'd forgotten to let the bath water out.

'Geraldine!' she shouted on her way. As she approached the bathtub she could see Janus – he was so much bulkier than the other two, no one could possibly mistake him now – leaning on top of James. The child was romping, over-excited by the party; he had no idea how strong he was, how heavy compared to his delicate brother.

As soon as Janus was aware of Lisa, he turned round and looked up at her, big blue eyes wide, rubbing his wrist. He began to cry, but Lisa, worried about James, ignored him.

James surfaced upright as Janus leaned back and Lisa snatched him out of the water and onto her lap. She didn't even stop to drain him, nor to take time to grab his towel. Holding him upside down, she saw some water coming out of his mouth, just a few drops. He appeared to be breathing normally, apparently none the worse for his tumble under water. Lisa glanced briefly at Janus, still rubbing his wrist. The silver bracelet was, she saw, cutting deeply into him.

That's what it must have been. The poor little mite was in pain; the bracelet was too tight on him, she could see the flesh bulging round it. He'd hauled himself up because the bracelet hurt, and so pushed Jiminy under the water. It was time to take Janus's bracelet off, otherwise it might actually stop the child's circulation.

Leaning over, her lips brushing the top of Jiminy's head as her arms embraced him protectively in his warmed towel, Lisa leaned down and unlatched the bracelet on Janus's wrist. The deep, red weal where it had been made her feel guilty that she had left it for so long. It wasn't really needed any more. She wondered how Meg had the heart to insist on Phyllis's brace when it was clearly hurting the child. Worried what Frank would say, she supposed. It had crossed her mind before that Meg was oddly nervous of going against Frank's wishes.

Janus smiled radiantly at her and splashed the water again, enjoying the expanse of bath all to himself. Lisa pulled out the plug and heard the gurgle of draining water.

She returned to James, now wriggling on her lap. Nothing, apparently, was wrong with him. He gulped a little more water out, sneezed once or twice, then seemed to settle down. She readied him as quickly as she could. Blue pyjamas. Could she risk leaving Janus on his own? Not likely to come to harm in so little water, she thought.

'Geraldine!' she hollered again. Only the draught of the open front door and the sound of Duffers running in and out. 'Seb,' she called. 'Seb, come and take Jiminy for me, will you?'

He was still singing at the top of his voice.

'Seb!' she shouted, louder now. But James began to cry, and Janus to splash the water swirling away into the drainage hole, threatening to wet Jiminy's pyjamas. She stood quickly with James in her arms and rushed him to the bedroom. 'Play with him, Seb,' she said, laying him on the double bed. 'You can have a game with him while I dry Jansy.'

James twined his arms round her neck, blew bubbles at her. Unwillingly she freed herself from him, tickled his chest, prattled to him and turned away. As she walked rapidly back along the corridor, she heard loud slaps in the bathroom, shrill shrieks. Janus was an unusually rowdy baby.

She reached the door, exhausted, took a deep breath and leant against it. As she stood, she could just make out the back of Janus's head. Surely he had been further down the bath?

She froze. As she looked along the bath, she could see another child, his back towards her, turning to face her. Two babies in the bath, splashing the remnants of the water.

'Jiminy!' she cried out. The sound came out like a choke, strangled at birth. 'How could you possibly get back in here?' she whispered to herself. The scene in the nursery last year came back again full force.

The tots just burbled at her, clapping their hands, squeaking delight. Lisa gaped at the two children, then hurled away towards the triplets' room. The suppressed memory was beginning to take hold and bring waves of panic.

'Baa baa black sheep, have you any—'

'Seb!'

He turned from the bed he was sitting on with James, in blue pyjamas, lying by his side. He was hugging James with his teddy.

'Where's Jeffrey?'

Seb started singing again. Lisa turned unwillingly towards the three cots lined up at the far end of the large room. Two empty; the third had a one-year-old, standing, clutching the bars, his red pyjamas intact.

She whirled round to look at Seb and his other brother. They were still on the double bed, James's head on a large pillow, his blue pyjamas covering him.

Gulping for breath, Lisa dashed back to the bathroom. She could hear the splattering as she ran, and a peculiar sort of rattle, an odd, unusual noise, between the grunts of babyish effort.

She forced herself to look towards the bath and shuddered, noting that the child turning to look and smile at her was similar to the Janus of earlier on, like him but slightly different. As her eye went down his trunk along the bottom of the bath, she gagged. The second baby was leaning forward, his back rounded, his face down. He seemed to be slumped there, inert.

Her heart thumped crazily as she swooped towards him and pulled his shoulders back. The eyes stared at her, just as blue as her triplets' – but lifeless. Horrified, she dropped the body back. The other child – Janus? *Was* he Janus? – had begun to cry, his arms stretched out towards her.

Lisa wilted onto the stool and laid her head against the bath edge. She must be hallucinating. Alec was right; she had to get more help. He'd warned her she was overdoing things.

The crying baby in the bath grasped at the rail and hauled himself up to standing. Lisa could see that an oddly yellow liquid was clinging to him. One of the plastic ducks, its head partially blocking the outlet, must have been the reason for some water remaining in the tub. But why was it this odd yellow colour?

'Jansy?'

The child was crying, catching hold of her, grasping at her clothing, hoisting himself up to her. And then she understood how he had changed; he'd become smaller, somehow. Not smaller – thinner! That's exactly what she remembered from last year.

A tiny hand grasped a finger, curled its own fingers round hers. She looked at the left wrist. There was no bracelet on it, and what had been puffed flesh round a deep, red line just a few moments before was now quite smooth, with no sign of a ridge. The little head, its wet curls twining into ringlets, turned innocent blue eyes towards her.

'Mumumum,' he babbled, his hands imploring her to mother him, his lips curved upward.

His skin, Lisa noted as though she were an onlooker, detached, watching from afar, was beginning to crinkle. Presumably the effects of the long time he'd spent in the water.

'Mumumum,' his lips pleaded with her, small hands held out to her. Maternal instinct stirred within her; he was her child, her baby. He needed her. Whatever had happened, he was her flesh and blood, a part of her. Avoiding the inert body in the bath, Lisa lifted the baby blabbering at her and wrapped him in his towel.

She turned to see a small hand, limp and flaccid, peeping from below the body in the bath. So poignant, so like her other children. Her heart leaped up, choking her windpipe.

One hand hovered towards the shape, then recoiled. Panting with fear, Lisa put forefinger and thumb down and felt a little leg. Moist skin. She let go and vomited into the lavatory.

She knew she had to overcome her horror, to act responsibly to preserve her family. She had to *know*.

She held Janus against herself, stood up, and stared, disbelieving, at the contents of the bath again. A one-year-old baby, hunched face down in the tub. Gold curls were massed, matted, on the back of his head, exactly like her triplets.

Lisa tipped the little torso back, so that the body lay, blue face upturned. She focused on him from the legs upwards: a boy, exactly the size and development of Janus, though thinner. Janus was thinner now, she remembered with a shudder. Large blue eyes open, vacant. Janus, her mind signalled again, then turned to the living image on her shoulder, gurgling at her. The eyes in the bath were not remotely like the gleaming, piercing, penetratingly intelligent eyes of her first triplet. There was no spark at all, of course.

It couldn't be true. Her mind simply refused to accept the evidence of her eyes. Was it a waxen effigy? Had the conjurer played a fiendish trick on her? She bent again to touch the body and found it all too fleshy. It was a real body; the unmoving body of a baby boy who looked exactly like one of her triplets. Except that he was dead; quite dead.

An inkling of her own, her children's mortality coursed through Lisa, caught at her throat, her limbs. She could not cope with this, could not breathe. She had to leave this room, this witness to the terrible events which made the future of her family seem bleak and hollow. Head spinning, a pain across the eyes scratching at her, she heaved for air, unable to breathe normally. Without a backward glance, she carried Janus to the nursery, instinctively pulling the bathroom door shut behind her.

Depositing him on the double bed she snatched up James and placed him in the cot lined up beside his brother Jeffrey. Two infants in two cots; the third one – he looked like Janus – on the bed. Seb singing.

Rubbing the third baby with the towel, shaking powder frenziedly around, she counted time and again. Two babies in the cots; one on the bed. Three infants; her triplets.

She was exhausted, must have seen double in the bathroom. She cuddled the child in his towel, cooing to him, feeling him wriggle against her restraining arms, nestling him to her.

'What's the funny smell, Mummy?'

Seb was right; there was a curious odour, as well as the odd yellow colour on the towel. Had she been prescient, choosing yellow to distinguish Janus from his brothers? She pulled out a pair of his yellow pyjamas, prepared to put his nappy on.

'Got to go wee wees.'

'No, Seb.'

'Got to,' he said and started toddling towards the bathroom.

She flung Janus back onto the bed and ran after her eldest son.

'In Mummy's bathroom, Seb!' she shouted out. 'There's water all over the other one.'

He held his hand in front of him, staring at her. She grasped him roughly, quickly, and pushed him the long walk down the corridor. Then she saw Geraldine.

The girl – what if the girl saw what was in the bath?

'About time, Geraldine,' she seethed at her, then couldn't stop herself from shrieking. 'You're supposed to be helping me. Take Seb to wee in my bathroom, the children's is completely flooded.'

Geraldine, smiling good humour, took Seb's hand. 'All right, Lisa. I'll see to him.' Her normally shrewd, inquisitive eyes strayed towards the front door. Her thoughts were still with Matthew.

'Go on, Seb,' Lisa hissed at him. 'Do as you're told.'

Almost hysterical, clenching her nails into her palms, she sprinted back to the bedroom. Janus was sitting in the middle of the double bed, solemnly tearing Seb's nursery-rhyme book into shreds.

Still two infants in the cots; one on the bed. She counted them off on her fingers, then breathed relief. Her triplets were safe.

Fastening a nappy on Janus, she tucked him under her arm and backed into the children's bathroom. She had to take him with her; he was different, thinner; and Geraldine mustn't see him. What's more, he didn't have his bracelet on. What if it happened again? As long as she held on to him he couldn't . . . *clone*, she thought wildly. As long as she held on to him they were safe.

'I'm finished,' she could hear Seb saying to Geraldine, could hear them coming back down the corridor.

Lisa inched further into the bathroom, then forced her eyes to look into the bath. The body was still there. Lisa squeezed Janus tight, but could not control her retch.

'Mummy. Where are you, Mummy?'

Janus began to kick and then to bawl.

'Shut up,' she screamed at him, then remembered that Seb was looking for her, no doubt about to burst into the bathroom, and that Geraldine was with him. She kicked the door shut and locked it. The large key clattered out and onto the floor.

'Take Seb to his room, Geraldine,' she shouted through the door. 'I'll come and see him in a minute.'

The girl twisted the doorknob. 'Anything wrong? D'you need some help? Why's Jansy making all that racket?'

'I *told* you it's sopping wet in here,' Lisa shouted at her. 'Just get Seb off to his room.'

'I would stay, Lisa, but . . .' Presumably Matthew was waiting for her. A stroke of unexpected luck.

'Just get Seb to bed, Gerry.' Lisa had lowered her voice, energy draining out of her. 'Then you can go. I'll see you in the morning.'

'I'm having lunch with Uncle Nige, Lisa; I did remind you. Betsy's coming. I made sure she remembered.' The girl rattled the knob again. 'What's wrong, Lisa? The door won't open.'

'For goodness sake! I sometimes need to go to the loo as well.'

'Oh.' An audible intake of breath, even through the door. 'Sorry.'

Holding Janus to herself to quiet him Lisa heard Geraldine and Seb trotting down the corridor. The bracelet; where had she put the damned bracelet?

Lisa forced herself to look at the bath ledges. She searched over every nook and cranny for the silver chain but couldn't see it. Her eyes now roamed round the other surfaces; the basin, the windowsill, the cupboard holding nappies, the laundry basket. The bracelet was nowhere to be seen.

There was another knocking on the door. Lisa, her mind fixed on the bracelet, gripped the child in her arms hard enough to precipitate a wail. She relaxed her grip and absently kissed his head.

'Anything else I can do?' Geraldine asked. 'Shall I take Jansy for you?'

The girl evidently realised something was up. But there was nothing Lisa could do about that, no way she could open the door to her. Geraldine might know something was wrong; she couldn't possibly know what it was. And she was probably thinking longingly about Matthew. With any luck he would be waiting for her.

'Are you okay? Jansy sounds rather miserable.'

'He's just grisly.' A deep breath in, a last determined effort to keep control. 'Must have had too much of the clotted cream and feels sick. Look in on the other two and see if they're all right,' she called out. 'I'm almost through here.'

Within moments the doorknob rattled again. Lisa bit back the urge to scream at the girl to leave.

'Is it all right if I go now?'

'Is Seb in bed?'

'He's reading his helicopter book.'

'Right, then, off you go.'

'Goodnight, Lisa. You too, Jansy.'

It was at this point that Lisa remembered what had happened to the bracelet. In her haste to take it off she had simply dropped it in the bath. It must be with the body.

Janus was wriggling under her arm. What time was it? Was Alec due back? Sick, shocked, distraught, she turned, knocking the baby's head against the bath. A shrill, long scream brought her back to reality. Had Geraldine heard that? There was no further clatter at the door; she must have left.

Holding her breath, averting her eyes, the kicking infant still under her left arm, Lisa placed her right hand into the bath and tried to feel for the bracelet. The slimy bath, its bottom covered in a glutinous mixture of soap, dirt and that odd yellow liquid revolted her. Unable to hold Janus she laid him on the floor. He began to cry pitifully. Not the raucous bawl of a few moments before, but the small, pathetic cry of a tired infant.

Desperate now, Lisa knelt beside him and pulled the plastic duck away from the plug hole, then turned, hugging Janus to herself, trying to quiet him. His drawn-out, tired mewl inspired her to lever herself onto the stool, to pick him up, to rock him. He's only an infant, she told herself. He could not possibly be held responsible for anything that had happened.

The final slosh of liquid running out of the bath energised Lisa into one last attempt to find the bracelet. The body of the dead infant lay, oddly thin and limp, its feet towards the drain. Retching, she had no choice but to return Janus to the floor. Forcing herself to action, she moved the body's legs away and at last saw the bracelet on the bottom of the bath. JANUS, the letters winked at her.

She clutched it, allowed the legs to plop back and turned to the living child. His eyes gleamed wet as he tried to writhe away from her searching arms. He was afraid of her. Her shouting, the way his head had bumped against the bath, the unceremonious manner in which she had dumped him on the floor.

She clasped him to her, tears of relief at his safety pouring down her face. She could not bear to look at the other child, the baby she'd only briefly known. Tears for his short, sad life welled into her eyes; she could not stop them.

A loud, rat-tat-tatting at the back door made her freeze. Frank back with the car already? She wasn't expecting him till much later on; he must not see her like this, must not come in. She wouldn't respond, just pray he'd simply leave the keys downstairs for her.

A short interval of silence as she tried to stop the flow of endless tears, then the sound of the old door being opened lurched her heartbeat into a faster pace.

'Missus! Us broughten t'car backalong,' a voice Lisa recognised as Don Chivers' called up the stairs.

Lisa sat rigid, cringing against the bath, pretending she wasn't there. Another series of loud knocks as the stockman tried to make himself heard.

'Us'll leave t'keys,' Lisa heard him shout.

Terror made her clutch Janus harder to herself. The child began to cry, then howl. She tried to hush him, tried desperately to find a dummy, a bottle, to fill his mouth, pressed a toy duck into his hand. He would not stop. The noise would almost certainly bring Don Chivers running up the stairs, into the bathroom. She had to get out of here.

Kissing Janus, Lisa forced herself up and out onto the landing, rocking the child now merely wailing on her arm. She looked down to see Don standing by the kitchen door, his horny, muscled hand holding her car keys.

Light, crinkly eyes swept up, spotted her and Janus, stopped still. He was about to put the keys down and retreat when Janus began to screech, to toss on Lisa's arm and try to haul himself away. Instinctively she put her hand up to the child, the bracelet dangling from two fingers, glinting in the hall light. She knew at once that Don had seen it. His eyes stayed mesmerised on her hand. She had to distract him, reassure him that Janus was as he'd always been, that nothing out of the ordinary had happened.

'He's overdone after the party,' she shouted down. Her voice sounded husky, unreal.

'Oh, arr.' His eyes now moved, flitting from her hand to Janus.

Janus had stopped shrieking, was quieting down. 'Bit better now,' she pointed out as she gathered the tired child tighter into her arms and rocked him.

Don did not leave, but stood, his grey eyes firm, unblinking, now riveted on the silver. Lisa slipped the bracelet out of sight under Janus's nappy. 'Thank you *so* much for bringing the car back so quickly,' she squeaked, breathless but determined. 'I told Meg there was no rush.' She brushed her arm across her face, pushed her hair back, acutely aware that she looked strange, out of control. 'If you could leave the car keys on the stairs?'

The man went on standing there, unmoving, staring at her tear-stained face. At last he put the keys on the first tread, then looked up at her again. 'Them bain't stout arter they fust'uns,' he finally brought out. He went on standing there, irresolute.

Using every ounce of willpower she could muster, Lisa stood firm. 'I won't come down,' she said jerkily, tasting blood as she bit her lip to keep herself from screaming. 'Jansy is very tired. I have to get him straight to bed.'

'Bain't long afore 'un goes,' the voice continued, low.

'Thanks again,' Lisa shrilled at him and began to edge away.

'Oftimes them be dead right soon; not'ing as be done but bury they critturs,' he called after her. 'Tha' be t'right t'ing as us 'ud do.'

Almost hysterical, Lisa ran back into the nursery and slammed the door. She couldn't stand the man; he was a ghoul, a harbinger of doom. She sat on the bed, clasped Janus between her knees, grabbed his left wrist. 'You're wearing this,' she wept at him. She slipped the bracelet on and clasped it shut. Utterly drained, all she could do was dress the shrieking baby in his pyjamas, then place him in his cot. She tottered to the double bed and lay down on it. She must give Don time to leave before she went downstairs.

16

Lisa, gasping and out of breath in the triplets' room, lay back on the double bed, waiting for her racing pulse to subside. She tried to drain her mind; without success. The bathroom images flashed lurid and clear.

She levered her torso up, great shafts of pain stabbing her brain. None of it could be true; she was slipping out of reality, her mind a turmoil of emotions. Exhaustion, perhaps. A whole year of looking after the children, no holiday. Add to that the party today, her fury at Geraldine's desertion, bathing the triplets on her own. Worn out, she had hallucinated. That's what it must have been.

She looked across the room, holding her head, trying to still bands of tightening aches. Three cots, she counted on trembling fingers, holding three infants. One year old today; her triplets were toddlers now. Janus, Jeffrey and James. She pointed them out to herself: yellow for Janus, red for Jeffrey, blue for James. All stretched out in their cots, all present and correct.

A vision of the lifeless baby in the bath flooded back. A silent, unmoving body, intense blue, staring eyes, gold curls exactly like her triplets'. A shaft of fear tightened her lungs, and her whole being shuddered. There was no noise or movement from the children. All three were lying still. Too still? A thudding in her ears as her blood surged, strong and overpowering, through her head, distending pain. She wanted to get up, and found herself held down. Her muscles refused to obey the impulses she sent to her brain. She let herself sink back, tears flowing. Had one of her little ones died? Was she denying it?

Slowly, the rushing in her ears receded; she succeeded in lifting an arm, pulled herself up to sitting and then stood. Fighting back dread, she lurched towards the cots, grasping at bars. The babies appeared to be asleep. She could hear them breathe, could see their clothing rise and fall, noticed their little fists were curled. James had his left thumb in his mouth and Lisa saw the bracelet on his wrist. JAMES, she read;

then read it again. It still said JAMES.

She turned to Jeffrey. He was lying with his left arm under the duvet. Lisa folded the bedding back carefully and raised up the little limb. The silver bracelet blinked JEFFREY at her. Breathing more easily, she slid the arm back under the duvet.

It was Janus's turn. She sagged towards his cot and grabbed the top rail. He wasn't asleep yet; he was lying, eyes wide, unblinking, evaluating her. The blue irises did not move; they stared at her. She felt the intensity and then, taken off guard, saw the gleam again. Lasering into her head, her brain, her mind. A tingle of alarm arched through. She braced her legs and forced her face towards the child.

'Hello, Jansy.'

The baby went on staring as before.

'Time to go to sleep,' she murmured, dipping her hand into the cot, stroking him. He twisted his head away, then turned back to stare again, unmoving, truculent.

His bracelet; she simply had to see it. She could not go back to the bathroom, and what it might contain, without first making sure. It was ridiculous; the child in the cot was only one year old. She was the stronger; she could pull up his arm and check his wrist. 'Just want to see your arm,' she cooed at him, softening her voice. His eyes grew less intense, began to move.

The insistent trilling of the portable on the bed startled her. She gawped, unable to move her feet. Her left hand clutched the cot rail in a vice-like grip. The ringing stopped; Lisa relaxed her hand and drew herself upright.

The phone began to ring again. Waves of panic flowed from her guts to her head; her blood, suddenly released, rose to her face, making her feel as though her skin were burning. She put her hands up to her cheeks to cool them. She had to take control. She hit her clenched right fist against her left arm, releasing fingers, and forced herself to go to answer the phone.

'Ha . . . hello!'

'Lisa! There you are at last. You sound odd. Is something wrong?'

'It's you, Alec.' She hiccupped, sat on the bed and leaned back on the scattered cushions interspersed with toys. 'I'm just utterly exhausted.'

'Of course, darling. Thought you might still be in the midst of things. The party. How did it go?'

'What?'

'The birthday party, Lisa. Is something wrong? What's going on?'

'The party, yes. All right, I suppose. I'm just completely drained.' Lisa sighed, a long, deep sigh of utter weariness.

'You sound terrible, darling. Are you all on your own?' He appeared anxious.

'Yes, thank goodness. It all went on a bit.' She eased back against the pillows, shutting her eyes, shutting out the present. 'Betsy had to leave before bathtime.'

'Didn't Gerry stay on?'

Fury suddenly overpowered her. If the girl had pulled her weight, all this would not have happened. 'Geraldine!' she spat the name out. 'She was worse than useless.'

'Now what?' She heard irritation creeping through Alec's voice. 'How did she get across you this time?'

Of course he'd take the girl's part, Lisa's mind fired bitterly. And probably rather more than that. Always that readiness to drive her home, however tired he was. Pleased, Lisa suspected, to get away, to have a drink at the Fitch-Templetons – or so he claimed – while she stayed behind to prepare their meal.

'She just left me to it,' Lisa wept, defusing rage. 'All by myself.'

'She didn't help you bath them?'

'And you're never here, not even on their birthday,' she suddenly sobbed, outraged. 'They're your children too, you know!' Alec's obsession with Flaxton was depriving her children of their father.

'So what did she do this time?' His voice had turned jocular, humouring her. 'Pop the balloons?'

'Ran off with the conjurer!'

'The conjurer?'

'A rather dishy young man. I saw the ad in the local paper; it was my special surprise. Went down a treat with everyone.'

At first there was silence. His laugh, when it came, was awkward, subdued, as though what she'd said was in bad taste. 'I'm sorry, pet. It's just the thought of Gerry popping out of a hat – like a rabbit!'

He sounded almost jealous . . . Was he actually having an affair with Geraldine? Lisa brushed the thought away; compared to what might be waiting for her in the bathroom, it was irrelevant.

'She left me coping with all four of them in the bath while she went gallivanting off.'

His voice had changed again. 'I'm sorry, darling, you're worn out. I'll read the riot act to her next time I see her, I promise.'

'Always bloody Flaxton first,' Lisa wailed. 'Even with Geraldine.'

Annoyance made her voice stronger, edged determination into it. 'At least it will be Betsy tomorrow morning.'

'Betsy? Why won't Gerry be coming?'

'She's having lunch with Nigel Carruthers.'

'With Carruthers? Geraldine?'

'He is her uncle, remember. Apparently he regularly takes her out to a posh lunch.'

'That's a constant, is it?' Alec sounded both surprised and, Lisa felt, upstaged. 'Does it happen often?'

Did he suspect a liaison between the girl and her uncle? Surely not. Lisa was too tired to pursue it. 'Every other week or so.' She shrugged it aside. 'It's one of the few appointments Geraldine sticks to. Anyway, I've decided to get rid of her. Maybe I can persuade Betsy to give me more time.'

'Dump Geraldine before you've had a chance to find someone else? That's brilliant, Lisa.' The icy tone.

'She's more trouble than she's worth,' Lisa shouted back. Her voice began to rise, crescendoing into hysteria. 'She's always getting everything wrong. She simply piles the dried laundry into the cupboard in a ball! She—'

'Steady on, darling.'

Lisa gulped, regained her breath. 'And that bloody dog of hers on top of everything else!'

'So tell her to leave the dog at home if that's the problem.'

'No, that's *not* the problem! Geraldine simply isn't up to it. I'll talk to Anne.'

'Anne?'

'Anne Marsden, Alec! The one who runs the playschool.'

'You think she knows a better mother's help?'

'We could send the triplets there for the mornings,' Lisa found herself saying. 'That would give me real time off. Meg's always telling me Anne's longing to have them.'

'Something we could think about,' Alec soothed her.

'They'll be safer, better off.' Why hadn't she thought of it before? 'If Anne can cope with the triplets now I can dispense with Geraldine.' She paused at that. 'Even the idea of it makes me feel better.'

'You sound completely overdone, pet. Why don't you ask Meg to come over?'

The very last thing she wanted. She cleared her throat, pushed her voice firmly into control. 'I'll be all right now, darling. Honestly. Just needed someone to let steam off to. You really don't need to worry.'

'You make me feel a heel,' he said, sounding glum.

'I know you'd have been here if you could,' Lisa sighed, her fury spent. 'I'm not really getting at you. Just that girl letting me down at the last moment.'

'That's why I'm ringing. I simply can't get back tonight.'

'Oh, Alec!'

'I know, I know.'

She breathed in deeply. It would give her time to think; there was no way she could possibly explain what had been happening over the phone. 'Never mind, everything's quiet now. I could use an early night.'

Coherent thoughts were beginning to form in Lisa's head. She'd check Janus's wrist, make absolutely sure the bracelet was secure.

'. . . be back around tea time.'

'Sorry, darling. I didn't quite catch what you said.'

'You sound terrible, Lisa. We've got to get you more time away from the children. A trained, live-in nanny after all, perhaps. We can afford it.'

'No!'

There was a pause; obviously Alec trying not to lose his temper. 'We won't discuss it now.'

Lisa, making another supreme effort to compose herself, suddenly saw Geraldine in front of her, smirking at Alec, pouting her lips. Sending the children to Anne's playschool would mean Alec wouldn't have the opportunity to see so much of the girl.

'There's nothing to discuss. Once I've got rid of Geraldine, there'll be one child less to look after!'

Another silence. 'I'm sorry, Lisa. I really can't stop now. We'll talk it through tomorrow. I'll take the children over at the weekend and give you a break, I promise.'

Take over? She'd tell him everything tomorrow. At last she would be able to share her terrible secret with the only other human being who could really understand her plight. Because he was their father, and as much involved as she was. And Alec would have to acknowledge what was going on. She had the evidence – the all too solid evidence – to show him.

'Mummy!'

Not now; she couldn't think about all that now. 'Seb's calling me,' she said, getting up from the bed. 'I'll take the phone through. You could just say goodnight to him.'

'Did you have a good party, Seb?'

'Lots more wabbits; white bwabbits.'

'Anything else?'

'And pigeons flewed round the playroom. I's going to crayon with Mummy.'

'Splendid. 'Night, Seb.'

Lisa clicked the receiver into standby and sank onto the rocker in Seb's room. 'You crayon, Seb. I'll watch you. Mummy's very tired after the party.'

He coloured in the picture they had worked on yesterday. 'Brown and white moo cows,' he said. 'Like Auntie Meg's.'

'You like the Jerseys best?' Lisa asked, aware that he was drawing several calves for each cow. Had he guessed what had happened? Known it would? He was the one who'd seen it all before.

'Want to go down,' he told her solemnly. ''Night, Mummy.'

She wished it were. At least there'd be no Alec to counter, no one to disrupt her while she tried to work out a solution to her – to their – dilemma. She'd need the wisdom of Solomon to get it right.

A kiss and hug for Seb, and she tottered to the door, grimaced goodnight. She crept unwillingly back to the triplets' room. Janus was asleep, just like his brothers.

Trembling, shaking a little, she raised his arm, looked at the bracelet on his wrist. It seemed to spell SANVI. What did that mean? Was this the clone, and was Janus lying in the bath?

The thought of a witch's curse filled her mind. They'd cut down the elders without a thought, deprived themselves of the ancient protection against witches. Why had they been so foolish as to ignore country lore? And the clover – she'd wished for twins on the four-leaf clover and it had given them to her with a vengeance. Twinned Janus time and again. If wishes were children, mothers would weep . . .

Lisa concentrated her eyes on Janus's bracelet. The letters looked peculiar, not quite right. SANVI. Was that a curse? Her thoughts darted aimlessly through her memory. Something Japanese? How could that be connected . . . Had the bracelet also cloned? Her hand now numb, the prickles of pins and needles in her fingers, Lisa dropped the small wrist. Janus lay like any child asleep: peaceful, deep breaths, showing downy cheeks, a small right fist above the bedding. She walked round the cot to look at his face, lifted his arm again.

Utterly, completely paranoid, she scolded herself, and laughed out loud. Of course the answer was quite simple, quite straightforward. The ornate lettering said JANUS: upside down! She'd put the bracelet back the wrong way round.

Proof, then; it must have happened. She'd taken the bracelet off, and put it on again, and it wasn't too tight. A grim, dark feeling of despair, of forces beyond her understanding, her control washed over her. She unlatched the silver chain, her head on fire. The infant stirred. Lisa, keeping her grip on the child as though her life depended on it, turned the bracelet round and fastened it on again. She looked at it. It spelled JANUS. And it was right. There was no mistaking him: strong, alert, demanding. He was, she realised, still with her. It was the clone who was dead.

Don's low, defeated voice came back to her: 'Not'ing as be done but bury they.'

She shuddered. What if there really was a body in the bathroom? What if the nightmare she had just been struggling through were real? Don's eyes had lighted on the bracelet, had stayed there, had drawn their firm conclusion. What if he talked, sent Frank round? She had to act now, show courage for her children's sake. She could not wait for Alec. She had to look into the bath, confront what it contained.

Lisa walked into the children's bathroom and turned to shut the door slowly, deliberately, too terrified to face the bath immediately. She put her left hand behind her, feeling for the stool. She'd sat on that just a short time ago to dry each one of her little brood. The memory she feared, the picture she wanted to erase, suddenly came back to her. Another baby, just like the triplets, in the bath with Janus.

How could that be? It made no sense at all. It was against natural law, against every experience she'd ever had or heard of. Except, of course, for what she'd heard from Don about the newborn farm animals. What had he said?

'Next time I looked t'were three on they. T'won't do.'

Indeed it would not do. If anyone caught a hint, a glimmer, a whisper of what had happened, she and her family would be overwhelmed. Cameras, microphones, members of the press. Her family would become a freak, a circus show.

Why was this happening to her?

'I reckon it be that Multiplier stuff,' she remembered Meg saying, the day that James – appeared. Is that really what had made Janus different from other children? That she had assimilated some of Meg's produce when she was pregnant? Had it, in spite of Meg's care, become contaminated?

Quite possibly it had, but it wasn't very likely to affect Janus now. Whatever had happened before, Flaxton had delayed the launch of Multiplier specifically to give them time to change the formula. Alec had blown his top about it often enough. And he'd complained that they'd had to dispose of the old formula completely. Scrapping the original supplies had cost Flaxton a fortune.

She thought back to what Meg had brought for the tea today. Janus wasn't allowed any dairy products; and, anyway, the clotted cream must be innocuous by now. A vision of the child's face in the bath, plastered with a dark red, sticky mass – the blackberry jelly! Blackberries were not in season yet; that had to be last year's jelly. And Janus was a lusty eater. He'd probably gobbled up quite a lot of it. But could that really have had such a catastrophic effect?

Janus had been bloated before the tea; very bloated. And aggressive. Just like the time when he was barely two weeks old, when James made his appearance. In those days he had drunk Meg's goat's milk. Now last season's bramble jelly, still impregnated with the old strain of Multiplier, might well have been the trigger for another cloning.

Elbows on her knees, head drooped forward on her upturned palms, Lisa felt hot tears trickle through her fingers. She had to think, work out what the consequences might be – for Janus, for the other children, for Alec, for herself.

That wasn't all. The Graftleys were involved as well. And Flaxton; she had been so busy thinking about her family that the implications for Flaxton had escaped her. She took on board, for the first time, what exposure of the effects of that first batch of Multiplier might do to the company. She did not need to be an expert in marketing to know that their products, though modified, would instantly be shunned, that they'd be bankrupt within weeks. Public awareness of cloning would finish them.

Did Flaxton – did Nigel Carruthers – understand the real fruits of their fertiliser? Did the company, even now, realise that cloning was going on?

If Flaxton did know, they'd very successfully hidden their knowledge from everyone, including Alec, That much was sure; no vestige of such a thought had come to him. And Frank? She'd heard Frank singing the praises of farming with Multiplier – because it paid. Frank wouldn't let such a dangerous cat out of the bag; he'd cover up.

And Don? Of course Don knew, better than anyone. So why would *he* collude with Flaxton? Because, Lisa guessed, Frank had convinced him that they had already put the matter right. The two of them had systematically slaughtered anything and everything bred on Crinsley Farm last year. The lambs, the kids, the calves, Meg's chickens, even the kittens – that's why Frank had made sure they were all drowned! He hadn't forgotten his promise to Seb at all.

It didn't end there. Lisa remembered the shocking slaughter of the rabbits she'd seen in the meadow. Quite likely Frank thought he'd eliminated all residuals. He couldn't know about Janus, had no idea about the human factor.

'Them bain't stout arter they fust'uns,' Don had declared. He meant, she supposed, that after a cloning animal reached a certain stage of development its clones were vulnerable. Janus's new clone must have been defective to start with. That's why he'd died so soon.

She sighed; all this was conjecture, pure conjecture. She couldn't verify any of it. All she knew was that there'd been an extraneous baby in the bath. Lisa inched her head round, eyes searching everything except the bathtub. Her hands began to fold towels, straighten out flannels, put toothbrushes away. She bent towards the floor and mopped up the water with the hand towel by the basin, flushed the vomit in the lavatory, began to clean the white porcelain, the seat. She could not put it off any longer now. She looked into the bath.

The first thing she saw was the bath mat. Soggy tufts of blue cotton were heaped in the tub, mounded but innocuous. How had it got there? Gingerly she pulled it back – and there was nothing. Nothing but a filthy bathtub, disgusting plastic ducks, a rather curious yellow colour staining the ring of dirt round the bath. Nothing more.

A surge of hope rippled her frame. Had she really imagined it all? Was Alec right, and she was heading for a nervous breakdown? She pinched herself; the pain was real enough. She was here, in her bathroom, now. She wasn't dreaming.

She looked around. The bathroom was still a mess, heaped linen on the floor. But she'd seen another little boy. Tears poured as she remembered his small, lifeless body. Had it somehow got under the jumbled laundry on the floor?

She flung pillow cases, cot covers, nappies around the small room. No sign of a body, of anything except the usual attributes of a children's bathroom. It wasn't there! She had been wrong; she must have been. There was no body, no clone. She'd imagined the whole thing.

Water – she desperately needed water. She turned the tap on full, felt the cold water over her hands, splashed it onto her face. She took great swallows of it, grabbed a mug and greedily poured the cold liquid down her throat, over her hair, her neck, her breasts. She felt contaminated and in need of cleansing. She let the water flow over her, liberating her, cooling her, permitting her to leave. There was nothing she could do here. There was no body, no incriminating evidence. She heaped the dirty laundry into a pile, placed it outside the door. Her breathing was becoming laboured again – she was overwrought, out of control.

She went down the corridor to her room, exhausted, unsteady on her feet. She opened the windows wide, breathed in cool, evening air, fanned her face eagerly. A deep, crimson glow across the skyscape thinned slowly into grey across the moors and dimmed the green into black. The willows stood silhouetted, a faint gold dripping from the top branches, firing them into a dying flame. So much beauty hiding so much pain. The whisper of a bat chasing nocturnal insects; the predatory hooting of an owl. Balmy, country noises to calm her down.

Lisa smiled to herself; the silence would heal her. There was too much upheaval in her life. Once the children spent several hours a day away, she would be able to enjoy time to herself again, be free to think of her paintings, how to progress her work. Even mothers needed time off.

A muffled sound she assumed was some nocturnal animal pierced into her consciousness. Rhythmic, continuous, it seemed to come from the bottom of the garden by the fruit trees Alec had planted earlier that spring. A rabbit, perhaps, digging a warren. Or a badger sett making a home inside their boundaries. The idea appealed to her.

The constant, steady slurf reminded her of metal cutting through earth. Was someone digging in the field? Using a spade at this hour? Preparing for the hunt, perhaps; she knew the hunters stopped up rabbit holes to stop the fox bolting into one.

'Doin' a spot o' gardenin', tha'n it?' a disembodied voice spoke up, fluttering on the damp evening air, clear as a bell. 'Bit o' extra cash.'

Lisa felt long, black shadows closing in on her as she stared across the moor. The voice sounded like Mark Ditcheat's, their neighbour beyond the rhyne. Whoever he was talking to did not reply.

'You be out late.' The demanding voice, evidently not to be deterred, sounded suspicious.

'Arr. Git t'plant t'tree.' Familiar gruff tones.

'Tree? This time o'night?' A laugh. 'Where be the fire, then?'

'Cum when him at t'house be Lunnon way.' It was Don's voice, she recognised it now.

Don was planting a tree in their garden? That was absurd; Don had no business being in their garden at all. Saunders did all that . . .

'Them be dead; not'ing as be done but bury they critturs'; the words Don had muttered only a short time ago reverberated in Lisa's mind. The cool, so welcome minutes earlier, was making her feel cold. Don was digging up earth to bury something – a 'crittur'.

She hadn't imagined it at all; there *had* been another cloning, another clone. Another child just like her triplets. And Don had taken it. Taken it off, just the way he did with the farm animals. He was digging a grave for flesh of *her* flesh, burying it because 'Tha' be t'right t'ing as us 'ud do'.

Lisa leaned her head against the window frame, drew in her breath. No doubt Don meant well, meant to help her. But what he was doing was without her permission, her consent. She wanted, needed, the body. To mourn him; he was her child just as much as Jiminy was hers. And she had to show him to Alec. How else could she convince him of something that was so unbelievable?

'Us be tellin' Frank yer be moonlightin'.' Lisa heard Mark cackle now. 'Us be seein' he at t'Young Farmer's meetin' ternight. Him be talkin' 'bout that there Multiplier. Got a promotion on.'

'Oh, arr.'

'Gie they trees Multiplier and yer be bound ter git good crops,' Mark volunteered.

'Arr.'

'Bin lookin' o'er they cattle,' Mark went on, his voice tailing off as he walked away. 'Can't be too careful . . .'

Cattle rustling was a thriving crime on the Levels; most farmers counted their animals morning and evening. That was why Mark Ditchcat was there.

Lisa remained at the window, listening intently. There was the slow shuffle of metal dragged over the local quarry chippings Alec liked to spread along his paths. No doubt that was Don hiding the evidence of his nocturnal digging. What should she do? Confront him? Demand to know why he was in her garden?

She hadn't the strength for that; she could not possibly do that. She had to let it be for now, talk to Alec about it when he came back, let him take the responsibility. She'd done enough; it was time for Alec to shoulder some of the burden.

Would Don tell Frank? Probably not; there was no reason to. As far as Don was concerned, he'd buried a body, just like he did at Crinsley

Farm. It was unlikely he'd tell anyone.

Soft, summery air billowed around her, stroked her shoulders, her cheeks, her hair, embraced her with the balm of the fresh scents of nature. She leaned her head against the window frame, watched the grey of evening light turn to wide streaks of rose, then darken into dusky velvet. Damp evening mist laid drops of water on her lips, her eyes; she breathed in deeply, felt the contentment of the country night suffusing her.

Calmer at last, she stole into Seb's room to see him fast asleep. She crept into the triplets' nursery again. Three babies, breathing, sleeping, *present*. She checked that they were in their cots time and again. She moved, as in a dream, to Janus's cot. She stood and watched as his head turned on the pillow, serene, the sleep of innocence.

17

The house, hushed and enveloping, hugged Lisa's secret within its massive walls. She reassured herself that her family was sheltered, protected by the solid structure. The dark outside intensified as she lit soft lighting in her bedroom, in the bathroom adjoining it. She felt the events of this afternoon fade from immediacy, felt released enough to pamper herself with a relaxing bath, to plunge herself into hot water laden with Badedas-perfumed bubbles.

Lying in the silken liquid, unleashing her experiences of the last few hours, Lisa wondered whether she was the only mother who had a child like Janus. She needed someone she could tell her thoughts to, someone to share her fears and her anxieties with. Above all, she needed someone she could trust to listen to her.

Thinking about it convinced her that she couldn't tell Alec about what had happened. Even if she could get him to take notice of what she was trying to tell him, he would never believe her incredible story. She thought back to the way he'd assumed that she, not Geraldine, had been the problem when she'd tried to tell him how the girl had let her down after the party. He'd taken Geraldine's part; he thought more about the wretched girl than her! If she now started telling him about Don, explained how he had buried the dead clone to help her and, indirectly, Frank, Alex would, she was sure, find the story completely unacceptable.

Her husband lived in his own world, away from hers, involved in his career, driven by his ambitions. He was not prepared to accept that she, or his family, had difficulties in their lives. Not because he did not love them; Lisa felt sure he loved them dearly. He simply needed everything in their world to be right, under control, properly ordered; rather like the digits in his ledgers, she supposed. He was an accountant, he dealt in figures, in matters of known fact. If she told Alec she had seen a fourth baby, identical to Janus, in the bath, that Janus had cloned a brother who had died almost immediately, then followed this by telling him she suspected that Don had stolen the body to bury it in their garden, Alec's most likely reaction would be to think she was unstable, about to have a mental breakdown. He might even think she'd already lost her reason and send an ambulance round!

What about Meg? Why not confide in her? Meg would believe her; she already suspected that Jeffrey and James had cloned in the womb. But something held Lisa back. The troubled brown eyes, the uncharacteristic shiftiness of late. Meg had her own burdens; Lisa hadn't the energy to work out what they might be.

An image of Trevor came into her mind. Trevor was used to the quirks of creative people; they were his living. She could talk to Trevor. He would let her chatter, pour out her misgivings; he would calm her down. But he was not the man to confide in about this afternoon's happenings. She had, after all, sounded him out before on that point. Though he had always been ready to help her in a friendly way, he would not wish to be involved, to share any real responsibilities. And why should he?

Perhaps Don's instincts had been wise. The old countryman, level-headed and experienced, had known what to do. Bury the evidence, let sleeping clones lie – undisturbed, undisturbing.

That left only one course of action open to her: she had to make absolutely sure that nothing like this could ever happen again. She must prevent further cloning at all costs. Janus – and it was, she was now very clear, only Janus she had to worry about – must always have something fixed to him which neither he, nor any casual meddler, could remove. Something extraneous fastened to his body – a foreign object, something which could not clone itself – would stop the cloning. But it had to be a tight fit, had to stop the cloner's body from being able to discard it, or split inside it. Metal, Don had insisted; metal was better than clothing. What could she do? She couldn't force her triplets to wear bracelets all through their childhood. In any case, the bracelets were already becoming tight and they were too intrusive.

She weighed up possibilities in her mind. Bracelets on the triplets' ankles rather than on their wrists, for example. No more useful than the present system, and harder to keep a check on. Perhaps a silver chain round each child's neck, small name tab attached, like soldiers' identification discs?

None of these ideas worked. And a chain could easily be taken off, might even be dangerous. There must be something suitable! A ring, perhaps? She laughed out loud at that. She could give Trevor a ring right away. That was the sort of problem he would be happy to discuss, to help her with. His pleasant, friendly voice would make her feel better. She dripped out of the bath, sheeted her body in luxurious towelling, lay on her bed. Reasonably relaxed, she tapped Trevor's number on the keypad.

A soft, low 'Hello' answered after the second ring. It didn't sound like Trevor; too young. Too come-hitherish, for that matter.

'That you, Trev?'

There was a pause, and then a high-pitched, irritated voice spluttered, 'Who wants him?' Leo, Lisa guessed at once. Leo discouraging all Trevor's entanglements other than himself. Thinking about it, Lisa felt sure even Leo could not be jealous of her, though Trevor had warned her about his possessiveness. The mother of four children under three could hardly be considered a sexual threat by anyone, Lisa decided firmly.

'It's Lisa Wildmore here, one of his clients,' she cooed. 'I just wanted a tiny word with him.'

'Lisa Wildmore?' There was a pause as Leo screened the information. 'Ah, yes, I've heard about you. The one with triplets!' His voice rang out triumphant, lightened with friendliness. 'How are you getting on?'

'Rather too busy,' she said, hoping not to sound curt. 'Trying to keep some semblance of normality.' Clearly she could not talk to Trevor now, but she could, at least, ask him about her very practical problem.

'Poor you. I'll get himself for you.'

Trevor came on the line. 'Lisa? Anything wrong?'

'Sorry, Trev. I didn't mean to intrude. Just thought you'd be the right person to solve a rather tricky issue for me.'

'Anything I can do, my dear.'

'The triplets have outgrown their silver bracelets, so they've got to come off. I'm still worried about the babies getting muddled up, and Alec only laughs at me. Any ideas about something less officious we could use?'

She heard the scraping of a chair, presumably Trevor making himself more comfortable. There was the sound of a slight scuffle, then a giggle.

'Trevor? Are you still there?'

'I'm looking at the perfect solution,' he told her gaily.

'Looking at it?'

'The elegant Leo. He wears a darling little earring in his left ear.'

A tiny earring; the sort that people wore to keep a pierced ear open. 'That's brilliant, Trev,' she sighed. 'You're absolutely marvellous.'

'Any time, darling. We're just off to the opera.'

'I won't keep you. Thanks a million – well, thank Leo!'

Lisa put the receiver down slowly, and carefully clicked it into place. She would have to think of some reasonable excuse to have an earring put in Janus's ear. Not only his, of course; Jeffrey's and James's as well. And then it came to her full force. The real reason was the best reason. They needed earrings so that people outside the family could tell the triplets apart. And if the children were to go to Anne Marsden's playschool, that's exactly what would be needed.

Just one more difficulty she had to solve. The rings had to be easy to distinguish. They were manifesting in her mind. Each ring could be made of a different metal, showing as different colourings. Colour-coded, just like their clothes.

Gold, Lisa worked out instantly, for Janus; the nearest metal colour to yellow. Very appropriate. Bronze for Jeffrey, perhaps, to approximate to red. And finally a silver ring for James. All she had to do was arrange for a jeweller to insert a tiny earring by that curious mark they had by their left earlobes; the mark which proved above all else that they were identicals.

A smile crossed Lisa's lips at last. She would discuss earrings with Alec tomorrow. Meanwhile she would dispose of any remnants of that afternoon. She walked determinedly to the children's bathroom, collected the bundled bath mat, the towels, the whole load of laundry soiled with the day's events. The yawn of washing machine stood open wide, ready to bleach the linen into innocence. She jumbled stained washing into the porthole. The machine dutifully swallowed the evidence, secreted it behind lathering suds. The soft hum of the motor, rocking its load, reverberated through the house, a lullaby for oblivion.

18

'You mean you've actually *sacked* Geraldine? Before we've even had a chance to discuss it?'

Alec looked absolutely furious. He paced up and down the room, pushing his fingers through his hair, arranging and rearranging the ornaments on the mantelpiece. Lisa could not make out whether his anger was at the prospect of losing the contact with Geraldine or because he was worried about the girl's connection with Carruthers.

'I wish you wouldn't jump down my throat like that. I didn't sack her. I know she's Carruthers' niece. What I did was put my foot down about that dog. I said she couldn't bring Duffers here again, and I told her that I'd put the triplets' names down for Anne's playschool.' Her frown lines bit deep. 'I told you, Alec, she makes more work than she helps with. And that business after the party was a disgrace, an absolute disgrace.'

'At least she's there,' he said dryly. 'You can answer the phone or go to the loo without panicking.' He bit his lip, narrowed his eyes. 'I don't know what's got into you lately. It isn't *sensible* to antagonise the girl.'

Lisa felt her husband's irritation tearing them apart. He was blind to the telltale signs of the strain she was under. She felt herself becoming alienated. Alec couldn't understand why Geraldine was unbearable. If he thought about it at all, he probably thought she was jealous of the girl's youth, her obvious good looks. So what on earth would he make of talk about cloning? She was right not to burden him with it. It was her cross to bear, and hers alone. Her job was to protect her children and her family. And there was still the faint – the very faint – possibility that she had imagined everything. It would be fatal to tell Alec and then find out that Don had had some quite innocent reason for digging in their garden. Perhaps Alec, or Frank, had asked him to do some work there.

'I've still got to have an ear out for her. What about what happened with the kettle? If it hadn't been for Seb being alert, Janus would have been scarred for life.'

'For God's sake, Lisa.' Alec's head jerked back as his eyes blazed at her. 'She's not likely to do anything like that again; that was weeks ago.'

The way he was always making excuses for the girl infuriated her. It was Geraldine's incompetence that had precipitated the crisis, after all.

Lisa couldn't hold back her anger any more. 'And that wretched animal,' she flared. 'You simply ignore that. It's *dangerous* for children to play on grass a dog has fouled. I had to put a stop to that.'

Alec looked at her sideways; she could almost hear his brain ticking over, deciding she was becoming neurotic. She'd have to sound reasonably composed if things were not to get out of hand. She softened her voice. 'And I haven't thrown her out, just alerted her to what I'm going to do. I explained I'd need some time completely to myself so that I can really get back to painting. And that means the triplets being at the playschool.'

'You still need help when they get back.'

'I told you, Alec, Anne is willing to give them lunch and arrange for them to have a nap. Betsy will take them for a walk after that.'

He sighed. 'When, Lisa? When can you send them to Anne's?'

'As soon as they can manage without a bottle,' Lisa told him gleefully. 'Next month. I'm pretty sure I can get them on to cups by then.'

'That'll be the day!'

'No, honestly. Trainer cups. The triplets are crazy to follow in Seb's footsteps, and Anne is simply longing to have them. They'll bring in other children, you see. I think she's already decided to make allowances.'

'And you think she can handle our whole brood?'

'It really isn't a problem, Alec. She has three assistants, and all mod cons, and a lovely garden which is completely walled in and very safe.'

'I see you've got it all worked out.' The narrowed eyes had broadened again, looked at her reflectively.

'And she's happy to take on extra help if she needs it.'

Lisa and Alec were walking round their two acres, admiring the new planting of daphnes: Mezereum glowing deep rose in May sunshine, Somerset carrying pinky-white blooms with a pervading scent, attracting the first crop of butterflies. Slightly to Lisa's discomfiture, Alec was leading the way towards the peaches and apricots. That was precisely where she judged Don had used a spade the evening before. Suppose Alec found evidence of Don's digging?

'Can you smell daphne collina? The fragrance is still absolutely glorious,' she said, trying to sound normal.

'What? Oh, yes.' Alec had popped his head round the tool shed door. 'I can't understand it, Lisa. I had a whole bag of lime I was going to put on the new espaliers. They're stone fruit; they need the minerals. I know I put a two-kilo bag in the shed!'

Lime. Had Don taken it? She knew lime had been used in the past to help bodies decompose, and as a disinfectant. She trembled as her mind conjured up images of the evening before. The little figure in the bath, bent over, Don's expression as he saw the bracelet dangling from her hand . . . She pulled herself together. 'Perhaps you left it in the garage.'

'I checked earlier on. It's not in the garage.'

Should she tell him, after all? He was her children's father, he—

'I *know* I put it in the shed. Did you take it?' He looked at her accusingly.

She wondered what possible use he thought she could have for the lime. Always that accusation in his eyes. No, she couldn't take him into her confidence. 'I'll pick up a bag for you when I go shopping,' she volunteered instead. 'You can put it on next week.'

'Oh, all right.' Alec hoisted a package of Multiplier under his arm, turned away from the shed and began striding down the garden in his boots. He carried a fork and made his way towards the espaliers. Lisa followed him hesitantly, unwillingly.

He stopped short at the bed planted with the new fruit trees and began to examine the ground. 'What on earth's been going on here? Someone's been messing about with the soil between these trees.'

The narrow border between the new espaliers against the wall looked freshly raked. Lisa remembered the scrape of metal against the stone scalpings. She looked nervously around for further evidence. Don would have had to put extraneous soil from the grave somewhere.

And then she saw it, a great clump of dense clay on top of good black loam. A grey, solid clod that leered at her. It glowed, sticky wet and pale, its ghostly outline all too visible. Would Alec notice? There must have been more of it. What had Don done with it? Carted it away? Her eyes roamed the area for a hiding place, lighted on the rhyne. Grey lumps of mud jutting out of the water in the ditch shallow with lack of rain. Don must have thrown the clay in for rainstorms to wash away.

'This really is too much!' Alec exclaimed. 'Look at this. The main leader's been broken.' He turned on her. 'Do you know anything about that?'

'I haven't been down here, Alec.' Her voice was low, subdued. She thought about the little body, unceremoniously got rid of. A child – her child, even if he did come about in a quite incredible way. A tear began to trickle down her cheek.

Alec was examining his trees carefully; he didn't notice her. 'Someone's broken several of the young shoots I was going to train,' he said. 'How can I grow espaliers if I haven't got decent leaders?' He squatted down beside the place where Lisa judged Don had buried the body. 'Did you allow the children down here? Was it them, crashing into my trees?' He turned round, annoyance making his face red. 'The place is big enough. I asked you not to let them play around down here.'

Her voice, at first unsteady, gruff, took on irritation. 'It wasn't the children, Alec. I wouldn't let them come down here on their own.' She couldn't think quickly enough, but tried to say something which would make sense, which would head him off. 'Maybe Saunders raked it over for you, darling.'

He turned right round. '*Saunders?*' he exploded. 'Since when does *Saunders* decide what needs doing?' He began to distribute granules of fertiliser from the yellow packaging. 'This will produce results, I'm sure.'

Lisa gulped, abhorrence flooding over her. A scene of small corpses, multiplied, crowded into her mind. She shook herself, trying to quench the tears trying to spill. 'D'you think, darling, it might be a good idea to let the trees establish first? Otherwise you'll just encourage the extra growth of young wood,' she said.

'Exactly what I'm aiming for,' he rounded on her. 'I've just explained, I want young shoots to train as leaders.' He scraped his fork round a tree trunk. 'Someone has been here.'

His attitude, his care about the trees rather than her, brought out her temper. 'Then I expect it was Duffers,' she shot back at him.

'Duffers?' He knew quite well what she was talking about. 'Oh, yes. Gerry's terrier.'

'Exactly. I told you I had to get rid of him. It isn't just a question of Geraldine being useless. That wretched animal kept digging up the garden. It's completely untrained. Perhaps Saunders noticed and tidied it all up again. He knew you'd be upset.'

'Dogs don't attack fruit tree branches, Lisa. You really are prejudiced against that girl and anything to do with her.'

She knew better than to attack Geraldine directly. 'I've seen that stupid animal dig right round trees and shrubs, exposing the roots and everything.'

Alec squatted down and examined the earth around the slender tree trunk. 'It *has* been disturbed. These trees are pot grown; that means he must have dug right by the trunk and broken some of the roots. You didn't mention that before.'

'I do have a few other things on my mind,' she suddenly snapped. The tears were really threatening now, oozing under her eyelids. Whatever she did or said annoyed him. He was being completely obsessive about the garden, unwilling to tolerate anything but his own ideas. It was impossible to talk to him.

Alec was squatting by the nectarine. He turned and looked up at her, his eyes dark and brooding.

'You always turn down help, Lisa. You reject my mother, and now you're longing to get rid of Geraldine. You have only yourself to blame if you get completely worn out.'

'What I would like to do,' Lisa explained to Dr Gilmore, 'is make sure no one can get the triplets confused. You know, there might be all kinds of occasions when that could happen.'

'Well, I suppose so,' he said, sounding dubious and looking at the toddlers crawling round their playroom floor. 'I always thought mothers never got it wrong.'

'I don't,' Lisa agreed. 'And nor do Alec or Seb; or even Betsy. And Meg usually knows the difference, too. I'm not talking about the people who're used to them. I'm talking about unexpected eventualities.'

'Like what?'

'I'm going to send them to a playschool on weekday mornings. Lodsham House is only five hundred yards down the road from here. They're one year old now, and it will be good for the whole family. But of course the assistants there have to be able to tell them apart.'

'So that's the plan, is it?' He smiled enthusiastically. 'That is a good idea. It'll give you some time for yourself.' He grinned as he looked from one small child to another. 'And I do see what you mean about mixing them up.'

'Alec and I may take a few days' break.' Lisa sounded nonchalant. 'We might leave Alec's mother in charge.' A bright, sudden smile. 'So I thought, if you have nothing against it from a medical point of view, I'd have their ears pierced.'

The GP was sitting across from Lisa, leaning back in his chair, tapping a pencil idly against the notepad he had in front of him. He looked up, startled. 'Pierce their ears? What good would that do?'

'Only the one. You may have noticed, their left ear has a little indentation on the lobe. I thought there would be no harm in piercing through that and inserting a different metal ring in each child's ear.'

'Just one? For identification purposes?'

'Yes, just a tiny band, as small as we can make it. Gold, bronze and silver. Just wide enough to make it easy to tell them apart.'

The doctor picked up Jeffrey and placed him on his lap, examining his ear. 'You know, that's not a bad idea,' he said. 'Not bad at all.' He jiggled the laughing child up and down. 'There's just one thing. I think you should use precious metals for all three. Bronze might well cause an allergy. Why not use platinum instead?'

'I hadn't thought of that. The problem is it's almost the same colour as silver.'

'Yes, I do see that.' He looked from one child to another. 'You could, I suppose, put a twist in one of the bands.'

'That would solve it,' Lisa agreed at once.

'I hope it won't affect them psychologically.' Gilmore smiled at the triplets, now all engrossed in building blocks. 'I'm sure you don't want to encourage them to be drifters!'

'As soon as they're old enough to say who they are, we can dispense with the earrings,' Lisa said. If he knew the whole idea was based on Leo, he'd probably think she was encouraging her children to become homosexuals.

'You seem to have it all figured out.'

'That's my job.'

The doctor looked surprised at her tone. 'And what about you? Are you getting on all right? Not too much strain?'

'Things have settled down a good deal.' Had Alec been discussing her with the doctor behind her back?

'Good, good,' Gilmore soothed easily. 'I think taking a break is an excellent idea. And if, in the meantime, you think you need something to calm you down, I can prescribe a mild sedative.' He opened his bag before she could even answer, and hauled a prescription pad out of it. 'I know you always like to know what I'm prescribing.' He smiled. 'Smallest dose of diazepam.' He saw her look nonplussed. 'Quite well known – Valium.' He scribbled illegible symbols on the pad, tore off a sheet and handed it to her. 'Just don't increase the dose without consulting me,' he said.

That sounded remarkably like Meg's instructions about valerian tea. And the names of the herbs Meg used were almost as unfamiliar to Lisa as Gilmore's drugs.

'Calm me down? Whatever do you mean by that?'

'Nothing at all, Mrs Wildmore,' he said hurriedly. 'Just a suggestion, in case you're having broken nights.'

'I don't take drugs unnecessarily,' Lisa reminded him, handing back the prescription. 'I prefer to stick to herb tea. Melissa is a wonderful relaxant. I grow it for myself.' She grinned at an idea that formed in her mind. 'Would you like to try some?' she asked pleasantly.

'That's very kind but I must get on. The children are looking really well. I do congratulate you.'

So Alec *had* been on to him, telling tales about her problems with sleeping, her fits of anger, her shouting. She'd have to go back to valerian tea for a short time. She couldn't afford to have her brain fogged by tranquillisers.

[illegible]

[illegible]

[illegible]

[illegible]

[illegible]

[illegible]

[illegible]

19

They weren't exactly shouting 'tally ho', but the effect was the same. The hunting horn reverberated in Lisa's eardrums, raucous and shrill. The Lodsham in full cry.

'It's the hunt, Alec,' Lisa called. To her surprise Alec's enthusiasm for gardening had grown. The manual work, he maintained, refreshed a mind cudgelled with too many figures. 'Help me to get the children in.'

'In?' He straightened up and looked at Lisa resentfully. 'Why shouldn't they watch the fun?'

'It isn't fun for the fox. I don't want them growing up with the idea that hunting is the way to spend their leisure.'

Alec shifted the hoe he was manoeuvring from his right hand to his left, and supported his weight on that. In spite of the work involved, he insisted on a herbaceous border to divide the lawn from the orchard. 'It's country life, pet. I know all that stuff about the poor, innocent fox. Just doesn't happen to be true. The sweet animal hunts himself. Meg's hens have been nabbed often enough for you to know it isn't all one way.'

'I'm more concerned about the effect it has on human beings than the pros and cons of hunting,' Lisa said loftily. 'After all, I do paint hunting scenes.'

Lisa picked James up and held him against herself. He was the one she felt most protective towards; a sweet-natured, gentle child she loved to be with. She could no longer safely carry two triplets, so she held her right hand out for Jeffrey. He trotted obediently towards her.

'If you could bring Jansy in for me,' she said, turning towards the side door. 'Come along, Seb, we're going to play indoors.'

'Seb can come down the drive with me. We'll watch them riding past. Frank's bound to be with them.'

Lisa looked over her shoulder, clamping her teeth together to keep calm. 'If you don't mind, darling, I'd really rather not.'

'I'll put Seb across my shoulders; he'll be quite safe.'

'I can't stop *you*. Just remember what Meg said last time: those hounds are fierce, really fierce. I'm nervous about those animals.'

Alec laughed; that friendly, indulgent laugh which infuriated Lisa. 'Honestly, darling, they're trained to tear the fox to pieces, finish it off as quickly as they can. Human beings are definitely not quarry.'

The sound of the horn was getting closer, its mournful monotone echoing round the moor.

'Alec, I'm going in now. They're really near. You weren't here last time. Those brutish hounds hurl themselves across our wall and swarm all over the paddock. They bay louder than any pack I've ever heard, they trample everything in their path. They're terrifying.' She darted her face towards Alec nervously, then opened the side door and placed the two toddlers on the hall flagstones. 'Hurry up, Seb.' Her voice, no longer diffident, brought the child running. 'I'll shut the door. You look after Jiminy and Jeffers while I fetch Jansy.'

Lisa closed the old door with a bang and turned round. Alec leaned his hoe slowly against the stone pillar by the rockery and watched Lisa walk up to Janus. The insistent baying of the hounds was getting louder, more threatening.

'Gee-gees.' The child planted firm feet astride and looked at her defiantly.

He had become podgy again, a sort of bloated, swollen look Lisa found distinctly worrying. She eyed him nervously; he was much larger than the other two, definitely plump. Memories began to stir. She pushed them aside and bent down to him, smiling, determined to be patient with his stubborn behaviour. 'That's right, darling,' she agreed, squatting in front of him, holding out her arms. 'Lots of gee-gees, and lots of big bow-wows. We have to get away from them. They'll knock us over.'

The urgency in her voice alerted the child to danger. He turned full blue eyes on her, lifted his arms and went towards her so that she could hoist him up. He was so much heavier than the others. The hounds bayed closer and the strength she needed to lift Janus surged through Lisa. The child clasped her neck tight as she sprinted for the door.

The first foxhound was already crashing over the rhyne and into their orchard. Lisa had seen the Master, vivid red coat glowing in morning sun, hacking his mount through Mark Ditcheat's field below the rhyne that separated their garden from his acreage.

'Hey! Get out of here!'

Lisa stood by the crack of door, extricating herself from Janus. 'Alec, please! Don't mess about. They're really vicious. Get out of their way!' she called, suddenly aware that the whole pack was charging towards her husband. 'Come *on*!'

The leading hound had turned into a dozen almost instantly, with reserves charging up. Their clamorous baying, their extraordinary speed produced some sort of primitive response in Alec. He began to trot, then run towards the door. He shut it just in time against the growling din of dogs leaping against it.

'See what I mean?'

'I'll have a word with Frank about that. It's ridiculous!'

'Frank? I thought there was a Master of Hounds in charge?'

'Whatever, Lisa,' Alec said crossly, clearly annoyed at this undignified retreat from his own garden.

'I wish you would get on to *someone*. Diana's for ever saying how marvellous that pack is. I can't think why. I'm surprised no one's done anything so far. I know most people follow in their cars, but there are the odd cyclists.'

'Presumably they know they're not to attack people on the road,' Alec said, frowning.

'You mean because we aren't part of a crowd they think of us as prey?'

'Shouldn't, of course, but something like that.' Alec was more than annoyed; he was shocked, alarmed even. 'Let's go and see what they're up to,' he said, leading the way into the living room. 'We should be safe enough looking out through the bay window.'

They stood, the six of them, watching the huntsmen ride across the moor spread below their eyrie. Janus stood close beside the glass, chubby fingers spread out against it, watching intently.

A straggle of indifferent horses roamed in and out of gates opened up to the road. This wasn't really hunt country; the divisions between the fields, consisting of rhynes haphazardly bordered by thick hedges of hawthorn interspersing sloe and willow, were laced with fearsome brambles. They made cross country hunting far too difficult. The hunt followers straggled along the lanes in convoys of Land Rovers, Volvo estates and Ford Fiestas augmented with old men on bicycles and young men in Cortinas that had seen better days.

'View halloo!' resounded into the Wildmores' living room. They couldn't mistake Frank Graftley's full, reverberating shout. He appeared, his hunting pink flashing across their sight, galloping Light Amber across the field at full pelt. The hounds pursued him at a furious pace, followed by two more huntsmen in pink. The Master of Hounds drew his hunter up and turned imperiously.

'Get 'em in!' he yelled to the whipper-in who was having trouble controlling the questing cry. Don Chivers, Lisa was suddenly aware, recognising his spare body, the shock of white hair under the hardtop, the way he flailed skinny arms. She was surprised to see him there; supporting the hunt was not what she thought of as his inclination.

'It's primitive,' Lisa said, turning to Alec. 'Unbelievably primitive. I'm glad they're far enough away so we can't actually see them tearing that unfortunate animal apart. Is Frank really keen on all that?'

'Keener than ever. His boys, too, of course. See them?' Alec, field glasses in his hand, pointed at the two older Graftley lads, Michael and Alan, on ponies.

'I didn't realise they'd allow them on the field.'

'Cub hunting.'

'Don's there as well, helping with the foxhounds.'

'You mean Frank's stockman? So he is. That's rum. Frank was saying only the other day that old Don didn't really hold with hunting. Said he prefers to get on with his chores.'

'He seems to be helping the Master.' She turned to Alec excitedly. 'I remember now – the man we met at the party. Gudgeon, I think his name was. He's the Master of Hounds. That's what Diana said.'

'Sir Wilford, d'you mean?'

'That's right. Sees a lot of Frank, I gather from Meg. Do you do business with him, then? Didn't much take to him myself.'

'He's on the Flaxton board.' Alec pushed his hair off his forehead. 'I suppose he and Frank come across each other at the meets. I had lunch with him the other day. He offered me one of his new hunters, actually.'

'Gudgeon, d'you mean? Or Frank?'

Alec positively cackled. 'Frank wouldn't give away a horsefly. No, Sir Wilford. I gather he thinks it would be politic for me to ride.'

'Thought you said you weren't too keen.'

'I'm not. Well, I never learnt. That's why I thought we might get Seb to take some lessons. On a pony, of course,' he said quickly. 'Thought I might join him.'

'Would you like that, Sebbie?'

The little boy's eyes rounded in excitement. 'Ride ponies with Daddy,' he said. 'And Mummy,' he added, looking uncertainly at Lisa.

'Daddy and Uncle Frank, I think.'

'And Mikey and Alan.'

As they watched, the hunting scene below them suddenly seemed to change. The normal, aimless sniffing of hounds following scent turned to tense excitement, then to something nearer panic. Two horses seemed to be being spurred towards the pack at the same time. They crashed into each other, unseating one rider who disappeared beneath the horses' legs. Frank Graftley's mare, nearby, reared on her hind legs. Lisa realised Frank was desperately trying to avoid a form lying prone, the riderless horse cantering off. The horn screamed loud staccato.

'What the hell's going on? Frank's going to smash into the chap who . . .'

Lisa did not take in the rest of what Alec was saying. A prick of panic tightened her chest as she watched, mesmerised. 'Someone's down,' she gasped. 'What on earth's happening? Why doesn't he move out of the way?' Was that, could that really be, Don Chivers on the ground?

'The hounds are swarming all over him,' Alec said grimly. 'Wonder who it is?'

'Something's gone terribly wrong,' Lisa found herself whispering, a conviction of a sinister turn of events making her shudder. 'I'm going to ring the ambulance.' And she was on the phone, tapping 999, before Alec had taken in just what was taking place before his eyes.

As she looked up, waiting for the connection, Lisa saw Frank galloping towards them, kicking gleaming riding boots into Light Amber. He avoided the crowd by the gate by jumping the mare over the rhyne beside the road, then cantered urgently towards their drive. 'There's Frank.'

'Must be riding in to ask us to get help.'

'We'd better get some blankets ready.'

'Let's settle the children in the playroom,' Alec said quietly, gathering Janus and Jeffrey up as Lisa asked for an ambulance.

She followed Alec into the playroom with James and installed Janus in the playpen, allowing James and Jeffrey outside it. Janus had become very aggressive again; she did not want to leave him, unsupervised, with his triplet brothers.

'You look after the triplets for me, Seb,' she said. 'You're in charge. There's been an accident, we've got to help Uncle Frank. Be a really big boy now. Make sure Janus stays in the playpen.'

'I know how to do it, Mummy,' he said. He'd always been remarkably good with Janus.

* * *

'Did you see 'un? See what happened?' Frank reined Light Amber up sharply and dismounted. He looked almost wild, blank eyes roaming and aimless. 'Best ring the ambulance, quick!'

'Already on its way,' Alec said calmly.

'Thank God for that. Any blankets?'

'We got some out for you. We couldn't really tell what was going on . . .'

'Don Chivers were whipping in. The hounds turned on him, tore at his boots and he fell off. Then two horses trampled on top of him,' Frank almost sobbed. 'He didn't get up.' He leaned against the stone pillar, removing his hardtop, mopping the sweat streaming down. 'He be done for.'

Lisa felt a chill shudder going through her as Frank confirmed what she already suspected – knew.

'Don was thrown? You mean your stockman?' Alec asked, frowning, surprised.

'Arr, that were old Don.' Frank's voice, usually so strident and sure, sounded tremulous.

Lisa looked at him sharply. Had she misjudged him? He'd always seemed so cold, but now there was no mistaking strong emotion.

'I'll get you something to sit on,' Alec said, watching in alarm as Frank heaved for breath. 'I always thought you said Don didn't join in the hunting.'

'The gaffer specially asked me to bring him,' Frank said, his voice throbbing. 'Got to get back to him.' Frank leaned against the pillar, breathing hard. 'Danged if I know what be going on. One minute Don were whipping in, the next Wilford Gudgeon's gelding were piled on top of him. Crushed the life out of him. He be a goner.' The swollen red face had drained to grey. 'In all my years' hunting I've never seen anything like it. Those hounds turned on him!'

Lisa's thoughts raced through her mind. Wilford Gudgeon had wanted Don to do the whipping in; and it was Gudgeon's horse which had trampled Don to death. Had that really been an accident, or had someone seized their chance, stamped Don out of the way?

'What's *wrong* with those hounds?' Lisa almost shrieked at Frank. 'They looked completely out of control.'

'Turned right on him, as though he were the quarry!' Frank's shoulders shook. 'Even the horses bolted with fright. That must be how it happened.'

'Supposed to be a good pack, isn't it?'

'Best there be. I reckon they scented blood, together with the scent Don carried.' Frank put his face in his hands. 'Don don't hold with hunting. I made him do the whipping in, said he were being soft. My God, you should have seen – no, bain't no good. It were just terrible.'

A memory was trying to surface in Lisa's mind. She couldn't quite put her finger on it. All she knew was that something was terribly wrong. Otherwise why would an old hand like Don be thrown, and even if he were, why would a horse trample all over him? And the hounds. Why would a pack of hounds, trained from birth to kill a fox, suddenly turn on a human being? Fox hunting had been practised in the countryside for centuries. Could foxhounds change character?

'Which pack is it?' Lisa turned to Frank.

'Pakenham Moor,' he said, something of his usual resentment coming through. 'Wilford Gudgeon – he's the one on the bay. Gaffer at Priddy; old manor house. He runs the kennels. He be a wonderful Master.'

Wilford Gudgeon again.

'That's what Diana said. D'you know him well?'

'See him socially, you mean?' Frank looked rueful. 'Not my patch,' he said as he drained the whisky Alec had brought for him. 'But I does come across him. Point-to-points and such.'

'Sir Wilford runs those hounds?' Alec demanded.

'I know he feeds them the right stuff. He gets his meat from us.'

'*You* supply feed for the hounds?' Was that what had been nagging at the back of her mind? Frank was supplying meat from herds grazed on his fields. Could that affect the hounds? Make them more aggressive, out of control?

'I do that,' Frank said as he turned irritably towards Lisa. 'What's wrong with that, then?' The eyes, brimful of feeling a moment before, looked at her coldly. 'You don't hold with hunting, I dare say.'

'Actually Frank, that isn't true. I know hunting helps keep the countryside in trim, makes sure the horses are up to scratch.' She drew a deep breath. 'And hunting ensures the hounds continue to be bred. None of that bothers me; it's only right.' She looked at the man in front of her. She'd no idea his hair had greyed so much. 'It's the followers that really worry me, I suppose. Not the riders, that's just sport. It's the people in cars and on foot. They seem to want to be in at the kill. To see a single animal hunted by a whole pack of hounds. I think that's absolutely disgusting.'

Frank didn't answer her. He'd closed his eyes, leaned back his head.

'Don – I can't rightly believe it. Don Chivers. Worked for my father afore me, and my granfer afore that.'

'Perhaps he'll pull through. He's very fit.'

'Pull through?' He turned on Lisa. 'Survive a horse tromping on him, torn by them hounds? Not a bloody chance in hell. He be done for, right enough.'

They heard the ambulance siren its way across the moor roads. Frank looked up, a little unsteady, and seemed to shiver at the sound. He caught Lisa watching him, braced his shoulders back and walked to the stone wall to look over it. Alec and Lisa joined him, and Lisa could see his trembling hands grasping the jutting topstones. He wasn't merely emotionally overcome; he was frightened, Lisa realised. Perhaps he was conscious of how easily he might have been in Don's place.

'Amazing how far you can see. It's still a good mile off.' Alec watched the large vehicle negotiate the hump bridge over Lodsham Drain.

'All those followers upalong are going to slow it up. Leastways they got enough sense to park on the verges.'

'I'll go and make some tea,' Lisa said. 'You'll need something sweet to help you over the shock.'

'Later,' Frank said slowly, remounting and holding out shaking hands for the blankets, his eyes shifting away. 'Got to ride back to cover him. Though we fell out betimes, Don were one in a million. I won't never see the likes of him again.'

20

'I could come down any weekend you like,' Sarah Wildmore said carefully. 'Really, I'd love to help with the children.'

'That's very kind of you, Sarah. We're fine.'

'It would be so nice to see something of the little ones.'

'I can't do everything!' Lisa suddenly snapped at her mother-in-law. 'My exhibition is next week, and the boys have just got over colds and been at home, and I haven't even got that awful Geraldine to help me now.'

'You finally sacked her? I didn't realise.'

'There's nothing for her to do! The boys are at playschool every morning, and Betsy picks them up for their walk after their nap.'

'So the poor girl's redundant.' Sarah laughed, but Lisa could hear the nervousness.

'As a matter of fact, she's been taken on by the person who runs the school. She's one of the trainees helping with the children.'

'Really? Geraldine? Did you give her a reference? I thought you said she was completely useless.'

'Inexperienced,' Lisa said warily. 'She has a lot to learn. Anne Marsden's equipped to teach her.'

When Nanette Fitch-Templeton had rung and asked Lisa to give Geraldine a testimonial, she'd hardly been in a position to refuse. 'She did so love being with your little ones, Lisa,' Nanette had flattered her. 'That's why she's so keen to get experience at Lodsham House. *Such* good training for her,' Geraldine's mother had insisted, trying to press Lisa into writing something the girl could use.

'I suppose so. She is still rather immature,' Lisa had answered evasively.

'I know, my dear, I know. These teenagers . . .' She trailed to a stop. Lisa could almost hear her try to work out the right approach. 'But she did learn so much from you, and she's absolutely desperate to try for the Norland training.'

The girl had never mentioned such a possibility to her. But Lisa had been in a quandary. Geraldine was, after all, Carruthers' niece. Alec wouldn't tolerate direct criticism of the girl.

'I stressed how young she was to Anne,' Lisa excused herself to her mother-in-law.

'Of course,' Sarah said softly.

'We parted on perfectly amiable terms. She often pops in at weekends.'

'I wondered about that.'

Did Sarah also suspect Alec was having an affair with the girl? Probably thought it a good idea, Lisa thought sourly. 'I'm supposed to entertain some of the Flaxton bigwigs,' she finished up, a little calmer. 'Neither Betsy nor Geraldine can give me much help with that.'

'Dinner parties, d'you mean?'

'That sort of thing.'

'If that's what's worrying you,' Sarah said, 'I could make myself useful. Why not ask me down next time you're roped in and I'll see to it. You play the little wife, I'll be the dowager.'

Lisa was annoyed with herself for making such a silly mistake. If she didn't fall in with that suggestion, Sarah would have concrete complaints next time she talked to Alec.

'Of course I know how much you have to do,' her mother-in-law intoned. 'But it's the sort of thing I'm really good at.'

Lisa could picture the scene with Alec. 'Shouldn't you be getting some more help for her, Allie?' she'd suggest to him demurely, insinuatingly. She always called him Allie; you'd think he was still a baby. 'It can't be right to keep my only grandchildren apart from me like that.'

It was not, Lisa thought irritably, as she parried her mother-in-law with promises of a visit later in the month, that she didn't know she was going through a bad patch. Who wouldn't, with four such young children under foot? Hardly grounds for 'seeking some sort of professional guidance', as Alec had so pompously put it.

The suggestion had, however, struck a chord with Lisa. Was she actually neurotic? Was her imagination playing tricks on her? Even to entertain the idea of cloning when there were plausible alternatives did sometimes seem absurd even to herself. But there were no plausible alternatives. It had happened; she had found James, not given birth to him. She did not believe she could be mistaken about a thing like that.

What annoyed her most of all was that Gilmore had taken it on himself to intimate she needed more help in the house. What on earth did an ordinary GP think he knew about it? A medical education hardly equipped one to run a home. Meg, too, had said she looked 'run down', whatever that was supposed to mean. Trevor was the only one who didn't get at her, who had something encouraging to say.

'You really are a marvel, darling. These paintings are *exactly* what the market wants,' he'd smiled at her last time he'd looked over a new batch.

Of course what none of them could even guess at was the real strain she was under. And that had nothing whatever to do with coping with so many young children. Don Chivers' death haunted her. She could not rid herself of the feeling that it had not been an ordinary accident. It wasn't just what had happened, it was the way it had affected Frank. He appeared shaken, even more furtive than before. The odd habit of looking over his shoulder, of dropping his voice as though afraid of being overheard struck Lisa as significant. Had he played some part in Don's death? Surely not. Why would he want Don out of the way? The man had been loyal to Frank and his family all his life, he would never have done anything to hurt them. It was Don himself who had been responsible for helping Frank cover up by killing suspect livestock, ploughing up suspect crops. If he'd wanted to make it all public he'd have done it there and then. And Don had disposed of the first batch of Multiplier. Built a huge bonfire, Meg had told Lisa, burned all of it, together with an old elder hedge which he'd grubbed out.

'Terrible waste,' Frank had complained. 'Money going up in smoke.'

No, Frank had nothing at all to gain from Don's death. In fact, Frank's reaction was more that of a man threatened, as though Don's death were some kind of warning. What really worried Lisa now was that Frank had suddenly shown more than his usual interest in the triplets; it reminded her of Don. She was pretty sure Don hadn't told Frank about the dead clone. And, even if he had, why was Frank only reacting now? Were her children in some sort of jeopardy?

Lisa shook herself. The earrings were in place, it couldn't happen again, she could relax. Each triplet had a tiny, delicate little band of precious metal slipped through an equally tiny hole in the left earlobe. Plain gold for Janus, twisted platinum for Jeffrey to distinguish it from the plain silver one for James. They were quite difficult to spot unless one knew just where to look for them. Lisa was positive that the thin gold band kept Janus from cloning. But in spite of the earrings, she knew the problem was still there, waiting to pounce, demanding some sort of permanent resolution.

Lisa had no difficulty distinguishing Janus from his brothers, with or without the earring. And she had the uncomfortable feeling that he knew what she was thinking, that she was worried about him, and for him. A new problem had surfaced recently. Janus was not only bulkier than his brothers, and unusually strong. He was also extremely bright – and far too assertive.

'I'll just put Jiminy and Jansy in the playpen,' Betsy called to Lisa as she was clearing up in the kitchen. 'Jeffers needs changing.'

Before she could shout a warning, Lisa heard the howls from the playroom. She ran down the corridor to find Janus gripping the playpen rail with one hand and bashing his gentler brother on the head with a brick with the other.

'No, Jansy!' she shouted at him.

She saw the child's gleaming, shining eyes turn to her, felt his frustration.

'That's very, very naughty!' she told him.

He grinned at her, confident of his strength, evidently content to wait for the right moment to show it.

'Stop that now, Jansy.' Lisa took the brick out of the child's hand and lifted up her delicate, docile little Jiminy to comfort him. He smiled at her through his tears. 'You're not to hit your brother.'

The toddler turned deliberately away. There was a hiccup as he heaved vomit all over the carpet the playpen was standing on.

'Jansy!'

'I expect he just had too much tea,' Betsy soothed, coming in with Jeffrey. Janus turned towards her and lifted up his arms, waiting for her to pick him up. 'He's too small to know when he's had too much,' she tried to appease Lisa, putting Jeffrey down. 'See, he's as good as gold now. We'll just get a cloth and mop it up, shall we?'

Janus allowed Betsy to lift him out and take him to the kitchen to fetch a cloth. When they returned he was smiling at her, putting fat little hands into her hair and laughing. She set him down by Jeffrey and climbed into the playpen, bending to clean up the mess.

'Look at that,' she said, turning to Lisa who was still holding James in her arms, stroking curly blond hair out of his eyes. 'Jansy's trying to help me. Isn't that sweet?'

Janus was reaching through the playpen bars, putting his hand in the mess. He coiled up a pugnacious fist and plastered the vomit over Jeffrey's face.

'Janus!' Lisa shrieked.

Betsy gently opened the small fist and cleaned it with the cloth. 'He's only trying to feed his little brother.' She smiled at Lisa. 'They can't know what they're doing.'

Lisa kept her feelings of helplessness from Betsy by placing James on the floor and walking him towards the playpen. As they approached, she saw Janus's eyes glow – that curious gleam which told her he was different from her other children. He stretched out his right arm, caught at her hair and pulled.

'Jansy! You're hurting Mummy!'

'Oh, dear,' Betsy was saying, dropping the mopping-up cloth to help disentangle Lisa's hair.

'It's all right, Betsy. I can handle it.'

Lisa grasped Janus's fingers and pried them apart. The strength in them amazed her, then frightened her. He was eighteen months old, she told herself repeatedly. Only eighteen months.

'Mau, mau,' he suddenly announced. 'Mau, mau.'

'Isn't that sweet.' Betsy's moon face split into melon halves. 'He's trying to say Mummy!' Tender eyes turned to Lisa. 'Is that his first word?'

It was not the way Lisa interpreted it. To her it sounded like 'more, more'. The question was, more what?

'Jansy, stop making that scrunching noise,' Lisa complained.

'You're becoming completely impossible to live with,' Alec seethed. 'All the child did was crunch an apple in his mouth!'

True as far as it went, Lisa thought to herself, but certainly not what was really going on.

Janus was sitting on the bench beside James, round blue eyes clamped on Lisa, determined jaws rhythmically chomping apple.

Crunch, crunch. The apple slices set out in front of the child disappeared at an alarming rate, and when he'd finished those he grabbed at James's.

Lisa's hand shot out to stop him. 'Those are Jiminy's, Jansy. If you want more, you can always ask.' She saw Alec's head emerge sideways from behind the paper, watching her.

'Mau, mau,' Janus said promptly, hand outstretched.

'More please.'

'Mau *pees*!'

'I'll cut you some.'

The knife, a small, sharp kitchen knife for paring vegetables, rapidly cut another Golden Delicious in half, decored it and sliced swiftly through the soft flesh, cutting crescents. Lisa pushed three slices at Janus and saw him grasp them and devour them. This time he stuffed all three into his mouth at once.

'Steady on there, young man,' Alec smiled at him, but Lisa saw a faint frown of worry on his brow. 'You'll choke yourself!'

He was greedy enough to do it. Lisa put the knife carefully away and watched Janus's reactions to the new supply of apple with growing distress. Trickles of liquid dribbled from the corners of his mouth and down his chin. As she watched him swallow, gulping large chunks of apple, Lisa saw him swell up even more. If he doesn't clone soon he's going to burst, suddenly flashed across her brain. And he can't clone if he's got an earring on.

She saw the child fingering his earlobe, pulling it down. He was quite capable, she suspected, of pulling the lobe off to get his way. And then – and then the clone would have a piece out of his lobe too.

Lisa began to feel herself slip into another world, an eerie, surrealistic world where cloning was the norm. Had she imagined it, or were there far more spiders spinning dense webs around her home, trapping more flies? She watched a large, black fly, slowed by the cool of morning, crawl slowly up a kitchen windowpane. Transfixed, she seemed to see its swollen body elongate, then buzz its wings and prise apart as it split and two more wings emerged from the centre. Two smaller flies crawled slowly up the pane. It reminded her of the stag beetle which had crawled towards the spilt milk. Don had squashed it, she remembered now. Pushed his heavy boot on it without a qualm. Because he'd known that if the beetle drank the milk it might start to clone.

A feeling of hopelessness enveloped Lisa. She wanted to share her terrible secret with Alec, to scream her horror at this catastrophe about to engulf the world, to sob her fears away. And if she did? He wouldn't believe her, he'd call in the caring professions, they'd find out she was telling the truth and – she'd lose her children. The phenomenon would still be there. What had been started could not be undone.

Lisa, trying to appease Alec, merely succeeded in widening her mouth into a nervous grin.

'You think it would be funny if he choked?' she heard him demand. He could be quite sarcastic.

'Of course not. I was thinking about something else.' She supposed it had been rather an odd reaction. If Alec knew what she was really thinking he'd call in a whole gaggle of psychiatrists.

'I'm glad you've got time to think,' Alec crabbed at her, putting down his paper and energetically spooning cereal into Jeffrey. 'I think your other sons need your attention. I've told you till I'm sick of repeating it: get some more help. We could arrange for Geraldine to come in a couple of hours on Saturdays.'

He wanted Geraldine back; he was using their children as an excuse to see more of her.

'With Duffers, I suppose,' Lisa snapped at him, her lips drawn tight. 'Two extra mouths to feed.' If she allowed Janus to eat whatever he demanded, would he actually burst?

'You would at least have help for part of the weekend,' Alec intoned. The accusing, persistent voice of someone who knows all the answers. 'I can't always help you out.'

'I have no problems on my own with them,' Lisa thrust at him. 'It's only when you're around that they give trouble.'

'I know,' he said, resigned. 'I put them up to it.'

'And, anyway, I think there's something wrong with Janus.'

'He's a toddler, Lisa. Just a little assertive, that's all. He's stronger than his brothers.'

So he'd noticed that. Lisa looked at her husband from under hooded eyes and forced herself into a gentle voice, even a covering smile. 'You don't understand, pet. I'm not talking about the way he behaves.'

'There's a physical problem?'

'Just look at him, Alec. He's all bloated.'

'You mean his ear? He's getting allergic to the earring. I told you that would happen.'

'I'm talking about the whole of his body, for goodness sake! He's positively enormous. He ought to see a specialist. Diana gave me the name of a really top man in Bristol, Walter Morgenstein. That idiot Gilmore insists there's nothing to worry about.'

'Honestly, Lisa, it's *you* who ought to see someone.'

'If you'll just take a decent look at him, Alec. Just for once, instead of instantly assuming I'm off my nut.'

Lisa pulled the table out on its casters, exposing a row of four little boys wedged on a bench against the wall.

'Can I get down now?' Seb asked politely.

'Of course, darling. Go to the playroom. We'll all go out for a walk later on.' She turned to Alec. 'If you can hang on for just a minute, help me get Jeffers and Jiminy into the playroom.' She pushed the table back against Janus to keep him safe.

When they returned they found him round-eyed and solemn, his fleshy hands pushing the table away from himself. He was about to tumble off the bench. Lisa held out her hands and smiled.

He started to bellow, flailing his little legs and kicking at her, tubby hands made into hard fists.

'Jansy,' she cooed, her voice soft and gentle.

He screamed again and started hurling both plates and cutlery onto the kitchen floor.

'That's enough of that, Janus!' his father thundered and picked him up, removing a plastic spoon from the child's hand. 'Let go of that.' Alec wrestled the spoon away. The child, defeated, sat on his father's arm, quiet now, alert blue eyes staring beyond him.

'He's terribly rowdy and aggressive,' Lisa said, resigned to picking up the debris from the floor. 'And he's not chubby just because he eats a lot. I know it's more than that; he's far too puffy. I want that chap in Bristol to take a look at him.'

Alec sat down and held the toddler out in front of him, his hands under his armpits. He couldn't fail to see that he was swollen, an odd, curious sort of sponginess along his arms and legs, a strange and quite unpleasing billowing of his trunk, a sort of bulging in the abdomen. It looked as though the problem could be abnormal water retention. The little pot belly, straining the yellow T-shirt, bulged out like a balloon.

'Sorry, Lisa, I do see what you're getting at.' Alec turned to her, holding the child against his shoulder now and standing up.

'If you think Geraldine will give up her time to come on Saturday mornings, that might help.' Lisa decided to placate her husband.

'She loves the children.'

Did Alec believe that? Did he really not know that the girl was making a play for him?

'She tolerates them, and she's quite good with Jansy, I admit. Plays with him on his own.' Probably, Lisa thought, she liked the macho in the boy, even at his tender age.

The child in Alec's arms started to wriggle, then to pummel his father's head.

'Right, Jansy, off we go to the playroom.'

Lisa's face became tense again. 'I usually put him in the playpen in the dining room,' she said. 'He's rather rough with Jiminy. And you know Jiminy, he's so sweet-natured, he lets Jansy do anything he likes. I prefer to keep an eye on him.'

'Really?'

'Really, Alec.'

'The playpen it is, young Janus.'

The child was pulling roughly at his hair, throwing himself backwards and forwards, his flesh oozing round his clothes.

Alec looked at his son. 'I think you have a point. Will you make the appointment with Morgenstein, or shall I?'

'I'll see to it first thing on Monday,' Lisa announced. 'Just put him in the playpen. Give him his flock of woolly sheep to boss; he'll be okay.'

21

'You're sure you can cope on your own, Betsy? You don't want me to ask Meg to come over for a bit?'

'I've only got to take them down the road.' Betsy looked positively hurt. 'And it's just the two of them for the afternoon, Lisa. No trouble at all. Seb's always very good when we pick him up later.'

'Right. Help me get Jansy into the car seat.'

It took them ten minutes to fasten the screaming, kicking Janus into the restraining harness. Lisa understood that he knew where she was taking him, and why, and didn't want to go. Every time she looked at him and remembered the happenings of only six months before, she was sure it would come about again. The bloating, the aggression, the greed. The process was accelerated this time; she was sure Janus was about to clone again. He had become steadily more contentious since she had made the appointment with the paediatrician two days before. The boy had overheard that; and she was sure he'd sensed that she had finally decided she had to involve the authorities.

No one could doubt that there was something wrong with him. Even Alec thought so now. But Alec also thought her unstable. She'd noticed the way he looked at her, seen the uncertainty in his eyes. And he refused to discuss the possibility that Janus might have more than some mild allergy. He was not prepared to countenance the suggestion that there was something seriously wrong with the child.

But even if he were to, Lisa realised, it would no longer be a solution to their problems. Alec was Janus's father, as involved as she was. What could he do that she had not already done? She needed to consult someone who would view the matter professionally, and Morgenstein seemed the perfect man. It even crossed her mind that the child might clone in front of the specialist. If she undressed Janus, took the earring out, he might clone then and there. Morgenstein would have to credit it. Furthermore, the doctor would be a witness to the fact that it was Janus, not Jeffrey or James, who was afflicted with the ability to clone. That would concentrate medical attention on this child. The doctors might even find a way to avert it happening in the future.

Janus began to kick again. Perhaps he guessed what it would mean for him if the outside world knew about his unbelievable attribute. She was near to tears as she realised what she had to do. She turned to Jiminy, drew him to her, hugged him tight. Then she lifted Jeffers up, high over her head, and swung him down again. The delighted child beamed.

'I'll do some painting with you when I get back,' she promised Seb, ruffling his hair.

It was time to concentrate on Janus. He was her very own child, her flesh and blood; what option did she have but to take him to Morgenstein? She had her other children to safeguard.

'It's fairly urgent,' she'd told the doctor's secretary. 'The child is getting really tense and hard to handle. There's this odd puffiness I can't account for.'

'Wednesday, Mrs Wildmore? Ten thirty all right?'

'Can you manage a little later? Say around two? I've got the three others, you see.'

'Dr Morgenstein will see you in his lunch hour. One thirty, Wednesday.'

'That is good of him,' Lisa had said gratefully.

She had to think of a plausible explanation for Betsy, alert her to the fact that she might be back quite late.

'The trouble is, Betsy, that Dr Morgenstein may have to run extensive tests. I could be held up till quite late, you know. Perhaps not back till teatime, or even after the little ones' bedtime.'

'You think it's as serious as that?'

Betsy's loving concern made Lisa wince. Was she wrong not to tell anyone around her, to plan to spring it on all of them? She felt it was the only way she could prove that her other children were normal, the only way to keep them safe. She *had* to see the specialist before she mentioned anything to anyone else.

Janus began to scream. Strapped in his car seat he could not move his body much, but he pounded everything within reach of his small, tight fists. He sounded frantic. Betsy offered him a biscuit; he tore it out of her hand and hurled it with extraordinary force against a side window.

'He'll settle down as soon as the car moves,' Lisa told Betsy, oddly calm now that her course was clear. 'I'd better leave. It can take more than an hour to get to Bristol, and then I've got to find a parking space.'

'I hope Alec's meeting you, you'll need some help.'

'He can't get away,' Lisa said. 'I've got to dash now, Betsy, or I'll be late.'

Betsy leaned into the car, stroked the little boy's head and kissed him on the forehead. He quietened at her touch. Then, as she withdrew, he began to scream again.

The motor purring into life lulled Janus into wailing. As they moved down the drive, Lisa could see Betsy in the rearview mirror. She stood by the front door, waving at Janus secured in his seat and facing backwards. Lisa caught a glimpse of the child out of the corner of her eye; he was plopping his hands, forlorn and miserable. She felt a clutching at her throat, a misting of her eyes. This was her son; a small, defenceless child she should be protecting with all her strength, not taking to the lion's den.

A loud hoot jerked her back to reality; she only just managed to pull into a passing place to avoid an oncoming motorist. Mark Ditcheat, she saw. He glared at her and wound his window down.

'Ought ter know better'n that!' he shouted.

Unnerved, with Janus keening thinly in the background, Lisa flicked on her favourite tape for driving. The rock and roll of Fats Domino appeared to tranquillise the child; she'd noticed that before. He'd finally resigned himself to the ride.

The moor road to Wells curved past the Graftleys' farm on her right, and on through Pewksham. The village, Lisa had always felt, was aptly named. A slippery, khaki skin of cow's excrement surfaced the road, requiring careful steering to avoid a skid into untidy hedges at the roadsides. No rhynes to enclose the fields in this part of the country.

A large herd of oncoming milch cows forced Lisa to stop the Volvo, allowing them to lumber past. Janus began to fuss immediately, banging the car seat back and forth, yelling at top pitch. An old, fat cow pushed a swollen belly at the car. Lisa could feel it rock. Large, bovine faces surrounded her and swayed the car from left to right. Long dribbles of saliva appeared on the bonnet, tails swished into side windows. Lisa felt vulnerable, engulfed, drowning in a sea of ruminants. She turned the cassette recorder volume up. A hooting behind her; she could see Frank, in his Land Rover, urging her on. He drummed a brawny arm impatiently, pointed ahead. Lisa, unnerved, nosed the Volvo through the herd. A peremptory rattle on the bonnet showed her the oncoming farmer, red with fury, mouthing obscenities at her. She put her foot on the accelerator and forged through.

Escaped, at last, to the main road, Lisa drove through Wells, then turned left and wound the Volvo up steep Milton Lane and through on to the Mendips along the Old Bristol road, the scenic route. The high plateau, the Levels spread out beneath in shades of green, consisted of sparser, more arid pastures enclosed by drystone walls. Lisa hurried past them, unseeing, her heart beating fast. Janus sat quietly now, his Buddha face towards the rear, eyes closed, apparently asleep.

It was a lull; he suddenly began to pound everything within reach, to scream, to howl. Lisa slowed down, her ears drowned in the noise reverberating round the car. Shrill screams stabbed through her brain, preventing her from thought, from action. She could not drive through this. Desperate, she looked for somewhere to pull over, and saw Frank's Land Rover gaining on her. Taking his produce to Pakenham Moor kennels, she shuddered to herself. The last thing she wanted was that Frank should stop. She rolled down her window and waved him past, then saw an entrance to the Priddy Woods on her right.

She had to find some way to stop the incredible row Janus was making. Whatever else was wrong with him, his lungs were sound. His shrieks were piercing now, continuous. Was he trying to force her to return home?

'Wee!' he screeched. 'Wee . . . ee . . . ee!'

There was no other vehicle parked in the small space by the style leading to the woods. Lisa drew in, relieved; no one but her to witness Janus's tantrum.

Janus's head swung back as the car stopped, and he calmed down. His eyes, squeezed almost to oblivion, reappeared slowly, deeply sunk in folds. It seemed to Lisa he had bloated even more. His neck was wedged thick and tight against his anorak, a florid crimson mass against the yellow. His eyes were slits of animosity as he watched her every move.

His cries, less staccato, still sounded like 'wee'. Perhaps he needed to pee; he was so terribly puffed-up, so obviously waterlogged. Perhaps he was also in pain, needed to be taken out of the confining safety seat.

Lisa unstrapped him. He offered no resistance but stayed motionless, silent now, staring beyond her.

'Time to get out, Jansy.'

The head remained impassive, glazed eyes not focused.

'Come on, Jansy. You need to go wee-wees and then we're going for a walk. You'll like the woods.'

He sat, fat legs outstretched, his arms unmoving by his side. Lisa pulled on the walking reins round his body. As soon as she relaxed the force he simply jackboxed back. He seemed unable to move.

'Come on, Jansy. Help Mummy get you out.' She moved him slightly and his foot wedged inside the seat. 'We've got to try!' Lisa was almost ready to scream herself. She took a deep breath, bent her knees and attempted to lift the child out. He seemed wedged where he was, immobile, his eyes showing pain.

'He *is* a big one, isn't he?' A young man parking his bicycle, a pair of greyhounds halting at his side, smiled at her. 'Can I give you a hand?'

Lisa flashed teeth at him as he, stronger than she was, eventually managed to lever Janus out and hand him to her.

'Hold on a mo,' he said, eyeing the style. 'I'd better help you over that as well.'

'Thanks,' Lisa called after him. His dogs had moved off at a rapid pace and he was keeping up with them.

'Any time!' he called back, waving tan leather. He'd let the dogs roam free.

Janus was standing, stolid, on the style. Lisa grasped hold of him, all forty pounds, heaved him into her arms and walked unsteadily into a small track at the side. The child began to moan, kick at her arms.

'Stop it, Jansy. We've got to go further in,' she told him, clinging on in spite of leg lunges into her abdomen. Changing tactics, Janus clawed at branches above him, began to tear at his clothes. They were a few yards into the woods now and, branching off into an even smaller track, Lisa searched desperately for cover. Her child was in pain, she had to help him. But what she suspected was about to happen needed to happen in privacy.

A stumble on a tree root brought her to her knees. Before she could balance herself, Janus had tumbled out of her arms and into the soggy undergrowth. She grabbed the walking reins and pulled, sinking down into woodland soil softened by decaying pine needles. Lisa looked around her. The spruces' arms stretched overhead, blocked out daylight, enfolded them in deep shadow. She grasped Janus, now crying softly and pulling at his clothes, between her knees. Slowly, gently, methodically, she began to undress him, slipping the reins carefully under the clothes as she took them off, keeping the child secure. He made no attempt to fight her.

He was naked now, held between her legs, the walking reins still round him, the earring still in his earlobe.

'Keep still, Jansy. I'm going to take your earring off.'

Apparently he understood what she was doing. He made no further attempt to get away; he was going to co-operate.

Lisa undid the tiny clasp and removed the earring, then carefully slipped it onto her little fingertip. A lurching terror gripped at her. The child was naked. He could now clone. She could not stop it; that would be going against his nature, it would be simple cruelty. But this time it would be different; this time she was prepared. Prepared? She almost laughed at that, her face a twisted mask of fear and frustration. If she were right, there'd be a second toddler this time; a child, a human being who could already speak a few words. How could that possibly be?

She didn't know; all she knew was that she had to allow Janus's body to do what it was programmed to do. Even as she watched, she could see him oozing around the walking reins. It would be torture not to free him.

'I'm taking off the reins now, Jansy.'

She clicked them undone. Janus's body was now entirely free from any artifact. There was nothing she knew of that would prevent him from cloning. He was, she saw, terribly swollen, podgier even than at the weekend – than this morning. The time was ripe.

'Go on, then, clone!' she told him sadly, eyes wet, nose moist. 'I'm not going to stop you.'

The child stood, motionless, and suddenly began to pee. A long, steady stream of liquid oozed out of him and she could dimly see the puffiness going down. Or was she imagining it? Had she imagined everything? Was Janus simply suffering from some soft of dropsy, and she had chanced across the self-cure? Perhaps Alec had been right; the child was allergic to the gold earring and had swollen up because of it.

The stream of liquid continued, threatening her handbag and the little heap of clothes. Lisa pitched herself sideways onto her knees and shoved everything to the side. Though the light was filtered through dark greens, Lisa could see the liquid was denser than urine, darker coloured. There was an odd, chlorine-like smell. She sat back on her heels, almost convinced that nothing further would happen.

She drew in a sharp breath. When she looked at Janus again she saw his body, thinner now, bones showing, elongating sideways. Desperate, she rubbed her eyes and looked again. She saw the shape before her extend, broaden out. Tears cascaded down, veiling her eyes. She watched her son metamorphose before her. The rotund toddler of a few moments before was turning into an oval shape, arms spread wide. He stood, silent, vacant eyes staring in front of him. As his shape continued to expand, he lost his balance, toppled onto his back.

Lisa felt a tight band drawing round her, a straitjacket of horror. It took all her strength to stop herself running away, to stay with her child. He was her son; she had to be there when the awesome act she was witnessing came to an end.

The pale shape was even wider now, the broadened head on top staring with eyes reaching further and further apart, fixed and unmoving. The mouth, Lisa saw, had become a huge round, gaping in a silent shriek. The whole form was spreadeagled on the ground. A shaking, writhing motion rippled through it as the distended head showed a fissure forming at the crown. By the fontanelles, Lisa thought sadly. And as she watched, every action played out in slow motion, a rift appeared, cleaving down, the bridge of the nose opening, splitting wide.

Riveted, unable to move her gaze, Lisa watched the neck divide, a snap of Adam's apple, a moan from the little form as the collarbone burst forward, ribs lengthening out, dilating. A deep furrow channelled into the breast, running down towards the navel. Would his belly split open, its contents spew over pine-needled earth? Would he die in agony before her? Was Janus now too old to clone, the process gone terribly wrong?

As Lisa, unable to move, watched helplessly, the long, deep fissure reached the child's genitals. There was a lurch, a rending tear as the shape split in two.

Lisa bent double, a pain inside herself, the pain of a mother watching, impotent, as her child is torn apart in front of her. Her heart pumped hard, adrenaline surged through and gave her the power to use her limbs. She crawled nearer the movements on the ground. There was no longer any doubt about it: there were two children.

Two heads, ears sprouting out between them; two pairs of eyes either side of a nose she recognised. Two necks, two trunks, two stumps of arms growing, like the horns of a snail emerged from its shell. Even as she looked, they sprouted to match the other sides. Looking down, Lisa could see two small sets of genitalia, leg stumps emerging left and right, growing apace, becoming two completely formed bodies.

Two entities; two individuals who had taken on the look of two familiar toddlers, eighteen months, identical. Indistinguishable, in fact, from Janus; a thinner, unbloated Janus. There were two naked toddlers on the woodland floor, on their backs, side by side. They lay still, panting, then seemed to draw within themselves. To Lisa's absolute astonishment they sat up, looked around, saw her, and smiled at her.

'Mumumumum . . .'

Two toddlers gurgling at her. A vision of the day, so long ago now, when she'd had her pregnancy confirmed came back to her. She had seen this happen before, she realised. Seb, standing in the meadow, had held two wings of a fritillary. She understood now why he'd been able to catch the butterfly. It was in the act of cloning, unable to flee. She could no longer hide the facts of cloning from herself, pretend it hadn't happened. She'd witnessed it.

This new form of reproduction was more serious than even she had conceived of. It was clearly not confined to Janus. She remembered the clover: leaves multiplied, flower petals crowded tight. The phenomenon had already spread, had infiltrated the lower forms of life. Infected eggs, larvae, seeds were all set to proliferate, to become a random burgeoning of life that could not be restrained. It was happening all around them: to insects, crops, farm animals, even to wildlife. Were other humans involved, or was Janus unique? What should she, could she, do?

Lisa looked round. Had anyone else observed this unbelievable event? She could not know. The scene she'd witnessed had petrified her, slowed her brain. She had not been aware of her surroundings, had simply watched, incredulous, as Janus turned into two.

She could still hear the young man calling to his greyhounds. The actual cloning must have been virtually instantaneous.

Two Januses were with her now; mobile, already sitting up, then standing back to back. And about to head, she guessed, in different directions.

22

Two pairs of limpid blue eyes gazed at her; two gentle smiles embraced her; two sets of arms lifted in unison to be picked up.

Which one was Janus?

A nearby bark warned Lisa that people were walking their dogs in the woods. The dim, dappled light flickering across the children's naked bodies under the trees made it impossible for her to see clearly, but one thing was unmistakable. Whatever else she had imagined that she'd seen, there were two children with her. One, by her knees, sat down, began to babble, to play with the damp earth, some pine cones, to crawl. The other, noticing, dropped to all fours, came nearer and started playing with his – brother? His flesh and blood, *her* flesh and blood. An unheard of new way for a human to reproduce, but the living proof was in front of her: cloner and clone.

Lisa looked down again at the two prattling, adorable toddlers. Neither of them really seemed like the podgy, swollen Janus of a few moments ago, but they were both the same, identical in every way. They seemed exactly like the toddlers she had left at home; indistinguishable from Jeffrey and James to people who did not know them well, but to her mother's eye clearly more like Janus before he'd become so rounded.

And supposing she *could* tell the difference? Supposing, somehow, she could figure out which one was Janus? What should she do then? She tried to regain control of her mind. Think! she told herself sternly. *Think* what to do.

A wriggle of yellow caught a glimmer of light. One of the little boys tried to pull on the T-shirt. He pushed it, hopefully, against his head and teetered towards Lisa. The yellow cotton glowed as a ray of sunlight cut through the branches. The garment, incongruous at a rakish angle on the child's head, began to slip. Lisa felt a spasm in her left side as if she had been stabbed. These were her children; artless, enchanting, irresistible. She loved them both.

Obviously satisfied with his effort with the T-shirt, the child began to try putting on the shoes lying just by his feet. He started slipping a tiny foot into the heel part of the shoe.

'Not like that, Jansy,' Lisa found herself saying, smiling at the child. Then checked herself. One of these toddlers was not Jansy; he was a newcomer. A single shoe – maybe that meant he was a Leprechaun . . . She brushed the fancy away. She had to know which was which. Had to – for the sake of the children who were not cloners. *Had to!* Which one? Her heart began to beat, faster and faster, as panic gripped her, trickled sweat. She must be able to tell Morgenstein which was Janus, identify the cloner.

How could she tell? Was there something to point to it? Should she wait for another cloning? No; it would not happen again for some time now. She'd worked it out. Somehow Janus had to gather his strength together; feed on more food than any of the other children, perhaps. Then, when he was ready, the signs would appear. He'd become chubby, waterlogged; then edgy, turn aggressive and, as he bloated even more, become positively unbalanced with the need to clone.

The second child tried to crawl onto her lap. How could she choose? What if she got it wrong? A light clicked in her mind. The other toddler, the one she had called Janus, had started pulling on his clothes – her instincts must have told her he was Janus! The new child, the clone, could not know how to dress himself, had not had the experience. That was it; she'd got it now. *That's* how she could tell the difference!

Thrilled, delighted with her reasoning, Lisa grasped the child who was not playing with the clothes and held him tight within her knees. She pulled the earring off her finger and pushed it into his earlobe.

'There!' she said to him. 'There you are; I'll call you Jacob. You wear this so I know which one you are.'

He cooed at her, put his arms round her neck and kissed her. Just like her little James, her heart began to sing to her. Just like her lovely, angelic, docile little Jiminy. She breathed her love back to the child between her knees, wrapped her arms protectively round him, pulled on his trainer pants, his little trousers. Then she put on his socks, pulled on the little yellow shoes.

All fitted to perfection; not strained, as a few moments before, but with a bit of give.

Lisa looked around for the T-shirt. The second child, the one she had momentarily forgotten, was approaching her, tumbling to his knees, crawling over to her, the yellow T-shirt trailing along the needled ground behind him.

'I'd better put that on Jacob,' she said, a sadness in her voice. Jacob was a clone; he'd be more delicate than Janus. The little boy squirmed determinedly towards her. 'You always wanted to be free to clone, Jansy,' she told him. 'Well, now you are. You can do it as often as you want. I'll see to it that you're not stopped again.'

She'd dress Jacob, then take them both back to the car and wrap Janus in the cardigan she'd left there. Slowly, methodically, she finished dressing the child who was wearing the earring. Carefully she brushed off the pine needles, the damp grass, small spikes of pine cone. He was dressed; the time had come for action.

She had no choice but to explain what had happened to Morgenstein – she could not hide the new toddler. And there was no law against cloning, after all! She would take both children to the doctor, ask him to check them both over, and then take them both home. That would be the time to explain everything to Alec. She had two children with her, and they were hers. There was no way she was going to give either of them up.

She slung her handbag over her shoulder and contemplated the two toddlers in front of her. She had to get them back to the car. How was she going to do that? She couldn't carry both of them together for any length of time, even if each one was ten pounds lighter than the Janus of a few moments ago.

A loud, ferocious bark distracted her attention away from her thoughts. Looking behind her, she saw the black and white body of a Dalmatian advancing on her. Her mind stopped functioning rationally. She snatched both children up and began to stumble, blunder across hummocky grass still wet with dew, pine needle carpet slick under her, the naked child slithery under her arm.

'Rover!' a male voice shouted, loud and commanding 'Stay, boy!'

The dog crashing at her heels stopped hounding, but still loped after her.

'Rover!' she heard again, the sound filling her mind, excluding rational thought. 'Heel, damn you, heel!'

Lisa was moving more slowly now; she couldn't go on like this. The naked toddler snaked out of her arm; she held his hand tight. She had to think. Stop and think!

'Mumumum,' he burbled at her.

She put the dressed child down as well, released her bag, sank to the ground and tried to take stock. Whether Janus was normal in the usual sense or not, he *looked* like any other toddler, he acted like one. More than that, he was identical to her other triplets, and he was her son. Could she deal with the aftermath of the world knowing he was a cloner? At least she could vouch for the fact that only these two were involved; but would her other two toddlers, safe with Betsy, escape the consequences of her decision?

Lisa pulled her knees up to her face, put her head between her hands, and wept. Great gulps of emotion welled through her. She could not help herself.

Little fingers grasping at her brought her back to the present. Straining her ears, she thought she could hear a rustling in the undergrowth, a yap that sounded oddly familiar. Was someone watching them? Startled, Lisa looked at the naked child playing with pine cones, then turned and saw the dressed child waggling away, her handbag trailing behind him. He giggled happily, his little legs, strong and fast, windmilling through the debris on the forest floor.

'Jacob!' she called. 'Wait! Wait for Mummy!'

He carried on unheeding. Irresolute, Lisa looked at the naked child who was now sitting down. She could catch the dressed child faster if she was on her own; she'd have to run and leave the other for the moment. He couldn't possibly stray far while she went after his brother. Galvanised into action, she sprinted after the small, yellow figure.

A surface root of a tree already felled trapped her left foot. She tumbled to the ground head first, momentarily stunned, then picked herself up and only dimly saw the yellow gleaming ahead, taunting her to go after him.

The child swayed on and Lisa followed him. Was there someone behind her? She had the oddest feeling she was being trailed, then concentrated once more on the child running away from her.

She saw him again, sprawled on the ground, like herself a victim of the roots. He dadadaed happily, his fall cushioned by pine needles, his little legs sticking in the air. One shoe was missing.

'You're as bad as Jansy,' Lisa gasped, grabbing the child, hitching her handbag to her left shoulder. 'That's got the car keys in it. Now then, let's go back and find Jansy.'

She picked the toddler up and tried hard to remember just where she had come from. There were no distinguishing marks; one spruce after another, all at the same stage of development, all dripping green. Was this the way?

A yellow shoe! They were stepping through the trees in the right direction. Lisa put the shoe on the child. Tiring rapidly, she put him down to walk. He dragged hard against her hand, the trees grew denser, the forest floor more slippery, less even. Lisa pulled the toddler along, ignoring his moans, looking stonily ahead, no thought now in her mind except to search for the second child.

How could she find him? What was there to lead her to him? A dog ran past her. The taut, off-white coat of a bull terrier, she noticed dimly. And she caught sight of a trouser-clad figure with the dog; he ducked into the shadows.

The child with her began to wail; he stumbled, half crawling, half dragged by her hand. Lisa panted, fatigue overwhelming her. All she had ever wanted was to be a mother, to take her children into the countryside, the woods, singing to them as they walked, hand in hand, through Hansel and Gretel land. The situation now was very different. She strained to pick up sounds that would lead her to the second toddler.

She made out the small, soft mewls of a young child crying. Jansy! Was she getting near him at last? Would she find him quickly? Would he come running up to her?

Lisa had a little lamb, his fleece was white as snow, chattered through Lisa's mind. Where was the other toddler, her little lamb?

'Jansy? Is that you, Jansy?' she called out, searching the undergrowth, peering into the shade.

A thin wail as she followed the direction of the cry.

'Jansy!' she called again hopefully, her voice becoming high and squeaky. 'Where are you, Jansy? Can you hear me?'

'*And everywhere that Lisa went, the lamb was sure to go*,' she murmured to the child with her, comforting herself. She could hear nothing but the heaving of her chest, the whining of the toddler beside her. He was tottering, hardly able to stand. She picked him up and held him close. He became quiet.

Lisa listened again; only the distant barking of dogs, the roar of traffic. No sound of crying now. Plop. She heard a big plop. They were deep in the woods, the ground was sloping downwards and she found it easier to carry the tired, almost inert, toddler. His arms embraced her neck. She kissed him.

The ground became wetter, spongier. She skirted a deep hole, almost slid down into it, and, as she wondered where she was, heard something slipping on the other side of her down, down . . . What was it? She couldn't see, she had no more energy, she let it go and sank to her knees.

The same odd, plopping sound, a yapping, something snuffling, a bark. Things falling into the pit. A stone, a squirrel scurrying nuts, a small rabbit hunted by a terrier?

There was nothing to see. The trees were dense and foreboding above her, the daylight only just filtering through. Lisa peered down into the void, through the pine-needled gloom, but could not distinguish anything. A small, keening sound, fading away. An owl? A child? Impossible to tell.

Exhausted now, no longer able to think, Lisa staggered to her feet, then reeled. How could she leave without the other child? She floundered round the trees, then noticed movement.

'Jansy?' she called again, some strength and hope returning. 'Where are you, Jansy?'

A stolid, striding shape, a gait she vaguely recognised, followed by something on all fours, slithered away from her. Not a child – much too large. A man walking his dog.

A chill shuddered through Lisa. Her head began to throb, her limbs to ache. She looked desperately round her. The trees, all the same size, waved mocking branches at her. They formed a circle of darkness which surrounded her, closed in on her, threatened to suffocate her.

A curtain crashed down on her mind. What other child? Lisa scolded herself. Jansy was with her. She had undressed him, allowed him to pee the bloating away. And he had turned into a lighter, brighter, delightful child just like her other three. He needed her to care for him, to look after him. That's what she had to do.

'You're my little lamb,' she whispered into Janus's ear. 'You're one of Lisa's little lambs.'

Resolute now, she hoisted him across her shoulders and took her bearings. 'We've got to find our way out of here,' she said. 'We'd better try to find some sort of road.' And Lisa began to walk towards the light, the path, and finally the broad avenue leading to her car.

23

'Mrs Wildmore,' Dr Morgenstein announced, affable, sweeping up to Lisa. Both hands were stretched outwards in an attitude of avuncular greeting.

Lisa shifted her toddler carefully onto her left arm and, politely, stretched out her right hand. The specialist covered it with both of his and smiled beyond her. His grey three-piece, she noticed, was immaculate. Her eyes swept to his manicured fingers. Could she now pull away her hand? Holding a weight of thirty pounds without her steadying right arm was beginning to cause problems. Lisa thrust her left hip forward in an effort to achieve balance. Looking down, she noticed Dr Morgenstein's shoes had been polished into brilliance. She pulled her hand away to stop the toddler, now leaning away from her, from falling out of her arms.

'Do sit down, Mrs Wildmore.' Dr Morgenstein motioned her to the upright chair on the far side of his desk and walked back to his seat. 'So this is the little man in trouble, is it?'

Lisa was uncomfortably aware of her muddy tights, her stained skirt. She manoeuvred the child she was holding to cover as much of her clothing as possible. The extra pair of shoes she'd had in the car gleamed incongruously clean. They were, however, out of sight.

'This is Ja-Janus,' she said, widening her mouth to cover her unease. 'He's one of my identical triplets.'

'Of course.'

'We have been rather worried about him lately. He did seem, well, sort of *bloated*,' she went on helplessly, aware that the child on her lap was nothing of the sort.

'I see,' the specialist encouraged her. 'Where, precisely, do you feel he's bloated?'

'Well, er, you see . . .' Lisa looked over the bare, polished desk at the man keenly assessing her. She watched, distracted, as his steel-rimmed glasses slid down his narrow nose.

'Yes? In your own words, Mrs Wildmore.'

'Actually,' Lisa blurted out rapidly, 'he was bloated all over until about a couple of hours ago.' She sounded feeble-minded even to herself.

'Two hours ago?'

'I stopped the car by some woods; he was crying quite a bit.' The doctor was watching her with interest. 'Well, screaming. He seemed to be in great pain.'

'I see.' He was making some notes on a pristine pad.

'His clothes seemed too tight on him. I took them off and he started peeing.'

'He hasn't been urinating as much as usual?'

Lisa searched desperately for inspiration. 'No, no; it wasn't that. He was just so bloated, but then he peed and peed and it seemed to go down.'

'I'm not quite sure that I entirely follow you, Mrs Wildmore. You've brought James along?'

'Janus.'

'Of course, Janus, yes. You've brought Janus along as an emergency because he seemed terribly bloated to you and this worried you. Is that right?'

'And he was in considerable pain, yes.' She looked at the docile child on her lap. 'And his behaviour had changed. He was becoming terribly aggressive.'

'You were sufficiently worried to seek specialist help rather than consulting your GP.'

'I've taken Janus to Dr Gilmore several times. He couldn't find anything wrong with him. I *know* there's something, but I can't pin it down. So I thought I'd bring him before the bloating subsided again.'

'It comes and goes?'

It builds up alarmingly just before he feels the urge to clone, Lisa thought grimly. But I can hardly tell you *that*.

'It seems to get worse over a period of time and sort of reaches a climax. Then it goes down again. As I said, I have mentioned it to Dr Gilmore. He suggested I get an expert opinion.'

'Of course, quite right. And you feel the child has released the extra fluid now because he urinated quite extensively on the way up here?'

'I know it sounds unlikely.'

'He could just be the type of person who holds fluids more than others.'

'His brothers are identical with him, and they don't do it.'

'No two human beings are ever exactly the same.' Dr Morgenstein pursed his lips severely. 'And of course it may just have been that he eats more salt food than the others.'

'I never use salt in cooking, I don't consider it healthy.'

'Even foods specially prepared for young children contain salt, I'm afraid. Marmite is often recommended, for example,' the specialist smiled slightly. 'So even if you don't use salt for cooking, he may have imbibed a fair amount.' Neat writing began to fill up the page in front of him.

Lisa used unsalted Marmite, and never allowed her children packaged food, but she decided to keep her nutritional knowledge to herself. Let him think she was an idiot, as long as he examined the child properly.

'But you will check him over?'

'Of course, Mrs Wildmore. I'm just making a few notes to start with. We'll give him a thorough examination, take specimens, the whole routine, in a few moments. Then you won't need to worry in the future.'

'My husband was getting worried, too,' she added.

'I can assure you I am taking the matter seriously,' the doctor told her as he rang the bell for his nurse. 'Just take, er, Jason,' he began, blinking at his notes as the nurse came in.

'Janus.'

'Janus. Get him ready for me, will you please, Miss Dobbs?'

It seemed the paediatrician was good with children. The child gurgled with pleasure throughout the whole of the half-hour check-up. He was not the Janus she had started out with that morning. That much was clear.

Twisting her wedding ring round her finger, Lisa tried thinking back to the events of the Priddy Woods. Her mind simply refused to do it. All she could picture was a small, yellow figure running away from her in the shrouded tangle of spruces.

Was Alec right? Was she the one who needed medical help, and not the toddler she had brought with her? That could not be the only explanation. Alec had also been alarmed by the bloating, had noticed the aggression. Even Betsy had admitted Janus was waterlogged.

'Nothing at all to worry about, I'm sure,' Dr Morgenstein assured Lisa suavely. 'Naturally we'll send all the samples to the laboratory.' He smiled benignly. 'A very healthy toddler, Mrs Wildmore. If you have two more like him, you're very lucky.'

'I know,' she said. 'I've got a marvellous family. And after thinking I was infertile, too!'

'You were worried about infertility?'

Had that been an unwise thing to say? 'Some years ago,' she brushed it off. 'When we were still in London.'

'You took fertility drugs?'

'About five years ago.'

'I see.' He made more notes. 'There is just one small thing.'

'Yes?'

'I see Janus wears an earring.' The paediatrician looked at her reflectively.

He thinks I'm a bit of a hippy, Lisa realised. A one-time layabout who's married a successful man.

'Is there any special reason for that?'

Lisa smiled her relief. 'Each of the triplets wears a precious metal earring in his left ear. It's just so that we can be sure of telling them apart. They really are identical, you see.'

'You mean you can't tell the difference?' He sounded interested for the first time.

'*We* can tell the difference, of course. It's to help the staff at the playschool.'

'I see. They already go to playschool.'

'They were longing to join their elder brother,' Lisa said defensively. 'Anyway, Janus wears a gold earring, Jeffrey wears platinum and James wears silver. I'm told precious metals don't cause allergies.'

'That may be true in general, Mrs Wildmore,' the doctor said gravely, 'but I do suggest you take Janus's earring off. I think you may have noticed an allergy to that. If there's no problem with the other two, you can always tell which one he is by the absence of an earring.'

Dr Morgenstein walked over to Lisa, patting Janus on the head, then put his finger on the child's left earlobe. He undid the clasp, slipped out the earring, and handed it to Lisa.

'I think you'll find that will solve your problem,' he smiled at her. 'But if you're worried again, don't hesitate to get in touch.'

Lisa slipped the earring on the small fingertip of her left hand for the second time that day, her heart missing several beats. She stood, unsteadily, to leave. The child on her arm smiled radiantly at her and clapped his hands. She was tiring rapidly.

‘I didn’t leave his walking reins with you, did I?’ she asked the receptionist as she was leaving. ‘They’re yellow, to match Jansy’s T-shirt.’

‘I don’t think you brought any in here, Mrs Wildmore.’

Morgenstein, Lisa thought as she drove home, was obviously going to ring Gilmore at the first opportunity and tell him that she, not Janus, was medically unsound. Morgenstein’s modulated, soothing voice spelled menace to her.

She looked at the smiling, dimply child strapped in his seat. He was gurgling happily, trying out the sounds of speech, the image of Jeffrey and James. This was her son Janus: her very own son. Love for him swept over her.

She must have hallucinated what she thought she had seen in the Priddy Woods, must have allowed her tears and the flickering shadows to mislead her. As for the walking reins – she’d definitely lost those. But that could have an innocent explanation. She’d simply left them where she had taken Janus’s clothes off, where she’d allowed him to pee, and then forgotten them.

She smiled radiantly. The little boy with her was perfectly normal. The doctor had said there was nothing wrong with him, been quite certain about it. Like his triplet brothers Janus was just a part of the wonderful family she’d always wanted.

Lisa sang out loud; she was completely sure she’d finally been freed from the cloner. She’d left him in the Priddy Woods, a product of her fertile imagination.

[illegible]

We'd [illegible]

[illegible] Part were [illegible]

[illegible]

we'd call in [illegible]

[illegible] searching [illegible]

[illegible] on how to [illegible]

Then [illegible]

and right [illegible]

[illegible]

24

'We watched the local news last night. Did you?'

Lisa realised with a start that the back door had opened and Frank was standing in her utility room, a wine-coloured tracksuit emphasising the paunch which had recently become quite noticeable. Phyllis and Paul were with him. He was, apparently, jogging them to Lodsham House School.

'Trying to get fit,' he explained, patting his cider belly. 'Thought we'd call in on our way and say hello. Haven't seen much of you lately.' He looked flushed, his chest heaving as he recovered his breath; he was still clutching his twins by the hands.

Lisa sensed Frank's small, currant eyes exploring her. He'd obviously come for a specific reason. She felt nervous, intensely aware of his presence and of the way he watched her every move as she directed Seb on how to put his jumper on.

'I can do it, Mummy! I always do it by myself at school.'

'All right, Seb. But you were getting your fingers caught in the threads at the back. Bestie would be upset.' Betsy Beste had hand-knitted the jumper for Sebastian.

'On HTV. They've come across the decomposing body of a young'un in an old pit. Just the remains of a bare body; no clothes nor nothing. Boy around eighteen months, they reckon.' Frank trotted out the information as though he had rehearsed it.

Lisa's hands turned to blobs of ice as she turned towards Frank. So it *had* happened. She hadn't, after all, imagined the cloning of two months ago. But why had Frank come to tell *her* this? Did he know what was going on? Is that what this visit was about? Or was it just coincidence?

Lisa tried desperately to pull herself together. She was jumping to conclusions. So there was a body; someone had come across the body of a toddler, a boy. That's all. Why should that be connected with her and her family? Unless there was a picture of the child in the local paper

. . . Heart thudding, she turned away from Frank and bent towards Seb again as he was stretching his arm through a sleeve, catching a finger on a loop of yarn.

'Make your hands into a fist, Seb.' Her voice sounded strangely squeaky, and she saw Seb look curiously at her. Her freezing hands felt numb; instead of pulling the child's arm out of the sleeve she made matters worse, puckering the loosely knitted fabric. She could not stop herself from looking over her shoulder. Frank's eyes, fixed on her back, were waiting for further reactions. That's why he hadn't phoned, she knew at once; he wanted to see how his news affected her. The narrowed, questing eyes surged fury through her, pumped blood. What was he playing at? He might suspect what was going on, but he couldn't possibly substantiate it. Nor would he want to. It would draw public attention to what had happened on his farm when he had tested out the original strain of Multiplier. Lisa stood tall, squaring her shoulders, and lifted her chin defiantly. He was bluffing, trying to flush her out. But why?

'No one's come forward, well *someone* must be missing their little'un and not said about it.'

Seb pulled his sleeve on for himself. 'Why didn't he have any clothes on, Uncle Frank? It's cold today.'

'We'll be late, Seb,' Lisa said briskly. 'Hurry up and get your anorak on.' She saw Frank was still staring at her and faced him out. 'Completely naked, did you say? Wouldn't that suggest one of those ghastly, well, child abuse cases?' She dropped her voice and motioned her head towards Seb, to indicate that he was listening. 'You know what I mean.'

'Arr, could be.' The eyes had sunk away.

She smiled at his retreat. He'd expected her to show fear, to give him the chance to bully her. She gathered three pairs of shoes into stiff hands, still anxious, feeling Frank's truculence.

'How are the triplets? None of us has seen them for a while.'

'Same as ever, hard work.'

'All right then, are they? Getting on well?'

'Come and see for yourself,' Lisa said coolly. 'They're with Alec in the kitchen, waiting for me to get them ready.

'Apparently,' Lisa said to Alec as Frank followed her, 'Frank's called to tell us about a rather odd snippet on the local news. They've found the body of a toddler in the Priddy Woods.'

'I never said that!' Frank said. 'Whatever made you reckon that?'

Lisa stopped short, the blood draining from her brain. 'Didn't you just say—'

'I never said nothing about Priddy Woods. I said they'd found the remains of a toddler in an old pit.'

Lisa swallowed hard. '*Lift* your leg, Jansy, don't kick.' She was squatting, her back to Frank, putting the triplets' shoes on, grasping their feet and pushing hard. Frank had followed her right into the kitchen, still holding on to his twins.

'Hello, Frank. We don't often see you at this hour.'

'Morning, Alec. Just purdled in to let you know the news. Makes us worry about the young'uns playing on their own.' He walked closer to Lisa. 'Weren't Priddy. It were farther down; Milton way. Could have been dragged from the Priddy side; that's more than likely, the police reckon. State the body's in, they say he been mauled about a fair bit.'

'Mauled about?'

'One of those dogs folk make pets of; maybe a stray, maybe an old lady walking her pet, not keeping proper control.'

'Foxhounds again?' Alec asked, startled.

'No, not hounds,' Frank said. 'More like a terrier. Warwickshire bull or suchlike.' He saw Alec frown. 'Could be a grockle, allowing animals to roam. Foreigners don't seem to know what they're dealing with. A dog's instinct is to hunt.'

Lisa noted that Frank still liked to blame local problems on tourists, or recently arrived residents.

'Can they be as specific as that?' Alec asked. 'A child killed by a terrier?'

'Not a feature left in his face, body completely mangled, the police say. But they've not said nothing about whether he were dead when the dog got hold of him.'

'It was a he, then? They were able to identify a boy?'

'They can tell from the bones. There was nothing else for them to get a hold of. Too young for proper teeth. Nothing they could identify.' He paused dramatically. Lisa could feel his eyes on her. 'Apart from a pair of unusual walking reins nearby. Yellow ones.'

Lisa's mind skimmed rapidly back over what had happened the day she'd driven Janus to see Morgenstein. She had lost Janus's yellow walking reins – but nowhere near Milton; she hadn't stopped there. She must have left them in the Priddy Woods, where she'd undressed the child. That proved that the body mentioned on HTV news could not have anything to do with her. But she still couldn't stop her shoulders trembling a shudder.

'It sounds horrific.' Alec, unaware of possible implications, looked over the top of his *Financial Times.* 'Still, we can't go by that bit of evidence,' he went on. 'We lost a pair ourselves a little while ago. But we haven't lost a child.' He chuckled. 'Not at the last count, anyway.' He put his paper down and smiled amiably. 'That's a very exciting item of news for such a quiet area. But someone must be missing a toddler and presumably will come forward to say so.'

'Not up to now.'

'Perhaps a visitor to the area.'

'Grockles? And didn't get on to the police?'

'It's a strange old world,' Alec said easily. 'Do excuse me, Frank. I've got to rush.'

If Lisa hoped that would be the end of the matter, she was wrong.

'They do seem to be getting more alike, not less,' Frank remarked. 'I could swear Jansy were much fatter than the other two last time I saw him. And he looks much more like Jeffers.'

'You're quite right.' Lisa bent towards her triplets, lifting them off the bench. 'He was. Not really fat, actually. Sort of bloated.' She smiled engagingly at Frank. 'He had an allergy, the specialist said.'

'Oh, arr.'

She shepherded the triplets towards the pushchair. 'You haven't come across them for some time, Frank. Most people think they all look alike – peas in a pod, they always say.'

'You're forgetting, Lisa. I've known them since they were born.' He knelt down by the children. 'Jiminy is easy to spot – delicate, like. But Jansy and Jeffers seem almost identical.' He looked back at Lisa over his shoulder, his eyes fine slits. 'Now I remember Jansy as quite different somehow. Bit of a bruiser, if you don't mind me saying. Both these two are sweet as pie; even the one with the gold ring.'

The one? He was pointing at Jeffrey. What was he trying to say?

'Just growing up, I expect. Dr Morgenstein says the result of the allergy could easily have been aggression.'

'You'd reckon he were an entirely different child,' Frank said laconically.

Lisa laughed grimly to herself. She only wished that Frank was right and she had a non-cloning child with her. The one she'd taken to see Morgenstein, she was quite clear, was Janus.

'Dr Morgenstein wanted us to leave off Jansy's earring.' She smiled at Frank again. 'But I'm happier if they all wear earrings, or we don't bother with any of them,' she went on, careful to keep her voice even and unexcited. 'We don't want Jansy to think of himself as different from the others.'

It sounded hypocritical, even to herself. She knew, better than anyone else, that Janus was very different indeed. The question was, what did Frank know? He couldn't *know*, Lisa repeated anxiously to herself. He could suspect, because of what was happening on his farm, and he could be trying to find out more. But why was he concerning himself with her children all of a sudden?

'So what I thought,' she confided, 'was that I'd swap them round: platinum for Jansy, gold for Jeffers. Sorry if that confused you,' she added genially. 'It wasn't meant for that.'

Was she imagining it, or was there anger in Frank's attitude?

'So you decided to play tricks?' he said. 'Can't make a fool of me! I knew right away that there were something different.'

'Looks like that paediatrician was actually worth his money. He seems to have worked out the problem for poor old Jansy,' Lisa said smoothly. 'Fancy an allergy causing a change in personality.' She straightened up and began to manhandle the pushchair towards the drive. 'We'd better go or we'll be late.'

Frank dusted his knees off and planted himself directly in front of the chair. 'Best give you a hand,' he said, walking round and grasping the handle. 'Want to watch out going down the drive; quite a drop there. The three of them are heavy now, the pushchair could run away with you.'

'I keep the brake on,' Lisa said, but let him take the pushchair. She took Seb's hand in hers, then looked around for Phyllis and Paul. 'You take Seb's hand,' she instructed the little boy and held Phyllis with her other hand. The child looked strained; she seemed to drag her bad foot more than Lisa remembered.

The rumble of a lorry coming up the lane behind them made Lisa pull the three children onto the safety of the verge. She expected Frank to do the same with the pushchair.

'Get to the side, Frank! The milk tanker's coming up fast!'

He stopped, but it seemed to Lisa that he made no effort at all to move the pushchair out of the way. In fact he seemed to be turning it into the road. She dropped the children's hands and leaped over, tugged the handle down away from Frank and dragged the chair back towards the verge. The tanker lumbered past with inches to spare.

'No need to panic, they're good drivers,' Frank said, standing stolid, looking her full in the face. He turned to the triplets again. 'They're identicals, right?' he continued, stepping aside and looking at them searchingly. 'Means they're equal genetically. You'll probably get the same trouble with Jeffers.' He stopped in front of the school gates. 'Leave you here,' he said. 'I'm going on.'

'Hello, Frank.' Geraldine was tripping down towards the gates. Her long, slim legs were displayed almost to her hips but, Lisa noted, her feet were shod in low-heeled, though stylish, leather boots.

'Morning, Gerry. You're smartish on the job.'

'Bit of a flap on. Three new children this week. Anne asked me to come in early to help her out.' She grinned at Lisa, no doubt to show how indispensable she was to her new employer. Then she turned to Frank. 'No Land Rover this morning?'

'Keeping fit.'

'You? Since when?'

'Got to get started somewhen.' He waved at her as he started off.

'Will you be over as usual later? What about the—'

'All taken care of, Gerry,' Frank interrupted, voice loud, drowning Geraldine's soprano. 'No need for you to worry none.' And he loped off without another word.

It struck Lisa as odd that Frank and Geraldine should be on such friendly terms. Geraldine stared uncertainly after the departing figure, then turned towards the children. 'Come on, you lot.' She took the large pushchair over from Lisa. 'You're wanted on parade!'

Anne Marsden had taken to having a sort of assembly now that her numbers had grown.

'Frank says there's been some horrifying news on HTV,' Lisa said, walking beside the girl, watching Geraldine's expression. 'The body of a toddler found near Milton.' She paused, seeing Seb looking up at her.

'He had no clothes on,' Seb said.

Geraldine's long legs strode on, her face turned away. 'Uncle Nige rang last night,' she called back over her shoulder. 'It sounded really gruesome.' She continued pushing the pushchair. 'Hurry up,' she shouted to the children. 'You'll be late!'

Lisa kept up with her, helping Phyllis. 'Thought you'd have worked out a theory, Gerry. You're always reading those mystery stories.' Somehow she had to try to find out if anything else had been reported – Geraldine would surely have gathered all the facts together. 'Slow down a bit,' she said, determined on an answer. 'Phyllis is having trouble keeping up.'

Geraldine turned, holding out a hand to Phyllis.

'Did they mention if there was anything with the child, something that might identify him?' Lisa went on as casually as she could. Her voice, still somewhat breathy, purred pleasantly. 'Good test of your deductive powers.'

The girl shrugged, apparently not interested. 'Uncle Nige said there was nothing, absolutely nothing at all. Not a stitch of clothing, not even a scrap of anything nearby. A real puzzler.'

Lisa was sifting her impressions, trying to evaluate what she'd been told. Something was very wrong somewhere; she couldn't quite put her finger on it, but she could sense it. Reluctantly she waved goodbye, about to leave.

The vigorous, assertive barking of a dog made her stop, tense, an odd jolt of memory coming back. That bark; she'd heard that bark before. Instinctively she turned to sprint towards her children. Janus was brandishing his left arm at Duffers. The terrier jumped at it, excited now, the barks turning into snarls. James, Lisa noticed at once, had begun to whimper, and Jeffrey leaned away. But Janus, apparently unafraid, pummelled the dog's snout with the metal aeroplane clutched in his right hand, lunging at Duffers's eyes. Lisa drew in her breath as she pitched towards the dog, aware of danger.

'Sit, Duffers!' Geraldine shouted, alerted in her turn.

Too late. The dog, provoked by the child, followed Janus's arm as he pointed it towards the wheels. The terrier jumped, seizing the arm in his flews, his paws on child and pushchair.

Geraldine snatched the dog's collar as Lisa, plunging forward, galvanised the pushchair into explosive movement. Janus, his left arm grabbed by the terrier's teeth, swiped with his right. Swirling the metal toy, he jabbed again at the terrier's eyes. The animal, his jaws round the sleeve of the yellow anorak, felt the attack from all sides and began to clamp his teeth, shaking his rear from side to side, then yelped raucous barks in sudden pain as he felt his paw trapped in the turning wheel. He let go of Janus.

Reluctant memories of Priddy came flooding back to Lisa: flashes of something buff-coloured, light, streaking through the dark spruces. Had Geraldine and her bull terrier followed her that day? That was absurd. She really was letting her imagination take over. Geraldine, she knew perfectly well, had been at Anne's, doing her job. But *someone* had been following her, she was sure of that now. And there had been a dog; the fleeting look she'd caught could have been a bull terrier. They were the sort of dogs who mauled their quarry.

'Get *down*, Duffers!' Lisa screamed at him, incensed and outraged. 'Down!' She kicked the dog hard to one side and bent to Janus.

'What's going on?' Anne was running towards them. She turned to Geraldine. 'What's Duffers doing here? You know he isn't allowed. Did he snap at one of the triplets?'

Lisa looked up to see a flash of fury as Geraldine turned to Anne. 'Jansy trapped his paw in the wheel!' the girl shouted, gathering the dog into her arms. 'He wouldn't begin to hurt one of the children. He's gentle as a lamb when he's not hunting.'

'He's *bitten* Jansy!' Lisa exploded, lifting Janus out of the pushchair, holding him to herself protectively, stroking his head.

'Only because his paw was trapped!'

Anne was already by Lisa's side. 'Jansy's been bitten?'

'I think the anorak took the brunt of it,' Lisa said, recovering, examining Janus's arm. The toddler, she noticed, showed neither fear nor pain; it was almost as though he'd provoked the dog deliberately. She levered the coat off carefully. The sleeve of his jumper showed no blood, but as she pushed it back, Janus rubbed his arm. Lisa could see tiny pinpricks of toothmarks on the smooth skin. Her heart sank; his flesh had begun to swell again.

'I'm sorry, Anne; I've got to get him to a doctor. I don't think it's serious but he could be infected.'

'Come in, my dear. Of course. I'll give the surgery a ring.' She turned to Geraldine. 'Lock Duffers away, Gerry. In the scullery. He's to be nowhere near the children, you know that perfectly well.'

Why wasn't Anne demanding the dog be sent away for good? Lisa thought angrily. Why was he here in the first place? He'd attacked Janus! And Anne had no right to have a bull terrier with children in a playschool. Was Anne condoning the animal's behaviour? Kowtowing to the Fitch-Templetons, no doubt, because she was running a business.

Something sinister was going on, Lisa was sure of it. She even had the distinct feeling that Frank had tried to push the triplets in front of the lorry earlier on.

Things were getting out of hand. It was much more dangerous than she had imagined. Janus was being stalked. Overwhelming waves of maternal feeling drowned out rational thought. She had to protect her little boy. She had to take Janus away, keep him safe. Her child, she realised with a start, could be in mortal danger. And his triplet brothers were sufficiently like him to be in danger too.

'It's no good, Anne. I'm really shattered. I'm taking the children home again.' She watched Janus's reaction, saw his eyes gleam their understanding. He knew; he knew quite well that she was about to remove him from the chase.

'Why not leave the others, Lisa? They'll be perfectly safe.'

Lisa turned the triple pushchair round and headed towards the gate. 'I'm not leaving any of them here today,' she said, as calmly as she could, her voice tremulous. 'I'm afraid all this has made me very nervous. I'll give you a ring later.' She took Seb's hand. 'Come along Seb. No school today.'

And as she walked her children home, Lisa thought again of Frank's strange visit, his oddly threatening attitude to her. Of course the body talked about on the news couldn't have any connection with her – that child had been found in Milton, several miles away from where she'd been. But something nagged at her, something that Frank had said, something that didn't quite fit.

'You're going too fast, Mummy!' Seb said, trotting beside her, trying to keep up.

She slowed her pace, relived again the feeling in the woods. Dark spruces, all identical, brooding overhead. A running dog, the plop of something falling, the snuffling, scurrying sound . . . She brought herself back to her children.

'Sorry, Seb,' she sighed at him. 'We're almost home.'

How could she convince Alec that she had to keep the children at home again for their own safety? Not all of them, of course. Only Janus. He was the cloner; he was the one they were after, the one who could betray the secret. He was the target. It was Janus she had to safeguard, to keep away from everyone. She knew that now.

25

'You want to take them out of playschool?' Alec stared at her, his mouth open. 'I thought the whole point was that their going gave you time to yourself.' He paused for a few seconds. 'Did Anne say she wouldn't get rid of Duffers?'

Lisa was feeling desperate. She had to keep Janus at home, and yet she couldn't explain why to Alec – that would just confirm his conviction that she was unstable. The way he was looking at her, his general attitude, convinced Lisa that he was wondering how to persuade her to see a psychiatrist. She had to be careful, try to sound both reasonable and yet convince him that her concern was genuine.

'She didn't say one way or the other. She told Geraldine to lock him up, and that she'd deal with it later.'

'So? Presumably she has.' His eyes flashed impatience.

'They're too much for her.'

'They? What on earth d'you mean by "they"?' Impatience was turning to irritation.

'The boys.'

'Jansy teased Duffers; animals taken to playschools have to be prepared to put up with that. What have the others done?'

'People lump them together.'

'We hardly need to encourage that,' Alec said dryly. 'Anyway, don't be so absurd. The woman's looking after twenty children under five. The fact that four of them are ours is neither here nor there. She can either cope with her job, or she can't.'

Lisa looked directly at Alec, her face the bland mask she'd cultivated now for almost two years, ever since the 'birth' of James. 'Even if she can, I can't cope with the strain. Janus is getting aggressive again, belligerent. As soon as he spotted Duffers he enticed the dog to him, tricked him into grabbing at his arm. Then he thumped him, deliberately pushed the metal toy into the dog's eye. Geraldine knows that, and she'll tell Anne.'

'You're being utterly ridiculous, Lisa. There was a small accident; unfortunate, but simply an accident. Jansy came to very little harm, and Duffers wasn't seriously hurt. Just bad luck that his paw got caught.'

Lisa tried a different tack. 'Jansy could have been badly bitten. That's a bull terrier, you know. Those dogs can be quite fierce. Extraordinary that such a young child is capable of handling him.' She couldn't help a smile of pride in her brave son. 'Jansy's incredibly strong and daring. Geraldine was quite shaken up.'

Alec was frowning. 'Duffers will have to go. I quite agree he shouldn't have been allowed at the school in the first place.'

'Of course he'll have to go! That's not the point. Anne knows what Jansy intended. She's always made allowances for him, she thinks the world of him, but I don't think she's up to handling him. You know what I'm talking about, you've seen it all before, Alec. The boy's getting back into his combative phase. This time he took it out on Duffers. I'm worried about what he'll get up to next.'

'He's a small child, Lisa, pig-headed, stubborn, not a sadist out to get innocent people or animals. You've said it often enough; that dog can be quite mean. Perhaps he started it.'

'Jansy gauged it exactly right. He may be small . . .' She stopped, considering this. 'Well, relatively small. He's incredibly strong for his age, and he's retaining fluid again.'

'You haven't put the gold earring back?'

'I've left that one on Jeffers. That isn't the problem. What really matters is the way he can work things out. He's only twenty months, and he's way ahead of most people.'

'You'll tell me next he's superman,' Alec said crossly. 'Honestly, darling, you're carrying this too far. It's got to stop.' He was pacing up and down the room, his face away from hers. 'I've asked you to have a word with Gilmore—'

'Do me a favour, Alec. Gilmore! What on earth d'you think *he* could do?'

'For a start he could give you a mild sedative. What I'd like to see him do is refer you to a psychiatrist.' He walked towards her, stretching out his arms. 'You're in trouble, darling, truly. You need help.'

She backed away from him. What could she do? He was reacting to her again, rather than to the situation with Janus. 'Oh, Alec. You think it's all me, but it isn't, you know.' Her distress was evident in her trembling voice. She took a deep breath, determined to sound sensible. 'Just think why we decided to get in touch with Morgenstein in the first place. Then think what happened about the dog. Janus did trap Duffers's paw in the wheels, you know. And what about the way he managed to sabotage Anne's eggs?' Janus had stolen into the kitchen and pulled the weekly supply of eggs to the floor. Not satisfied with that, he'd stamped on them; trampled them into smithereens.

Alec tried again to approach her, to put his arms round her, to try and hold her to him, she supposed. She had to get her point across, not be sidetracked away from it. She moved away towards the window and started pulling the curtains shut.

'He didn't sabotage them, Lisa. All he did was pull the trays down from the kitchen table.'

'Intentionally. He knows the kitchen's out of bounds.'

'It isn't going to be dark for a couple of hours, why are you closing out the light?'

'I'm just getting them to hang straight.' She shook the heavy material impatiently.

A cloud of dust brought on a fit of sneezing in Alec. He blew his nose. 'The business with the eggs was something that could easily have happened with any of the children. I'd say it was more Anne's fault than Jansy's. She had no right to let them be unsupervised anywhere, let alone get into the kitchen on their own.'

'That's exactly what I've been trying to tell you, Alec. She isn't up to looking after Janus.' Sweet reason wasn't going to work; she might as well sound as obsessive as he thought she was. 'I'm keeping him at home,' she announced, abrupt and with finality. She swished the curtains apart and crashed open the sash window. 'The others can continue to go to school, I'll look after Jansy myself. Then I'll *know* there won't be any more problems.'

He looked hard at her, shrugged. 'There is one thing you might be right about,' he said.

'You think I might actually be right about something?'

'Do stop being so hostile, Lisa. I'm only trying to do my bit. I wish you wouldn't exclude me so.' He smiled at her, tentatively putting out his hands again. She stood rigid by the window. 'What I mean is, Janus is definitely puffing up again, rather quickly at that. Perhaps he's allergic to the platinum as well. I told you we ought to leave him without an earring.'

'My fault again!'

'I didn't mean it that way. What I suggest is that *I* take him to Morgenstein this time. If he's allergic to both metals, it's more than just a simple allergy.' He paused, looking at her, evidently uncertain. 'There could be another problem, Lisa.'

'Such as?'

'The child could be autistic.'

Lisa laughed at that. 'My goodness, Alec, autism shows itself by lack of verbal communication. Janus is pretty good at expressing himself!' As though she hadn't considered such matters; as though, in a sense, she wouldn't welcome a known disorder. 'Anyway, the great man's already spoken, and the tests were negative. There's nothing wrong with Janus, physically or mentally. It's all my fertile imagination.' She turned and laughed again; an unsteady laugh.

'Do be fair, pet. You said yourself the bloating had gone down by the time you got to the paediatrician. The boy's coming up to it again. I'll make an appointment. He won't evade the issue with me.'

There was nothing further to say as far as Lisa was concerned. She felt fairly confident that the doctor would insist on the usual three weeks before an appointment. Alec could hardly plead an emergency. And meanwhile – meanwhile she'd work something out to safeguard the child. All her instincts told her he was in danger; real, physical danger.

Alec cleared his throat. He seemed apprehensive. 'You might just bear in mind that Morgenstein did suggest it was an allergy, he didn't dismiss the whole thing out of hand.' He smiled, then started sneezing again. 'We'd better take the earring off Janus,' he finally brought out.

'No!' It was out before she could stop herself.

'You're reacting completely over the top,' Alec said slowly, almost gently. 'You must see that. What possible difference can it make? After all, there's no mistaking which one he is.'

An ear-piercing scream managed to infiltrate through the thick walls, followed by a chorus of lesser sounds. Lisa sprinted for the door, only to be restrained by Alec.

'Mother is with them, Lisa. She'll manage.'

Putting his arm round her shoulders, he steered her through to the conservatory and out, over to the children playing in the sandpit.

'Hello, Mummy. Jansy's been naughty,' Seb said as soon as he saw them. 'Granny said he had to play by himself.'

Alec looked at Lisa triumphantly and walked over to Janus. The child was standing just outside the sandpit, rhythmically smashing his toy aeroplane against the terrace stone.

'No, Jansy,' Alec said, removing the toy. Carefully, deliberately, he undid the clasp of the platinum earring and slipped it out of the child's ear.

Lisa stared at the ring, now disappearing into Alec's wallet. What could she do? She'd have to check on Janus constantly. The child, she realised dimly, her mind racing her instincts, was unlikely to undress himself during the day. At night she'd go into the nursery and clamp something onto him. She'd have to think the problem through at leisure, when Alec was out of the way.

'And Mother's very keen to give you a day to yourself, you know. I wish you'd take up her offer.'

Sarah Wildmore was staying for several days. She looked up from the sandcastle she was perfecting. 'Why not have tomorrow off, Lisa? Really, I'll be happy to take the boys on. And Betsy won't mind helping me, I know.'

'You're not used to it, Sarah. It will wear you out.'

Sarah laughed good-naturedly. 'You think I'm too old. Well, even at the advanced age of fifty plus I ought to be able to cope for a day!'

Lisa gave in to her mother-in-law, relieved that Betsy was prepared to help out on a weekday morning. She'd drive to Bath, look in on the Touchstone Gallery. They were really doing well with her watercolours.

In any case, there was one thing she could rely on: Sarah would not allow Janus to take his clothes off. Besides, he wasn't critically swollen yet. Lisa felt pretty confident that he was not yet ready to clone again.

Queen Square car park was only a few minutes' walk from the Touchstone Gallery. Lisa's heels clicked briskly as she hurried through crowds of ambling tourists. Bath was overflowing with visitors; Trevor was absolutely right to place her pictures here.

'Do you need any help?' a young woman asked her as soon as she'd opened vast Georgian doors and walked through.

'Just looking,' Lisa said, smiling.

She tried to see 'Heron Among the Willows' as though she'd never come across if before. Windswept willows lining a river, two herons standing on its bank, a third scooping fish, Glastonbury Tor outlined behind them – pastel colours, a gentle, English light. Time to make a change; time to show the truth behind the pretty façade.

She saw the willows change shape. Thrusting green shoots turned into gnarled, broken branches weeping towards a sodden, murky whirl of overflowing banks. Leaden skies stretched into drab fields turned into pools reflecting grey. Earth colours instead of pastel; almost monochrome. Blasts of ashen air across the moor; cattle hump-backed against the wind, resigned to mud.

'That's a Wildmore,' the girl said, coming up behind her. 'She's one of our most successful artists. Lives locally, you know. Down near Wells. She specialises in scenes of the Somerset Levels.'

'I see,' Lisa said dutifully.

'They're still very modestly priced,' the girl went on. 'That won't last long now. They're simply walking off the walls, so the values are bound to rise. This one's available for twelve hundred pounds – a bargain.'

Lisa's face reddened. 'I'm sorry,' she turned to the assistant. 'I should have introduced myself—'

'Lisa!'

The door leading to the back of the gallery had opened. At first Lisa could not distinguish who had greeted her. A silhouette of a man, quite young, bejewelled, elegantly dressed, preceded a shorter figure.

'Darling! Why didn't you let me know?' Trevor stepped forward, rushing his arms at her, planting a kiss on one cheek, then the other.

'Trev! I'd no idea you were going to be in Bath.' She grinned, delighted. 'I'm on parole. My mother-in-law is coping – or at least I hope she is. Last-minute decision; couldn't resist popping in.'

'Marvellous, darling. Now let me introduce you to one of your most ardent fans. This is Leo – Leo Blanchet. You've spoken on the telephone.'

'What fun!' Leo greeted her, wine-coloured velvet blazer toning an iridescent tie. 'So this is my best-selling artist.' Melting black eyes examined Lisa openly under raised brows. 'Pretty as a picture.'

Trevor's laugh neighed round reechoing walls. 'Leo's just taken over the Touchstone. His little place in Albemarle Street is overflowing, so he's branching out.'

'Fancied the West Country,' Leo tossed in. 'Bath is perfection. Good for the Festival, as well. Are you a devotee?'

'Only in theory at the moment,' Lisa explained. 'I'm rather taken up at home.'

Leo's eyes slid away. 'Of course.'

'You'll join us for lunch?' Trevor said eagerly. 'I'm sure you'll know the best place for us to go.'

Lisa could see the velvet ripple as irritation stiffened Leo's shoulders. 'That's sweet of you, Trev. Actually, I was thinking of—'

'We really must celebrate. After all, Lis, much of the success is down to you!' Trevor, standing between them, placed his arms round both sets of shoulders. 'I know you two have loads in common.'

Leo's nose lengthened perceptibly. 'Provided you can steer us to a good place for lunch,' he said, eyes cold. 'Can't abide hormone-laden roast with soggy veg. Can Bath provide something wholesome *and* exotic?'

'Bath can do better than most,' Lisa said. 'The Hole in the Wall's only five minutes' walk from here. A choice of vegetarian main courses, fish or game, all organic. I'm sure you'll approve.' She looked at Leo carefully. 'But if you prefer something more theatrical, you could try Popjoys.'

'Done that,' he said. 'Not bad; teensy bit trad.'

'Then try the Hole,' Lisa said, stalking out of the gallery. 'I'll point you in the right direction.'

'Hold on.' Leo ran after her. 'Sounds really good!' He twirled himself in front of her, bowing low. 'Do come, we'll make a real party of it.' The black coals blazed over her, dancing approval.

Lisa led the way across Queen Square, up Gay Street towards the Circus. She was struck again by the brilliance of honey-coloured stone curved to reflect the light. One day she must catch that. 'Across to George Street,' she told them, pointing right, jay-walking the busy road and sprinting on. 'Up these steps, the entrance on your left.'

Sinking into the lounge easy chairs, Lisa agreed happily to champagne. 'We really do have something to celebrate,' Trevor said. 'Leo signed the papers this morning.'

'So, tell me about yourself.' Leo's fingers flashed several rings. A large opal caught Lisa's eye. 'Like it? Belonged to my aged pa. Died recently.'

'I'm sorry.'

'No need. Alzheimer's took him some years ago. Blessed release.' The dark eyes grew deep. 'The stone lived up to its name. Opals always shine brighter on the dying. Positively gleamed last time I saw the old roué.'

'So what's the news from pastures green?' Trevor was already reading the menu. 'I see they're quite inventive on vegetarian, Leo.'

'Too green, perhaps,' Lisa said. 'Thought I'd pop into the reference library before I head back.'

'Planning on using new pigments?'

Lisa smiled. 'I do feel stale. Thought I'd try earth colours. More of a sombre mood.' She turned her shoulders briskly towards Leo. 'Hope it won't ruin sales, but I mustn't get into a rut.' She twisted back to

Trevor. 'I wasn't actually thinking about pigments when I said green.' She twiddled the stem of her glass, fizzing the bubbles. 'They're overdoing the fertiliser bit, in my opinion. The grass looks – unnatural, somehow. Too much cerulean blue.' She looked for a response, but Trevor had lifted the menu and blotted her out.

Leo's black eyes leaped into brilliance. 'You've decided to check up on them?'

'Exactly. Our neighbours' farm is the testing site for a new organic product.'

'Trev was telling me, said you weren't mad keen.'

'There's just too much of everything. "Bain't natural" is the local expression.'

'The venison looks good, or there's saddle of hare,' Trevor interrupted loudly.

'Too much?' Leo folded his menu and beckoned to the waiter. 'Like your triplets, you mean?' He said it softly, almost purring it.

Lisa froze. 'I was thinking of the farm animals.' Her feet, crossed casually at the ankles, flexed into pointed toes.

'The grass is as green as a peacock's preen?' Leo suggested, not smiling.

'Exactly,' Lisa agreed. 'Emerald green. It's even crept into my paintings. The untreated moors are actually a somewhat drab colour, khaki mixed with gull grey.'

The waiter was hovering beside them. 'So, are we ready to order?' Trevor swished his menu shut. 'What's for you, Lisa?'

'That's what's really bugging me,' Lisa told them. She took several gulps of her champagne. 'I think the fertiliser doesn't just increase the desirable. The kittens, for instance—'

'How about starting with the brandade of smoked mackerel?' Trevor interrupted, then turned to the waiter. 'That good?'

'Speciality of the house, sir. Mr Perry-Smith's original recipe.'

'Very nice, thank you.' Lisa turned back to Leo. 'The litters are much bigger. And I know cats start out blind, and that's perfectly normal, but we rescued one from a rather large litter a neighbour was going to drown and it had a lot of trouble with its eyesight right from the start. It keeps getting worse. The poor thing's virtually blind now.'

'Leo?'

'The brandade will be fine. And you think the fertiliser contributed to that, somehow?'

'Followed by venison moussaka?'

'Sounds delicious, Trev. You order,' Leo said, turning back to Lisa. 'How, precisely?'

'It seems to aggravate defects – that's my theory, anyway. The mother cat was swimming in local milk.'

'Not *Silent Spring*, more of an *Overabundant Autumn*?'

'So you've read Rachel Carson. You'll know exactly what I'm talking about then. It's possible that overdoing the fertiliser could have worse consequences than the poisoning nightmare she described.'

'"The sedge is withered from the lake,/

And no birds sing."'

'*You're* quoting Keats?' Trevor sounded almost animated as he turned to Leo. 'I thought you said you only read modern poetry?'

'It's as though he wrote it for us.' Leo turned back to Lisa. 'You think that excess could overburden the ecology, make us obese on a planetary scale?'

'A graphic way of putting it, but yes, I do. Most people assume more is better. It could, in fact, be catastrophic.'

'Come on, you two. If we could concentrate on the wine?'

'We trust you implicitly, Trev.'

'I just wanted to see what the genetic section might have on—'

'For goodness sake! You're being really boring. This is supposed to be a celebration.'

'Sorry, Trev.'

'Look behind you, Leo. That's a fabulous collection of horse brasses.'

'What?' Leo turned round to look behind him, then stood. 'They are exciting, aren't they?'

A large collection of amulets, showing their pedigree by traces of constant cleaning, were displayed over the whole surface of the wall.

'Any good horseflesh in your area, Lisa? Your hunting scenes are much prized, so presumably there's some good sport.'

'Actually,' Lisa said, the noise of clattering hooves coming into her mind, 'Frank Graftley breeds hunters. Very successful at the local point-to-points.'

'I really must come down to visit you,' Leo said, walking back. 'I'm in the market for a hunter.'

'Frank has some outstanding breeding stock. But I have to warn you, many of his foals go lame.'

'No lucky horseshoes?' Leo raised neat eyebrows. 'I thought that was the big protection.'

'Perhaps they nailed them with the ends pointing down, and the luck's run out,' Trevor suggested, laughing heartily. 'Let's address the positive. This mackerel is outstanding.'

Horseshoes – *that's* why Frank, who'd killed off everything else on his farm, could get away with selling, not killing, the foals. They couldn't clone, of course. They were shod, permanently tagged in their own, unique way.

'Perhaps you'll invite me down sometime. The country sounds intriguing.' Leo smiled at Lisa, calling the waiter to order wine. 'Better make the most of venison while it's still from the wild.'

Janus needed something like a horseshoe, some sort of equivalent, to stop him cloning. He was an innocent victim, doomed to clone in the way thalidomide victims were doomed to have stunted limbs. Was there an antidote? The earring hadn't stopped the bloating, or the aggression. What triggered actual cloning, anyway? And would it continue throughout Janus's life?

'What about the Fleury '85?'

'Sounds perfect,' Lisa said. 'Of course you must come down to see us. Next time Trevor drives down, come with him.'

'Jansy really is a handful,' Alec's mother greeted her as soon as she returned. 'He pushed Jiminy into the mud by the drain. Quite dangerous, Betsy says. A sort of mini quicksand.' She smiled apologetically. 'I'm afraid we're short one blue boot. And while we were dragging Jiminy out, a whole lot of cows started towards us, would you believe.'

Lisa smiled, relieved at Sarah's ignorance. 'Not cows, Sarah, bullocks – steers, as they call them locally. Nothing to worry about there. They're just curious, or think someone's come along to give them extra food.'

'You could have fooled us!' Sarah flopped onto a sofa, tossed off her shoes and stretched her legs out along the seat. 'Betsy and I were quite worried.' She wiggled her toes.

'Worried? Why? What happened?'

'The whole lot started to move towards the children—'

'I told you, they thought they were bringing them some extra food.'

'Kind of bearing down on them, snorting and beginning to trot. We'd just pulled Jiminy out, and were quite a few yards away. Betsy left Jiminy to it and began to run towards the animals, trying to head them off, hollering as she went. It would have been funny if I hadn't been so nervous. I shouted at Jiminy to stay where he was and rushed after her, shrieking as loudly as I could.'

'You really were worried.'

'That's when the most extraordinary part of it happened. Jansy picked up a fallen branch and brandished it at them. It was really quite a big one, I couldn't believe he could lift it. But he did. He not only lifted it, he bashed one of the animals on the nose. It stopped the brute in its tracks.' A brittle laugh, a deep breath. 'You should have seen it. It stopped and stared, then backed. Jansy took another swing at it, while Betsy and I were panting and shouting just behind him, and they all turned tail.' She finished up out of breath. 'I could use a stiff drink.'

Lisa poured out a Malvern and malt.

'Easy on the water.' Sarah drank deep. 'So the child isn't all bad. An excess of energy, I take it. When's Alec taking him to the specialist?'

'In a couple of weeks.'

'The sooner the better, I suppose. Not that I'd want anyone to break his spirit or anything like that. Sorry, Lis. I'd put it all down to your being neurotic but the child really is quite – well, let's say difficult. Betsy made all kinds of excuses for him, but the fact is he pushed Jiminy deliberately. I saw him do it.'

A scheme was beginning to form in Lisa's mind. 'He's going through a bad patch,' she dismissed the incident. 'Whatever that specialist maintains, there's something physically wrong and it's bothering the child. More than an allergy, I mean.'

'You think you know what the problem is?'

'I think it may be earache.'

'Earache? You mean that bit of infection he sometimes gets?'

'The nurse at the surgery told me they often insert grommets to relieve pressure. It may be that that's what needs doing.' A small, plastic tube through the eardrum, left in till it fell out after eighteen months or so; that would be brilliant. She'd ask Gilmore to arrange an appointment with an ear, nose and throat consultant as soon as possible. There should be plenty of time before the next cloning.

26

'Kitty bumped, Mummy. Poor Kitty's hurt.'

'Yes, darling, I know. Kitty can't see. Auntie Meg's vet came over yesterday and said he couldn't make her better. Remember?'

'Kitty's not ill!' Seb shouted at her, stamping his feet. 'Kitty can't see!'

'She can't manage without seeing, darling. We talked about that, didn't we?'

'Don't want Kitty deaded!'

'You know it happens, Sebbie. You know everything dies.'

'Old things die. Kitty's not old.'

'Not always, darling. Sometimes a pet is too sick to live. It's kinder not to let them suffer. The vet is coming this morning to put Kitty to sleep; you know we talked about that yesterday.'

'She isn't tired.'

'I think you should say goodbye, Sebbie. Give Kitty a big hug.'

'Seb help Kitty,' he mumbled, head buried in the cat's fur. He held his pet tightly to himself, trying not to allow the tears. '*My* Kitty. You can't dead her.' Grief welled out; under his eyelids, down his cheeks, long gulps of grief.

'She'd always be hurting herself, Sebbie. It wouldn't be fair on her. She might jump on the cooker and burn her paws . . .'

'Poor Kitty,' he kept saying. 'Poor Kitty.'

Jeffers and Jiminy, infected by their brother, also began to cry. Even Janus, Lisa saw, his eyes solemn, had a single, large teardrop running down his cheek.

Lisa gently took the calico cat from Sebastian and put her in the willow basket, shutting the lid. 'She needs a sleep now, Sebbie.'

He tried to get back to the cat, wriggled out of her restraining arms. Even Seb could show a nasty temper when he was upset.

'Why not have a game on Daddy's computer?' Lisa distracted him, taking his hand and leading him to Alec's study. 'There's just time for one before we have to leave.' She turned the machine on and inserted the latest game disk Alec had brought him.

Seb sat on Alec's chair, an unusual look of anger in his eyes, and thumped his fingers over the keyboard. 'Why's Jansy staying home?' he asked.

'He's going to see Dr Morgenstein again,' Lisa evaded the issue. 'As soon as he comes back from holiday.'

'Jansy's not in bed,' Seb said. 'Jansy's not ill.' His look was openly hostile. 'Is Jansy going to be deaded?'

Lisa had to clear her throat several times before the words would come. 'Don't be silly, Seb. Daddy is taking him to the doctor soon,' she managed. 'Then he can go to school again.'

Luckily Morgenstein could not see Janus until the following month. This gave Lisa much-needed time. She thought she could delay the cloning, possibly even prevent it altogether, if the bloating could be controlled. She had to find some way of releasing the extra fluid without allowing Janus to clone.

Lisa put her arms round Seb. 'Come along, Sebbie. Time to get ready.'

'I'm not finished!' he insisted, overturning Alec's chair, banging the table. 'I've nearly won!'

'When you get back, Seb. We have to go now; we'll be late.'

'It isn't fair!'

Lisa walked all four children to the school, then walked back with Janus. He was often difficult, destructive even. But the fits of bad temper were not as uncontrolled as before. She could only be thankful that something seemed to have changed.

Without the competition from his brothers, Lisa had been surprised to find herself drawn to the child. He was extraordinarily perceptive, and positively gifted. His drawings were remarkably accomplished. An early artistic talent, Lisa assumed. The bond between them, so often disturbed, was cementing into more than the usual love between mother and child. Lisa also felt admiration for her son, pride in the way he handled an attribute he had to live with but could not regulate.

Lisa saw him take Seb's place at Alec's desk; she must have forgotten to turn the machine off. 'You're too young to be playing with the computer,' she said gently, looking at the screen as Janus knelt on the chair and flicked deft fingers over the keyboard. 'Let's do some drawing.'

The child ignored her, clicked keys, brought up one screen after another. No real harm in that, Lisa thought to herself, relieved to have time to clear the breakfast. He couldn't mess up Alec's files, they needed a password to be accessed.

When Lisa finally returned, about to switch the computer off, the screen that greeted her spelt FLAXTON PLC in enormous letters. There was a list of names and figures beneath. These must be Alec's private files, the figures he was putting together for the company. He was working towards a public offering of Flaxton shares – the company was going public within weeks. Lisa had had neither time nor energy to give thought to that aspect before. With a start she realised she must, from now on. She had to work out what she could do to stop Flaxton selling Multiplier.

'How did you get that screen, Jansy?'

'Daddy files,' the child said easily.

They were top secret. How could he know Alec's password to get to the Flaxton files, let alone the one for the spreadsheets? That couldn't be coincidence.

'Look, Mummy.' Janus leant backwards and twisted his head towards her, beckoning at the screen. 'Pretty,' he said, encouraging her.

She examined the colour monitor. It was not displaying a spreadsheet; what she saw there was a series of carefully constructed diagrams. Janus must have brought up the biological files, the ones that dealt with the components which made up Multiplier and Flaxton's other products.

'You like those?' she asked the boy. They did look pretty, the structures displayed in different colours. Perhaps if she approached a government agency and told them about the disks . . .

'Yellow,' he said, pointing to the background colour. 'Jansy.' He tapped his fingers over the keys and brought up another screen.

'How do you know what to do, Jansy?'

'Just know.' The screen had changed again. The colours, though rather lurid, showed several similar structures on different backgrounds. Colour-coded, just like her triplets' clothes.

'Look, Mummy,' he said, again. There was an urgent tone in his voice.

Lisa stared as Janus flicked from screen to screen. They all seemed virtually identical to Lisa. The boy was positively excited. Long strings of symbols spread across the monitor.

The child was looking, rapt, at the different characters. Molecular structures, perhaps; or chromosomal charts.

One screen seemed to interest Janus more than the rest. He pointed at it with his fingers, traced out the lines, took her index finger in his hand and traced them with her. They meant nothing to Lisa; just a diagrammatic form of some chemical compounds she did not know, and was not interested in.

'Very nice, darling,' she said, as she turned off the computer.

Lisa was more concerned with Janus's body. The swelling, so rapid once it had started in the past, had slowed down in the last few days. He was definitely puffing up again, parts of his body painfully swollen. But he was nothing like as belligerent, nor as waterlogged, as in the two weeks before the cloning in the Priddy Woods. Something was different. But what?

He was curiously intent on eating only certain foods. He appeared to adore the large supermarket just outside Glastonbury, refusing the organic produce grown in their own garden, the good food proffered by neighbours. He simply would not eat it.

Lisa, reluctantly, had consulted Gilmore. 'They all go through a stage of refusing food,' he'd told her. 'Don't worry about it. The more you worry, the more he'll hold back.'

None of the boys had ever been fussy about food. Lisa had always boasted how they ate everything within sight, clearing their plates, aware of competition from their brothers.

She had the feeling that Janus was trying hard to tell her something. It was possible that he knew what brought on the cloning. It happened to his body, and he was trying to avoid it. As far as Lisa could judge, he was trying to avoid any food grown locally.

'Where's Bestie, Mummy?'

'It's Saturday, Seb. You know that.'

'Where's Daddy?'

'He won't be back till late. I told you, we're going on a picnic.' Lisa opened the back of the Volvo estate and piled in the pushchair, a picnic basket and her bag of bits and pieces. 'You sit between Jeffers and Jiminy in the back, Seb. We're going to Brean Sands. We can play on the beach and look for wild flowers on the cliffs.'

It was one of those glorious late autumn days that occur surprisingly often in Somerset. Sunny, mild, almost like summer.

The children at the back sat quiet. Jiminy, she could see in her rearview mirror, was nodding off. He seemed to need more sleep than the others, particularly lately. Seb and Jeffers were counting the number of tractors they passed; Seb counted and Jeffers repeated the numbers after him.

Janus had bloated up again alarmingly in just ten days. Perhaps the pre-cloning had escalated because there was nothing fixed to his body. She was sure the time had come again; she was about to put her theory to the test.

Strapped into the seat at the front, Janus kicked steadily sideways, squirmed himself into impossible positions. He spilt the apple juice he screamed to have and spat the biscuits he demanded onto the floor. Lisa, exasperated and near breaking point, plodded on regardless. He knew what she had in mind; she was sure he could read her thoughts. She concentrated on her driving, across the moors and down towards the sea.

They found the water calm and glittery, the short grass on the cliffs sprouting its mantle of vivid green. A small, level headland was ahead, approached by a lurching track that no one else would be keen to navigate in the off season. The shoreline here had rocks among the sand. Debris was strewn around. She drove the car up the path towards a place that overlooked what had clearly become an unofficial dump. They wouldn't be disturbed.

Lisa unstrapped the three boys at the back and allowed them to run free. Janus she carefully kept on walking reins, holding him secure as she tried to formulate a plan.

'Let's walk down to the beach and build some sandcastles,' she encouraged her little brood.

They trooped down cheerfully, scooped sand, collected shells and pretty stones. Seb built a sandcastle, Jeffers decorated it with shells, Jansy was collecting stones. Stones . . . he could hit the others with stones, Lisa panicked, odd lurchings of prescient danger flooding through her mind.

It was not, apparently, what he had in mind. Janus set the stones out carefully; he selected different colours for different positions. The speed, the way he seemed to know precisely what he was doing, astonished Lisa. She watched him build a complicated looking honeycomb.

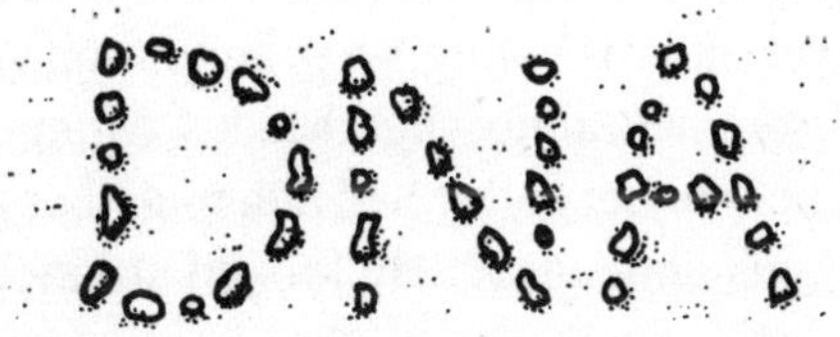

He looked expectantly up at her. 'Dinnay,' he told her, pointing. 'Jansy made Dinnay.'

'It's very pretty, darling.'

'*Dinnay*, Mummy.'

'We'll have the picnic now, shall we?' she said. 'Let's go up to the car to get the basket out.' She grabbed Janus by the hand and firmly kept him by her.

'You go first, Jeffers. Jiminy?' She turned to see the little boy still sitting on the sand.

'He's asleep, Mummy. Shall I wake him up?'

In her confusion she let go of Janus and ran down towards the beach again. 'Jiminy?' she called, a spike of worry scratching her back. 'Jiminy? Are you tired? Shall I carry you?'

The toddler just sat there. But when she came up to him, he stirred, and then smiled that glorious, sweet smile that only Jiminy seemed to have. Love for the little boy came flooding over her; she scooped him up, raised him to her neck, and walked slowly up the little path.

'Help Jeffers with the last bit, Seb,' she asked her eldest son. 'He might slip backwards.'

'I've got him, Mummy,' Seb shouted gaily. He loved to help with the triplets. 'Shall I get Jansy now?'

'No, I'll see to Janus.'

The child looked at her solemnly. 'I know how to do it, Mummy.'

'Just make sure Jeffers is all right, would you, Seb?' Lisa said, softening her tone.

There was no need to help Janus. He scrambled up behind them, then butted ahead, elbowing into Seb.

'Jansy!' Lisa called, unsure how to control him while she was carrying James. 'Don't push!'

He turned. Was that a wistful look? He seemed to be trying to shrug his clothes off.

'Look, boys.' Lisa, puffed from the climb and herding the three boys in front of her, still carrying James, pointed to a stretch of inviting grass. 'Let's sit down over there.'

The little boys began to troop obediently towards the spot. Lisa was suddenly overwhelmed with exhaustion. The burden of coping with Janus, and the secret she was hiding, were beginning to take a huge toll. She felt completely drained, almost lightheaded. Sitting down gratefully, she placed James next to her and called Seb to gather the others round.

'Wee wees,' Janus announced. He looked strained, puffed, white.

He was about to clone again, Lisa could sense it. She couldn't face the consequences of another cloning. Not now; not ever again, maybe. She had to try the method she'd thought through. She prayed that it would work.

'Wee wees!' Janus repeated, urgent and loud.

Lisa tightened the reins, pulled the loop round her wrist, and turned to Jeffrey. 'Come here a minute, Jeffers.' She pulled the child towards her and unclasped the gold earring. She smiled at him, pushing him off, and turned to Janus.

'All right, Jansy,' she said, gathering him into her arms, holding him to her, kissing him.

'Wee wees,' he cried out.

Quickly she stripped the child naked and set him to pee. A long, deep yellow stream came out of him. Lisa's tears overflowed as she remembered Priddy Woods, and the bathroom scene so long ago.

She let him pee for a time, saw the deep yellow turn even darker. Before he could finish, she pulled Janus to her, grasping his arms, and tried to push the gold earring back into his ear. He wriggled, twisted to get away; the odd, yellow liquid sprayed everywhere. On Lisa's legs, on Janus's clothes. She did not care; she *had* to get that earring in.

'Mummy,' Seb tried to get her attention. 'Mummy! Come quickly! Jiminy's gone!'

Her mind, in limbo between the world of reality and out of it, stayed focused on Janus. 'Keep still, Jansy.'

He was still peeing, visibly slimming down. She struggled with the earring. The hole in Janus's earlobe had grown smaller in the last few days, virtually joined up. Would she manage it in time? He couldn't clone while she held on to him. Could he? She shuddered. Perhaps he could. Perhaps, once the process had started, he could not stop.

Lisa forced one last effort. Even as she held it she could feel the ear-lobe reduce. Resolute, she pushed the earring through. She had drawn blood; a small trickle of blood. Blood and sweat mingled into a slippery ooze. She heard the click of the fastener shutting, and let Janus go.

'Mummy!'

Lisa returned to full consciousness of what else was happening round her. She noticed, alarmed, that the other two toddlers had wandered off. Where were Jeffrey and James?

Her body drenched in sweat, she pushed herself to her feet to follow Seb. The reins she'd taken off Janus were still in her hands but he was not. Then she remembered; she'd unlatched him to let him start the cloning process. She dashed back to him and scooped him up. There was just one of him, and he was quiet now, submissive.

'Jiminy! Jeffers! Where are you?' she called frantically.

'Jeffers is over there, Mummy, building a house.'

She saw the red-clad rear lifted high as he collected stones and shells to build some sort of fortress. Where was James?

'Mummy! Got to fetch Jiminy.'

'What d'you mean, fetch Jiminy?'

'He's down there, Mummy. Look!' Seb took her arm, walked her to the edge of the cliff and pointed down.

'You mean he fell down there?' She choked; she'd neglected her little Jiminy, allowed him to get hurt. The sweetest, most delightful of her children.

Seb pulled at her hand again. 'Over here, Mummy.'

'No, Sebbie,' she gasped at him, feeling the dizziness of vertigo, not capable of any movement, forward or back.

'He's down there, Mummy,' Seb assured her again. 'He slidded down.'

Lisa cautiously approached the ledge, put Janus down, laid herself on the grass and forced herself to look at the rocks below. A heap of blue; the body of a toddler. Her Jiminy. Had Janus deliberately drawn her attention away . . .?

Absurd. She was being utterly unfair. The child had been about to clone again; she'd *had* to counter that. It was not Jansy's fault. He couldn't help himself, he needed her as much as her other children did. More, perhaps.

Lisa made herself get up, intending to run down the small path and on to the beach below. And then she saw that right by her was a slide; a long, sandy slide no doubt made by children in the summer months. That's what Seb had tried to tell her. James had used that.

'Look after Jansy and Jeffers,' she told Seb as she took her anorak off and sat on it, sliding down quickly, landing by the child on the beach. He half sat, half lay, quite still as she approached him.

Heart pounding, disgusted with herself, appalled, she understood that the burden she was carrying had been responsible. It was too much for her, it was no longer safe to keep this harrowing knowledge to herself. She had to confide in someone, trust some other human being with her grim secret. But who was there to confide in? Sobbing, she rushed towards the inert body and saw Jiminy stir, sit up and rub his eyes.

'Mummy,' he said, holding out his arms and smiling at her.

He couldn't be badly hurt; he wasn't even crying. Why had she thought that he was dead? She gathered him up, nuzzled into his neck, covered his head with kisses. He gurgled at her. He seemed as chirpy as before; a cheerful little boy, full of smiles and clapping hands. Heart beats subsiding, Lisa lurched up the small, steep path towards the other children.

'I couldn't stop him, Mummy. He slidded down.'

'He must have been tired,' Lisa said, her voice unsteady. She took Jiminy's earring out. Perhaps he was allergic to the silver.

She could not shake off a feeling of danger, of impending loss. Dark forces, she sensed, were gathering again. This time she was afraid they might well overwhelm her.

'We'd better get home,' she told her quartet, settling Jiminy into the car, then dressing Janus. 'It was a bit too late in the year to come to the beach.'

27

'Where *is* everybody?'

Alec's voice rang out, cheerful, reverberating through the lofty hall and up into the big stairwell leading to the bedrooms. Seb appeared instantly at the top. He hauled his body onto the banister rail and started sliding down the first section, backwards, towards his father.

'Hello, Daddy.'

'I've told you not to do that, Seb.'

He grinned. 'It's like the beach, Daddy. Jiminy slidded down to the beach.'

'You've been to the beach? Today?'

'We was going to have a picnic, but Mummy helped Jansy pee, and Jiminy fell asleep and then it was too cold.'

Alec looked up the stairs, surprised to see Lisa there, a bathtowel in her hands.

'Bathing them? At this time?' He hoisted Seb onto his shoulders and vaulted up, galloping and trotting by turns, then running into the children's bathroom.

'Hello, you lot,' he said, bending down and kissing each toddler's head, then turning to Lisa who had her back to him. 'It's only half past four! I came back early especially to take them off your hands.'

Lisa could feel him looking at her intently and tried to gather her strength together.

She couldn't manage it; her face, when she turned to look at her husband, was ashen.

'My God, Lisa! What on earth's the matter now?'

'We went to Brean,' she said quietly, holding her breath to stop herself from shaking, then breathing out slowly. 'We were just about to have a picnic, and Jiminy slid down a sand run onto the beach and seemed a bit stunned. I thought I'd better bath them all early, and check that he's okay.'

Alec looked carefully at his triplets, happily splashing in the bath, then back at Lisa. 'I can't even see a bruise on any of them,' he said. 'But I must say, you've got a point about those earrings. If it weren't for the gold earring, I'd say Jeffers looks just like Jansy. Well, a thinner Jansy, somehow. His ear's a bit red.' He looked from one child to another. 'So which *is* Jansy? Neither of these other two has an earring on!'

He stooped, tilting up the face of one child without an earring. 'Hi, Jeffers.' He turned to Lisa, his eyes perplexed. 'Why did you take his earring off?'

'Jeffrey's, you mean?' A forced laugh which could hardly have fooled a stranger, let alone Alec. 'It must have slipped out when they were playing on the beach,' she lied bravely, her voice barely audible.

'Slipped out? What d'you mean, slipped out? And slipped into another child's ear? This boy has a gold earring!'

Alec lifted the child with the gold earring out of the bath and looked him over carefully.

'He looks like Janus,' he said. 'Except he doesn't seem to have any of that bloating which has been coming on again. He seems almost back to normal.'

'Yansy,' the child smiled at him.

'He even says he's Janus,' Alec said, alarmed. 'You haven't been changing earrings to test me out or anything, have you?'

'Jiminy slidded down to the beach,' Seb said, taking his father's hand and holding it. 'Jiminy was gone.'

Alec turned amiably towards Seb, smiling. 'Turned into a toad, did he?' he asked him jocularly.

'Turned into a bwabbit!' Seb shouted happily. 'Turned into lots of bwabbits!'

'That conjurer seems to have made a lasting impression,' Alec laughed. 'You've all decided to play tricks on me, haven't you? You've changed the earrings to trick me, eh?'

'Turned into another Jansy,' Seb told him solemnly.

'Just because he's lost his earring? And which one's he?' Alec pointed to the child without an earring he'd just called Jeffers.

'Jeffers!' Seb laughed. 'You know he is, Daddy. You just said so!'

'And what about the one with the gold earring?'

'That's Jansy,' Seb said pragmatically.

'So you did change them.' Alec's lips drew tight. 'I really wouldn't have thought you'd have the energy.' He forced a smile, trying to keep his temper. 'Why did you take Jiminy's off?'

'He wasn't well. I got really worried about him.' She looked helplessly at Alec. Would he ever understand? 'I thought maybe it was his way of showing an allergy to the earring.'

'Oh, right. Good thinking.' The cold, calm, modulated voice which drove her mad. 'Let's just forget about the earrings.' He was, Lisa saw, about to take the gold one out of Janus's ear.

'Don't!' Her shriek of horror stopped Alec in his tracks.

'What on earth d'you mean, don't? Janus is definitely allergic to gold!' He stared at her. 'So you didn't just play around? You did put the gold earring back on him deliberately?'

'I needed one for Jansy. Jeffers is all right without his.'

'You've decided to change Jansy back to gold again? Is that it? After all the trouble we had?'

'It's not like that at all,' she said, soft and low. And then the tears came. A trickle at first, then more and more. She could not stop them. 'Later, Alec. I'll have to explain it to you later. Let's get them bathed.'

'Mummy's tired,' Seb told him. 'Because Jansy peed and Jiminy slidded down.'

At last, Lisa saw, Alec realised that this wasn't a game, that she was in deadly earnest, trying to tell him something. He looked at her, the tears still rolling down her cheeks, unchecked.

'Right,' he agreed. 'Later.'

Mechanically he helped her bath, dry and dress the children in their night things. They avoided speaking to one another.

'I'll give them tea,' Alec said crisply. 'You get some rest. Doesn't help any of us if you overdo it.'

There was nothing further she could do. Looking bleakly at her family, Lisa left them to make herself some valerian tea and went to lie down on a sofa in the living room. She felt exposed, alone, vulnerable; she closed the shutters tight and lay back on the sofa. Her eyelids drooped, but she heard the sounds of Alec romping with the children, putting them to bed. Such ordinary sounds . . .

Exhausted, strained, she drifted away into her thoughts, seeing the Priddy Woods, two toddlers where there had been one, identical. Could anyone believe a thing like that? Would Alec have her certified? She heard his footsteps, determined, bouncing down the stairs, and shut her eyes. The living room door burst open.

'Just what is going on, Lisa?' Alec walked into the room and turned the overhead light on, flooding her out of the shadows. 'I'd have to be an idiot not to know something is. Let's have it. There's more to it than

I realised. Seb keeps saying that Jiminy, who does look rather pale, is "another Jansy". It doesn't make sense to me, but he must mean something by it. What's that supposed to mean, "another Jansy"? Have you been encouraging him to play conjuring tricks?'

'Seb lives in a dream world, you know how imaginative he is. I've no idea what you're talking about.'

Dare she take the plunge, tell Alec? He was, after all, as entangled in the situation as she was herself.

'Something is going on, Lisa. I know I've thought it's you cracking under the strain, but this is different. This time Seb's talking what sounds like rubbish.'

The urge to confide in him, the only human being who would, after all, be really motivated to support her, was overwhelming. She had to tell him if she was to survive, and help her children to survive. Their father was the obvious person to share the burden with her. He was involved with them intimately now. The triplets weren't strangers, newly born infants. They were his sons, he had grown to love them. He would be as unlikely to betray them as she was.

'All right, Alec. I'll have to tell you this time. He's your son as well as mine, and I can't keep it to myself any longer.'

'Tell me what?'

'You'll think I've really flipped.'

'Try me.'

'Seb is quite right, James was "another Jansy". When he was born.'

'Come on, Lisa! What *are* you talking about?'

'I put the gold earring in Jansy's ear because he was about to clone again. I lost the silver one.'

'*Clone?* Jansy was going to *clone*?' He looked distraught. 'For God's sake, Lisa, what is that supposed to mean?'

'Split into two identical beings. Reproduce himself.'

'Reproduce his complete body?'

'He can only clone when he's completely free of anything which isn't part of his body,' Lisa rushed at him. 'If there's nothing, and he's naked, and the time is ripe, he simply splits.'

Her husband just looked at her. 'Splits,' he repeated mechanically, evidently humouring her. 'Of course.' Ice-cold, detached. He did not believe anything she had said. 'Go on.'

'The first cloning was in the womb, just before I gave birth. The doctors said it couldn't be twins because the scan only showed one foetus. They were quite right. The first baby, Janus, split into two identical babies just before they were born. That's why they weighed exactly the same. The only difference between them was the shape of the head – you must remember that yourself. Apart from that, the two foetuses would have been identical. Witherton, of course, thought they were identical twins.' She looked at Alec. 'Which, in a sort of way, they were.'

'I see. And then?'

'The second time was when I had the triplet,' she said. 'You assumed I had given birth – what else were you to think? So I let it ride, almost convinced myself. The truth, after all, is so incredible. But it did happen. Apart from me, only Seb knew. Janus cloned, split into two separate human beings. Seb saw the two babies together in Janus's cot. He can tell which is which.'

'Let me get this straight,' Alec said, keeping his voice a monotone. 'You didn't give birth to a third triplet; you found two identical infants, together, in Janus's cot?'

'It was hot, remember. Janus must have kicked his nappy off, so there was nothing attached to him – and then he cloned.' She paused and saw that Alec was simply waiting for her to go on. 'The real truth is so unbelievable, so utterly unheard of among vertebrates, that everyone believed that I'd had a late triplet. That has been known.' She smiled slightly. 'Then I had to work out what was actually happening. I finally cottoned on. I had to fasten something to the cloner's body to stop him doing it again. Actually, Don Chivers put me on to it, though I didn't understand what he was telling me.'

She looked again at Alec; he was staring at her, speechless, waiting for her to go on.

'I did mention it to you. Don came to warn me after the twins were born.' She stopped to collect her memories. 'I thought it odd at the time that he should be interested in the twins; in fact I got quite cross with him. He was only trying to alert me, trying to draw my attention to how he coped with the farm animals.'

'Animals? You're comparing our children to farm animals?'

'Remember when Don said if he didn't tag the newborn lambs immediately after they were born, that there'd be more?'

'You're suggesting our children should have been tagged as soon as they were born,' he said, slowly and deliberately. 'Just like Frank's lambs.'

'We all have bodies, Alec. Humans are no different from animals in that respect.'

'And that's what you arranged – first the bracelets, then the earrings. Those were their tags.'

'Exactly.'

'And you think Janus swells up just before the cloning,' Alec said quietly, searching her face, looking into her eyes.

'And becomes more and more aggressive.'

'What happened when you went to see Morgenstein?'

She told him what had happened in the Priddy Woods. 'At first I thought I'd lost him, Alec – when I ran after Jansy. In the end I thought I must have imagined it all. Then, a couple of months later, Frank told us about the mauled toddler on HTV news. Now I'm sure that was him.'

She could see the pity in his eyes. He didn't believe anything she had told him. Why should he? How could he? This type of reproduction outside the womb was unknown among the higher animals. As every secondary schoolchild knew, binary fission was the reproductive system used by amoebae and other primary animal organisms, not by humans. But that was precisely what had happened to Janus; it was just scientific jargon for what amounted to cloning.

'Tell me about this afternoon,' Alec said wearily. 'After all, it's different this time. There are still only triplets, not quads.' He looked at her quizzically. 'Unless, of course, you're maintaining Janus did away with one of them?'

'It's not funny, Alec. The new clone could be dead moments after cloning. They don't always survive, you know. I found that out from Don as well.' Her weeping, so long suppressed, burst forth into a fountain of tears, a wailing of sobs. She could not go on; could not bring herself to tell the story of the cloning in the bath, the death, the disappearance of the body. It was too much.

'If you don't mind, darling,' Alec comforted her, 'I'm going to ask Gilmore to prescribe something for you. You really can't go on like this. Try to tell me what happened this afternoon.'

He waited while the sobs lessened, while she sipped the herb tea and calmed herself.

'We were just going to have a picnic, when Jansy said he had to pee.'

'Honestly, Lisa. He does it all the time.'

'Not like this. He went on and on and on, just like he did in the Priddy Woods. Not really pee; a viscous, deep yellow fluid with an odd smell.'

A spark lit up Alec's eyes. 'And the puffiness went down?'

'Exactly. He wasn't quite so bloated, so I knew he was about to clone again.'

Alec sat in his chair, his right knee over his left leg, trembling slightly. 'So did he?'

It seemed to Lisa nothing was real any more. 'Did he what? Pee? I told you, loads of it, all that revolting yellow.'

'Did he clone, Lisa? You said he was about to clone!'

'I took Jeffers's earring off and jabbed it into Jansy's earlobe before he finished peeing.'

'So that he couldn't clone,' Alec said gently, looking at her.

'Yes.' She gulped again, pouring tea down herself. She could feel it affecting her, sedating her. 'I had to be quite brutal. The hole was smaller, almost closed.'

'Then what happened?'

'Seb said Jiminy had gone. I was concentrating so hard on Jansy, pushing the earring in, I didn't notice what else was going on.'

'And was he?'

'Gone, d'you mean?'

'Yes. Had Jiminy gone?' Alec said, his voice rising somewhat.

Fear began to clutch at Lisa again. He wasn't crediting a single word; he simply thought she was insane. She saw his face through tear-filled eyes, swimming in front of her, his glasses, magnifying his eyes, goggling at her.

'Jiminy was down on the beach. I thought he'd fallen over the precipice.'

'And?'

'I told you. He'd slipped down a sand run, but he was okay.'

'And Jansy?'

'He can't clone with the earring in his ear, and he can't take it out by himself.'

'He's allergic to gold, Lisa!'

'You still think that's all it is?'

Her husband looked at her, then walked towards the drinks cupboard. 'Better drink this.' He poured a stiff whisky. His voice had taken on a gentle, caressing tone. 'You look all in, darling. What on earth possessed you to take them to the beach all by yourself?'

'It was such a lovely day.' She shuddered. 'I thought Jiminy was dead. Seb was shaking me; he said Jiminy had gone. And when I looked, I saw two triplets. The third one was down on the beach. I thought the heap on the sand was Jiminy's body; it seemed to be quite still. When I went down he was half sitting, half lying there. Then he began to move.'

'He was all right in the bath, no sign of any injury.'

Lisa nodded. 'He seemed to be okay, though I couldn't be sure. But he isn't himself. I expect you've noticed that.'

'He did seem very tired. That's it?'

'Isn't that enough?'

Alec took a long, hard look at her.

'You don't believe any of it, do you?'

'I believe you think these extraordinary events happened. I don't think they did, no.'

'You didn't immediately know which was which, either. They're more alike than ordinary identicals.'

'Because Jiminy isn't well, you said so yourself. And Jansy is much less bloated.' He sighed. 'That's because I took his earring off; it's finally showing a result. Morgenstein did spell it out for you, Lisa. Janus is allergic to metal.'

'Just try to think there may be something to what I'm telling you, Alec. First I had twins unexpectedly. An identical triplet turned up in a most unusual way. Janus swells up all the time, and he is very much stronger, brighter and more assertive than his identical triplet brothers.'

She sighed as her eyes filled again with tears. They seemed to pour from her in a never-ending stream. Just like the way Janus peed, she found herself thinking. His way of crying about his fate, perhaps.

She had done all she could to share her terrible secret with her husband, the father of her children. He thought she was, at best, deluded. She'd tried to enlist Trevor, too. He hadn't wanted to know. Neither of them believed anything she told them. Because it had never happened before, they thought it could not happen at all. But who, she thought to herself, believed in test tube babies just a few years ago? That had been considered impossible.

She couldn't tell Meg; Meg was Frank's wife. There was only one person she could trust, one human being who knew what she was saying was the truth. And he was far too young to help her.

There was nothing further she could do to convince Alec. Until the next time. That's when she'd confront him with the evidence. At least when Janus cloned again his father would have been forewarned.

28

'Out of the blue.' Frank stood on the terrace, passing thick fingers through hair matted by his hardtop.

'You can tether Light Amber in the field.' Alec's lips were compressed. 'Use the electricity pole; she can't come to any harm with that.'

The grey jodhpurs winged stiff and wide as Frank walked slowly towards the paddock. 'Get going, Amber. Haven't got all day.'

'You need a drink,' Alec said gently. 'Tether her, then come and sit down. I'll get it for you.'

'How on earth could it have happened?' Lisa asked.

Even though she hadn't known Susan Andrews all that well, she was shocked – dumbfounded – to hear she had died. Susan had been a staunch support for Lisa during the two weeks after James was 'born', and she'd helped out intermittently after that. She'd sorted out the best feeds, arranged the switch from goat's milk to soya. There had always been a bond between them, a feeling of comradeship. But the midwife had never probed, never asked direct questions.

'Weather's been that wet.'

'But Susan must know these roads well enough to drive blindfold. She's out on her rounds here all the time.' Meg had repeatedly warned Lisa about the dangers of slipping into the rhynes or the Sheppey in rainy weather, but she hadn't expected someone to die because of that.

'Don't matter how well she knows 'un, those verges give when wet.'

'Too exhausted to feel the car sliding, you mean? Tired out by yet another late-night call?'

'Could be; don't think that's what it were. She's been a bit depressed. Meg reckons the night hag were about.' Frank shivered slightly, in spite of having ridden over. 'Misled her, Meg says.'

'Night hag? What on earth is that?'

'Barn owl.' Frank looked uneasy. 'Saying is that seeing the night hag means she's after newborn babes. Susan's been that worried. We reckon the banks gave way without her noticing. Her old Beetle must have slipped, right by the bridge. Knocked her out, I daresay. Police said she drowned.'

There was no question that Frank was deeply disturbed. It seemed out of character to Lisa. The man was pretty callous, death was something he lived with every day, and he hardly knew Susan.

'I can't believe it. She was so strong and capable. She always looked as though she could handle anything,' Lisa said, trembling, remembering Susan's brisk practicality.

'She were up on Blight Moor, delivering Jennifer Sims. Another emergency, month or so early. Twins.'

'Twins? Jennifer Sims has had twins?' Lisa looked at Alec, but talk of more twins did not seem to alert him to anything unusual. Susan, Lisa remembered, was Don's nephew's wife. Had Don talked to her about the large number of multiple births on Crinsley Farm?

'They're very small. Probably that's what fashed Susan, made her less careful, like.'

'Did Jennifer know she was going to have twins?' Lisa's voice sounded strained. Was this another pre-birth cloning? And if so, was Susan's death really an accident? Could it have been a way of silencing a witness, someone who might draw attention to the appearance of unexpected twins? Her clinical notes could have shown cause for an investigation. And that could lead to Flaxton . . .

Frank lowered the glass he was about to put to his lips and stared at Lisa over it. A deep, penetrating stare she found distinctly unnerving. Challenging her; he was challenging her to say something. She dropped her eyes hastily.

'I reckon so. They do those scans nowadays. Anyway, it were all sorted out as far as Susan goes. She'd sent for the flying squad. They'd taken over and she were driving home. Bit of a mist on the moor. Nothing special.'

'How could someone like Susan Andrews possibly drown in the Sheppey? It's still fairly shallow, in spite of all the rain,' Alec said, clearly puzzled.

'Who knows?' Frank said, truculent. 'Happened, didn't it?'

'I still can't understand why no one saw her,' Lisa thought aloud, then bit her lip to stop herself from saying anything more.

'Pitch dark that night; no moon nor nothing,' Frank went on, dogged. 'It was the rear lights as gave her away. Tim Graves spotted that old Beetle. Otherwise no one would have noticed till morning.'

'Is there going to be an inquest?' A vivid image of Don's eyes, troubled, sad, came into Lisa's mind. Don had died in an odd accident as well.

'The full works,' Frank said shortly. He poured the whisky down his throat and reached his glass out for more. 'But what I really came about was Don's widow.'

It was as if he'd read her mind. 'How d'you mean, Don's widow?' she asked, startled. 'Something's happened to her as well?'

'Eh?' He stared at her, then shook his head. 'She's fine, just needs a bit of financial help.' He looked at Alec carefully. 'What I thought was that Flaxton might get around to offering her a little something. You know, spread the word about how generous they are.'

'You want me to put it to them.'

'Maybe you could find some clever money angle that would suit them.'

'And get you off the hook.'

'Not right to let her starve.'

'What I suggest *you* do, Frank, is let her keep that cottage she and Don lived in. They must have been there for years.'

'Eh? That's a tied cottage. I'll need it more than ever now Don's gone.' He stared out across the moors. 'Great worker, Don. I've been taking on three others to fill his place; even so they can't hold a candle to him.'

'Pay you to build. No young man would want that old cottage, anyway. Not modernised enough, and too far off the road.'

'Reckon I'll have to do it up. Anyway, Ella wants to join her sister down in Cornwall, wants to be shot of this place. Says they've had nothing but bad luck this last year. Blames it all on Don cutting down those elders by the cottage. "Never cut them down without permission", she told 'un. "Never burn them or there'll be a death." Don cut them down and burned them. Made quite a stink, just like corpses, Meg said. She thinks he worried so much he weren't paying proper attention the day of the hunt.'

'Meg did mention Don wasn't at all happy with the new fertiliser,' Lisa said. 'That he'd burned the first batch with the old elders.' Was there something to these superstitions after all? she wondered. She swept curses aside; something atrocious, but not paranormal, was going on. She was sure these 'accidents' had been arranged. She was only too right to be apprehensive on Janus's behalf, to keep him by her at all times.

'Meg said about that?' Frank was on to it like a bullet. That sharp, calculating look. 'No call for that. Don saw the benefit of Multiplier just like the rest of us.'

Lisa, annoyed with herself for betraying Meg, wondered again how she could ever have thought of Frank as an easy-going man. 'Well, you know, Frank, she doesn't like it for her hens.'

'Not doing no harm,' he said, glaring at her. 'We're getting more eggs than ever we did.'

The man would do anything for money. Could he be implicated in Susan's death? Not really. His reaction had been one of fear, not guilt. Frank was distinctly frightened, and for himself. Just like he was after Don's accident.

Lisa couldn't stand his small, currant eyes staring at her a moment longer. Some instinct told her to attack his weak spot, talk about the little girl he bullied Meg into keeping in irons.

'How's Phyllis? Meg said the brace was coming off at last.'

His face jerked round, eyes slunk into his head. 'We got those doctors to do another operation. They don't rightly know what they're about. Don't want no cripple for a young'un. She's a real goer, though. Don't make no difference what brakes you put on her, she still gets about as best she can. Plucky little maid.' His voice was steady, under control.

'And doing so well at school,' Lisa put in. 'You must be very proud of her.'

'Trevor! This is a surprise.'

Lisa pricked up her ears. Alec had leant over her to pick up the receiver before she could reach for it.

'Of course you can; we'd be delighted. You driving?'

The noises from the other end of the phone suggested he was not.

'Look, I'd pick you up, but Lisa isn't up to scratch.' She saw her husband fiddling with the cord, turning his back to her, voice lowered. She couldn't quite catch what he said. 'There's a bus to Wells, I'll pick you up from there. Five past every hour. What? From the bus station, yes. Can you catch the eleven-five? See you.'

'Trevor in Bath again?'

'Day after tomorrow. Wanted to spend the night. I grabbed the chance to have a chat with him. You won't listen to anything I suggest, maybe you'll listen to what he has to say.'

'I've mentioned a couple of things to him myself, about the animals and that.'

'Animals?'

'You know that fertiliser's a disaster, Alec, and that the clonings have been happening on the Graftleys' farm. It's just that their stock is always slaughtered before any of them get a chance to clone, and—'

'Hold on a minute, Lisa.' Alec walked up to her, looked into her eyes. 'What, exactly, do you imagine Multiplier does?'

She took a deep breath, braced herself. 'I think it's a catalyst for irreversible changes in the embryonic stage of a living organism.'

'That's pure conjecture, Lisa.'

'In particular, I think it stimulates the germ of living matter in a different way from any compound used before.'

'Fair enough, it does. It energises both plant and animal growth, and encourages the shedding of extra ova—'

'No, that's not it, that's my whole point, Alec. What it does do is activate a single, *fertilised* ovum to split in two—'

'So what's the big deal on that?'

'Let me finish. To split in two not only inside, but outside the womb, even when the organism is complete. You must see that that's potentially catastrophic.'

'It would be if it were true!' He laughed. 'And just how did you get infected by all this?'

'I ate Meg's produce. It was supposed to be clear of Multiplier. There must have been seepage, or maybe Frank used it behind Meg's back. To get more eggs, or something.'

'You've got a splendid imagination, Lisa. We all know you're a superb artist.'

'No, Alec. I researched it.'

'Wells Library, I suppose.'

'Bath Reference, actually.' She sighed. 'I know what effects it has. And so does Frank. He's killed off virtually everything that moves on that farm. He wouldn't even allow the *kittens* to survive.'

'Kittens?' He paused for a moment, looking at her. 'For goodness sake, Lisa! All farmers drown kittens when they have too many.'

'Frank promised Seb one, and he still drowned the lot.'

'So he forgot. Anyway, what about the horses? How come he sells horses, then. Why are they exempt?'

'They're shod, Alec, that's why. I told you, an animal can't clone if something's fixed to its body.'

'You've got an answer for everything,' he said slowly, then drew in his breath. 'This really is absurd, Lisa. If anything of that sort were going on, the Graftleys would have mentioned it. What about Meg?'

'I'm pretty sure Meg only knows about cloning in the womb. She told me about one of their ewes having seven identical lambs. But Don knew about it happening outside the womb as well. He knew right from the start, I've told you that. Maybe Susan knew as well. She is – was – married to Don's nephew, you know. And now both she and Don are dead.'

'And Frank? Why's Frank keeping quiet?'

'He stands to gain enormously by keeping it a secret. If it came out, he would be ruined. Money, Alec. The stuff your life revolves round.'

'Do me a favour, Lisa!'

She shrugged. 'You heard Don yourself. He said that the lambs only multiply if he doesn't tag them. But he's dead; he can't back me up.'

'This is utterly insane. Such unbelievable consequences would all have come to light by now. That's the idea of a testing site!' He laughed. 'You don't suppose for a moment that Flaxton would just carry on if there were side effects like that?'

'They aren't just carrying on. The launch was delayed for ages because they needed to modify the stuff. You told me that yourself.'

'Quite right. There were too many multiple births.'

'*Not* multiple births! I told you, splits – in the womb and out of it. They're trying to cover up the evidence.'

'*What?*'

'If even a hint of their being involved in this horror got out, it would be a disaster for them. Ruin their plans for expansion, scotch their going public.' She took Alec's hand in hers, looked at him earnestly. 'Just think of it, all kinds of wildlife cloning, insects as well as mammals, you know. Millions of them, completely uncontrolled.' She stopped, dropped Alec's hand. 'I think they murdered Don. He had proof, you see.'

'Don died in a hunting accident, Lisa.'

'Maybe they even had Susan killed.'

'Susan? What was *she* supposed to know?'

'About unexpected twins,' Lisa said, thinking back. 'It shouldn't really happen nowadays.'

'Country women have bees in their bonnets about home births,' Alec said sourly. 'Like some nearer home that I could mention.' He grinned.

'Probably don't bother with proper check-ups.'

'And they're watching me and Janus.' It was becoming clearer to her now. 'They had me followed to the Priddy Woods.'

She played it all back in her mind's eye again. The deep hole she'd skirted in the Priddy Woods as she'd wondered where she was, the sound she had heard of something slipping on the other side of her . . . down. What had that been? An odd, plopping sound, a yapping, something snuffling, a bark.

'*They* were the ones who hid the clone so I couldn't find him again!' Lisa cried out. 'And then, no doubt, they got a terrier to maul him to death.' She could not restrain the anguish in her voice.

'For God's sake, Lisa!'

And then it came to her. Of course. She knew where to find the proof. She could *show* Alec a clone. A gruesome one, but a clone, all the same. She turned to him again, eyes bright.

'I can prove it to you, darling.'

Why hadn't she thought of it before? Don had buried the dead clone's body in their garden; the remains would still be there.

'Prove it?'

'Yes, prove it beyond any doubt.' She drew herself up – she had to be brave. 'I haven't told you about the cloning in the bath.'

'I see.' The pitying look again. 'There was a cloning in the bath? Tonight, d'you mean?'

'Tonight? Of course not. Then there'd be a clone . . .' She stopped. He was just humouring her. So let him. This was her big chance to convince him. 'On the twins' first birthday,' she smiled at him, excited now. The body might be putrid, but it would not yet have completely decomposed. There would be traces. It had all happened, after all, less than a year before.

'*Twins*' first birthday?'

'The first anniversary of the day Janus and Jeffrey were born; the day we chose for celebrating the triplets' birthday. There was a cloning in the bath. That time when Geraldine just left me to it.'

'After the party.' He paused. 'When you were so exhausted.' This time he was taking notice.

'That's right. I took Janus's bracelet off because it was cutting into him. Then he cloned in the bath, while I was seeing to the others in the nursery.'

'So what happened to the clone?' Alec asked softly.

'He died almost immediately . . .' Her voice broke as she remembered the little face turned back to look at her. She forced herself to carry on. 'I was quite beside myself, I had no idea what to do. Meg had borrowed the Volvo, and Don brought the car keys back. He saw me all upset, and with the loose bracelet dangling from my hand. He just put two and two together. That's when he told me clones often don't survive and the only thing to do is bury them. So I knew he'd guessed what had happened. I didn't really want to believe him, so I went back to the nursery, and you phoned. When I finally got round to the bathroom again, the body had gone.'

'Gone? You mean disappeared?'

'At first I was relieved. I thought I'd imagined everything. So I went to my bedroom, stood by the window, drinking in the night air to calm myself. That's when I heard a voice. It seemed to be directed to someone at the bottom of our garden. Mark Ditcheat in his field, I recognised. And then I heard Don answer. Don was there, pretending to plant a tree.'

'Must have been dark by then,' Alec said. 'How could you tell?'

'I could hear everything, every syllable, every movement of the tools Don was using. You know how sound carries on the moor, especially at dusk.'

Alec was staring at her. 'Why didn't you ring me?'

'You were somewhere in London, Alec, unavailable as usual. And Don was there, and he already knew what was going on, and I was terrified for our children. So I just let it ride.'

'You didn't even try to tell me.'

'It was the only way to make sure no one took the others from us, Alec. What was the point of telling you then? I thought I could prevent it happening again.' She turned to him, deep tension on her face. At last – at last she could prove she wasn't crazy. 'He buried him between your new fruit trees, the apricot and the nectarine. You remember, one of the nectarine leaders got broken and you got annoyed.'

'Several of them were broken. And you said that that was Duffers digging about.'

'True enough, but Don may have broken some as well. I had to cover up for him.'

'And now you don't?'

'Now I have to convince you I'm not mad. Janus is getting ready to clone again; it's his nature, he can't help it. If we leave him without an earring, or some other device, he'll manage to get his clothes off and split into two identical children which we won't be able to tell apart.'

'Lisa,' he said. 'Lisa, darling. We have to get some help for you.'

'Just humour me one more time, Alec. It won't take long. All we have to do is unearth the body.'

29

'Are you sure you want to go through with this, darling?'

'There's no other way to convince you. You're not going to believe me unless I *show* you.' Lisa tried to sound reasonable, practical. Inside herself she felt a fear, a terror, even. Alec had sprinkled Multiplier around the fruit trees. A ghostly shroud formed in her mind, then split in two, two into four . . . Wraiths dancing in dark branches, she told herself. Flashes of torchlight flittering reason away. She bit her lip; drew blood.

'Sort of ghoulish, isn't it?'

'I don't know what you're worried about.' Lisa forced herself into a matter-of-fact response. 'You think I'm off my head, that there's no toddler's body there. It's all a figment of my fevered, fertile imagination; a chimera. No need to worry then, is there?' she finished up triumphantly.

'Just as you like, Lisa. Between the apricot and the nectarine, you said?'

'Right. You planted them in early spring last year, if you remember.'

'Of course I remember. Saunders dug the ground really well. Put me on to Scotts nursery, said Moorpark and Lord Napier would be the ideal cultivars for this area. What makes you think Don chose the ground between those two trees? Because prunus species grow so fast?'

'Nothing to do with the trees. I expect he noticed the ground had been dug recently. He probably thought it wouldn't show up new disturbance. And that border is the furthest from the house.'

Alec was striding down towards the stone wall facing south, with the rhyne on the west separating Mark Ditcheat's field from their property. It was already getting dark. They carried a Tilley lantern.

'And he probably thought no one would be digging this bed again for years,' she added. 'It must have seemed the perfect place.'

'Here?' Alec turned to her. 'You're quite sure? I don't want to disturb the soil for nothing.'

'There,' Lisa insisted. 'The last two trees before the rhyne. It's not hard to work out the right place. It was the nectarine leader which was damaged.'

'Leader?' Alec said, emphasising the word sarcastically. 'Leaders, you mean! I suppose I should have guessed it couldn't be just the dog. Peregrine was also damaged.'

'Don never went near the peach, I'm sure. That wretched Duffers must have done the rest, just as I said.'

Alec began to clear the topsoil. 'I hope that's right. I hardly want to dig up the whole row!'

What state would the body be in? Would there be a whole skeleton, the skull's sockets accusing her? Had the little boy, his life so short, rested in peace? She choked back her feelings.

'I know where he buried it – him,' Lisa insisted. 'I'm not likely to forget.' She shuddered as she remembered what she had gone through that day: her horror at hearing Don's voice, the realisation that he was digging a grave in their garden. And now retrieving the body was just as important. Without it Alec would not believe her. She would once more have to manage on her own, considered seriously deranged, conveniently set aside as unable to distinguish between fact and fiction. Until the time when Janus cloned again. Next time it might not be possible to protect Janus, and her family, from disaster.

'Mark Ditcheat was in his field, counting his cattle. Don was right by the end of the wall, otherwise Mark probably wouldn't have noticed him.'

Alec began to dig. Slowly, methodically, he spaded up the compacted soil and placed it on the path. It took energy and time to lift off the top spit.

'According to you, this is where we should find the first clues,' he said, wiping his forehead, looking from Lisa to the clumps of earth. 'If you've got it right, I should come across something any minute.'

They stood in silence, green boots trampling in soil, looking at one another across the moths flickering around the lantern light. Bats swooped up insects. 'Bats are demons', Lisa remembered Meg telling her. 'They spirit away the souls of folk dying at night. They're not about during the daytime.'

'Positive you want me to go on with this?' Alec said softly.

'Want?' Lisa suddenly sat down on the grass beside the path. She felt enervated, unable to support herself. 'Of course I don't *want* you to do it. But it's the only way you're going to be satisfied.'

Alec changed spade for fork and placed it into the second spit of the shallow trench he had been digging. 'Right, then. Here goes.' He hoisted earth again; searching, careful, one slow forkful after another, soil spreading black on to the path. Stained earth. 'Was he wrapped in anything?'

'Two pillowcases were missing.'

'Rotted by now, I suppose.'

'I would have thought there'd be large bits and pieces,' Lisa said tremulously. 'Is that a bit of something?' She could see a dim reflection among the dark earth.

Alec stooped down. A glint of white, hard and brittle. A piece of broken china. Squeaks of metal against metal as Alec hit a small tin. A ring of silvered paper caught on a tine, then reflected gold in the lantern light. Lisa was momentarily reminded of the earrings; had she put . . .? She bent down to pick it up. Just metal foil which undid itself into a strip.

'Saunders said there was any amount of junk when he was digging here. A previous owner must have used it as a dump.' Alec worked his fork into dense soil again. Clod after clod of rich loam methodically enlarged the growing mound already on the path. There was no sign of anything but earth, interspersed with a few pieces of broken crockery and glass, some bottle tops.

'There's nothing, Lisa.'

'There has to be,' she whispered. 'Don buried him here.'

'Nothing at all.'

'Perhaps we need more light.'

He held the lantern up and shone the bright torch round and over everywhere. No sign of cloth or body, no sign of bones.

'You're not going deep enough.' Lisa grabbed the fork from Alec's hand and began to dig. In her eagerness her strength increased. Careless of her ungloved hands, she levered the fork in deep and wide.

'There's nothing except good black loam, Lisa.'

She straightened up at last. The bed between the fruit trees had been dug out at least two and a half spits, three in some places. Don would have buried the infant well down, but not lower than that.

'We'll have to try the space between the next two trees,' Lisa insisted eagerly. 'Moorpark and Peregrine. Perhaps you're right. It was quite dark. I must have got it wrong.'

'Moorpark was bashed about more than either of the other two, so it could have been on the other side of that,' Alec said, starting to spade again. 'This soil's much harder going than the other site,' he announced after the first spit, sour and tired. 'It's not going to do the trees any good.' He spaded great hulks of grey clay, which covered the path.

Clay! Lisa remembered now. The lower spit Don had dug had been clay. Grey, solid clay which he had heaved in chunks into the rhyne to disintegrate. She'd been right. The first site had to be the place where Don had buried the clone, because there was no clay there. Had the little body already turned to earth? Even his bones? His skull? Could he really have disintegrated so quickly?

'You might as well stop digging, Alec. I know it was between the last two trees in the row, the apricot and the nectarine. I know because the subsoil is heavy clay. Don dug great clods to make room for the body. He threw them in the rhyne to hide them; I saw them there. I noticed because of one he'd overlooked.'

Alec straightened, resting on his fork. 'There was nothing there, Lisa. We dug the whole distance between the trees. Absolutely nothing! No sign, no vestige, of a body, or even of material. It couldn't possibly decompose completely in such a short time.'

'Don must have put the lime on it. You must remember that. You couldn't work out what had happened to the lime.'

He smiled; a small, wan smile. 'I do remember that,' he agreed, 'but it's hardly proof of a child's body, now is it?'

He got to work to fill the second hole, neatly cleaned the path and raked it level. 'There's something I should mention,' he said. 'Not very pleasant, but it is a point.'

'You've found something?'

'I don't like talking about it in this way. We're here to unearth the body of a human being – a child. It sounds so brutal.'

'What, Alec? What are you talking about?'

'Well, if there'd really been a body . . .'

'Yes?'

'It would have decayed.'

'So?' she almost shrieked at him. 'So what?'

'The soil would have sunk down.'

Lisa thought for a moment. There was something in what he said. 'I expect Don wedged some of the clay round it.'

'Think so?' He looked at her, obviously startled. 'Even so, the soil above it would have settled. There'd be a dip.' His voice was low and sombre. 'I'll bring a load of scalpings down,' he told his wife. 'Tidy all this up.'

Multiplier; Alec had used it liberally. Perhaps, Lisa thought despondently, exhausted, unable to fight any more, instead of reproducing the body, the wretched stuff had reproduced the animals – the worms – which hastened its rotting. That's why there was nothing there; that's why the earth was such rich loam. What other explanation could there be?

30

'Lisa! It's good to see you. Come in, do.'

'Thanks, Anne.'

'All on your own? How on earth did you manage that?'

'Trevor's down for the weekend. He and Alec and the boys have gone to climb the Tor. They're going to fly the kite Trev brought for them. And give me some time off!'

'Cup of tea?'

'That would be lovely.'

'Milk and sugar? Or d'you take honey?'

'No sweetening.'

'It's an acquired taste, I know, but I expect you're used to it.'

'What is?'

'Goat's milk in tea. Meg says you had it all the time you were carrying the triplets. Must be why they're so sturdy.'

'You use Meg's goat's milk?' Lisa had half risen from her chair, goggling at the milk jug Anne was pouring from.

Anne stared at her, surprised. 'You didn't know? Right from thc start. Frank brings it over in the Land Rover every morning, when he drops Phyllis and Paul off; and the cheese.' She laughed, slightly embarrassed. 'I didn't mention it to you because I thought you knew – well, I just assumed it. Of course I use it. Everyone says it's better than cow's milk for young children. The mothers really like us to—'

'You've been giving them Meg's goat's milk all this time?'

'Honestly, Lisa, aren't you making rather a thing of it? It isn't a secret, or anything. It's supposed to be much better for the children. Quite a few of them are allergic to cow's milk.'

Lisa sat down heavily in the chair just by her. She stared ahead of her. Was that why Janus had cloned again so soon after the cloning in the bath, had bloated up again so quickly after that? Because Anne was feeding him the goat's milk loaded with Multiplier? No, that couldn't be why. The fertiliser had been modified.

'So how is Jansy? Any chance of your letting him come back soon? I never blamed him about Duffers, you know. That was Geraldine's own fault. I told her Duffers could only come if he behaved whatever the children did. This is a playschool for young children, not a kennels. And you know he isn't allowed here any more.'

'I know,' Lisa managed to say. A thought struck her. 'What does she do with him?'

'Frank always takes him when he brings the milk. Actually, he often did before. Duffers is locked up until then.' She smiled at Lisa. 'As for the eggs, that was just high spirits. My own silly fault for not keeping my eye on him every second. He's a real challenge.' She stopped, almost out of breath. 'And I miss my little sessions with him.'

The incident when Janus smashed the eggs suddenly took on a new significance for Lisa. Did he know what made him clone? Was he trying to avoid contamination? But the eggs couldn't be the problem, any more than Meg's goat's milk. Frank and Don had slaughtered all Meg's chickens last year when cleansing the farm of the old strain of Multiplier. Perhaps the ground was still contaminated, the grass eaten by the goats, pecked at by the hens, carrying it into the food chain. But was that enough to trigger another cloning? Or was there something else?

'Seb told me Janus liked drinking tea,' Lisa said.

Anne laughed. 'Extraordinary child. He always liked to pretend he preferred it black.'

'Black? Jansy likes to drink it black?'

'"No milk", he always said. I've never heard of such a thing with such a little one before. Sat there, just like a grown-up, holding his cup and refusing to have milk.' She smiled uncertainly at Lisa. 'It was very weak tea, practically hot water. Sometimes I put a slice of lemon in it for him, and I always added a large dollop of our own clover honey.' She looked at Lisa nervously. 'But of course I made sure he had his morning milk with the others,' Anne hurriedly went on. 'We didn't let him get away with anything. I added a bit of honey to that, too. He didn't seem to like it.'

'What about the eggs, Anne? Do you get your eggs from Meg?'

Anne frowned. 'I thought she was a special friend of yours. Are you trying to tell me there's something wrong with her produce?'

'I'm just worried about the bacteria in eggs,' Lisa explained, her mind sharply working through possible threats to Janus. 'You know – salmonella. They say that free-range chickens are the most suspect. And there might be listeria in the soft cheese made from goat's milk.'

She smiled pleasantly at Anne. 'Did you use that, by any chance?'

'You're really worried about the stuff, aren't you?'

'Only as far as Jansy is concerned.'

'You think Jansy may be allergic to the bacteria?'

Suddenly the word clover pushed itself into Lisa's consciousness. Clover honey – Anne's hives were set right next to Crinsley Farm. The real culprit among the foods Janus had eaten at school wasn't Frank's produce, it was the honey! That would be last year's crop, made by Anne's bees gathering pollen from Frank's fields. So if Anne had been sweetening Janus's tea with it, and even added it to his milk, it would be what had caused the rapid bloating. Lisa's heart began to turn as she thought of the problems Janus had had to deal with. Perhaps that was the reason he'd stayed thin since he'd been at home. He'd peed the extra stuff away at Brean, and because he hadn't been to playschool he wasn't imbibing any contaminated food. He'd stayed with her, safely consuming supermarket food.

'It's possible. Alec's really concerned about his behaviour. He even thought Jansy might be autistic, but I know that's absurd. After all, he's usually very sociable, and very keen to take part in everything. It isn't autism.'

'He's always easy with me,' Anne insisted. 'I've no idea why everyone's so down on the little lad. Bright as a button, with quick reflexes. Means one's got to be on one's toes when looking after him.'

'He doesn't take up too much of the girls' time?'

'He's demanding, but he entertains the other children. Why don't you send him back next week? You really need time off.' She looked uncomfortable. 'I don't mean to be rude, Lisa, but you look terrible.'

'You think you could cope with him?'

'Of course I can, my dear. No problem at all. We're all longing to have him back. He is such a leader, you know. He really brings the others along.'

'He ought to stay off the milk, and the clover honey,' Lisa said, her voice dropping low. 'Some people are very allergic to clover.' She hesitated slightly. 'And the eggs and cheese. Maybe he can't cope with the very stuff which is good for the others. I'd better send his food round with him. Can you arrange he only eats that?'

'I'll see to it, my dear. If you think there may be trouble with bacteria, I'll drop eggs for the time being anyway.'

As they were sipping tea, Lisa noticed the sun had turned blood-red. A huge globe hung in the sky above the Levels, an evening mist veiling it. Just after five; they'd all be back by now. She must go home, help get some tea, help bath them.

Lisa felt some of the weight she carried had been lifted from her shoulders. Anne liked Janus, wanted to have him back. And Trevor; Trevor had agreed with Alec that she was overwrought, that she'd been fantasising. After all, Trevor had pointed out, she was creative. Didn't she use that wonderful imagery in her work? Wasn't that the point of it?

There had been no buried body. That was the fact which even Lisa found difficult to come to terms with. Perhaps Alec was right and she had dreamed the horror, the whole thing.

'Thanks, Anne. Come over later and have dinner; after eight, when the kids are off. Have you met Trevor? I think you'd get on well.'

'I'd love to, my dear.'

When she got back, Lisa was surprised to see there was no car in the drive, or in the garage. It was now misting thick across the moors, the light fading fast. Had the men taken the boys out for a cream tea? She checked her answering machine. No messages.

Something began to make her nervous. Something was happening to her children, she sensed it, felt it in her bones. She paced about the living room and began to fret. The gloom was coming down fast. She decided to drive to the Tor to look for them. She couldn't miss them on the moor road if they were heading back.

The traffic in Glastonbury was unusually busy; Saturday, Lisa reasoned to herself. She heard the wailing of a siren, felt the usual frisson of apprehension down her spine. A car crash, perhaps; sympathy tightened her throat.

Winding her way up Fisher's Hill and along Bere Lane, she turned into Chilkwell Street. She could already see a small crowd jamming the turning into Well House Lane and caught a glimpse of revolving blue lights. That's where the accident must have been. Alec's car was probably locked in. The simple explanation of why they weren't home yet.

Driving slowly now, wondering where to park her car, a sense of panic welled up from somewhere deep, crept into consciousness, began to grip her. What if it hadn't been a car crash? What if one of her children had had an accident? Was that why they hadn't returned, why they hadn't phoned?

Simply abandoning her car in the middle of Chilkwell Street, Lisa pushed into Well House Lane and elbowed over to the ambulance. Her heart leapt. Trevor was standing by it, his hands clutching Sebastian and Jeffrey. He caught sight of her.

'Lisa!' she saw him mouth.

She had to get closer. 'Let me through!' she shouted, slipping between bodies, forcing herself forward.

'How did you hear?' Trevor asked as she reached him.

'Hear? Hear what?'

'My dear.' He took Jeffrey's hand and put it into Seb's. 'Hold on to him, Seb. I've got to talk to your mummy.'

She saw him step towards her, his dark blue jeans black against the headlights. She saw his eyes gleam wet, catching the flashing blue light, the tears rolling down his cheeks, haloing them.

'My poor darling.'

The black legs moved as though he were a raven; his nose glowed like a beak. His arms rose up, the black anorak taking wing. She moved away, cowered away from him.

'I am so very sorry. We really took such care, I don't know how it could have happened. It was so quick—'

'What?' she shrieked. 'What's happened? Where's Jiminy?'

'Jiminy slidded down, Mummy!' Seb was crying at her. 'Jiminy slidded a long way down and lay quite still!'

'He had his coat off,' Trevor was saying, holding her, hugging her. 'To sit on. We thought he looked tired. And it was slippery, you see. He simply started sliding down.'

'Where's Janus?'

'I'm sorry, my dear. It was Jansy who took the brunt of it when he slipped down.' He held her tight again. She felt confined, imprisoned, coerced against her will. She wrenched away, pummelled at Trevor, fought him off. He let her go, talking at her, hands hovering after her, trying to soothe her. 'He's a remarkable little boy. He tried to catch his brother and held on to a bush. That broke his fall.'

'Janus is dead?'

'No, no, my dear. Janus has had an accident. He's—'

'It's Jiminy, isn't it?' She looked at Trevor, standing silent now, head bowed. 'Isn't it?' she screamed at him. 'My little Jiminy, he's gone?' She pushed his hands away, stood apart from him, moving back into the crowd making way.

'Jiminy started sliding down on that shiny blue anorak and Jansy was in front of him and sort of broke his fall. Jiminy fell on top of Jansy, who saved himself by grabbing at a thorn branch. He's broken something,

I'm afraid. I think maybe his leg, but I'm sure he'll be all right. A green fracture.'

'He pushed Jiminy?'

'Jiminy crashed into him, Lisa. There was no way Jansy was responsible. And he was such a brave little chap. He—'

She could no longer think. She let out one long scream of anguish. 'Jiminy's dead! My Jiminy!'

It seemed to Lisa that hundreds of eyes began to stare at her, to gleam at her, to point.

'I'm a doctor, let me through.'

And as she watched, unable to move, a young man came towards her, grasped her arm, held it tight. 'Is this the mother?'

Alec was coming, too. Tall Alec, slow walk, bowed down, glasses slipping down his nose. His arms held a small, blue-clad figure lying limp.

'Lisa,' she saw his lips move, wet globules weeping down his face.

'Don't touch me!' she screamed at him. 'Get away from me! I told you. I told you and you wouldn't listen!'

The young doctor took out a syringe and plunged it into her. A sedative, she supposed, as she slipped out of consciousness.

31

'Where am I?'

There was no answer to Lisa's question. She woke up to find herself in a strange room, in even stranger surroundings.

'What is this place?' she whispered, noting the high windows, the empty walls. There was no reply. 'Is there anyone there?' she shouted.

The quiet came back at her, pressing on her straining ears.

White, it was all white. An intense stillness seemed to lie over everything, air muffled, light dim. She lay quiet, the sound of her breathing filling the room, a rushing in her head. It seemed to her that the world was so silent she could hear her blood flow.

At last her ears, attuned to the tiniest murmur, heard a soft whirring. What was that? Some sort of instrument of torture?

The whirring stopped. There was a louder noise, a sort of hum, a bang, followed by what sounded like footsteps. Unmistakable now, heavy treads along a corridor somewhere outside her room. As Lisa looked towards the door, she could see a square of something that should be glass but which reflected back at her. And then the square swung away as the whole door opened wide to let a figure through.

'Awake, I see, Mrs Wildmore. Feeling any better?'

Lisa stared at the woman who'd simply walked into the room without knocking.

'Where am I?'

'There's nothing to worry about . . .'

That sickly, patronising tone. It stirred Lisa first into anger, followed rapidly by fear. Where were her children?

'I asked you where I was.' She sat up, leaned back as she felt her head ache with the effort. 'I didn't ask you whether there was anything to worry about. Perhaps you'd be good enough to tell me.'

'Of course, Mrs Wildmore, it isn't a secret. Gladstone Nursing Home. I'm sure you'll—'

'And where is that?'

'Just outside Bath. I'm sure you'll—'

'What am I doing here?'

'I'm afraid I can't answer that question. Dr Pleadling will be here shortly. He'll clear everything up for you.'

This was absurd. 'You are suggesting that I simply wait until some doctor graciously appears?' Was she being held against her will? 'Unless you give me a good reason to stay, I'm leaving.'

'That won't be possible, Mrs Wildmore.'

She *was* being held. The nurse, or whatever she was, approached her slowly. Was she about to administer some drug? An injection perhaps? She'd had one earlier. Had she talked of cloning while she was under the influence of drugs?

'Is this a prison?'

'Of course not, Mrs Wildmore. It's just that we thought—'

'We? Who's that supposed to mean? *I* had nothing to do with my coming here. Where's my husband?'

The woman stopped uncertainly at the end of the bed, then started coming nearer again.

'You touch me and I'll have you up for assault.'

'Hostile reactions will not be helpful to you, Lisa. The review of your case is coming up today, you know.'

'My name is Mrs Wildmore,' Lisa said furiously. 'Are you holding me here for some reason? On what grounds?'

The woman squinted at Lisa through heavy, lowered lids – Big Nurse in *One Flew Over the Cuckoo's Nest*, Lisa thought grimly. Then shock at what she took to be her situation made her feel ice along her veins. Better to play along, pretend to do exactly as they wished. They might perform a lobotomy on her. Slight shoulders heaved in a shudder. And then she shuddered once again as memory came flooding back.

'Jiminy! Where's my Jiminy?' she sobbed. That's what it was. She saw the scene again: blue lights flashing, an ambulance, and Trevor telling her that Jiminy was dead.

The nurse had obviously rung for assistance. Several more people entered the room, including a young man.

'Mrs Wildmore? I'm Dr Pleadling. You were admitted as an emergency.' He smiled, his teeth gleamed white and even. As she looked, Lisa thought she saw his lips draw back. The teeth now seemed to snarl at her.

'Emergency?'

'You'd had a terrible shock, perhaps the most dreadful experience anyone can have. I am so very sorry. Your husband—'

'My baby, where's my Jiminy?'

'There was nothing anyone could do, Mrs Wildmore.'

'*Where* is he? Why the hell don't you answer my questions?'

'You've been under sedation for two days—'

'*Jiminy!* Where's Jiminy?'

The doctor sighed and signalled to two nurses to go over to Lisa.

'I'm asking you where my son is,' Lisa said, breathing in and making a supreme effort to remain calm. 'Just answer the question. Doping me into oblivion is not going to do anything for me – or you, in the long term.' She saw his eyes sweep over her.

'He had a terrible accident.'

'I know that! Where is he?'

'He's in the Chapel of Rest at Morrison's, in Wells.'

'He's dead.'

'I'm sorry, Lisa.'

'You don't know me,' she said coldly. 'My name is Mrs Wildmore. Where's my husband?'

'He will be here in an hour or so. We had to admit you, you understand. Naturally you were completely grief-stricken.'

'Grief-stricken?'

'Overwrought, unable to cope.'

'If everyone who lost a child was sent to a mental institution, they'd be full,' Lisa said coldly. 'I suppose Alec didn't like the way I insisted someone had killed my Jiminy.'

'No one killed him, Mrs Wildmore. You have to believe that.'

'Have to?'

'For your own sake. He didn't even die of the fall.' The young man brought a chair up to her bed, sat next to her and took her hand.

Lisa withdrew it instantly.

'Please do believe what I am trying to tell you.'

She stared at him, eyes stony.

'Your little son had a coronary.' He reached out for her hand again; she hadn't the strength to take it away.

'My Jiminy? He was a toddler! A heart attack?'

The doctor's hands were clasping hers. 'I'm very sorry. A congenital condition, a sudden failure of the valve.'

She took her hand away, drew it up to herself. 'He's very ill?'

'He was liable to the instant death syndrome.'

'He's dead? Jiminy's dead?'

'It's very unusual, but it does happen. It means he had a sudden heart attack. His body must have slumped forward; that's how he came to slide down the Tor. It's very steep, of course.'

'You're telling me it was going to happen anyway?'

'I'm so sorry. No one could have known about it beforehand.'

That could be true. She remembered the way the little boy had nodded off, in the car, on Brean Sands. And she remembered how she'd found him on the beach, unharmed apparently, but harbouring a fatal disease. A long, low moan of anguish reverberated round the room. The tears began to stream.

'And Janus?' she asked. 'What about Jansy?'

The doctor looked puzzled.

'My other son,' she said. 'One of Jiminy's triplet brothers.'

'Of course. He showed remarkable courage, quite incredible for a child of that age. He tried to grab James to break his fall, and he snatched hold of a thorn branch. That's why he didn't come to worse harm himself.' He tried a smile. 'I'm afraid he did get hurt in the process.'

'Hurt? Badly hurt? Jansy's hurt?' Her Jansy; her brave little Jansy had tried to save Jiminy.

'He broke his leg. A compound fracture, I'm afraid.'

Her eyes began to fill with tears again. 'Where is he?'

'In the Bristol Infirmary. He's doing very well. A brave little chap.'

'He's in a cast? His leg, I mean.'

'I'm afraid so.'

'Will he be all right?'

'It's wonderful what they can do in orthopaedics nowadays. Yes, there's every reason to believe he'll get over the fall completely. His bones are still growing, and pliable. They've put a plastic splinter in to hold the bones together.'

'A plastic splinter?'

'I'm sorry, Mrs Wildmore. It's nothing to be alarmed about. It doesn't hurt. He'll be—'

'But the splinter will stay in place?'

'The bones grow round it; there should be no complications at all. I'm sure he will heal without any detriment to his movements.'

A piece of plastic in Janus's leg, set in to stay with him for the rest of his life. The thoughts flitted quickly through Lisa's mind as the stress she had been suffering for so long now began to ease, to lighten her burden. Her monstrous problem – Jansy's problem – had been solved.

Someone, somewhere, had seen to it. God, perhaps. Janus would never clone again. She need not even bother to think about it. A feeling of euphoria, of light-headedness, made her lean back against the pillows, relief renewing grief, welling more tears.

Her Jiminy, her sweet little boy, had gone. He had been too good to be true; he wasn't destined for a long life and she'd lost him. Bitterly she remembered how she'd wished for twins; and twins is what she now had.

'I see,' she croaked. Her throat felt parched and cracked. Life without her Jiminy; two children who looked like him but were not him. How could she survive that? Her tears had stopped, she seemed to be dried up. She looked at the young doctor hopelessly. He wouldn't be able to help her.

'Could I possibly have some tea?'

'Of course, Mrs Wildmore.' He turned to a nurse. 'And your husband, as I said, will be with you in a short time. We've been in touch with him, told him you were awake at last.'

'You had me committed? Actually committed under a section of the Mental Health Act?' She stared at her husband. 'You actually did that, Alec?'

'An emergency admission, darling. You were completely beside yourself, honestly. You shrieked that Flaxton had sent someone to get Janus, that he'd killed Jiminy, that you'd make sure they couldn't do anything like that again. All kinds of crazy things. I really had no choice in the matter. There were the other children to think of, you know. And it was only for seventy-two hours.'

'So how long have I been here?'

'Two days. Dr Pleadling is perfectly happy for you to leave with me if you wish.'

'I can go any time I like?'

'A couple of small formalities . . .'

'I see.' She looked coldly at Alec; he had betrayed her. 'What about phone calls? Am I allowed to make one now?'

'You want to phone someone?' He shrugged. 'Trevor, you mean?'

'Yes.'

'Of course, darling. This isn't a prison. I wish you'd understand my position. I had to think about the boys.'

'Jiminy is dead.'

He put his arm round her, drew her to him. She pushed him away.

'Our little son is dead, I know.' She saw tears gathering in his eyes. 'I know how much he meant to you. I loved him too.'

She let him hold her hands. Her eyes, now dry, looked beyond him to the high windows. 'They told me he had some sort of heart failure.'

He leaned towards her, held her to him. This time she let him, felt a shudder through her body, an ache, a wrenching pain. The blessed relief of tears came again.

'Something like that – sudden death syndrome, they said. That's why he needed so much rest. And poor old Jansy's hurt. He has a badly broken leg.'

She looked at Alec. 'Splintered, they told me.'

'He'll be okay, Lisa. He's very strong. Honestly, you needn't worry.'

'I wasn't,' she said, realising that he had not believed, did not even remember, anything of what she'd told him about Janus. He had absolutely no idea of the significance of the splinter. He thought her deluded; not mad exactly, but definitely deluded.

'What about Seb and Jeffers?'

He smiled for the first time. 'Seb really is absolutely wonderful. My mother's come to stay and he's helping her. She's coping very well. Betsy comes every day, and Anne does her bit at school.' He looked at Lisa. 'She seemed to think you didn't want the boys drinking the goat's milk, is that right?'

'That's quite right,' Lisa agreed, 'but it's not really critical one way or the other. It's Jansy who shouldn't be drinking it. I think he may be allergic to it.' The drugs, the relaxation of her terror, were making her feel exhausted. 'Perhaps I'd better try to get some rest.'

Jiminy was dead. Somehow she had to believe that, accept it. Or try to. And Janus was safe for the moment. She would ring Trevor to find out about her rights.

'Of course, darling. That's the whole thing. You're simply exhausted. The exhibition on top of the children . . .'

Lisa ignored the glaring omission of the cloning. 'Earlier on, were you implying that my leaving here depends on what Pleadling reports?' she asked. 'The small formalities?'

'It's not quite like that.' Alec looked distinctly uneasy. 'I'm sorry, Lisa. I had to act, for your sake as well as the rest of us.'

'So tell me what is going on.'

'Your case comes up before what they call a Mental Health Review Tribunal. That's within seventy-two hours of admission. They have a duty to discharge you if it is not necessary to keep you in the interests of your health or safety, or for the protection of other people.'

'And you think I qualify to leave?'

'The fact that you may hold peculiar beliefs as far as others are concerned is neither here nor there, apparently.'

'That's okay, then. I can believe in cloning if I want to!'

Alec got up from the bed and walked towards the window, then back again. He put his arms round her. 'You can believe anything you want, my darling. I'm sorry, my dearest, I really wasn't trying to make things worse. It was just such an awful, terrible shock. For me as well, you know.' He kissed her eyes, her hair, her mouth. 'They're *our* children. I know I've left you to cope with too much of it. I should be there far more to help you out.'

'I thought maybe you wanted to leave, run away with Geraldine.'

'The girl means nothing to me, Lisa. I never for a moment considered going off with her. She makes eyes at everyone. She's very pretty, I enjoyed driving her home; a little light relief. Pressures of work, that's all.'

'And an unresponsive wife. I know, I do understand about that.'

'Another visitor for you, Mrs Wildmore.' There had been no knock; the nurse who had looked in on Lisa earlier on was ushering Meg into the room.

Alec, his arm round his wife, looked startled, but recovered himself quickly. 'Meg! How nice of you to come. Lisa is leaving later today. I'm just off to make sure they get the red tape sorted out all right.' He leaned down and kissed Lisa on the forehead, then the lips. 'Got to go now, darling. You cosset yourself. I've brought you some chocolates and a glossy mag.' He got up and moved towards his briefcase, opened it and returned with an enormous box of Bendick's Bitter Mints and a copy of *Vogue*. 'Back around four. Try to get some rest before then.'

'You going to the office, Alec?'

Meg stood aside as he made for the door.

'Meetings, you know.'

'I meant the office here. If they sort out the paperwork now, I can take Lisa back with me.'

'Really? You've got time to wait? That would be great!'

'So how are things really?' Meg asked softly, as soon as the door was closed again. 'Best keep our voices down. Didn't much take to the way that creature barged in on you.'

'You noticed that.'

'I notice quite a bit, Lisa. I don't always let on. Somehow I hoped as it would all go away. But it's different when you lose one. I know. That happened to me.'

'You've lost a child? Oh, Meg, I'd no idea.'

'Not quite the same as you, she was stillborn. But she was still my flesh and blood.'

'That's why you came?'

'Not only that.' Meg took a deep breath. 'I know about the triplets; I know because that happened to me, too. Reckoned you'd been trying to tell Alec, and that was why you landed in here.'

'Happened to you?'

'Phyllis. Same thing that happened with Janus happened with her. The scan showed two babies, boy and girl. When Phyllis was born, about ten minutes after Paul, she turned out to be two. Exactly the same. Identical.'

'You mean . . .' So Phyllis was a cloner, too. That's why Frank insisted on that clubfoot operation right away. And that's why he'd been so insistent on the brace.

'I mean it happened, same way as with the animals. She split in two just before the birth. Only difference was the other one was born dead. Just minutes after Phyllie.'

'*Born* dead?'

The clone was always weaker than the cloner; Phyllis already had a defect. Perhaps that was why her clone had not survived.

'That's right, stillbirth. Horrible, really, and I didn't even know her. But she was still a part of me. I grieved for her.' Meg smiled sadly at Lisa. 'Can you credit that?'

'Of course I can,' Lisa hastened to assure her, putting out her hand. 'Of course. And now I know why you haven't had any more. I thought it odd, what with you being so involved with motherhood and everything. After all, you and Frank can afford any number of children!'

'I haven't told anyone else. Only Frank knows, and Susan, of course. I told you Susan delivered the twins – the triplets.'

'She didn't tell anyone?' So she'd been right; Susan had worked it out, and paid for that knowledge with her life.

'We asked her not to. What would have been the point? Only grief for us, and no good to the baby.'

'And Frank disposed of the body.'

'He did, my duck. Susan wrapped it all up, and he buried it.'

'And Don always knew.'

'Right, my love. Don knew from the start that there was something wrong.'

'And he's dead.'

Meg looked at her full face. 'And so is Susan.'

So she wasn't crazy at all, and she wasn't the only one who suspected Flaxton. Meg knew about human clonings in the womb, but she didn't know about Janus. As Lisa was about to speak, Meg placed a finger over her lips.

'Pays not to say nothing,' she whispered. 'That's what I was going to talk to you about.'

'Not telling anyone?'

'Get away from here. Fast as you can. Get away from all the terrible memories.'

Meg was warning her off, telling her to take her family away from Lodsham, away from Somerset. Was there anything else she was warning her about? Her head began to burn, to ache.

'We cut the elders down,' Lisa said sadly. 'Rex Smollett told us not to.'

'It's worse for you, Lisa. He was such a lovely little'un. You need to look after them specially. I hear Jansy has a badly broken leg.'

'He'll be all right,' Lisa assured her. It was becoming clear to her that Janus was much stronger than Phyllis. He'd cloned Jeffrey in the womb, and Jeffrey was a sturdy lad. James, of course, was cloned outside the womb. That's where the difference lay. Her poor little Jiminy hadn't stood a chance.

But now even Jansy wasn't in danger any more. He'd never clone again. Flaxton would know that, would know he was no longer a threat. He had a plastic pin inside his leg.

32

'Flaxton want me to go to Scotland,' Alec explained to Lisa. His voice was eager, almost boyish. 'They've offered me a pot of gold to do it.'

'Flaxton? You mean you'd actually be part of the Flaxton set-up?' Lisa stared at Alec in disbelief, examining his face to see if he were joking. He seemed to be quite serious.

'Not really any different from what I'm doing now. Just better paid.' He laughed, a genuine sound of delight. 'It's a wonderful chance, Lisa. Flaxton need their own accountancy department now that they've taken over Grammidge.'

'Grammidge.' Lisa had some vague memory of the mention of that name. 'Who, or what, is that?'

'A fine old company based in Glasgow. Haven't kept up with modern methods, I'm afraid, so they were ripe for a takeover. That's why Flaxton want me up there as soon as possible, to sort all that out for them. Remember, they're going public.'

Flaxton plc; that's what Janus had brought up on the computer screen. What else had he tried to show her? She had to stop this happening, had to stop Flaxton expanding. But how?

'You mean you'd give up your partnership at Grew, Donsett?'

He shrugged his partnership away as though it were of no account. 'Don't you see? It's the perfect out.' His eyes crinkled as he turned to her. 'We can get right away from what happened here.' His arms enveloped her, pressed her to him. 'Better for all of us to try to leave the past behind us, try to forget.'

'Jiminy's dead,' Lisa said, her voice flat. 'My little Jiminy's gone. How do I forget that?'

'You have to go on, Lisa. For the sake of the others. You'll be better off away from here; leave the sad memories behind.'

'Leave them behind? And precisely how do we do that, if you work for Flaxton?'

'It's not what you think, pet. Flaxton are expanding, they're changing out of all recognition. They don't just manufacture fertilisers now, you know. They're into drugs and plastics, as well.'

'Oil derivatives, you mean?'

Alec was clearly finding it difficult to keep his temper. He swallowed hard, breathed deep. 'You don't approve of their organic fertilisers. Now, I suppose, you're going to tell me that oil products pollute the planet.'

'They do.'

'We can't live on the earnings from your watercolours,' he said, his mouth thin and tight. 'And your precious pigments are made by Flaxton, too.'

'I don't buy their paints.'

He brushed that away and tried to sound less harsh, humouring her again, she sensed. Hands gentle, slow movements, a live incendiary to be defused. 'Unless you're telling me we should go self-sufficient, crofting or something.'

Lisa's eyes brightened. 'Would you consider that?'

'No,' he said shortly. 'I would not. We have three sons to educate.' He smiled again, his eyes gentling into softness. 'And the new little one. Perhaps a little girl this time.' He kissed her hair. 'You always wanted a large family.'

The sun was beginning to slant into the living room. Now that the trees had lost their green, the turkey oak outside the bay was letting in the sun. Lisa considered again how clever the nineteenth-century builders had been. This room was carefully sited to get all the winter sun, but shaded in the summer. She looked at the familiar view spread wide in front of her. The dream which had started so well almost five years ago had turned into a nightmare. What were her longings now?

Alec was doing all he could. He spent time with his family, he courted her, treated her as he used to do. And he'd agreed – even brought up the idea himself before she'd put it to him – that they should try for a new baby. The pregnancy test was positive. They were to be parents again. As Alec said, perhaps they'd have a daughter this time. She could lavish her overflowing maternal feelings on a new baby. Away from here she'd have the chance to heal old wounds, if not eliminate scar tissue.

'Well?' Alec was pressing her. 'What d'you think?'

'What do you want me to say? You've already made up your mind.'

'I want to do what's best for all of us, Lisa. I'm not shutting you out, or refusing to listen to you. The point is, d'you have any better ideas?'

'What about Multiplier, Alec? You can't just go on helping them to sell that time bomb, or even allow them to leave it on the market.'

'Time bomb?'

'Think, Alec! Think what happened to us. It could happen to millions of organisms all over the world. It may already be too late to stop it, but we could at least try.'

He sighed, but smiled again. 'I have thought about it all carefully, pet. I haven't just assumed you hallucinated everything.'

'But you still don't believe a single word of what I told you.'

'I think it's conceivable we had triplets because of the original strain of plankton used,' he said slowly. 'But that's been completely modified.' He took a folder out of his briefcase and opened it up. 'See? An entirely different type of plankton.'

Lisa skimmed over the text, turned a page. The carefully coloured charts looked familiar – just like the ones Janus had shown her on the computer.

'And there had to be other factors involved, darling. Apart from taking fertility drugs, having multiples is hereditary, you know.'

Only fraternal multiples, Lisa repeated to herself. Could Alec really believe she hadn't thought all that through? But she wasn't going to argue the point. No one, as yet, knew precisely what triggered the forming of identical multiples. All the same, whatever it was, it certainly didn't happen just before birth, or after it.

'The scan, Alec. Aren't you forgetting about the scan? We *saw* it, you know. There was only one foetus,' she reminded him.

'I thought we'd agreed that he was hidden behind the second one.'

'There were *three* infants. You're going to tell me next we only had twins, that I imagined Jiminy altogether.'

'I know how hard it's been, darling. I know how much you loved that little boy. And so did I.' He came over and stroked back her hair, twisting the little tendrils round his fingers. 'They say time heals. We've simply got to get away from here. From all the unhappy past. I really thought that you'd be pleased.'

'That you're going to work for Flaxton?'

'They're on the way to being another faceless, multinational company. They don't count one way or the other.' He sat down next to her. 'Frank and I have been over the ground time and again,' he went on, taking her hands in his. 'There's just no evidence about doubling up after the births. Honestly, Lisa. He would know.'

Frank? He'd talked to Frank about cloning? Frank had as much to lose as Flaxton if what had happened became common knowledge. He was raking in loads of money from testing Multiplier, from his increased yields. And still he wasn't satisfied. He plotted to gain every extra penny that he could. He'd never cross Flaxton, he wouldn't dare. How could Alec trust a man like that?

Lisa felt a cold knife of fear slice through her. Frank knew all about cloning, even if she couldn't prove it now Don and Susan were dead. Frank had deliberately covered up what had been happening on his farm. What other reason would he have had to kill everything off so systematically? And what else had he been up to? Shuddering, she remembered the milk lorry, the near miss with the triplets in their pushchair.

'It all happened on his doorstep,' Alec went on, putting his arms round her shoulders, steering her to a sofa.

'The most significant result happened on ours, Alec.'

Alec sounded irritated. 'There were more multiple births, Frank doesn't deny that. But that's something which only affects animals with a specific genetic make-up. The new strain of plankton doesn't have that effect. All that first strain of Multiplier did was to bring out the latent tendencies, encourage what's there already.'

'Like cigarettes bring out a latent tendency to lung cancer?' Lisa said softly.

'Come on, Lisa, everything has its negative side. Flaxton are monitoring the new formula meticulously, there really isn't a problem. Shall I make you a coffee, or something?'

'I'm fine, darling.'

'Try to forget all that. So what d'you think? How about leaving, getting away from here?'

She had to admit Alec was right in some ways. Much better not to be reminded by the sight of the Tor outside the nursery window, or looming up across the moor. Even meeting Meg and her children flooded her with memories, brought back scenes of happier times. It certainly would be better to make a fresh start.

'What I thought was wonderful about it all is that we can still live in the country.'

'I thought you just said Glasgow. That's hardly the country.'

'The Hebrides,' Alec told her. 'The Western Isles. You remember our honeymoon on Islay. We said then how marvellous it would be to live there. I thought we might look for a house there. The plane to Glasgow only takes about half an hour.'

'You mean you'd commute by plane every day?'

'Perhaps not every day; stay in Glasgow Monday to Friday, then come home for the weekend.'

They'd had a blissful time there on their honeymoon. Islay, known as the queen of the Hebrides, was a glorious place. They'd gone bird watching, run over the sands, collected shells, sampled malt whisky, made friends. She liked the idea of going back. Her whole being responded to the call.

'What, exactly, do Flaxton want you to do?'

'I'm an accountant, Lisa. They want me to be their financial director. Glasgow is their headquarters now.' He smiled. 'It's very flattering. They've been so taken with my work, they want me on their board.'

'So you would be in a very strong position. You'd be able to fix the company if you wanted to.'

'Fix them? You mean ruin them?'

'If you found out I wasn't demented; if Janus clones again. You could stop them manufacturing?'

'In theory I could do just that.'

'And what about your mother? An island in the Hebrides would be even harder to get to than Somerset.'

'I know. She'll just have to settle for it. That's where my career is taking me.' He paused for a moment. 'You can do your painting anywhere. They say the light is wonderful in Scotland.'

'And what about the children's education? Have you thought about that?'

'Scotland has an excellent education system,' Alec said firmly. 'Particularly in the primary schools. If anything, they'll be better off up there. And safer; we can let them roam without worrying. Remember what happened at Milton . . .' He tailed off, aware at last of possible undertones, possible implications.

'You're not really asking me,' Lisa said. 'You're telling me we're going to move to Scotland – the Hebrides. Out of the way. You're ashamed of me, is that it? You want me settled on Islay where I won't embarrass you.' Her eyes went blank.

'Give me a bit of credit, darling.'

Was she being unreasonable? Alec did have to earn some money. Whatever he did, he wasn't going to be able to challenge Flaxton openly. If she could convince him of what had happened, he could destroy the company from within. That was her best course.

'Actually,' he went on, 'it wasn't only my idea. Meg suggested it. I do believe she put Carruthers up to offering me the job. She told me she thought you'd never get over Jiminy if we stayed. I hadn't really thought that through, I must confess.'

'Meg told you that? Thought I'd get over it better somewhere else, did she?'

'That's what she said.'

'It didn't occur to you she thought we ought to leave for other reasons?'

'Other reasons? What other reasons?'

Lisa crossed her left knee over her right. 'You'll think it's just another aspect of what you choose to call my over-excited imagination. The events on the Tor – d'you really think they were entirely accidental?'

She saw his eyes glaze over, heard the deep intake of breath. 'I went over it endlessly with Trevor, pet. After all, he was there, on the spot. Presumably you don't think he's got an axe to grind?'

In fact she did. Trevor, more even than Alec, was eager to forget that day. Seb had told her that a red-haired young man had played with them that afternoon, had taken the kite and soared it high against the wind. He had even carried Jiminy up the Tor. But Trevor evaded Lisa whenever she tried to find out more about this helpful stranger. Where had he got to? Why hadn't he come forward to talk to the police after the accident? Trevor, apparently, had been as taken with the redhead's looks as Alec had been with Geraldine's.

'So what did Trev say?'

'He agreed with Meg. If anything, he was even keener. It was he who pointed out to me about the painting; the light, and the colours, he said, are wonderful in Scotland. He thought your scope would improve tremendously.'

Lisa did not doubt that. Now that he'd flooded the market with scenes of the Somerset Levels, he'd want her to try something new. Hebridean seascapes, pictures of gulls hovering over shipwrecks – a welcome change.

Alec leaned towards her again, uncertain but smiling. 'Darling, why don't we at least have a try at it?'

'You mean you'd come south again if it didn't work out?'

'I promise. I absolutely promise that if you don't like it after a year, we'll leave.' A brighter smile. 'I tell you what. Flaxton offered me a really grand house on Islay. Belongs to one of their major shareholders. He's moved to Jersey or somewhere tax efficient. We could try out living there, not buy a house until we're sure. That means we could leave at any time.'

Lisa saw the force of that. 'I suppose so,' she said listlessly. 'I don't know that I care.'

He laughed, slightly embarrassed. 'It comes complete with a rowan tree.'

'A rowan tree? Is that significant?'

A faintly sheepish look. 'Very, apparently. It's just the thing for breaking evil enchantments. A safeguard against calamity.'

Lisa could see that her husband was doing his best to do what he thought she wanted. But the very idea of possible omens made her feel ill.

'It's a woman's tree,' Alec went on, unaware. 'So the future will be up to you. A woman who curses a rowan tree brings death on her husband. So I shall be trusting you to look after it for me,' he finished off.

'We won't cut it down, then,' Lisa said softly, smiling up at him, snuggling towards him.

Islay. They could make a completely new start on Islay. The plan was beginning to grow on Lisa.

33

'Mrs Wildmore! This is a pleasure. Busy again, I see.' Ian Parslow scanned his notes, then lifted his eyes to hers. Penetrating, green. They gave nothing away.

Alec had insisted Lisa consult Parslow again, go through that whole battery of tests once more.

'We don't want any unforeseens this time,' Alec had smiled at her.

'But Parslow was the one who called it "a perfectly normal pregnancy"!' Lisa was now sure he had seen something unusual at that very first meeting.

'He'll be especially on his guard this time. He's the top man, darling. Everyone we know uses him. We can't do better.'

Lisa had agreed reluctantly. Parslow could keep information from them, but he couldn't really harm her. The baby would, in any case, be born in Scotland.

Would he even refer to the last time he'd seen her? Presumably there'd been some sort of feedback about the triplets. At the very least Gilmore would have let Parslow know in the new letter of referral.

'Here I am again, Mr Parslow,' Lisa said, as amiably as she could. 'Alec and I are trying for a little girl.'

The obstetrician bristled at once. 'I can't arrange that at this stage, I'm afraid.' Thin lips drew back to show it was a joke. 'At any rate, not in the present state of medical knowledge.'

He did not flaunt quite the dismissive manner of almost three years before. Instead of talking from afar, he walked right over to Lisa and shook her hand. He moved her to the couch and hooked up the ultrasound. 'But maybe you can. I was absolutely astounded to hear about your triplets. That must have been quite a shock to you.' He looked at Lisa, a long, deep stare. 'And such unusual circumstances. I gather the third one was born two weeks after the other two.' There was no smile, no hint of an apology. 'Quite remarkable.'

'I did—'

'Word of your special powers has spread!' His strong baritone drowned her attempt to speak. 'Lady Carruthers particularly mentioned you when she consulted me the other day; suggested that, as I'd been so brilliant with you, I might be able to arrange for her to have twins.' He smiled. The cat who'd licked the clotted cream. 'Told me not to overdo it, though. Apparently triplets would be too much for her.'

He hadn't heard about Jiminy's death from Gilmore, Lisa felt sure. And Diana Carruthers wouldn't have mentioned it to him, either.

'I'm not expecting miracles,' Lisa told him, a little coolly. 'I just thought you might be able to say whether this one's a girl.'

Parslow scrutinised the monitor carefully. 'I think that's pretty clear. Your ultrasounds are always so distinct, my dear. A little girl it is.'

'You're sure?'

The green eyes looked cold. 'It isn't absolutely foolproof at this stage, but I would say ninety-five per cent certain.'

'Could you just show me . . .'

'Certainly.' He took the blunt end of a pencil and traced out the relevant parts. 'I think the simplest way to tell is by the absence of the male genitals.'

Why was this man's behaviour to her so different from the Parslow she'd met before? His apparent regard for her made her quite nervous. Was it simply because she knew Diana? Was he really such a snob? 'Do you foresee any problems?'

'A perfectly normal pregnancy.' Parslow turned from the scan and faced Lisa directly, that affable expression spreading over his face. 'I do assure you, Mrs Wildmore, there is no reason for anxiety.' Another sharp, quick glance at the monitor. 'None at all.'

That old spiel again. Had he seen the foetus within a foetus of her nightmare? Was she carrying another cloner?

'I can't see why you shouldn't carry a beautiful baby to term.' He looked at his notes again, then back at Lisa. 'Of course I have given some thought to what happened last time. I simply couldn't believe the letter from your GP.'

'You may remember, I thought it would be twins.'

'I do remember; we both got it wrong.' His lips smiled but his eyes were darts. 'Though you were nearer the mark.'

Lisa clenched her nails into her palms, crunched her teeth together.

'There really is only one explanation,' Parslow continued, voice loud and overriding. 'The two others must have been lying directly behind the first one, right on top of one another.' Another attempt at a smile.

'An extraordinary fluke. I remember being surprised at how clear the image was – much denser than normal. I'd no idea I was seeing it in triplicate!'

'That's really what you think happened?'

The darts turned into daggers. 'Absolutely. There's no other way to explain it.' He stared intently at the monitor, then looked at Lisa again. 'But this time we'll make doubly sure. If you'll bear with us, we'll do another ultrasound in a month or so. The foetus will have moved position. No question of the same thing happening again.' He wrote something on his notepad. 'We'll do our best not to waste your time. Take samples now for all the other tests, and repeat those, as well. Can't be too careful, can we?'

Why did that sound like a threat? 'Not the amniocentesis,' Lisa said quickly, assertive, positive.

'No, certainly not that, my dear. I do agree.' Almost on the defensive. 'It wouldn't be useful, in any case. The findings would be too late for possible termination.' He smiled. 'I'll send the results to your GP as soon as the lab returns them.'

'There is just one thing, Mr Parslow.'

'Yes?'

'I did feel you saw something – unusual – last time. I was quite sure of it. Not medically unsound, of course. Just . . .'

The eyes had veiled; he tried to smile, but merely twisted his mouth. 'There's nothing in the notes, Mrs Wildmore. As I remember it, there was no problem whatsoever.'

'Not a problem. I just thought you might have seen something out of the—'

'Nothing at all.'

Lisa wondered just how he could maintain that in the face of what had developed, but decided there was no more to be gained by prodding him. He'd simply put her down again. 'I rather hope it's only one, this time.'

Parslow, evidently relieved, actually grinned at her. 'Well, I'm certainly not making any rash predictions,' he said, 'but there's a sporting chance.' There was a pause as he walked towards the window, his back to her. 'What are you taking now? Any medication at all?'

'I don't believe in drugs, particularly when I'm pregnant.' She felt composed, assured. 'I don't smoke. And I won't bother with alcohol for the next few months. Just wholesome food, grown without any artificial stimulants.'

'Very commendable, if you can find it.'

'I've taken up vegetable gardening.'

'Not too much of the heavy work, remember.'

'If I feel overdone, I drink herb tea, made from dried roots or leaves. Grown on a local farm.'

'Indeed. Herb tea?' Parslow's quick eyes showed interest. 'What sort of herbs?'

'Lady's mantle is my favourite at the moment,' Lisa told him. 'Just the leaves. Very important during pregnancy.'

'Anything else?'

'Dandelion if I need a diuretic.'

He was watching her attentively. 'An interesting idea.'

She paused, wondering whether to let him know, then decided she might as well get his opinion. 'And valerian root tea if I'm overwrought. No chemicals of any sort, you see.'

The doctor rubbed a smooth, strong chin. 'It isn't quite as simple as that, you know.' A chair was placed beside her. 'I really think I must warn you against relying too much on folklore.'

'You don't approve?'

'I think you're playing with unknowns here. It's fashionable to think that plants are "natural" and can't do you any harm. We know that's wrong, of course. Some are known killers – hemlock, for instance, and belladonna. The green nightshade berries can be deadly, they contain powerful poisons – scopolamine, hyoscyamine and atropine, among others. I'm afraid "natural" isn't equivalent to "safe".'

'I know that, Mr Parslow.'

'All matter is made up of chemicals, we can't escape that. A number of the well-known drugs we use are synthesised from plants. But for every discovery of useful drugs from such sources, like aspirin or digitalis, we need to sift hundreds of plants or other organisms to find another safe one.'

'But—'

'I really don't want to preach, but it is important for you to bear some facts in mind. Natural plants contain any number of chemicals. They're in the tissues and juices of the plants. What bothers me is not the beneficial ingredients in some of the herbs – I don't deny there are pharmologically active ones – but that the dosage is uncontrolled.'

'You mean I don't know how much I'm taking?'

'Exactly. Neither how much, nor how little, or exactly what. On the other hand, if the desired ingredient is isolated, purified in the laboratory, it can be administered in properly calculated doses. That's what we do with modern drugs.'

'But the new drugs are much more powerful, and the drug companies make enormous profits.'

'There has to be a financial benefit, the research has to be funded.' The green had turned to a dark emerald. 'It would be much wiser if you stuck to proven vitamins and minerals. For what it's worth, that's what I'd recommend.'

'So you think what I'm doing is dangerous?'

'Mostly I'd think it was harmless. The valerian needs to be taken in strict moderation – I'm sure you already know that.'

'Yes,' Lisa said softly. 'I do.'

'I'd certainly prefer to prescribe a mild sedative.'

'Like thalidomide, you mean?'

'Below the belt, Mrs Wildmore. Tests are far more stringent now. Mine certainly are.' He looked at her, pupils pinpoints of power. 'I expect you've heard from Lady Carruthers.'

'Diana is expecting twins?' Lisa asked, an image of the split in her womb surfacing.

'I would never discuss a patient,' Parslow said severely. He smiled; a genuine, warm smile. 'What I thought she might have told you is that Flaxton have just made a substantial grant available to me. They are funding my team of embryologists. We're observing the effects of particular chemical signals on DNA.'

DNA – Dinnay! She saw the pebbles Janus had written in the sand at Brean – *that* was why he'd shown her the coloured screens from Alec's disks, that's what they symbolised. The DNA of a particular person. He'd found the description of *his* DNA.

'Mrs Wildmore? Are you all right?'

Lisa pulled herself together. 'Of course, Mr Parslow. I was just taking in what you were saying.'

Flaxton were funding Ian Parslow's research? She felt trapped, hemmed in. Had they obtained a sample of Janus's tissue, tested his DNA and found that he was a cloner? Were they now using Parslow to get samples from her new foetus? Perhaps he had worked out a way to obtain the cells he needed in spite of her refusal to have the amniocentesis. Was that why he was asking her to come back for a second set of tests? She would, of course, refuse.

'That's Flaxton's special field,' the doctor continued, unaware of her thoughts. 'These are exciting times.'

34

[illegible]

Do we really [illegible]

Alex [illegible]

[illegible]

She [illegible]

[illegible]

Stranger still, [illegible]

[illegible]

34

'Do we really have to go?'

Alec turned slowly, adjusting his silk tie in the mirror, his suit immaculate. 'One minute you say I'm having a secret affair with Geraldine, the next you refuse to join in when you're invited. The girl's eighteen, her parents are giving a special party at the Bath and West, and she particularly wanted you and the children to be there.' He did not hide his exasperation. 'Now what's wrong with that?'

There wasn't really anything wrong with it. Geraldine had taken immense pains to make herself appear sympathetic and friendly since the accident on the Tor. She'd offered to spend free time with Janus. She seemed to be prepared to put up with the problems he experienced accommodating his broken leg, and she had taken endless trouble to help him adjust to coping with his cast.

Janus, Lisa had noted with interest, had steadfastly refused all overtures of friendship. 'Don't like Gerry,' he said on virtually every occasion that the girl hoved in sight. 'Won't play with Gerry.' And to the girl herself he always said, 'Don't want you here. Go away.'

In spite of this, Geraldine had insisted on playing, or trying to play, games with him. To distract him when the pain was at its worst, she'd explained to Lisa. And Janus had suffered her there when he was in too much discomfort to fight her. The girl had gone even further. She had volunteered to help him with the exercises the doctors had prescribed to keep his body fit.

Stranger still, it seemed to Lisa that the girl's interest in Alec had decreased. She talked of several younger men and of a special boy friend. Nevertheless, Lisa was not fooled into thinking of her as a simple little helper at the school.

Geraldine's interest in Janus, Lisa had worked out for herself, was to keep tabs on him. In other words, as long as Janus was in a cast, as long as he was known to have that plastic splinter in his leg, he wasn't a threat to anyone.

Should the situation change, well then that would be different. Flaxton would hear about it right away, and take what action was necessary. They were playing a waiting game. Lisa had taken care to ensure they understood that Janus was no longer a danger to them. She went out of her way to discuss everything about Janus's medical condition with Geraldine, even inviting her to accompany them to the check-ups at the hospital.

What Lisa did not tell anyone, though she was acutely aware of it, was that the only way she could prevent that awful bloating, those first telltale signs of imminent cloning, was to keep the child to a strict diet of food produced by means other than organic. It was ironic that she, of all people, should now insist that Janus eat produce grown with artificial fertilisers. Controlled, as Ian Parslow had put it.

A very special set of circumstances had brought Janus about. She was sure she now knew how to contain his terrible attribute, how to stop his ever cloning again. He had a permanent pin in his leg; that solved the tagging problem. All she had to do was control his diet, make sure his energies were fully used. Perhaps Gilmore could be persuaded to prescribe a chemical diuretic to discharge any accumulation of extra fluid.

'You want us to meet you at the Bath and West at four?' Lisa brought herself back to the present.

'Three thirty, Lisa. The Fitch-Templetons particularly asked me to make sure that you get there on time. They have some special treat planned, and it's supposed to start at four.'

Alec walked over to his wife, his handsome features composed, his trim figure impressive in his suit, his brown hair reasonably plentiful. A good-looking, successful man; the father of her children. He had a presentation box in his hands. So he was giving Geraldine something special; evidently the flame wasn't entirely quenched.

'I thought we might give Geraldine a string of amber,' he said. 'She really has been splendid about Janus. Perhaps we can persuade Jansy to make the presentation.' He held the box out to her, smiling.

Lisa opened it. A string of iridescent opals blinked up at her, a matching pair of earrings at the side. These were in a different class from amber. Did Alec think she couldn't tell the difference?

Opals – known for their mythical powers. Stones of tragedy, of death. Some king of Spain, she remembered, had presented an opal ring to his wife on their wedding day, and she had died soon after. Did Alec know that?

'I think you gave me the wrong box,' Lisa said coldly, handing it back.

His eyes smiled love at her. 'This one's for you. To match your delicate complexion.' He came towards her, taking the necklace from the box. He held the milky stones up in his hands. 'May I?'

'Oh, Alec.' She melted. How could she have doubted him? 'They're lovely, really beautiful.'

The iridescent stones curved round her slender neck. Her skin, translucent and with the sheen of country life, glowed back the gemstones.

'Put on the earrings as well,' Alec suggested.

She placed the teardrops on the lobes of her ears. Soft, wavy gold wisped over them.

'I'll put my hair up,' Lisa said, holding it behind her. The face in the mirror smiled back at her, the blue eyes dark.

'You look a million,' Alec murmured into her ear. 'Sorry I've got to go. Geraldine's necklace is here.' He held another package out to her. 'See if you can get Jansy to give it to her for all of us. And don't forget, three thirty sharp.'

This time the opals had done their work even before they were presented, Lisa thought sadly. Her little Jiminy was dead already.

'You and Jeffers in the back, Seb.'

'It's my turn to sit in front, Mummy.'

'It's easier for Mummy to arrange Jansy's cast in the front,' Lisa explained again. 'It's coming off soon. Then you can take it in turns, as we used to do.'

The little boy said nothing, but Lisa could feel him think of Jiminy.

'Here we go, then, Jansy. You hold the present for Gerry, will you? Remember what we practised. When it's our turn to give her our presents, you give her this. From all of us.'

'No!' The little boy took the box and threw it hard against the floor of the car. The gold wrapping paper, so carefully arranged, split at a corner.

She saw Jeffrey scramble down to pick up the box, then gently stroke his brother's hand, holding the box away from him and offering it to her. Could Jeffrey feel his brother's pain? She took the box and handed it to Seb to hold.

Janus sat unresponsive, stone-faced, staring out of the windscreen. The two boys in the back began to chant numbers.

Lisa strapped the children into their seats. Her heart pit-pattered as she thought of the last time she had driven them alone. Brean Sands. Her little Jiminy had been with them, then. Sleeping in the back, already showing signs of the unexpected, unheralded illness lurking within him. Why hadn't she known? Could she have saved him if she hadn't been so taken up with Janus?

He sat, the child who had at one time been so aggressive, silent and docile. His leg was hurting him, she knew. The break, though mending brilliantly according to the doctors, was giving him constant pain, sapping his strength. He was no longer raucous. He had become thinner, almost skinny. Had the accident on the Tor been a real accident? Lisa could not stop herself from wondering. Something she couldn't quite put her finger on. Who was the redhead who had seated Jiminy on the slick blue anorak? That's why her little boy had slipped to his death that day. Whatever the doctors said, who knew how long he might have lived?

Who was that young man Seb had talked about? What had he been doing there? Had he given James a push? Why would he? Unless, of course, he had mistaken James for Janus. Was that possible? Was the young man a hired assassin, paid to kill the cloner before the world found out about him, before he could clone again?

Grief had prevented Lisa from thinking properly about the accident, and the grave-digging episode which had gone before it. Why had the grave been empty? Not because Multiplier had hastened decomposition, she now realised. It was because someone had removed the corpse and replaced it with loam. As Alec had pointed out, there was no dip, no indentation, no slippage of soil; so no body had decomposed. Nor was there clay, like the second spit between the other two fruit trees. Alec had dug up only good black earth.

Someone must have removed the body. That could only be someone who worked for Flaxton, someone who knew what was going on, someone who knew how to replace a body with soil. That's why the fruit tree leaders had been broken; that's why there were unexpected bits and pieces in the soil. It all made sense now.

'It's a Flaxton lorry, Mummy.'

Lisa, distracted, pulled herself together. She had been driving fast, oblivious of what was happening around her. The narrow roads could only be safely navigated by one car at a time. She'd have to pull in at a stopping place to allow the distinctive yellow lorry with its black Flaxton logo to pass her.

'That's the second one today.'

'Second what, Seb?'

'Second yellow one, with the pirate sign.'

'Pirate sign?'

'Like the jolly roger, the skull and crossbones.'

Lisa laughed. Seb had been reading *Captain Pugwash* books. It was true that the black logo, a large X supporting a central F, was reminiscent of the symbol of pirates of old. Modern ones were not so different, Lisa thought nervously. They all hunted for treasure, and killed if anyone got in their way.

She began to pull out of the passing space, then saw that there was a large herd of cows advancing towards her. She looked at the clock: nearly three. She'd be late. She'd forgotten to allow for afternoon milking; normally she would not be out on the moor at this time. Mark Ditcheat's herd, being humped – hunted, the locals called it – back to the farm for milking.

The road was narrow, but Lisa decided not to back into the passing place. The cows could quite easily go by, one or two at a time. She watched them lazily as they began to walk past, their dumb, silent faces looking indifferently through her windscreen. They were large animals. One bumped the car, and Lisa quickly shut the windows. Otherwise the flies which followed the cows everywhere would get in.

The big herd lumbered past slowly. Five past three. She might just make it in time if she speeded up as soon as the cows thinned out.

She turned from looking at the two children in the back and saw one cow heave against the Volvo as another bulled onto her back. The placid herd was beginning to lurch and move more rapidly. Lisa could see, across the many black and white backs still to come, the yellow of a large lorry pushing them towards her.

The cows pressed closer, surrounding her, crashing both sides, trampling the verges of the rhyne beside her. The mooing sounds of peaceful milch cows turned to lowing, the lowing crescendoing into the beat of hoof against tarmac and stones.

'It's another yellow one!' Seb said excitedly. 'That's three!'

They were stampeding. The driver of the yellow lorry was hooting his horn, banging the side of his lorry with a stick. Where was Mark Ditcheat? He was supposed to have one person at the back, one at the front, to guide his herd. None of them ever did that, but Lisa could not remember a time when there was no one at all to guide the animals.

A sudden, splintering crack. Lisa, horrified, thought her windscreen had been hit, then saw it was her outside mirror. A stone, presumably, kicked up by a hoof, had shattered the glass into a jagged, spiked star. Lisa saw images of cows reflected a hundredfold. She wound the mirror round to reflect the inside of the car; the mechanism was intact. Suddenly she caught sight of Janus in the mirror – a myriad Januses, tight-lipped, staring ahead.

A vision of a new world came to her. Not the sad, repetitive, contained *Brave New World* Huxley had foreseen, but something infinitely more terrifying. An exploding world, out of control, volcanic. Insects reproducing at exponential rates, invading cities, even bodies. Plants devouring the earth, smothering buildings. Large animals with no space to move. Even humans spurting out clones, great groups of stereotypes, their defects accelerating with each cloning. A horror spreading out its tentacles over the whole planet.

She could see that killing on a worldwide scale would be the only defence. Squads of exterminators wasting all life within their path. Troops of cloner hunters, armed with guns. The final solution. She wound the mirror back to the present.

The Volvo rocked from side to side and Lisa gripped the wheel. Would the frightened animals actually tip the car over and butt them into the rhyne?

'They're pushing us, Mummy!' Seb was pounding his little fists against the window behind the driver's seat. Lisa began to sound her horn, the loud Volvo horn she used to alert her way out of her drive.

The cows, driven between the lorry and herself, became confused. Some turned back on themselves, others began to shy away from her.

'Ho, ho, ho!' Janus began to shout, and Jeffrey immediately joined in with him. Seb amplified the cry, and the animals, surprised, steered clearer.

She'd have to take the cow by the horns, Lisa told herself grimly. She and her children would drive through. Once more a feeling of oppression, of forces arraigned to harm her, took hold of her.

Was someone really out to get her children, to kill the remaining triplets? Even though they were now completely harmless?

Lisa jerked the car into gear, blared her horn and began to nose through the milling animals. She could see the yellow lorry parked in the next passing place, the driver shaking his fist at her. She didn't look at his face, kept her eyes ahead. Sweating now, furious herself, she poked the tank-like Volvo through the tail end of the herd and accelerated away as fast as she was able.

'They tried to knock us over,' Seb said angrily. 'He shouldn't have been hooting at them like that.'

Lisa's knuckles whitened on the wheel. Those Flaxton drivers were getting out of hand. This time she had the shattered mirror to show her husband. She'd tell them all about it at Geraldine's party. Never mind that it was a special occasion. Fitch-Templeton was, after all, now also a director of the firm. And the rest of them would be there. If they really needed Alec, wanted him to sort things out for them in Glasgow, they'd have to humour her. Pass the word to their drivers to behave. It was time to put an end to this nonsense.

35

Alec was waiting for her at the main entrance to the showground, together with a young man in a chauffeur's uniform.

'You're late, Lisa.'

'Sorry. We had to negotiate Mark Ditcheat's herd. It was a disgrace—'

'Later, darling. Jenkins will drive us to the lake. We'll take the children on from there,' he said brusquely. 'Jenkins can park the car.'

There was something odd about the young man who smiled too widely as she handed him the car keys. He'd swept off his cap as Lisa climbed out of the driving seat. His hair, jet black, seemed to have been oiled. He had smooth, curiously milky skin freckling brown, and green eyes. An unusual colour combination, Lisa's trained eye registered as she leaned forward to buckle her seatbelt in the back. The chauffeur shifted his cap forward, evidently hot, and as he did so Lisa was surprised to see that the hair on the back of his neck, low down where it merged into his back, was ginger. Something impelled her to look at his hair again.

Jet black – too black, she thought. It looked as though he dyed it. And the eyebrows, too? She looked into the rearview mirror. Was black a fashionable colour? And then she saw what had been worrying her subconscious. The eyebrows were the same jet black as the hair, but the eyelashes were light ginger, like the soft down on the back of the hands gripping the steering wheel. This young man did dye his hair!

When they reached the lake, Alec got out first, then allowed Lisa to deal with Janus. He was not able to walk at all; she put him in the special pushchair they had bought for him, and pushed him towards the bank of benches erected round the lake.

'Jansy!' Geraldine caught sight of the Wildmores and came towards them, smiling bright teeth. She did not even glance at Alec. Dark, glossy ringlets overwhelmed bare shoulders, russet sequins on black lace corseted her exquisite figure into a tight hug, and her long, lycra-clad legs shimmered silver dust into Italian sandals.

The child in the pushchair leaned away from her. His big, wide eyes assessed her stability and noticed a flaw. Lisa saw the eyes gleam into life, then jog the pushchair into stonier ground. Catching his drift, she veered off the carefully cut turf.

'Not there, Gerry!' Alec tried to warn her.

But Geraldine, already caught in the rough field, began to teeter, then skip precariously as her long, skinny heels sank between the ruts. Alec offered an arm. Too late. There was a crack as the left heel broke off.

'Oh, dear,' Lisa commiserated. 'What a shame. Such lovely shoes.'

'That's not going to worry her!' Nigel Carruthers, welcoming them, roared with laughter. 'She's got at least another hundred pairs to choose from!'

But not here, Lisa thought gleefully to herself as she watched Janus's lips curl up into a rare smile.

'Just the man I wanted to see,' Lisa greeted Flaxton's MD. 'I've been meaning to tell you about those drivers of yours. They rush your yellow lorries across the moors as though they were torpedoes! We're late because they stampeded a whole herd of cows into us. It's disgraceful, and dangerous.'

Carruthers smiled urbanely at her. 'I am so sorry, my dear. It's the latest Mercedes engines, I'm afraid. Bit tempting, I daresay.' He smiled charmingly at her. 'You know what young men are!'

'But you will have a word with their foreman?'

'Lisa!' Nanette Fitch-Templeton sailed over and took Seb and Jeffers in each hand. 'I'm so glad you could come. And just in time. We've got a special treat for all of you.'

She led the way down to the showground lake now fringed by wide terraces, backed by a rockery straight from the Chelsea Flower Show. A fountain of bubbling water gushed out over a pair of dolphins frisking enjoyment.

'Look, Seb,' she said to the little boy. 'All your friends are here. Go and sit with them at the front. Look after Jeffers, now.' She turned back to Lisa. 'And we'll make sure Jansy has the best view. You'd like that, wouldn't you, Jansy?'

He twisted away from her, banging the side of his chair. Nanette turned back to Lisa.

'How's his leg getting on?'

'The cast is coming off in a couple of weeks. Then we'll have to work hard at exercising his leg, to get the muscle tone back, but once that's there, he'll be fine.'

'No permanent damage?'

'The doctors say he may feel the change in the weather, but even that's not as bad with plastic as with metal.'

'You mean the plastic will be there permanently?'

'I'm told the bone grows round it and it becomes part of his make-up.' Lisa smiled broadly. 'No different from having a filling in a tooth, I suppose.'

Was it her imagination, or did Nanette heave a sigh of relief? 'How wonderful,' she breathed. 'Now we can enjoy the show.'

The dolphins were twirling in the lake, throwing themselves in and out of the water, spraying the audience. Two lithe young men appeared, one with a plastic pail, the other with a ring and ball.

The dolphins began to go through their routine, catching the ball on their noses, diving through the ring, jumping out of the water to catch fish. Lisa was not sure what Fitch-Templeton did for a living, apart from the Flaxton directorship he'd recently taken on, but it was evidently paying dividends. The party had been put on for the benefit of his fellow directors and the larger shareholders; the lake had been widened into an immense pool especially for the dolphin display.

As a finale, one of the dolphins balanced a large, wide platter on its nose. The first young man kept it steady while the second placed a cake with eighteen lighted candles on the platter. It wobbled precariously but did not tip over. The audience cheered and began to sing 'Happy Birthday to you, dear Geraldine'.

Speeches followed, presentations were made.

'And I'm delighted to announce that Alec Wildmore will be joining the Flaxton board,' Nigel Carruthers was saying, turning to wave at the Wildmore family, 'as from today. As you know, he is organising our takeover of Grammidge. We'll be gaining a gifted new financial director. He'll see us into our new future; he'll mastermind Flaxton going public.'

Dutiful claps, subdued 'Jolly goods' around the packed stand.

'There is a price, I'm afraid. We're going to lose some wonderful neighbours in the autumn.'

Diana Carruthers, next to Lisa, whispered her regrets. Apparently she'd miss the Wildmores.

'The family have decided not to live in Glasgow, but to make their home on Islay.' He turned, smiling at Lisa. 'They've got used to our country ways and want to benefit from the beautiful countryside there. But we'll always be glad to welcome them in Somerset,' he said. 'What about a reunion here, this time next year?'

It seemed the Wildmores were popular. Rather more popular than Lisa had supposed. Or were these people simply glad to hear that they were leaving?

'It's our turn to give Geraldine a present,' Alec whispered to his three sons, carrying Jansy up to the front. 'Now then, Jansy. You be the one to give it to her. All right?'

The child's eyes seemed slit against the sun, the dazzle coming from the water. 'No,' he said.

'But, Jansy—'

'Don't want,' he said, quite clearly. It was, Lisa realised, his first public announcement. His voice rang true and clear.

Alec ignored what he said entirely, lifted him out of the pushchair and placed him over his shoulders. The leg, wrapped in its cast, stuck out defiantly. They processed up to the front, Seb and Jeffrey following behind.

Alec stood on the platform and made his speech of acceptance for the new job. That finished, he turned to the personal side.

'We all know how much Gerry's been helping our wounded warrior,' Alec said easily, 'and I know he'd like to express his thanks to her for all the trouble she's taken.'

He took the presentation box out of his pocket and handed it to Janus. The child held it high, then hurled it towards the dolphins with all his might. It sailed in a splendid parabola across to the middle of the lake. Janus had not lost the strength of his arms. If anything, it had increased; he had manipulated the pushchair as though it were a wheelchair.

To everyone's astonishment one of the dolphins leapt at the box and caught it on its nose, and held it there. The applause was deafening. Geraldine, now barefoot, walked over to the pool and took her present.

'It's absolutely lovely,' she said, taking out the glorious necklace of different coloured amber, their shades of yellow, russet and titian mingling into a cascade of adornment. They fitted her outfit to perfection.

Alec took a second box out of his pocket. Geraldine opened it to bring out a cluster of matching amber; earrings which blazed against the raven tresses of her hair. She looked absolutely stunning.

'And now, just to conclude this lovely celebration, I would like to make another special announcement. This one concerns my family and myself,' he went on, enjoying being the centre of attention. 'Wonderful news.' His voice dropped a tone. 'You all know about the tragic accident on the Tor, and how we lost our darling little son, one of our triplets. It was a terrible blow to all of us, and most particularly to his mother.'

The sea of faces smiled embarrassment, hats nodded, hands clapped demure sympathy.

'My family and I will be sad to leave Somerset. In spite of what has happened, we have splendid sons who were born here. We can't change the past, but we can look with confidence into the future. And a new future is there for us. I'm absolutely delighted to tell you all, it's been confirmed. We have a baby daughter on the way.'

'You've seen Parslow?' Diana whispered to Lisa, eyes wide.

'All those tiresome tests,' Lisa agreed, smiling away unease. Was there any way in which Parslow could have harmed her already? She didn't think so.

A faint ripple of surprised applause stirred through the audience. Nigel Carruthers rose to his feet.

'A toast to our very good friends,' he boomed, raising his glass, crashing his palms together.

It was then that the applause became thunderous.

36

'Will Uncle Trev be there?'

'Hold on a minute, Seb. I'm on the phone. Sorry, Dr Gilmore. Why do you want to do a blood test?'

'For Mr Parslow. I can take the sample from you, Mrs Wildmore, and send it up to him; no need for you to go to Bristol.'

'I thought he'd already sent my samples in and had the results?'

'That's just what I was saying to you. All Mr Parslow's files have been destroyed.'

'Destroyed? How?'

'There was some sort of break-in at his laboratory, very distressing. All his records gone, his samples smashed. Terrible business.'

Lisa was delighted about her records. Maybe fate was taking a turn in her direction for a change. 'But I thought he sent *you* my results? Can't you just send them back?'

A short pause, a clearing of Gilmore's throat. 'It seems he did some tests which wouldn't be relevant to y . . . the records here. Aspects of his research.'

So Parslow had not changed his spots – just his manner. 'He used *my* samples for his research?'

There was no reply.

'Without asking my permission first?'

'I'm sorry, Mrs Wildmore. I can't comment on that.' There was a chill in his voice. 'All I'm doing is—'

'I'll be in touch, Dr Gilmore,' Lisa said coldly. 'Thank you for ringing.' And she put the receiver down.

'Will he, Mummy? Will he come?' Seb was asking her, pulling at her sleeve.

'Will who come? Oh, yes, Uncle Trevor. Sorry, darling.' Lisa remembered, too late, that she'd forgotten to ask Seb's favourite uncle designate to join them for his fourth birthday party. 'I think he's in Bath, Seb.'

'Can you ring him and ask him to come?'

'I could try,' she said, annoyed that her preoccupation had stopped her working that one out. 'He might just be able to make it.'

Seb stood tall and eager in the hallway as Lisa tapped the number in.

'Trevor Sayles, please.' Lisa twiddled the cord restlessly as she waited for the connection. 'Trev, at last! You're obviously getting far too important.'

'Well, there you go, Lis. I have this lady client who paints wonderfully evocative West Country scenes. The galleries are flooding me with requests for shows!'

'I know, I know,' she said lightly, though there was some truth in what he said. 'If only I had more time!'

'Is something wrong?'

'Nothing you can't put right. Seb wants to invite you to his birthday party. We hoped you'd be able to drive down from Bath and be with us this afternoon.'

'Right away, you mean?'

'That would be great. Alec's already on his way.'

'I'd love to join you.'

'We're off next week, so Meg's giving the party. She says I've got too much else on my hands, with the move and everything.'

'Good old Meg.'

'Not so much of the old, she's my age. Anyway, here's Seb.'

'Hello, Uncle Trev.'

'Many Happy Returns, Sebbie! So what's your favourite present?'

'I like your paintbox,' Seb answered diplomatically. 'I'm going to try it out soon.'

'And the favourite is?'

'I haven't got it yet. Daddy's giving me a pony. When we get to Islay.'

'A pony? All to yourself?'

'Jeffers can ride it sometimes, but Jansy can't until his leg is better.'

'I can't compete with that!'

Lisa took the receiver back from Seb. 'We'll see you later, then?'

'I wouldn't miss it for the world,' Trevor said, a warm tone in his voice. 'I can leave here in about ten minutes. See you at four.'

'That's wonderful! Seb's thrilled. At Crinsley Farm, remember. Look out for Alec's Audi outside their house, then you won't miss it.'

'I'll be there. Well, courtesy of Lodsham herds.'

Lisa took Seb's hand in hers. She walked him out into the garden, her heart singing at the happiness in his eyes, and went over to Janus and Jeffrey playing in the sandpit.

Jeffrey was chanting 'Baa Baa Black Sheep' at the top of his voice. Janus, his cast-wrapped leg stretched out in front of him, was making shapes in the sand. Perhaps he'll be a sculptor, Lisa fantasised. She was astonished at the boy's precocity. He chiselled the sand quickly, expertly. Four identical sand rabbits, their ears laid back, crouched sentinel by the large warren he had built for them.

'They've got to hurry up, Mummy. We'll be late!'

'It won't take me long to get them ready,' Lisa assured Seb. 'Come on, Jeffers. You first.'

'Can you make a pony?' she heard Seb ask Janus.

'Pony,' Jansy said, sweeping the bunnies back to sand and assembling the massive body of a quadruped, its swollen belly curved, kneeling on its front legs.

Lisa's deft fingers changed Jeffers into clean clothes and shoes. She walked him to the sandbox. 'See he doesn't get himself dirty now,' she instructed Seb.

It took a little longer to ready Jansy. His face, at one time so podgy, looked wan. Unwinking blue eyes were solemn now, round with awareness, the sockets sunk deep with pain. Lisa's heart went out to him. He had paid heavily for trying to save his brother.

'Let's get you ready now, shall we, Jansy,' she said, smiling encouragement. Changing trousers caused him distress.

'Jansy going to party,' he agreed. 'Play with Phyllie.' He beamed at her. The cheerful, open smile of a two-year-old for his mother. No vestige of that crafty gleam that used to plague her, though his eyes were still brightly intelligent. Slowly, methodically, they moved in unison. It was not unlike having a handicapped child, Lisa thought suddenly. Jansy needed her help; he could not walk without her, he was dependent on her. But even when his leg was healed, they would remain partners, conspire to keep his secret secure.

That was no longer difficult, of course. He would never clone again, even when the cast came off. Not ever. Their nightmare was over at last. Whether Alec believed her or not no longer really mattered. She had three sons: Seb and her twins, Janus and Jeffrey. And, she hugged to herself, a new life stirring within her, a baby daughter.

Her hands, busy brushing the sand from Jansy's hair, twined his blond locks round her fingers, then wiped him clean. As she slipped the yellow shirt over his head, her mind went back three years. Seb's first birthday, when Gilmore had confirmed she was pregnant again. That was the time she'd found the four-leaf clover and wished for twins on it.

And that, she thought ruefully, squeezing her lids shut on the moisture in her eyes, is what she'd ended up with. Twins, not triplets. Her wish had come true. She'd never wish again; not for a single child, not for anything specific. She'd gladly take whatever fortune chose to give, and take it gratefully.

That day had been, she remembered fondly, a burnished summer's day. The soft, fresh air had enveloped her gently in a warm embrace. She had been eager, then. Hungry for more children, ambitious to prove her womanhood. This time she was content to allow life to flow through her, with her.

She placed a bottle of champagne in the pushchair beside Janus. They would celebrate their last Somerset birthday party with the Graftleys, with Trevor. She could see the tall meadow grass across the road beckoning, waving its welcome. She'd push Jansy in his chair, and walk the other children through the fields, over the Graftleys' home meadow. It would be fun to see how many varieties of butterfly they could count, to pick the blooming wild flowers, to enjoy the trinity of clover leaves, to see the vegetation and the wildlife back to normal quantities. The new strain of Multiplier was not causing problems. The skylark sang his song for her; high, glorious, gliding the wind.

'Come on, Jansy. Let's get you comfortable in the chair.'

He did not want to be strapped in. The well-worn meadow path was smooth, safer than walking round by road, but even so she wasn't going to risk a tumble for Janus at this stage.

'One, two, three, go!' Lisa sang out, shepherding the children down the drive, her mind busy with the new life to come. She would never forget her Jiminy; but she was ready, now, to live again. 'You wait here for a moment,' she told Janus, 'while I see the other two across to the field.'

As she spoke, the approaching roar of a lorry speeding towards the curve of their narrow lane held her back inside the drive.

'They go much too fast,' she told her children, exasperated. 'Gerry's daddy promised to have a word with them. They've no right to risk everyone like that. Even the animals aren't safe.'

The deep yellow of a Flaxton lorry hurtled past, quickly enough to make the logo appear to grin.

'It's the same driver,' Seb shouted. 'I'm going to tell my Daddy on him.'

'The one who hooted the herd into us?' Lisa asked, startled. 'Are you sure?' She had brought the incident up with Nigel Carruthers at the Bath and West showground, and she'd tackled Fitch-Templeton as well.

'Of course, my dear,' his bland, soft voice had tried to reassure her. 'I'll see to it first thing tomorrow.' She'd seen him swallow up her hair, her willowy figure, her neat ankles. His narrow lips had curved a cusp of twisted red. 'We're fitting tachometers to each vehicle now. That will discourage them from going over the speed limit. The fines are quite horrific.'

'Not that one,' Seb told her. 'It's the one who parked our car at the Show. I can tell because he wears those funny glasses. Like the man who carried Jiminy up the Tor.'

An icy finger snaked down Lisa's spine. 'Really, Seb? Are you quite sure?' The old, familiar terror gripped her in its tentacles. The lorry had hurtled past at a quite idiotic pace. She shuddered as the memory of her dead child came back, felt the horror of it. Alec was right; they had to leave. Abandon the sounds, the sights, the incidents which could bring it all rushing back at her, engulfing her, drowning her.

All was quiet now; no sound of traffic, not even the chugging of a tractor. At least the lorry had passed; it would not come this way again today.

Lisa held the two children in each hand and looked first right, then left, then right again. All clear; no new sound, only the wind in the willows whistling by. She marched them over the road, unlatched the rusty gate, swung it wide and saw them into the safety of the field.

'Stay there,' she told them. 'Go on a bit further, but not too far. See how many different butterflies you can count. I'll just fetch Jansy.'

As she turned, she saw the massive structure of her home for the past five years. Large windows outlined in Bath stone, the high red brick walls they'd softened with climbing roses; stolid, serene. Had bad luck really haunted them because they'd cut down that old elder hedge?

Her eyes followed the drive down to Jansy's chair. The little boy, evidently bored with waiting, had begun to rock it. His white-cast leg was moving up and down, his body back and forth. He must be getting stronger, Lisa thought happily. The pain must have lessened, perhaps gone away. He'd soon be well, running about like her other sons.

He was swinging his body, jolting himself back to reach the brake Lisa had carefully put on, intent on unlatching it. The strong fingers gripped back and down. She saw the chair begin to move; slowly at first, then gathering speed. She began to run, then sprint towards her child.

'Don't move, Jansy!' she cried. The terror of losing him gave her voice sufficient mastery to make him hold himself back as he looked towards her. The pushchair, no longer given impetus, turned and slowed into the curve of the wall by the drive, edging rather than rushing its way.

'*No*, Mummy!'

She heard the alarm in his voice, the warning; then took in the reverberating throttle of an accelerating motor. Her eyes turned up the lane.

'Sto . . . o . . . p!'

The shrill, penetrating yelp which Janus hurled across the road at her screamed terror into her mind. Twisting her body sideways, veering along the verge, her knee knocked jutting stone and unbalanced her. Hip crashing down hard, she faced the road, unable to move, the lorry charging at her.

The next few seconds played out in slow motion. The buttercup of the lorry reflected on the driver high in his cab. Young, powerful: milky white, freckled skin, shafts of bright sunlight stabbing spears of bronze through thick black hair, mouth broadening into strong, white fangs about to grind. And in that instant Trevor's words turned into images for her: that was the one, the handsome one who'd carried Jiminy to his death, hair now dyed black to hide the red. He'd turned the lorry round, waiting his chance to ambush them. And it had come. Flaxton's huge transporter was his weapon, aiming to crush, to pulverise. To kill.

The thunder of dust-stirring bulk tore along the road, the bug-yellow snout, its eyes, its face, its body – the giant lorry charged at her and her child. He missed her by inches.

'Jansy!' she shrieked.

The snorting, heaving monster juddered between her and her child. Smoke from the exhaust filled her mouth, her eyes, her ears; stifled her. An intense, sudden stab in her abdomen drowned pain, drowned thought. Tears streamed her eyes clear as she peered desperately for a sign of Janus. Where was her child, her son?

She saw the pushchair advance towards her, the yellow T-shirt hunched, a headless bulge looming through clouds of dust. Had the driver killed Janus? Was the chair bringing his lifeless body to her?

'Mummy! Mu . . . u . . . mmy,' she heard him sob. He was alive.

The pushchair gathered speed. She saw two small fists dragging – flailing – along the road. Janus was bent double to gain momentum, was rushing himself towards her, mobile, unhindered.

The steam-rollering yellow had passed, the grinning mask of death had overshot its target. Sharp pains in Lisa's belly began to squeeze; she groped herself upright and lurched towards Janus.

She caught hold of the pushchair handle as she heard the screeching brake of the lorry up ahead. The drive to Mark Ditcheat's farm flashed into her mind, quite near along the lane. He'd turn there, try again; or simply back towards them.

'Let go, Mummy! Run!' Strong hands waved her away, implored her to leave. Her son; her son Janus was trying to save *her*, to make himself the target.

She pushed the handle down and careered the pushchair on two wheels along the track. There was time; precious minutes to rush her children to the safety of Crinsley Farm before the driver could return.

Panting, blood trickling from her legs, Lisa pushed Janus beyond the iron gate and crashed it shut. The hasp clicked tight to keep the lorry out.

'Run, Seb!' she called. 'Take Jeffers and run! Don't wait for us!'

They scampered off ahead of her as she heaved Janus and the pushchair between rank vegetation. Tall meadow grasses bent away, grass kernels flicked into her mouth, her eyes. She charged on blindly, saw the farm buildings shadowing close, rushed the wide open gate to follow Seb and Jeffers across the cobbled farmyard.

The pushchair rocked a wheel between two stones, held fast. Janus lurched his weight to the other side to free it. Lisa, exhausted, forced one last effort, prayed there'd be help. The big barn doors to her right yawned wide, Frank standing there, beside a bale of hay.

He pulled the foil-paper ring off his favourite brand of cigar. The gold and silver of the wrapper sparkled sun into her eyes, her brain. She recognised the glinting ring of paper, heard again the squeal of tin against the fork as Alec dug the lower spit of the grave between the fruit trees.

So it was *Frank*. Frank had plundered the little body Don had buried, Frank had filled the grave with innocent earth.

Memories flocked fast. Lisa saw herself driving Janus in the Volvo, the Land Rover behind her, urging her on, Frank's clenched fist, the anger as he tailgated her up Milton Lane and past the Priddy Woods. He must have followed, seen the cloning, enticed Janus away. Then doubled back to abduct the clone, to set Duffers on to a defenceless, naked child. Her child, her son. Frank had stolen him, killed him.

Lisa saw Frank grin at her now. That same, mean grin she'd seen in her nightmare long ago. Frank with a pillow in his hands, lowering it over the cot, pushing it down, pressing hard . . .

'Stop!' Lisa heard herself screaming in her dream. 'You'll smother it!'

Frank turning to her, his small eyes spots of venom. 'Bain't human.' His cold, firm voice. 'Bain't nothing there but vermin. Old Don'll be shooting the whole lot of them damn critters.'

Not *her* baby, as she'd thought. His own – Meg's baby. Phyllis's clone had not been born dead. Frank had killed it, smothered it, before Meg even knew of it. Betrayed Meg, too. Forced her to keep the brace on Phyllis's leg, cowed her away from confrontation.

Why was the man leering at her now?

Pounding through her ears Lisa heard the roar of a lorry surging up the drive, caught the blaze of Flaxton yellow reflected in Frank's eyes, ready to pounce again, with only Frank as witness. She turned, saw the jet hair framing a snarling, twisting face, dark glasses mirroring her and her child, revving the motor to destroy them for ever.

Fury drove strength into her hands, into her body. With one deep lunge she pulled the champagne bottle out and kicked the pushchair towards the farmhouse. She reeled her arm back, heaved hard, propelled the missile at the windscreen and pitched herself towards the pushchair.

The bottle shattered; great spurts of exploding, frothing liquid foamed the windscreen opaque. A hard, glittering scree of glass blazed towards her. She heard Frank's frenzied shout, then a tormented bellow as the lorry displaced air and ploughed into the hay barn at full speed. A scrunch as hot metal made contact with tindered grass, belched out a shower of sparks flashing flame which then ignited into hell. Lisa felt the full blast of the explosion throwing her body forward, down.

She landed on soft grass, lay numb. Then felt the movement in her belly: a shift, a split – the great divide. It was not Janus they'd been aiming for. They wanted her – her and her unborn child. That's why the Flaxton assassin had lain in wait to crush her, to annihilate her. They knew there was another cloner in her womb!

She sensed her daughters starved of blood, felt the deep tugs as they struggled to survive. And then all movement stopped. Her little girls had died. Her heart seared the pain of that loss as her eyes opened to search for Janus. Billowing black smoke hid him from her as she struggled to find him. Where was he? Had Flaxton finally managed to rid themselves of him?

The roar of hay on fire behind her spurted the effort to find her child. Dimly she could make out a figure beside her, kneeling by her. Alec's lips covered her face with kisses, his hair entangled with hers, his hands mingled with her blood.

'Lisa! Darling, don't die! Stay with us, Lisa! We need you.'

'Where's Jansy?'

'He's with us, darling; he'll be all right.'

Janus needed her, she had to live for him. She knew her daughters had died for them, so that she could be with Janus, protect him from his curse, the curse she had so unwittingly wished on him. She had to live, take care of him, make sure no harm would come to him.

'I want to hold him.'

There was no pain now. All Lisa knew was that they were safe. Alec handed her son to her, lifted them up, rushed them away into the calm, stone darkness of the farmhouse. He kicked the door shut tight against the inferno outside.

Janus lay, panting, at her side. Small fingers fondled her face, his eyes gleamed tears, smiled pride. It was when she saw the love in Janus's eyes that Lisa knew, without a shadow of a doubt, that her struggles of the past two years had not been in vain. He was her son – she had protected him, safeguarded his liberty, made Alec aware of what had been happening. Together they would prevent Flaxton, and others like them, from putting humanity in jeopardy again.

* * *

What my dear, sweet mother did not, could not, know was that it was just another beginning.

My parents never dreamed I understood things they did not, that I could predict events far beyond their comprehension. They did not realise that my mind, caged in the frail body of a child, was formed way beyond its years, was able to generate thoughts beyond the minds of others. I tried to warn them not to seek advice but they did not listen, could not hear me. To them, my piping voice was just a noise, a fact of childhood.

We left the green fields of Somerset behind us, just as planned, but not their legacy. We could never rid ourselves of that, you see; it is within me, a part of me. And though I pass my genetic make-up on to my – well, let me call them brothers, for want of a better word – I am the sole custodian of my special attribute, the one that haunts me.

On Islay my father began to safeguard us, to obliterate the past, just the way my mother had always done. Painstakingly he plotted his revenge, let retribution against Flaxton take root. He infiltrated their stronghold bit by bit. A whisper here, a comment there. The cancer spread, the figures showed the profits dip, then slump away to nothing.

It was too late for my father to undo the damage Flaxton had already done. The force unleashed could no longer be contained. It lives within our universe, biding its time.

For us that time came all too soon. I remember it so well, the way I remember everything, every tiny detail, right from the moment of my conception. It was six months after Frank's death that my parents took me for a check-up. That's when it all came back to haunt us, that's where it all began again. The doctors insisted that they had to do it, reproached my parents for leaving it so long. They cajoled my father, murmured admonishments in soft, caring voices to my dear, sweet mother.

It didn't hurt; I healed up fast. They weren't to know what they had done. That was the time they opened up my leg, you see. That was the day they took the plastic splinter out.